The Gritty Truth

The Whiskeys

MELISSA FOSTER

ISBN-13: 9781948868471

THE GRITTY TRUTH

Cover Design: Elizabeth Mackey Designs
Cover Photography: Michelle Lancaster

WORLD LITERARY PRESS
PRINTED IN THE UNITED STATES OF AMERICA

A Note to Readers

If this is your first introduction to the Whiskeys series, each book is written to stand alone, so dive right in and fall in love with Quincy and Roni.

Ever since writing TRU BLUE, I have been anxiously awaiting the proper time to write Quincy's love story. I always wait until my heroes and heroines tell me when they are ready for their happily ever after. Quincy didn't whisper in my ear when he met Veronica "Roni" Wescott. He *hollered*, refusing to be ignored. Their love is too strong to be destroyed, but grab the tissues, because this book will tear you apart, and just when you think you've read all you can handle, it'll hit you again. But I promise to put you back together with true romance, hard-core love, and a swoon-worthy happily ever after.

Out of this epic love story came two unexpected stories: IN FOR A PENNY, a novella featuring Penny Wilson and Scott Beckley (and Bones and Sarah's wedding!) and RESISTING JON BUTTERSCOTCH, a second-chance romance featuring everyone's favorite flirt, fifty-shades-of-sweetness Jon Butterscotch and Tatum Helms, whom you'll meet in Quincy's book. Information about Penny's novella is included at the back of this book. Keep your eyes peeled for information about Jon's story. Remember to bookmark my new and upcoming release page.
www.MelissaFoster.com/new-and-upcoming-releases

You can download the Whiskey/Wicked family tree here:
www.MelissaFoster.com/Wicked-Whiskey-Family-Tree

See more of The Whiskeys books here:
www.MelissaFoster.com/TheWhiskeys

Remember to sign up for my newsletter to make sure you don't miss out on future Whiskey releases:
www.MelissaFoster.com/News

For more information about my fun and emotional sexy romances, all of which can be read as stand-alone novels or as part of the larger series, visit my website:
www.MelissaFoster.com

If you prefer sweet romance with no explicit scenes or graphic language, please try the Sweet with Heat series written under my pen name, Addison Cole. You'll find many great love stories with toned-down heat levels.

Happy reading!
~ Melissa

Chapter One

THE RHYTHM OF Beyoncé's "Halo" flowed through dance instructor Veronica "Roni" Wescott as she spun and leaped across the room at On Your Toes dance studio. The sight of Quincy Gritt's name on a text message had sent her body into an exhilarating flurry of desire, and she'd needed to try to get a grip before eight adorable little girls bounced into the studio for their class. Roni was acutely aware of her jerky movements, and pushed herself harder, striving for the perfection she knew she could never again achieve in the same way she knew there was not enough music on the planet to obliterate thoughts of the blue-eyed Charlie Hunnam lookalike. But she had to *try*. Drawing upon the tricks she'd learned when she was younger and navigating the derelict-ridden streets of her neighborhood, she forced herself to focus on the goal, not the noise in her head. She gave herself over to the music, allowing it to pull her through the contemporary dance she loved, pushing away the ache of shattered dreams and muffling thoughts of the man whose friendship and flirtatious texts kept her up at night. When the final crescendo rang out, she slid to the floor on her side, lowering her cheek to the smooth wood, and closed her eyes.

"Bravo!"

Roni's eyes flew open when she heard the voice of her best friend and fellow dance instructor, Angela Keiser. They'd been friends since third grade, when they'd met in a dance class at that very studio.

"Girl, you are killing it," Angela said as she strolled into the room in her white dance skirt and a midriff-baring top. Her long blond hair was braided and coiled into a bun at the top of her head, like a modern-day Barbara Eden in *I Dream of Jeannie*. Half of their best-friends necklace twinkled around her neck, as always.

"Thanks. Is your class over?" Roni pushed to her feet and grabbed a towel to blot her face.

"Yup. I'm heading out in a few minutes, but I have to say this, and I know you're sick of hearing it. You *really* need to dance in the Winter Showcase, and *no*, Elisa did not put me up to convincing you."

Elisa Abbot owned the studio, and Roni had taken dance lessons from her since she was five years old, until a few years ago. Three times a year Elisa held productions, or *showcases*, in which students and teachers performed for the community. Elisa had been all over Roni about dancing in the Winter Showcase, which was taking place at the end of January. When Roni was growing up, she had danced her heart out for those events, and danced solo more often than not. But thanks to a freak car accident, her days of rising to the top of any production were gone.

"*Pfft*. No, thank you," Roni said as her phone chimed like a traitorous secret teller, reminding her that she had a text from Quincy waiting to be read.

"You're way too good a dancer to hide away in here." Angela eyed Roni's phone on the table and said, "And too damn *hot* to keep hiding from Quincy."

"I'm not hiding from anything or anyone." Roni pushed past her and snagged her phone.

"No?" Angela crossed her arms with a challenging expression and said, "So that lingering text is not from Loverboy?"

"I told you to stop calling him that." Thankfully, Angela didn't call him that when he occasionally came to pick up his niece, Kennedy, from Roni's dance class, which Kennedy had started attending in September.

Angela knew her so well. She had been the one to drag Roni to the charity bachelor auction at Whiskey Bro's bar five months ago, and she had won the date with Quincy specifically for Roni, despite Roni having begged her not to. Though now Roni wasn't altogether sorry her bestie had done it.

"And I told you to stop being ridiculous and go out with the guy," Angela insisted. "You guys text all the time anyway."

"No, we don't. We text *sometimes*, and we don't talk about anything deep. He flirts and asks how my day was. We talk about dance and his job at the bookstore, our favorite foods, and shows we're bingeing, and sometimes we send funny pictures to each other. I don't know anything *real* about him."

She'd been thinking about that a lot lately, curious about who he really was and why he was okay keeping their conversations light and flirty, when most guys would have pushed harder, then given up. Sure, Quincy had tried to get her to go out with him at first. Angela had won him for Roni for that purpose, after all. But when she'd said she was too busy to date, he hadn't pushed, and when her grandmother had passed away over the summer and she'd said she wanted to grieve alone, he'd given her time to do so. He'd texted more often to make sure she was okay, but he had never pried into her life, which she'd appreciated. Then last Friday, he'd texted about going out after Halloween, *I think it's time we take our masks off and get to know each other better*, and now she was as nervous as she was excited about that idea.

"Sure you do," Angela said. "You know he's smart and hot as hell, and we've both seen how sweet he is with his niece. We also know he never reacts when the moms gawk at him because he's too busy paying attention to the kids or *you*. He's obviously a good guy, Roni, and I bet he's all kinds of *bad* in bed."

"Ohmygod. I'm sure Joey appreciates you noticing that." Angela was engaged to Joey Carbo, the co-owner of Jazzy Joe's café, where Angela and Roni often had lunch. They'd been eyeing each other for months before he'd finally asked her out, a little more than a year ago.

"*Please.* Joey doesn't get jealous. He *knows* I'm madly in love with him. Just tell me *why* you won't go out with Quincy. We paid a *thousand* dollars for you to win that date with him."

"Had I known that the reason you brought all your friends with us to the auction was that they'd pitched in toward buying me a date, I never would have gone," Roni said. "And I *told* you not to spend that money on him."

"It was for charity," Angela said.

Roni glowered at her. "Now I'm *charity*?"

"*No.* The *event* was for charity, silly. You're my sister from another mother, Roni, and I want you to be happy."

"I *am* happy," she said halfheartedly.

"Sort of. But you've seemed lonely since your grandmother died, and I'm with Joey all the time, so we don't get to hang out as often anymore."

Roni *was* lonelier without her grandmother. She had no idea who her mother was, and her father had taken off when she was four, leaving her to be raised by her grandmother. And with her grandmother's support, she'd spent her whole life preparing for a career as a professional dancer and had even made it through Juilliard. She'd been on her way to the future she'd always dreamed of when the accident had stolen it out from under her, taking with it the only group in which she'd ever felt like she belonged. But at least she'd *still* had her grandmother, and a place in her life. When her grandmother died, Roni had been left feeling adrift in a world she knew very little about outside of dance.

"I know you're close with Elisa, but it's different with a guy," Angela said in a softer tone. "Life is better when you have someone you care about to share it with. The fact that Quincy respected your need for space when you were grieving but found ways to let you know he was there for you should tell you the type of guy he is. And for the record, I still think you should have let him come over to comfort you during that time instead of holing up in your apartment alone."

"I could barely deal with it," Roni reminded her. "I needed time to grieve, not pressure to be funny or sexy for a guy." The truth was, she'd poured her grief into dancing late at night when no one else was around, and Quincy's texts had been a bright light during her darkest days. His texts had always been thoughtful, but during that time he'd taken extra care to ask about how she was feeling and if she needed anything.

"I get that, Roni, but I worry about you. That's why I won the date with Quincy for you in the first place. You've had so much happen over the past few years, and you're wasting away in this studio. You literally come downstairs from your apartment, and you're *in* the studio until you go back upstairs after work."

"Sometimes you and I go out to get lunch," Roni said, but it sounded pathetic, even to her, and totally worthy of Angela's eye roll.

"Come *on*. You're the prettiest, smartest, and most talented person I have ever met, and we both know you'll never go out and meet a guy on your own. You should thank me for handpicking him for you."

"I never asked you to do that, and I don't need a man to be happy."

"I know you don't, but I've known you forever, and I've never seen you react to *any* guy the way you do to Quincy. Everyone saw the way you locked eyes on each other when he was walking through the room before the auction. When he strolled up to the table and set those sexy blue eyes on you, you grabbed the edge of your seat like a lifeline."

Roni's pulse quickened with the memory. Her body had gone white-hot, vibrating with unfamiliar exhilaration. The only time she'd ever felt anything that powerful was when she danced.

"I gotta tell ya, Roni, I worry that the car that hit you might have broken more than just your bones. I think it knocked your hormones out of whack, too. If I were you, I'd be all over him."

Laughter bubbled out, and Roni said, "My hormones are *fine*, as proven by the way his *texts* make my heart race. I swear, one glance from him, even after all these months, gives me butterflies. What the heck is that all about?"

"It's called *chemistry*."

Roni scoffed. "That level of chemistry is way out of my league. The guy *exudes* testosterone with his tatted-up arms and scruffy jaw that says he can't be bothered to shave more than once every couple of weeks. Then there's his light-brown hair brushing his collar, making you want to grab hold of it, and…" Her hands fisted, itching to do just that. She loved his hair. "And he's got some kind of dark, passionate thing brewing in his eyes. You've seen it. I have no idea what *that* is. He looks a little haunted and guarded, but also daring, which is super confusing. Not to mention the way he asks after me all *sweet* and *charming* like he's not really pursuing me, meanwhile he's building a friendship that's bursting at the seams to be more."

"I know plenty of girls who would let him charm their panties off," Angela said with a giggle.

"No kidding, Angela. *That's* the problem. When that text first rolled in, before I tried to dance off my nervousness, I was *this close* to telling him I'd go out with him. But then I remembered that the minute he looks at me, my body heats up and my brain turns me into a sex-craved maniac. I'm afraid to talk to him because of all the X-rated thoughts he sends spinning in my head." Heat skated over her skin, bringing rise to goose bumps. She thrust her arm out and said, "*Look.* That's from just talking about him. See why I can't go out with him?"

Angela laughed. "You do realize that you keep talking about things that most women would give anything to find."

"Yeah, well, in case you've forgotten, most twenty-four-year-olds have a lot more experience carrying out all those dirty thoughts than I do."

Angela's expression softened. "Roni, I know you're self-conscious about your scars, but you've got to start somewhere. What if he's the right person to help you find your way *through* those dirty thoughts?"

"It's not about my scars. I mean, I'm not going to be

thrilled about any guy seeing them, but…" She lowered her voice and said, "He's a whole lot of man for a girl like me, who's only been with *one* guy. And that was short-lived, so it's not like we did all that good stuff you talk about." She'd gone out with a guy a few times when she was at Juilliard, and she'd slept with him just to get it over with, because she was the only virgin she'd known, and she was curious. The first time had sucked. The next few times had been okay, but nothing to write home about. She sighed and said, "You have to remember, Ang, I've lived and breathed dance my whole life. While you were out dating, I was here practicing. When you were going to prom, I was here, preparing for the Summer Showcase."

"I know, and it paid off big time," Angela reminded her. "But I think you forget that you're a whole lot of woman and you can handle *anything*. I'm not saying you have to sleep with him or even get serious. But he made it clear on Halloween that he wants to take whatever this is between you two to the next level. Go on *one* date with him. Give him—and yourself—a chance to get to know each other better. The fact that you've maintained a friendship all this time tells me how compatible you are."

"Like I said, I was *really* close to saying I'd go out with him."

Angela motioned toward Roni's phone and said, "And yet you haven't even read his text. Don't you think you should?"

"Might as well. My body is already throwing a party." She opened his text, and they both read it. *Hey, beautiful. Missed you last weekend. I've got a few nights this week with your name on them. Hit me up so we can connect.* She melted a little inside every time he called her beautiful.

Angela sighed. "He asked you out last weekend? What was

your excuse? Cleaning your grout with a toothbrush?"

"He texted over the weekend and asked me to go for a ride on his motorcycle. But I've never been on a motorcycle, which made me nervous to start with, and the idea of holding on to him for dear life was too much to handle. I said I had to shampoo my carpets."

Angela gave her a deadpan look. "Seriously? You don't even have carpets." She grabbed Roni by the shoulders and said, "Where is that fearless girl who worked her ass off and went off to Juilliard like nothing could break her?"

"She got hit by a car." A pang of sadness moved through her.

The sounds of girls giggling trickled down the hall, soothing that longing and filling Roni with happiness.

Another text from Quincy rolled in, and they both read it. *Time's running out to make your move.*

Angela lifted her eyes to Roni's and said, "You're not going to let him get away, are you?"

Roni's chest constricted at the thought of losing their connection. "I don't want him to go away, but I'm too nervous to go out with him. Can't we just be texting friends forever?"

Angela's face contorted in confusion. "Let me get this straight. You want to be friends *without* benefits, and you don't want to really get to know him? Like acquaintances who text silly pictures and ask about each other's days?"

"Suits me perfectly! I have to go teach my class." Roni hurried out of the room, trying to ignore the sour aftertaste of her lie.

QUINCY LEANED ON the counter at Luscious Licks, his friend Penny's ice cream shop, staring at his phone.

"A watched pot never boils," Penny said as she wiped down the counter, eyeing him curiously. Her hair was piled on her head in a messy bun, held in place with a straw and a tiny clip, as per usual.

"Trust me, this pot is burning like an inferno." He shoved his phone in his pocket as amusement rose in Penny's big blue eyes. People thought Penny looked like a lighter-haired Zooey Deschanel, but when Quincy looked at her, he saw a treasured friend he'd protect with his life, the girl who had taught him everything he knew about friendship. "I just can't figure out why she'll text at all hours, but she won't go out with me."

"Ah, we're talking about Roni, the only other girl in Peaceful Harbor besides me who *doesn't* want to go out with you, aren't we?"

Quincy wasn't immune to the single moms and young women at Between the Pages, the bookstore where he worked, or half of the other women he saw around town, vying for his attention. He just didn't give a shit about them. At six foot three with a hard body and a face that was easy on the eyes, he was going to have women chasing him whether he wanted them to or not. But as a person in recovery from a drug addiction and someone who ran Narcotics Anonymous meetings, Quincy knew the importance of self-care and surrounding himself with the people who supported his recovery. Fucking random women wouldn't do a damn thing for the man he strove to be besides reminding him of the guy, and the life, he'd left behind. Roni was a whole different story. She was the only woman he'd ever felt a connection with that ran deeper than friendship, and it wasn't even something he could pinpoint or explain. He felt it in his bones, as if they were meant to be together.

"She *wants* to," he said confidently. "She just won't."

Penny cocked her head. "That's what you used to say about me."

"Yeah, but we both knew that was different. We could have taken our backs to the mattress and had a great time, but we probably would have lost this." He motioned between them. They'd been friends since he'd gotten out of rehab almost two years ago, and yeah, he'd been cocky and Penny was hot, and they'd become fast flirty friends. But while everyone else had thought they'd end up together, Quincy had known better. He'd never had true friends until he'd gotten clean, and now he valued friendship above all else. He'd never risk losing that with Penny, and the truth was, that initial attraction hadn't been life altering, the way his attraction to Roni was.

"I'm just giving you crap," Penny said. "I'm glad we never hooked up. You're my best guy friend, and I don't know what I would do without you."

"You'd probably make a lot of really bad decisions," he teased.

"I already do that. I allow you in here, don't I?" She smirked. "You've let that hot little brunette string you along for months. I thought you were just dicking around with her."

"*Biding my time*, not dicking around. You know how important it was to me to pass the two-year-clean mark before I got involved with anyone." The day after Halloween had marked two years since he'd entered rehab and last used drugs.

"Yes, but you've been playing the texting game for months. What makes you think she's even interested? She turned you down when you first tried to get her to go out with you, and she isn't even the person who won the date at the auction, remember? Her friend won it for her."

"Of course I remember. That's a night I'll never forget." The first time he'd seen the gorgeous brunette with black-framed glasses, full lips that begged to be devoured, and a body made for worshipping, their eyes had connected and he'd been sure the room would go up in flames before he ever reached the stage. After her friend had won the date with him, he'd gone to introduce himself, and he'd learned that Roni, the woman with the most beautiful eyes and sinfully plump lips in Peaceful Harbor, Maryland, walked with a slight limp and was either painfully shy or smartly cautious. He'd been so intrigued, he hadn't stopped thinking about her since.

"I can feel it," he said. "There's an energy between us that's unfuckingbelievable."

Penny pointed at him and said, "The next time someone asks us why we aren't dating, can you *please* tell them we don't have *that*? That's the greatest feeling in the world."

"How do *you* know? You've never said anything about a guy giving you those vibes."

"A girl has to have her secrets." She chuckled and went to wipe down a table. "Speaking of which, does Roni know yours?"

"My past isn't a secret, Pen. You of all people know that. But it's not the type of thing you toss casually into a text, either."

"That makes sense." She began wiping down another table. "What are you doing tonight?"

"Studying. You?" Quincy was taking online classes toward a degree in accounting.

"No plans, but I'm sure I'll find something to keep myself busy."

The bells above the door chimed, and their friend Scott

Beckley walked in, eyes trained on Penny. She looked up and said, "Hey, Scotty. *Scott.* Geez. I've been hanging out with the kids too much."

"Hi," Scott said, heading for her. "I thought I'd come by to get a taste of my favorite treat."

"Hey, Scott," Quincy said, and Scott's head jerked his way, as if he hadn't noticed him standing there.

"Quincy. Hi." Scott crossed the room and clapped a hand on Quincy's back. "How's it going, man?" He was a formidable, rugged guy with sandy hair and a quiet strength that told of the years he'd fended for himself after escaping his abusive parents at the age of seventeen.

"Good. You?"

"Couldn't be better." Scott glanced at Penny and said, "Just came in to grab some sugar before heading over to Sarah's. I'm babysitting the kids tonight."

Scott had recently reunited with his estranged sisters, Sarah and Josie. Sarah was engaged to Wayne "Bones" Whiskey, a doctor and member of the Dark Knights motorcycle club. Bones had adopted Sarah's three children, and they were getting married next spring. Quincy's old roommate, Jed Moon, had fallen head over heels in love with Josie and her son, Hail, and Quincy was going to be best man at their wedding on Christmas Day. Jed was also a Dark Knight, and he worked as a bartender at Whiskey Bro's bar and as a mechanic at Whiskey Automotive, both of which were owned by Bones's family.

"Cool. Kiss the kids for me. I've got to take off." Quincy headed for the door, turning back to say, "Will I see you guys at the scavenger hunt this weekend?"

The Dark Knights motorcycle club was hosting a scavenger hunt to raise money for the Parkvale Women's Shelter, which was located about half an hour outside of Peaceful Harbor and run by the wife and daughter of another Dark Knight. Josie and Hail had stayed at the shelter when they'd first come to the Harbor. Bones volunteered, handling medical check-ups for the women and children who stayed there, and Sarah often went with him to talk with the women about her own journey out of homelessness.

"Of course." Penny set down the rag she was using and motioned to Scott. "This guy is my partner, since you're holding out for your text mistress."

"Don't give him a hard time, Penny," Scott said. "It takes some guys longer than others to connect with the right woman."

Quincy's friends were a tight-knit group. They all knew that he and Roni had been texting, and he'd made it clear he only had eyes for her. "Now, there's a man who understands that it's all about timing." Quincy enjoyed keeping things light with Roni, getting to know her on a level that didn't include exposing his past or the crimes he'd committed. But lately he'd hung on those texts, wanting to get closer to the woman behind them. It was time to open the floodgates to his past and see if she was willing to walk through them to be by his side or if she'd turn tail and run away. As he reached for the door, he said, "I'm a man with a plan."

"Hey!" Penny called out, stopping him in his tracks. "Why don't *I* know about this plan?"

"A guy's got to have his secrets." Quincy chuckled as he headed outside.

He straddled his motorcycle and rode to his apartment above Whiskey Automotive on the outskirts of town. As he turned down the long driveway, the sight of the four-bay garage brought a rush of mixed emotions. The painful clench of his gut and the swelling of his heart battled for dominance. Quincy chose to endure the familiar reality check on a daily basis rather than find another place to live.

There had been a time when he had lived through so many low points, he'd thought he was the only person on earth without a *rock bottom* to hit. But two years ago on Halloween night, he'd finally slammed into it. He had been severely beaten by a drug dealer and had collapsed unconscious on the lawn of the auto shop, where his brother, Truman, nine years his senior, had been working and living in the apartment Quincy now rented. Truman had spent six years in prison for a murder Quincy had committed and had gotten out only a few months before that night, when for the millionth time—and hopefully for the *last*—Truman had come to Quincy's rescue. He'd gotten Quincy the medical attention he'd needed and had convinced him to go to rehab.

Quincy climbed off his bike and spotted Truman standing in one of the bays wiping his hands on a rag. He was talking with Bear Whiskey and his sister, Dixie. The Whiskeys—Biggs and Red and their adult children, Bones, Bullet, Bear, and Dixie—were like family to Quincy. Bear was a part-time mechanic at the auto shop and a talented motorcycle designer for Silver-Stone Cycles, Dixie's husband Jace's company. Dixie managed the auto shop and the bar, and she was also the face of Silver-Stone's new Leather and Lace brand of women's clothing.

Truman lifted his chin in greeting as Quincy sauntered into the bay.

Dixie flipped her long red hair over her shoulder and said, "Hey, Quincy."

"Hi, Miss January," Quincy said with a chuckle.

Dixie glowered at him. She was tall, tattooed, and gorgeous, and she graced the pages of next year's Silver-Stone calendar. She was also a badass who took no shit from anyone, which was what made teasing her so much fun.

"I'm breaking into your apartment and burning that calendar," she hissed.

"Go right ahead. I've got three more," Quincy said, though it was a lie. He didn't even own one. He'd bought a handful of calendars to support her, but he'd given them out to the guys he worked with at the bookstore.

"Dude, that's my *sister* you're plastering on your walls," Bear snapped.

"Jealous?" Quincy teased. "Put your ugly mug on a calendar, and I'll hang that up, too."

"I'm glad you're here, bro," Truman said. His biceps strained against the sleeves of his shirt, blue ink covering his skin from knuckles to neck. His deep-set eyes had become less haunted in the years since Quincy's stint in rehab, but they still held the prison-power to instill fear in the strongest of men with a single stare. His thick dark hair and beard added to his intimidating appearance, but Truman was the kindest man Quincy knew.

"What's going on?" Quincy asked.

"Gemma got hung up at work, and Red's got Lincoln down for a nap." Truman's wife, Gemma, owned Princess for a Day Boutique. "Do you have time to pick up Kennedy from dance class?"

Truman and Gemma were raising Truman and Quincy's much younger siblings, five-year-old Kennedy and three-year-old Lincoln, as their own, giving them the family stability and parental love Truman and Quincy had never had. Red was as much of a surrogate grandmother to Kennedy and Lincoln as she and Biggs were surrogate parents to Truman and Quincy.

"As if he'd say no to a chance to ogle Roni." Dixie planted her hand on her hip and said, "He's been trying to get that chick into his lair for months."

"Trust me, Dix. If I was in a rush to get her in my bed, she'd have been there a long time ago." But Dixie was right; Quincy was always up for a few minutes with sweet, sexy Roni. He looked at Truman and said, "No problem. Whatever you need."

"How about taking my baby overnight so I can have sex with my wife without having to jump up every time he makes a noise?" Bear's wife, Crystal, had given birth two and half months ago, and they'd named their son after Bear's late uncle Axel, who had mentored Bear in auto mechanics.

Dixie smirked and said, "The way you paw at your wife, she probably needs the break."

"She loves it." Bear flexed his tatted biceps and said, "She's got Peaceful Harbor gold, baby."

Truman threw his rag at Bear and said, "We got work to do, poser."

"I'll see you guys in a bit." Quincy headed to the old truck Truman had fixed up for him. He'd long ago bought car seats, since he tried to spend as much time as he could with the kids.

The dance studio wasn't far from the shop, and he walked in a few minutes before Kennedy's class ended. He slipped past the mothers waiting in the lobby and headed down the hall, following the sound of music to Roni's classroom.

Roni stood at the head of the class, gorgeous in a skintight white bodysuit that disappeared beneath the waist of her sheer black skirt and leggings. He'd noticed she didn't wear glasses when she taught, giving him a side view of her high cheekbones, slender nose, and gorgeous mouth. Kennedy was in the front row, dressed in all pink, her dark hair pinned up in pigtails, and she was giving Roni her full attention. Love stacked up inside Quincy for the sister-turned-niece, whom he'd fought to keep alive in crack houses and on the streets before their mother had overdosed.

"Right hand out to your side. Left hand out to your side," Roni said, doing the motions as the girls copied her movements. "Cross your arms over your chest, hands up by your shoulders, and sway your upper body, leading with your shoulders."

She moved with such fluidity and grace, Quincy was mesmerized.

"Let's try it together now," Roni said, repeating the movements slowly and patiently, her eyes moving over the girls, a compassionate gaze coming to rest on an adorable redhead leaning against the back wall, her hands tucked behind her. "Okay, ladies, let's try that three more times on your own."

As the girls practiced, Roni went to the redhead in the back of the room and crouched beside her as she spoke. The little girl shook her head, frowning. Roni touched her hand, still talking quietly. The girl nodded. Roni pushed to her feet, taking the child's hand and speaking loudly to the class. "Good job, ladies. Okay, let's—" Her eyes found Quincy, and she stumbled over her words.

A slow smile crept across his lips, loving her reaction, which was the same every time he picked up Kennedy. He winked as she struggled to regain control. She was so damn cute, smiling nervously for him, then tearing her eyes away with such force, he wondered why she bothered when it would be so much easier to give in to their chemistry.

Roni walked the redhead to the group, then hurried to the front of the class and said, "Excellent class, ladies. Give yourselves a big hand." The girls cheered and clapped, although the redhead didn't join in. Roni stole a glance at Quincy.

Hello, sweetheart.

"Don't forget to get your things from your cubbies," Roni said, inciting a flurry of activity.

"Uncle Quincy!" Kennedy ran over, her pigtails swinging.

Quincy hoisted her into his arms, and she threw her arms around his neck, kissing his cheek. After all he and the kids had been through, being loved by them was one of his greatest blessings. He was lucky to have many *greatest* blessings in his life, and he'd never take a single one for granted again.

"Hey, jelly bean," he said, snuggling her. "Mommy got held up at work, so I'm giving you a ride home."

"Yay!" Kennedy cheered.

As parents filtered into the room to pick up their kids, Roni watched over the children like a mother hen, sneaking peeks at Quincy.

"Did you see me dancing? Awen't I good?" Kennedy asked.

"You're the best. Why don't you get your stuff while I talk with Miss Roni?"

She clung to him like a monkey and said, "I want to come with you."

He couldn't exactly charm Roni the way he'd hoped to with a little one in his arms. *Time to get creative.* He carried her across the room to Roni, who was saying goodbye to one of the other kids. The second she was done, Kennedy said, "Miss *Woni*, my uncle wants to talk to you!"

A nervous smile played at Roni's full, kissable lips as she set her hazel eyes on him, causing a squirrelly feeling in his chest, and said, "What can I do for you, Uncle Quincy?"

"Let me take you out tomorrow night." *Come on, baby, just say yes.*

Her eyes darted to Kennedy. "I'm sorry, but I have to work."

"Wednesday, then?"

She lowered her eyes for only a second before they flicked up to his, as though it was hard to look away, and she said, "I have class."

Time to bring out the big guns. He looked at Kennedy and said, "Jelly bean, help me out here. I want to have a playdate with Miss Roni, and she doesn't want to play with me."

Roni's cheeks flamed. But her widening smile told him to pull out all the stops.

"Uncle Quincy has the best playdates!" Kennedy exclaimed. "He plays for *hours*. We play dolls and dwess-up. Sometimes we play football, but he has to play on his knees because he's so big. We play house and we dance, and he even lets me put wibbons in his hair."

Roni laughed, and he'd give just about anything to hear more of that sweet sound.

"Ribbons?" she asked.

Oh man, maybe Kennedy isn't helping after all.

Kennedy nodded. "Yes, and if you're good, he'll take you to Penny's ice cweam shop. He loves ice cweam. He always says he can eat it all night long. Right, Uncle Quincy?"

He cocked a grin. *Best wing girl ever.* "That's right, kiddo. *All night long.*"

Roni's eyes flew open wider, and she snapped her mouth shut.

"You should have a playdate with him, Miss Woni!" Kennedy said excitedly, and wriggled out of Quincy's arms. "I'm gonna get my stuff!"

"You're *so* bad," Roni whispered, looking around them and laughing softly.

"That used to be true in the not-so-great sense. But I assure you, now I only use my bad side to be *very, very good.*" He stepped closer, the temperature between them spiking. Roni was tall, five six or seven, he guessed, the perfect height to take her face between his hands and kiss her. She smelled enticingly feminine, but he kept his hands to himself and said, "What's a guy got to do to get a date with you?"

"I don't really date, Quincy." She said his name breathily, as if it lingered on her tongue.

"Neither do I," he said honestly, and glanced at Kennedy, putting her shoes on by the cubbies. All the other kids were gone. "Maybe it's time we start. What time do you get off tomorrow?"

"I have a late meeting for an upcoming production."

"What about Wednesday?"

"Sorry. I'm here until eight. I like you a lot, but…"

"No *buts*, Roni. You can't hide behind your phone forever."

"Yes, I can," she said with a shimmer of playfulness. "I don't get flustered when we text. It's easier when"—she waved at his body—"all *this* isn't standing right in front of me."

"Then maybe I need to up my texting game."

"*No!*" she said quickly, laughing.

"Laughing is a good start." He closed the small gap between them, and her chest brushed against him, desire rising in her eyes. Her breathing hitched, but she didn't look away. Another good sign. He ran his fingers down her arm, and goose bumps rose beneath his touch. She made a sexy, *needy* sound, awakening the monster behind his zipper. "One date, Veronica, and I promise to keep my hands to myself." He leaned in and said, "Unless you ask me not to."

She opened her mouth to respond, and he cut her off. "Do you really want to make up another excuse? Because your eyes tell me that you feel the incredible, *inescapable* energy between us just as strongly as I do."

"Mm-hm." She pressed her lips together, holding his gaze for a beat before whispering, "I feel it, too."

"That's all I need to know."

Kennedy ran over and grabbed Quincy's hand. "Can we go now?"

"Of course, sweetheart." Quincy winked at Roni and said, "Ticktock, beautiful. See you soon."

Chapter Two

SOMETIMES QUINCY FELT like he was living the lives of two different people. The hardworking, easygoing guy who was pursuing Roni and the recovering substance abuser currently running the Wednesday-night Narcotics Anonymous meeting in the basement of the Peaceful Harbor Lutheran Church. But there was no escaping the fact that they were one and the same man and one could not exist without the other.

The hum of the overhead lights might be annoying to some, but for him it was the sound of stability and consistency, things he'd gone years without and now craved as badly as he'd once needed drugs. It was almost as strong as his urge to get closer to Roni.

The sound of the lights filled the silent moment of introspection for Simone Davidson, sitting across from him sharing her story with the group. Simone was painfully thin, though she'd put on a few pounds since getting out of rehab last month. Her curly auburn hair billowed around her face. A scar ran down the left side of her face from her ear to her chin, ending just below her lower lip. A battle scar, from one of the many times she'd tried to escape the hands of her ex-boyfriend. Her jeans and sweater were clean, and her brown eyes were clear, though shadowed with ghosts of her past. She picked nervously at her fingernails, which were also free of dirt. Quincy had never noticed the cleanliness of people or their clothing until he'd gotten the drugs out of his system. Now it was one of the first things he noticed, searching for signs of trouble even outside of the meetings. Most of the time he wasn't even aware he was doing it.

He'd known Simone back in his dark days, when his every move had been driven by the next high, before she'd become the girlfriend of Patrick "Puck" Fulton, the drug dealer whose posse had once beaten Quincy senseless. When Simone had come to Quincy for help, he'd known he was taking a chance of being harassed by Puck, but he'd flirted with death before, and he wasn't afraid of it—or of *Puck*. Not only was Quincy's head clearer and smarter than any dealer's, but his body was stronger, and his will to overpower anything that tried to drag him down was unstoppable. Knowing Truman, the Whiskeys, and an entire club of fearless bikers had his back sure helped, and it also made him the ideal person to take on the dangerous role of being Simone's sponsor.

Simone lifted her gaze to the others sitting around the circle and said, "The other day, I was walking through a gas station parking lot on my way to the bus stop, and this guy standing next to a fancy sedan was staring at me like he knew me. He looked familiar, but I couldn't place him. He was wearing a suit and pumping gas. He kept watching me, and it made me nervous, but after living in fear for so long, I refuse to be scared any longer. I promised myself I would confront my fears, so I walked up to him and asked him why he was staring at me."

She looked down at her hands, picking at her nails again.

"He said he was surprised I didn't remember." She lifted her eyes and said, "He was one of the guys my boyfriend had pimped me out to. He said we had sex dozens of times. I knew I had lost memories and time when I was using, but it brought it all to the surface, making me wonder how many other men I'd been with, how many hours, weeks, and months I'd lost track of. I used drugs for five years, almost to the day, believe it or not. That's about forty-three thousand eight hundred hours, and yes, I calculated it. I can say with great certainty that I can't recall the majority of those hours."

There were no flinches, gasps, or comments. There were no judgments. Drug addiction was ruthless, and the people there were all fighting similar battles. Quincy couldn't help but wonder what Roni's reaction would be if she was there. He quickly pushed those thoughts out of his head, wanting to keep even thoughts of her away from the ugliness of drugs.

"Those hours are my brass ring," Simone said. "I want to get to a point where I can say I've been clean longer than I was using, and I want to remember every minute of it…"

As Simone went on with her story, Quincy remembered his first few weeks after rehab, which had passed in a blur of NA meetings, self-doubt, and loathing warring with confidence and determination and hundreds of unanswerable questions. But probably the worst parts of those, and many other weeks, were the daily looks in the mirror, the accepting of responsibility for the pain he'd caused, and the deep-seated fear *and* hope he'd seen in his brother's and friends' eyes. He'd seen those same things in his own eyes. *Thank God Roni never saw me like that.* Quincy was one of the lucky ones. He had, and continued to have, unrelenting support from Truman, the Whiskeys, and the rest of their friends, giving him plenty of reasons to fight for a better life. But he often wondered how people battled the beast without those pillars of support.

"Hour by hour," Simone said, as if she were answering his question. "That's what I tell myself. When I think about how many years I wasted, too high to think or feel or speak, it just..." Tears slipped down her cheeks, and she looked at Quincy.

He nodded his encouragement, though he wanted to embrace her and let her know she had what it took to stay clean. Quincy knew how important hugs and encouragement were, both of which had disappeared from his life after Truman had gone to prison. These last two years of his recovery, Quincy had greedily accepted and happily doled out as many as he could. But this wasn't a group of friends chatting or a therapy session. It was Simone's turn to share her painful experiences and try to find her way through them, and in doing so, she might also help others. While hugs were encouraged, members were asked to save conversations and comments for after the meetings, which was exactly what Quincy would do.

"I don't want to go back to being the person I was, and I'm not sure who I'm supposed to become. But I'm going to figure it out," Simone said more confidently. "Thank you."

Jacob, the guy sitting next to her, reached over and embraced her, patting her back supportively.

Quincy glanced at the clock and said, "We're out of time. I'd like to thank everyone who shared tonight. When you walk out that door, remember the reasons you walked through it. The only person who can change your life is the one in the mirror, but you don't have to do it alone. If you feel yourself slipping, lean on your sponsors. That's what we're here for. There's a list of daily meeting locations on the table. You *can* do this, but you have to want it." He pushed to his feet, and everyone else followed, holding hands and bowing their heads as they said the Serenity Prayer.

When they were done, a couple of people left without a word; others thanked Quincy as he put away the chairs, and then they headed outside, where he knew they would linger and talk as late as they could. For people in recovery, too much downtime or time alone opened dangerous doors, behind which the beasts were clawing to get through.

"You did good tonight, Sims. I'm proud of you," Quincy said as she put on her coat. "How'd it feel?"

"Like I was sitting there naked."

He remembered that feeling all too well, but feeling vulnerable was so much better than being wasted. "That about sums it up, doesn't it?"

"Yes, but it also felt good, you know? Getting it out there. I still can't believe the things I did, the way I treated people. The way I treated myself."

"Recovery is not for the weak. We need clarity in order to accept what we did and find ways to forgive ourselves so we can move forward. We've all been there. Just remember, we are *all* far from perfect. That guy in the suit you talked about? He's no better than you. In fact, he's worse. He took advantage of your drugged-up state, and now you're done with drugs. You're working to better yourself, and he's probably still paying for sex."

Her lips curved up gratefully. "You always say things that make it easy to believe I wasn't a bad person."

"My sister-in-law once told me that even good people do bad things. I didn't believe it then as wholly as I do now, but I draw upon her words often. They're simple, but they're true, and a good reminder when things get tough."

"I'll remember that. Thank you. I'm going to do this, Quincy," she said vehemently. "I've never had anyone to turn to, and I appreciate you helping me get into rehab and set up at the women's shelter. I got a job at a convenience store that's on the bus line that goes by the shelter. I start tomorrow."

"That's fantastic." He'd rather she worked in Peaceful Harbor, where the Dark Knights had been patrolling like rabid watchdogs for generations. Puck wouldn't dare cross the bridge into Peaceful Harbor. But he'd talked with Simone about it a few weeks ago, and the buses didn't run regularly enough to ensure she could get to and from a job there. Luckily, the Dark Knights also patrolled the area around the Parkvale Women's Shelter and kept tabs on drug dealers and anyone else who might be a threat to the residents of the shelter. The patrols weren't as widespread as they were in the Harbor, but at least they had eyes on her.

"Have you heard anything more from Puck or his guys?" Quincy asked.

"No. After what Diesel did to him when he came after me at the shelter, I don't think he'll be back."

Desmond "Diesel" Black was a Nomad, a traveling member of the Dark Knights who didn't claim any chapter as his own. He was a massive man, with cold dark eyes and absolutely *no* people skills. He bartended at Whiskey Bro's when he was in town, which kept trouble out of the bar, and he was in charge of patrolling and coordinating the other Dark Knights who kept watch over the shelter. A man would have to have a death wish to mess with him.

"I couldn't have gotten this far without you, Quincy. I don't know how I'll ever repay you."

"Yes, you do," he said seriously. "You'll stick with the program, every minute, every hour, every day, and you'll call me if you need me. I've got your back, Sims. Whatever you need, day or night." He pulled her into an embrace and said, "You can do this. I believe in you."

RONI WAVED TO the last of the teenage girls from her hip-hop class and locked the studio door behind them. She headed back to the classroom to get her phone, hoping Quincy had texted. Even though they'd never texted on a daily basis, she'd thought she might hear from him after the things he'd said and the way he'd acted on Monday. But she hadn't heard from him yesterday or today. She told herself to temper the hope that had been building for the last hour and grabbed her phone from the table, deflating at the sight of the blank screen.

With a heavy sigh, she turned off the lights in the classroom and made her way toward the front, turning off the lights in each of the other rooms on her way. She felt stupid for getting her hopes up, but the way he'd looked at her like he didn't want to miss a *second* of seeing her had felt special and maybe even intimate.

But what did she know about special and intimate?

A guy like Quincy probably had dozens of friends *with* benefits.

For the millionth time, she wondered why he was even bothering with her. It wasn't like she was fantastic at flirting or gave off seductive vibes, the way Angela did with Joey without even trying. As usual, she had only one answer, and Angela had nailed it. *Chemistry.*

She rolled her eyes at herself for even thinking she was special to him. Those friends with benefits she imagined surely had even *more* chemistry with him. The butterfly-inducing zing of electricity between them probably only felt special to her because she didn't have enough experience flirting with guys to realize it was normal.

But it sure didn't feel normal.

She hit the last of the studio lights in the lobby and stared out the glass doors into the front parking lot, missing her grandmother. If Gram were alive, she'd tell Roni what she always had about matters of the heart. *Sparks start fires, and fires feel good when they're small enough to warm you, but inevitably they either die out or burn everything in their path. Forget the sparks, Veronica. Look into the heart of the person. If you see gray, run the other way. If you see red, take the man to bed. But if you see a clear blue sky, you've got yourself a unicorn, and that just might be your good, kind, hardworking guy. The one you're meant to be with forever.*

Roni stared into the darkness, picturing her grandmother's serious eyes staring out from behind her wire-framed glasses, her face mapped with wrinkles and worry lines, her short gray hair curling around her ears. The familiar weight of loneliness settled into Roni's chest.

She startled at a knock on the glass, her hand flying to her chest as Quincy stepped in front of her, those all-seeing eyes holding her gaze. Neither of them moved, but a smile lifted his lips, making her smile, too. He reached for the door, his brows lifting in question.

"*Oh.*" She unlocked the door, and he pulled it open. *My goodness.* He was gorgeous, tall and broad in a worn black leather jacket over a gray sweater and faded jeans. His hair was brushed back from his face, making his features even more striking.

He parked one black boot against the bottom of the door, holding it open, and said, "Hey there, beautiful."

His voice was rough and sweet at once, making every inch of her tingle. "Hi. What are you doing here?"

"Taking you on our date."

She laughed nervously, feeling a little giddy. "Our *date*?"

"You lost your chance to make your move, so I'm making mine. These are for you." He lifted his hand, showing her a fistful of wildflowers, which he must have picked for her because the stems were scraggly and dirty.

Oh, how she loved that! She couldn't have stopped the dreamy sigh that slipped out if she'd wanted to. "Quincy, they're beautiful. Thank you."

"You said wildflowers were your favorite, like the ones on the field by the bridge, right? That's where these are from."

She couldn't believe he'd remembered that from their first few weeks of texting back in May. A wave of emotion stole her voice. He stepped closer, bringing the rich, masculine scents of leather, earth, and *man*, with an undercurrent of something she had come to know as uniquely *Quincy*, and her pulse quickened.

"You should get your things," he said confidently.

"My things?"

"Keys? Purse?" His gaze moved slowly from her face all the way down to her toes, appreciation rising in his eyes as they followed the same path back up her black leggings, lingering long enough on her white ballet wrap shirt to make her traitorous nipples pebble to greet him. A wicked grin appeared as he met her gaze and said, "As much as I hate to ask you to cover up, you'll need a jacket."

Despite her rattled nerves, she was surprised that no part of her wanted to make up an excuse tonight. "Okay. Do you want to come in and wait? I have to run upstairs to my apartment for my jacket."

He cocked a brow and said, "You can wear mine." He shrugged his jacket off and held it open for her to put on. "I'm not taking the chance that you won't come back down."

She laughed softly, loving his sense of humor. "Won't you be cold?"

"Not likely with you by my side."

Even though she knew she wouldn't be cold with him by her side, either, hearing him say it so openly made her a little nervous.

He must have noticed, because he said, "I already promised to keep my hands to myself, and if you're worried, text that blonde you're always whispering with when I come around. Tell her I'm taking you out."

"Her name is Angela," she said, feeling silly for being so cautious. "I don't need to text her. I trust you, Quincy. A psycho killer probably wouldn't take the time to text for months on end. Let me just change out of my ballet slippers."

He cocked that brow again, and she explained. "I keep a pair of slip-ons right behind the desk." She pointed to the reception area.

His eyes remained glued on her as she changed her shoes. She grabbed her keys and stepped outside. He helped her put on his jacket, which was about five sizes too big, but cozy warm and smelled delicious, like him.

He held her gaze as he rolled up the sleeves and said, "You

look hot in my jacket."

She felt her cheeks flame. "So did you." Unable to believe she'd had the guts to say it, she turned around and locked the door to avoid his heated gaze.

"Do you have to go through the studio to get to your apartment?"

"No." She pointed to the door a few feet away and said, "That door leads up to my apartment. Where are we going, anyway?"

"You'll see." He put a hand on her lower back, guiding her along the front of the building.

When they turned the corner, walking toward the back of the building, she said, "There's nothing behind the building but a parking lot and loading docks. Should I be worried?"

"Never when you're with me."

That big hand of his pressed against her back, guiding her forward, and when they rounded the corner, her breath caught. The frame of his truck was illuminated with strings of tiny white lights. The tailgate was down, and the smallest firepit she'd ever seen sat on the metal bed, a teepee of wood perched in the center. Just beyond, he'd spread out blankets and colorful pillows, and in their center were several take-out containers from her favorite restaurant and two to-go cups.

"Quincy, this is *amazing*," she said as they neared the truck. "It's like those romantic Instagram pictures that I thought never happened in real life. I can't believe you did all of this for *me*."

"Yeah, I can't either." An incredulous laugh rumbled out.

The pit of her stomach sank. "What does *that* mean?"

"Oh, shit. I didn't mean that the way it came out. I meant that I've never done anything like this before. But I've waited a long time to go out with you, and I didn't want to take you just anywhere, like out for pizza and to see a movie."

"I like pizza and movies," she said, surprised that *he* sounded nervous, too.

"Cool. I do, too."

"But I like this a million times better," she admitted, and the smile she earned told her exactly how happy that made him.

"I'm glad, because I wanted our first date to be special, and honestly, I have no idea what I'm doing. This is the first *real* date I've ever been on."

"No way" fell out before she could stop it.

He nodded. "*Way.*"

"I don't even know what to say to that. I figured you had women lining up at your door to go out with you."

"I do, but that doesn't mean I take them up on it."

The way he said it wasn't bragging or cocky. It was unabashedly honest, and between that, his nervousness, and the romantic date he'd arranged, Roni's trepidation fell away. He set the flowers on the bed of the truck and helped her in, then climbed in behind her.

She picked up the flowers as he knelt to light the fire, and he said, "I had no idea wildflowers were still around this late in the year, but I gave it a shot and got lucky."

"In Maryland they can bloom through the middle of November, especially when the weather is as warm as it's been lately. I've actually never been given flowers before. It feels wonderful," she admitted.

He cocked his head, giving her his full attention, and said, "I haven't given them, either, and it feels great for me, too."

Oh Lord, she loved that.

He turned back to the fire, trying to get the kindling to light, and she told herself not to make too much out of his confession. "I love that you picked them from the very spot I mentioned. I'm surprised you remembered."

The fire crackled to life, the flames reflecting in his eyes. He shoved the lighter in his pocket and said, "I've got a good memory for important things."

He thought she was *important*! Maybe she was special to him after all.

She looked at the to-go cups and said, "Is one of these for me?"

"Mm-hm. The one on the left is water with lemon."

Her favorite drink. "Oh gosh, you remembered everything," she said.

"I hope so. I got you a club salad with extra avocado, honey mustard dressing, and a side of grilled Brussel sprouts. To be honest, I had to check our old texts to remember what kind of dressing you liked."

Inside she was doing a little happy dance, and she felt comfortable enough to tease him. "You did? Maybe I should rethink this date after all."

He laughed.

She held up the flowers he'd given her and said, "Would you be offended if I put these in my water?"

"Hold on a sec." He jumped out of the truck and went around to the front, grabbed something from the cab, and climbed back in with a plastic cup that had WHISKEY AUTOMOTIVE printed on the side and a bottle of water. He poured the water into the cup and held it out. "It's not fancy, but it'll do."

"It's perfect." She put the flowers in the cup, and they settled in on the blankets.

Quincy leaned over and touched the best-friend charm on

her necklace, the brush of his fingers on her skin sending prickles of heat through her. "Who's got the other half?"

"The one I'm always whispering with. Angela."

"Lucky girl." He held her gaze so long, the air between them sizzled. When she shifted her eyes away, he began taking the tops off the containers and said, "Hungry? This food isn't going to eat itself."

She was in awe of everything he'd done. Even the way he'd surprised her was special. "This looks amazing, Quincy. Thank you for going to all this trouble."

"Thanks for joining me." As they started eating, he said, "How long have you taught dance?"

"Officially, a little more than a year."

"What do you mean, officially?"

"I did some teaching when I was growing up. I've danced at this studio since I was five, two days a week at first, like Kennedy. But I loved it so much, dancing was all I wanted to do. I'd make up songs about whatever we were learning in school and dance in the halls, and at home while I did my chores."

"I bet you were adorable," he said, and the warmth in his eyes told her he really meant it.

"I don't know about that, but thank you."

"So you danced two days a week growing up?"

"For a bit. Eventually I wanted to take three dance classes each week. But my grandmother, who raised me, was a waitress and a seamstress, and she didn't earn much money. She was good with it, saving every tip, every extra penny. But even when I was young, I knew dance classes were a luxury. So to earn extra money, I started helping neighbors in our apartment building. I walked their dogs, played with kids while their moms were busy. I'd do whatever they'd let me do to earn the difference in tuition between two and three classes per week."

They ate as they talked, and Quincy watched her intently, listening to every word she said, like her grandmother used to. Like he *cared* about her answers.

"I loved studying under Elisa, the owner of the studio. She danced professionally all over the world for more than twenty years, and she retired when her mother got sick. She came back here to take care of her, and after her mother passed away, she opened the studio. She's an amazing person, and an even more incredible dancer. I'll never forget the day she pulled me aside after one of my classes and suggested I take private lessons. I was ten, and when she said I reminded her of herself, it was the *biggest* compliment I could imagine, and I burst into tears." She took a sip of her water and said, "I'm such a dork."

"You're not a dork. You're *passionate*, and that's wonderful." He ate one of his fries and offered her one.

"Thanks. I love fries." She loved that he shared even more. "Do you want some of my salad or sprouts?"

A flicker of wickedness shimmered in his eyes. "I'd like *everything* of yours." He stabbed a cherry tomato with his fork and popped it in his mouth, holding her gaze as he said, "Mm, sweet and juicy."

"*Ohmygod.*" She turned away, her cheeks burning.

"You're sexy when you blush."

She caught his grin and couldn't stop her own from appearing. He was so easygoing and likable, she didn't even try to hold back her sass. "And you go from sweet to naughty in the space of a second."

"I'm not going to apologize for that, but I can see it embarrasses you, so I'll try to tone it down. Did you take the private lessons?"

"In embarrassment? *No.* I was born this way."

He laughed. "Girl, you *are* somethin' else."

"When you figure out what that is, please let me know." *Wow.* This was fun. He was bringing out a confident side of her she hadn't seen since the accident. "To answer your question, I did take private lessons, and eventually I danced five days a week, but it took some creativity to afford it. My grandmother started making the outfits for recitals and productions, free of charge. Elisa would provide the materials, and Gram would make them."

He stretched one long leg out in front of him and bent the other, leaning his arm on his knee and turning his body toward her, and said, "Gram sounds awesome."

The way he said *Gram,* as if he knew her, felt nice. "She was. My dancing was as important to her as it was to me."

"I can't imagine having that type of passion for something as a kid, much less that type of support. What was your grandmother like?"

"*Tough.* She didn't mollycoddle, but she wasn't cold, either. She'd kiss me good night, and she showed up for *every* dance recital, but mostly she showed her love by fostering my dancing and raising me when she hadn't expected to. She could be hard on me, pushing me to get straight As and to stay on the right side of the law, which of course I appreciate. But if I said I couldn't figure something out, she'd get this look that I used to call her *don't give me that* face." Roni tried to mimic her grandmother's expression, tilting her head, narrowing her eyes, and pursing her lips.

Amusement rose in Quincy's eyes, and she liked that look on him as much as she liked the heated one he'd worn only moments earlier. "That's quite a face."

"Right? Gram was tiny, too, five feet tall on a good day, but she was fierce. When she made that face, I knew I was on my own. That was okay, though. I loved school, and I was good at it, so it just made me work harder and learn to be a problem solver. But I remember when I was much younger, wishing she was more like my friends' grandmothers who would make elaborate meals and dote on them. Gram cooked like it was a task, not a pleasure, making sure I got the right vitamins and minerals. We always had three food groups, and everything was overcooked, regardless of what it was. She could make a mean apple pie when she was in the mood, which wasn't often. But that made it even more special. She always said she filled them with love. It's no wonder I like apple pie so much. Just the smell of it makes me feel good all over. But being hard on me, and pushing me to make a better life for myself, was Gram's way of showing her love." She ate a forkful of salad, as more happy memories warmed her.

Quincy covered her hand with his, giving it a gentle squeeze. "You must miss her."

Roni nodded, her throat thickening. "I do. A lot. Before you knocked on the window, I was thinking of her." She looked down at his hand, aware of the roughness of his palm, the warmth of his thumb stroking her skin. "I never really thanked you for checking on me in the weeks after she died. That was really nice of you." She looked into his compassionate eyes and said, "I looked forward to your texts. They helped."

"I looked forward to your responses. I wanted to come over so you weren't grieving alone, but you were so adamant about wanting to be by yourself."

Although she hadn't admitted it to Angela, part of her had

wished she hadn't been too nervous to let him come over. "Sorry. Other than Gram, Angela, and to some extent Elisa, I've never had anyone to rely on. I don't know how to *do that*."

"I think we have that in common. But I've learned that it's okay to trust people, to let them in and rely on them. If I can learn to do it, maybe you can, too."

Their eyes held for a long silent moment, heat and something deeper filling the space between them. His face was so close, she could see thin white scars above his left eyebrow and along his cheek. She wondered how he'd gotten them but was too distracted by the desires simmering inside her to hold on to the thought. She felt his fingers twitch on her hand, and he licked his lips, his eyes drilling into hers. She wondered if he was going to kiss her—and was surprised by how desperately she wanted him to. His fingers tightened around her hand, and her pulse quickened.

Kiss me...

QUINCY'S FINGERS ACHED to tangle in her hair, to cup her jaw and *feel* her beauty *and* her passion as he devoured the mouth he'd been fantasizing about for all these months. Damn, he loved her full lips. Angelina Jolie had nothing on her. But he'd promised himself he would take it slow so as not to scare her off. The problem was, Quincy had no idea how to do this. He knew how to *fuck*, and he knew how to be a friend, but he had no experience with the deeper emotions consuming him every time he saw Roni or texted with her. He had the urge to protect her, and at the same time, he felt a visceral need to be closer to her—and he wanted to explore *all* of it, to learn everything about her, to touch her, to hold her naked body while they lost themselves in each other.

What. The. Hell?

He'd never picked apart anything like this, much less a physical connection. But he had a feeling that sex with Roni wouldn't be sex as he knew it, just like this date was different from anything he'd ever experienced or imagined. He and Penny had spent plenty of nights talking, but in all the time he'd known her, he'd never once felt anything even close to this. If he didn't put on the brakes, he was going to take that kiss, and whatever this was would be over before they even got started.

He reluctantly moved his hand, instantly wanting to reclaim the connection. Instead, he took a swig of his water and cleared his throat in an attempt to calm his desires.

Yeah, that didn't work.

He'd known since the first time he saw Roni there would be no *tempering*, but hell, he had to try. He went for a change in subject to steer his brain to a safer track and said, "Where did you grow up?"

"Not in this idyllic town, that's for sure. I grew up over the bridge, in an awful, drug-infested neighborhood. My grandmother had lived there all her life and refused to move. But she wanted me to get out as soon as I graduated high school, which was why she pushed me so hard."

"It's strange that she wouldn't have moved you out of there when you were younger."

"The area wasn't like that when she was growing up, and she said she wasn't going to let anyone run her out of her home."

"That's gutsy. Did you stay clean?"

"Of course. I've never even smoked a cigarette. My grandmother smoked a pack a day right up until the month she died. She would have throttled me if I'd so much as *tried* to smoke."

"That's good. That's love." That's what Truman had done for him before going to prison. "Are your parents still around?"

Her gaze drifted to what was left of her salad, and she pushed the food around with her fork. "I don't know who my mother is. My father left home when he was eighteen, and six years later he came back to live with my grandmother with me in his arms. I was about a week old. He was a drinker and a gambler, and he was in and out of my life for the first few years. He stole from my grandmother and he was *mean.* One day he showed up drunk, demanding money and tearing the apartment apart. My grandmother pulled a gun on him and told him to get out and never come back or she'd have him arrested."

Bad memories resurfaced of the night Quincy had shown up at Truman's place asking for money to pay off his debt to Puck. He'd never forget the disgusted, and so fucking disappointed, look on Truman's face as he'd sent Quincy away and said, *You made this fucking mess of a life you're living. Unless you want to get out of it, don't show your face around here again.*

Roni lifted troubled eyes and said, "I haven't seen him since I was five."

He looked at Roni, with her sweet demeanor and clean life, hating that she'd experienced such ugliness and wondered if he was selfish for wanting to continue getting to know her. But he wasn't that drugged-out guy anymore. He'd proved that every day for the last two years, and he would continue to do so until they buried him six feet under. Pushing that hesitation aside, he said, "I'm sorry you went through that, and I'm glad you had your gun-toting grandmother."

"I told you she was fierce."

Damn, he loved how her smile lit up her face. He'd planned on laying out all of his ugly truths for Roni tonight. He'd owned up to his past to plenty of people, without hesitation. But he'd never been faced with sharing that darkness with someone he wanted to become involved with. He knew that once he did, it had the power to change everything, including the way she was looking at him as she sipped her water, and he wasn't ready to give that up just yet.

They made small talk as they finished eating, and then Quincy said, "If I remember correctly, there is one thing Gram didn't teach you."

"What's that?"

"How to roast marshmallows." He reached behind a pillow and pulled out a bag of marshmallows and two sticks he'd whittled into sharp points.

"Are you kidding?" She let out the cutest squeal and went up on her knees, his jacket dwarfing her lithe frame as she threw her arms around him, hugging him tight.

He was glad he'd waited to tell her about his past, because *nothing* was better than the look on her face or the feel of her embrace.

"You are full of surprises!" she said as she drew back.

You don't know the half of it.

"Come on, beautiful. Let's get you hot and sticky." The blush that earned rivaled the flames in her eyes. He was wrong before. *That* look was miles ahead of the last one.

They roasted marshmallows until the fire was nothing more than embers, and Roni tied him in all kinds of knots as she moaned with each bite of the sticky treats and licked melted marshmallow from her fingers. It was torture keeping his hands and mouth to himself. They made small talk and laughed at silly jokes, and man, he really dug her laugh. They talked about his job at the bookstore, and he told her how much he loved it and that his favorite part was reading to the kids for story hour. When he asked her what it was like teaching dance, her face lit up as it had earlier, and she raved about the classes she taught— contemporary dance (her favorite), hip-hop, and ballet. Her tone warmed as she told him that she and Angela had known each other since they were kids, and he sensed something bittersweet when she mentioned that Angela was engaged and they no longer spent much time together outside of the studio.

"I bet you two drove the boys mad when you were growing up," he said, setting down his stick while she roasted another marshmallow. He'd thought his life these last two years had been pretty fucking amazing, but Roni's sunny disposition, sexy innocence, and sassy sense of humor made it feel like he'd been only half living.

"Angela did, but I was always at the studio dancing or helping with classes. I didn't have much time for boys. To be honest, I still don't."

"So I've noticed." He leaned his arm against hers and said, "Thanks for giving me a few hours tonight."

"I still can't believe you did all of this for me." She lifted her marshmallow away from the fire and pulled it off the stick. Her eyes swept over the twinkling lights framing the truck bed, the trash from their meal they'd put in bags and moved to the side, and settled on the wildflowers, lingering there. When her gorgeous eyes found him, the intensity in them stoked the flames that had been simmering between them for months. "I'm really glad Angela won a date with you for me. This has been the best night I've ever had." She licked her lips, her cheeks pinking up as she said just above a whisper, "I like you, Quincy."

"Even though I make you nervous?"

"It's a good nervous. Butterflies-in-my-belly nervous." She held up the marshmallow for him to eat and said, "This one's for you."

His fingers gently circled her wrist as he lowered his mouth over the marshmallow, eating it in one bite and sucking the sugary treat from her fingers. Her eyes turned to pools of liquid heat, her chest rising with heavier breaths. He leaned closer and brushed his lips over hers, whispering, "How about this one?"

"*Quincy*" fell wistfully from her lips.

He slid his arm around her waist, drawing her even closer, and said, "I promise to keep my hands to myself, but my lips want yours."

"*Kiss me.*"

He slid his tongue along her lower lip and kissed the edge of her mouth. "So sweet," he whispered, and traced the bow of her upper lip. "I fucking love your lips." She made a needy sound as his mouth descended upon hers, and he reveled in her softness, the feel of her tongue gliding over his, tentative and somehow also eager. He was aware of *everything* about her—the way she held her breath for seconds at a time, releasing it with a hungry whimper, the feel of her arms circling him, drawing him closer, allowing him to take the kiss deeper. Her mouth was a treasure trove of pleasure. Her fingers dug into his shoulders as she opened wider for him, drawing a groan from some untouched place deep inside him. His hand skimmed down her hip, and damn, she felt incredible. He remembered his promise and forced his hand to remain there. He had the overwhelming desire to be closer, even if fully clothed. He leaned into her, taking her down on her back, but she broke the kiss, eyes wide.

"Quincy, I *can't*."

The worry in her voice tore at him. He gazed into her eyes and said, "I'm not trying to do anything more than kiss you. I just wanted to hold you while we kissed. We can stop."

He started to sit up, and she grabbed his arm, a spark of surprise glimmering in her eyes. "*Wait.* You're really okay just kissing?"

She was so sweet and innocent, he wanted to wrap her up and take care of her as badly as he wanted to kiss her. "Yes. I've waited a long time to kiss you, and I'm in no hurry to do more. I know you're nervous. I am, too. I've never wanted to hold a woman when I was kissing her. Not like I do with you. This thing between us is…" *More powerful than the lure of drugs ever was.*

"Electric," she said.

"Yeah."

"And scary."

"A little. Yes."

She licked her lips, trust settling in her eyes again. "Most guys wouldn't admit that."

"Most guys haven't lived the life I have. I value honesty, and I don't break promises, Roni. I want to see you again. I want to do the scavenger hunt with you Friday night if you're free, and see you next week, and the week after that. I'm not interested in a quick roll in the hay."

"I believe you. I like kissing you. I just didn't want to give you the wrong impression."

God, this woman… "I like kissing you, too, and I like that you're as honest as me. I could kiss you into tomorrow."

A bashful smile curved her lips. "I have to be up for work early tomorrow. It's one of my long days. But maybe you could kiss me for a little while longer?"

"Jesus, Roni, you get me all twisted up inside."

She wrinkled her nose and whispered, "Is that good?"

"*So* good, baby, you're redefining the word." He lowered his mouth to hers, and all those twisted knots inside him fell away.

Chapter Three

"WOULD YOU SLOW down?" Angela said as she and Roni hurried down the block Friday afternoon.

They were picking up lunch from Jazzy Joe's and stopping at the bookstore where Quincy worked, so Roni could say a quick hello. She and Quincy had texted a lot more often the last two days, but they'd both been busy with work, and last night he'd had a date with Kennedy and her little brother, Lincoln, which he'd said he tried to do fairly often. She loved that he made his niece and nephew a priority. But after Wednesday night, when they'd lain in his truck kissing and talking until nearly midnight—*mostly kissing*—she couldn't wait to *see* him. And not only for those steamy kisses, although she hadn't been able to stop thinking about them, either. She didn't have a lot of experience with kissing, but she was quite sure Quincy's butterfly-inducing, toe-curling kisses could win gold medals. By the time they'd finally said good night, she'd been hot and bothered. And now she missed *him*. She missed his face, his laugh, the way he looked at her.

"I know you're dying to see Quincy," Angela said as they turned the corner and the bookstore awning came into view.

"But it's not like he's going anywhere. You said he's working until four, then picking you up for the scavenger hunt."

"I know. I'm just—"

"A stalker?" Angela teased.

"*No.* But who are you to judge? When you started dating Joey, you saw each other *every* day. I just want a *peek.*" She stopped walking and said, "Wait. Do I *seem* like a stalker? Is it weird that after all these months, texting isn't enough anymore?"

Angela laughed. "No. I was kidding. The only thing you seem like is a girl who has finally let the guy she's been dreaming about all summer into her life, and one taste was not enough. That's a good thing, Roni. Maybe you'll even dust off your cooch and get some action. Now, come on, let's go see your guy; then we can go see mine."

"Ang! I have a *guy!*" she said giddily, making them both laugh. Her nerves flamed as they neared the entrance to the bookstore, and she grabbed Angela's arm and stopped walking. "Now I'm worried he'll think I'm clingy."

"Clingy would have been begging him to come by after he took the kids out last night. You just want to say hello. Besides, didn't you say he texted you something sappy about counting down the hours until the scavenger hunt? He's totally into you." She pulled open the door and waved Roni in.

His text hadn't been sappy at all. Her pulse quickened just thinking about it. *There's this guy at the bookstore bragging about taking out the hottest girl in Peaceful Harbor tonight. I gotta show you this guy.* He'd texted a selfie with the message *Can't wait to see you tonight, beautiful.* His sense of humor made him even harder to resist. Not that she wanted to resist him anymore.

She spotted Quincy, and those butterflies took flight again.

His hair fell in front of his eyes, and he raked his hand through it, pushing it behind his ears, giving her a great view of his handsome face. She loved his honest eyes, but what was it about his face that she liked so much? She'd been asking herself that for two days. There was no doubt he was gorgeous, with a square jaw and inescapable ruggedness, but looks went only so far. Roni knew how quickly outward appearances could change with accidents or age. She'd learned from her grandmother to see people for who they were on the inside, because even attractive people could be rotten. The answer dawned on her. The person Quincy was on the inside was what made everything else about him even more alluring. And the best part was, she had a sneaking suspicion that she might be the only person who was privy to his tender, romantic side.

She watched him reading to about a dozen toddlers sitting on the floor in front of his chair, their adorable faces tipped up as they hung on his every word. Two more children stood by his side, peering at the pages he was reading. One had a hand on his shoulder, and another was leaning against his other side. Quincy looked out at the kids as he told the story, speaking in silly voices and asking questions. He listened as intently to their answers as he had to her the other night. A little blond girl holding a stuffed hedgehog tried to climb into his lap. He lifted her and put his arm around her without missing a word of the story. The little girl rested her head on his shoulder.

Melt. Melt. Melt.

Angela dragged Roni away from the entrance, and they stood near a skinny girl who was also watching Quincy. Angela pointed to a handful of women standing huddled together, whispering, at the edge of the carpet the children were sitting on, their eyes locked on Quincy. "How many of those women do you think borrowed their nieces or nephews just so they could see Quincy?"

Roni noticed a few other women sitting on chairs, some with babies or toddlers in their lap, and there was definitely a difference between them and the whisperers. "Do you blame them?" Roni asked as casually as she was able, trying to ignore the jealousy clawing at her.

The skinny girl said, "He gets gawked at all the time, but he's all about the kids."

"Do you have a child over there?" Roni asked.

"No. The guy reading is a friend of mine," the girl said.

Angela's brows slanted. "A *friend*? Is he your boyfriend?"

Roni glared at Angela.

"No," the girl said. "He's just a friend helping me through a rough time. He's a good guy, and he's single, if that's what you're fishing for."

"She's *not* fishing," Roni said, embarrassed that Angela had even asked. She needed to get out of there. "We have to go. Have a good day." She hurried out of the bookstore with Angela on her heels, and as soon as they cleared the door, she turned on Angela. "Why did you say that? Quincy isn't that kind of guy."

"I didn't think he was, but why not make sure?"

"Because it makes you sound like you don't trust him, and *I* do trust him. Besides, you don't know who that girl is or what she'll say to Quincy. What if he saw me and she says I was checking up on him? I'm not even the one who said it, and I'm not checking up on him. All I wanted was to see him."

"I'm sorry," Angela insisted. "You're right. It seemed like a good idea at the time."

As they headed for Jazzy Joe's, Roni said, "You're the one who sang his praises, remember?"

"Yes, and you're right. I'm sorry. Like I said, I saw an opening and thought it was worth asking. And now we know." She put her arm around Roni and said, "You're my girl. I'm going to be a little protective of you."

"I appreciate that, but I don't think he's a womanizer, and I don't think I need protecting from him. But I might need protecting from myself. He looks at me like he wants to eat me alive." She pulled open the door to Jazzy Joe's and said, "And I kind of want him to."

RONI SPENT THE day volleying Angela's excited chatter and her lectures on safe sex. She couldn't believe she'd even told her bestie she wanted to be devoured by Quincy. It wasn't like she was going to jump into bed with him when they went to the scavenger hunt tonight, but that didn't mean she didn't think about how much she loved being in his arms, how good his hands had felt moving over her hip and down her back, and how much she liked when he'd caressed her face, gazing so deeply into her eyes it felt even more intimate than their kisses. Those things had her wondering what being closer to him would be like, how good his naked body would feel pressing down on her. A knock at her apartment door jarred her from her thoughts, sending tingles of anticipation racing up her chest.

Quincy was there to pick her up for the scavenger hunt. She took one last look in the mirror at herself in black skinny jeans, ankle boots, and her favorite cropped lavender sweater and thought she looked darn good.

If only she wasn't so nervous.

She hurried through the living room, trying to calm herself down, and pulled open the door. Her entire body sizzled at the sight of Quincy's slow grin and those clear blue eyes drinking her in.

"Hello, beautiful." He stepped inside, slid his arm around her waist, and pulled her into a knee-weakening kiss. "I've been waiting all day to do that."

"Me too" slipped out, as honest as it was shocking.

"Then maybe we need another." He lowered his lips to hers. "And another." He kissed her slow and tender, keeping her close as he said, "I'll never get enough of kissing you."

She didn't even try to think as she went up on her toes and pressed her lips to his, because *she* couldn't get enough, either. He crushed her body to his, and she felt every hard inch of him. By the time their lips parted, she was on fire.

"If we keep doing this," he said in a voice full of restraint, "I'm going to break that promise I made about keeping my hands to myself." He loosened his grip, which was probably a good thing, because she was debating asking him to break that promise. "How is it possible that you look even hotter with your glasses on?"

She absently touched the black frames. "I only wear contacts when I teach or dance."

"Good for me, then. You were wearing glasses the first night we met, and that's the image I see of you, sitting at the table, trying to figure out what that flash of electricity was between us. Just like I was." He brushed a feathery kiss over her lips and closed the door, his eyes sweeping over her off-white living room couch with light-pink and lavender accent pillows, the glass coffee and end tables, and her secondhand teal-and-oak settee. "I like your place," he said as he walked over to her bookshelf by the settee, eyeballing her fiction novels, books on dance, and photographs of her with her grandmother, Angela, and fellow dancers.

"Thanks. There's not much to it." She'd never had a guy in her apartment, and it had never felt overly girlie. But Quincy was so potently *male*, the way he strode across the room, big and broad in his leather jacket and black boots, it was a stark contrast.

"I disagree," he said. "Your home says a lot about you. It's feminine and organized, and all these pictures tell me who and what is important to you. Maybe one day we'll end up in a frame on this shelf, too."

She hoped they would, too.

He picked up a picture of Roni and her grandmother and said, "I assume this is Gram, the famous apple-pie-making tough cookie?"

"You really do remember everything."

"When it comes to you, I do. How old were you in this? Fourteen? Fifteen?"

"Fifteen. That was taken after the Summer Showcase. Contemporary dance is my absolute favorite, and I performed solo to 'My Immortal' by Evanescence. Gram said she cried during my performance." Her throat thickened with emotion as she took in her grandmother's proud smile.

"I wish I could go back in time and watch all of your performances." He set the picture down and said, "Is Angela coming to the scavenger hunt?"

She was still stuck on him wishing he could have seen her dance, and it took a second for her to tuck that sweet sentiment away and respond. "No. She had other plans."

"That's too bad. I would have liked to *officially* meet her," he said as he looked at more pictures.

"We stopped by the bookstore to say hi on our way to pick up lunch today, but you were busy reading to the kids. You were really good with them."

"I love kids. They get so excited over everything." He picked up another picture as if he didn't want to miss a single one. "Why didn't you stick around? I would have loved to see you."

"We had to pick up lunch and get back to the studio for our classes."

He showed her the picture he was holding, a wolfish grin lifting his cheeks. "You look hot in this leotard. You're probably going to have to model that for me one day."

Heat darted through her core, and she felt it spread up her neck and cheeks.

"You're damn cute, Roni." He chuckled softly. "Your grandmother looks proud in every one of these pictures. How long ago was this one taken?"

"That was my first performance after I went away to school, about six years ago. It was the only time she came out to visit, and we had the best weekend together, even though she hated the city. She said it was too busy and too loud. But the truth is, it wasn't home. She loved being home."

"I get that. Most people want to travel, but I'm with Gram. I prefer my life to be chaos free. I'm perfectly happy here in the Harbor, around family and friends." He set the frame on the shelf and said, "We should probably get going so we're not late."

She grabbed her short suede jacket from the hook on the wall. Angela had given it to her last Christmas and said it made her look *hot*. Quincy took it from her, holding it up for her to put on.

"Aren't you a gentleman?" she said as she slipped her arms into it.

"Apparently with you I am." He raised his brows, his eyes taking a slow stroll down her body. "That's a killer jacket. You look incredible."

"Thank you." She put her keys in her pocket, and as they headed down to his truck, she thought about how much she liked that dating was new to him, too. It was nice knowing they were both exploring it for the first time.

He helped her into his truck, and when he settled into his seat, he said, "Are you ready to enter my world?"

"I thought we were going to the scavenger hunt."

He started the truck, but he put his arm across the back of the seat, giving her his full attention. "We are. It's hosted by the Whiskeys and Silver-Stone Cycles."

"I read that online."

"Well, the Whiskeys are like family to me, and I'd like to introduce you to them, and to my buddy Jed, and the rest of my friends, if that's okay with you. Jed and I used to be roommates, and I'm going to be the best man in his wedding over the holidays."

"Sure," she said, though the idea made her even more nervous. "I'd like to meet your friends."

"Great. Since the Whiskeys are hosting, and Biggs Whiskey is the president of the Dark Knights, there will be a lot of bikers there. Do you know who the Dark Knights are?"

"I'm sure everyone in Peaceful Harbor knows about them. They do a lot for the community. But even if I hadn't heard of them, they made a lasting impression at the auction."

"I forgot about that," he said. "I was going to warn you that some of them look intimidating, but they're good guys."

"Are the two guys who nearly got in a fight over the redhead at the auction going to be there? They scared me." The redhead hadn't been on the manifest when she'd taken the stage and gone up for auction, and the calmer of the two men, who were both well over six feet tall, had bid tens of thousands of dollars on her. The rougher-looking guy with the thick beard and tattoos covering every inch of his skin had reminded Roni of a rabid dog ready to attack when he'd started the argument. Though the bidder had appeared calmer, she had no doubt he'd have done anything to win that redhead.

Quincy touched her shoulder and said, "They'll be there, but you don't have to worry about a fight breaking out. That was an isolated incident between Bullet Whiskey, the angrier of the two guys, with the thick beard, and Jace Stone, one of the owners of Silver-Stone Cycles. Bullet thought Jace wanted to just mess around with his younger sister, Dixie, the redhead."

"She looked like she could handle herself, and I don't think *any* guy would bid that much money if he wasn't serious about a woman."

"I know, but Bullet's protective of the people he loves. We all are. But they're friends again, and Jace and Dixie got married over the summer."

"Really? That was fast."

"Oh, I don't know. I think when it's right, you know it from day one." He gave her shoulder a squeeze and they headed for Whiskey Bro's.

Chapter Four

THE PARKING LOT of Whiskey Bro's was packed with motorcycles, trucks, and other vehicles. It was no wonder Roni had been uncomfortable when she'd gone to the auction. Even with the bright banner announcing the scavenger hunt hanging across the front of the old wooden building, it still looked as rough as many of the bikers it catered to. Crowds of people ranging from young families and professionals to tough-looking bikers wearing leather jackets with Dark Knights patches milled around tables set up on the grass. Quincy parked around the side of the building and helped Roni out of the truck.

"What's that building?" she asked, pointing to another weathered building behind the bar.

"The Dark Knights' clubhouse. They meet there Monday nights."

"If you're so close to the Whiskeys, why aren't you a member of the motorcycle club?"

"It would be an honor to become one eventually, but membership requires a big commitment. Between school, work, Kennedy and Lincoln, and a few other commitments, including a certain new woman in my life, I have enough on my plate.

Tru isn't a member, either; neither is Jace or my buddy Scott, who you'll meet tonight." He put his arm around her as they made their way to the front.

"Will Tru and Gemma be here with the kids?"

"Definitely." He scanned the crowd, looking for his brother. Dixie was standing by a registration table with Crystal and Finlay, Bullet's very pregnant wife. He spotted Truman talking with Jed and Bear and said, "There's Tru," as they headed over. "Nervous?"

"A little."

He pulled her closer and kissed her cheek. "I've got you, babe. We're going to have a great time."

"There's the big man," Bear said as they approached, giving Quincy an approving nod.

"I think you mean the *best* man," Jed said. He looked more like Quincy's biological brother than Truman did, with dirty-blond hair, a short beard, and blue eyes. "How's it going, bro?"

"Do you really have to ask?" Truman winked at Roni and said, "Hey there, Roni. Good to see you."

Roni said, "Hi."

"Roni, these are my buddies Bear Whiskey and Jed Moon. They work at Whiskey Automotive with Tru, and Bear is married to Jed's younger sister, Crystal."

Jed said, "It's nice to finally meet you."

"You too," she said sweetly.

"We've been watching this dude draw hearts around your name for months," Bear teased.

"Jackass," Quincy said with a laugh.

"Actually, Bear, I'm glad to hear that," Roni said, her eyes finding Quincy's. "Because I've been doodling his name, too."

Jed and Truman chuckled.

Damn, that felt good. "That's it, babe. Claim your man." Quincy kissed her cheek, earning an adorable blush.

"First she's got to find a *man*," Bear joked.

Quincy lunged toward him, and Bear stumbled back, nearly running right into his mother as she came through the crowd cradling baby Axel in her arms. Wren "Red" Whiskey looked like a younger Sharon Osbourne, with short red hair and wise eyes. As usual, she was dressed in black, from her leather jacket right down to her jeans and boots. Red was tough, as any biker's wife had to be, but she was also warm and loving and more of a mother to Quincy than his own mother had ever been.

"Careful there, big boy," Red said as she joined them. "I've got precious cargo."

"Sorry, Mom." Bear reached for Axel.

"*Aw.* Is that your baby?" Roni asked, leaning closer to get a better look.

"Sure is. This is my little man, Axel," Bear said.

"He's adorable. I *love* babies." Roni wiggled the baby's bootie-covered foot and said, "Hello there, Axel. You are precious, aren't you?"

"And so are *you*," Red said, sidling up to Quincy and placing a hand on his back. "Are you going to introduce me to this beautiful young lady, honey?"

"Sorry, Red. This is my girl, Roni." *My girl* hit him hard, and he loved the way it felt to say it. "Roni, this is Red Whiskey—Bullet, Bones, Bear, and Dixie's mother."

Red gave him a *don't be silly* look. "If you're going to list my children, you'd better add yourself, Tru, Jed, and half the other guys around here." She turned a welcoming smile to Roni and said, "It's a pleasure to meet you, sweetheart. You're the lucky lady whose friend won a date for you with this wonderful young man at the auction, aren't you? The one I hear has kept him on the line for all these months."

"Guilty as charged," Roni said. "I don't go out often."

"Well, sweetheart, you've got yourself a winner here," Red said. "Our Quincy has a heart of gold. He told me about your grandmother's passing, and I'm very sorry for your loss. If you ever need to bend an ear, people say I'm a good listener."

"Thank you," Roni said, eyeing Quincy curiously.

"I also heard that you're teaching our Kennedy some adorable moves down at Elisa's studio," Red said.

"Yes, that's right. Kennedy is a doll, and she sure does love to dance," Roni said. "How do you know Elisa?"

"I know *of* her. Knowing who the business owners are within Dark Knights territory is important so we can protect them. See that gnarly but insanely sexy old man with the cane and scraggly beard?" Red pointed to Biggs, talking with Jace and Bullet. Biggs was six five, his skin like leather from years of riding his motorcycle in the hot sun. He wore a long-sleeve black shirt under his black leather vest, which had the Dark Knights patches on the back. Biggs had suffered a stroke several years ago and was left with a slight drooping of the left side of his face, mostly hidden by his scruffy white beard and mustache, and a limp that required a cane. "That's my husband, Biggs. His grandfather founded the Dark Knights. We've been protecting Peaceful Harbor for decades."

"Okay, listen up, everyone!" Dixie announced through a megaphone, then waited for the crowd to quiet down. "Welcome, and thank you for supporting the Parkvale Women's Shelter by joining this scavenger hunt. We'll be starting in ten minutes. If you haven't preregistered or picked up your scavenger hunt list, you can do so here at this table. You will have two hours to complete as many of the items on the list as you can. Every item is worth a certain number of points, as noted on the list, and you must take a picture with each one. The team who earns the most points will win a two-hundred-and-fifty-dollar gift certificate from Silver-Stone Cycles' online shop."

Applause and cheers rang out, and Roni said, "She's even more gorgeous than I remembered."

"Dixie is the face of Jace's company for his new Leather and Lace clothing line, and she's the model in next year's calendar," Quincy explained. "She has to do appearances several times over the next year, and I'll fill in for her while she's gone, handling the accounting and admin for their family businesses."

"Wow, you weren't kidding about being close to them," Roni said.

"The second-place winner will take home one-hundred-dollar gift certificates from Whiskey Bro's and Whiskey Automotive," Dixie announced, inciting more cheers. "Remember to be safe out there. We'll meet back here at eight o'clock to announce the winners and enjoy a buffet feast prepared by my very talented—and very pregnant—sister-in-law, Finlay!"

Bullet hollered, "That's my lollipop!" causing an uproar of laughter.

"Did he say *lollipop*?" Roni asked.

"Yes, he did. That's what Bullet calls his wife, Finlay, the pregnant blonde standing next to Dixie. Finlay owns a catering company and cooks part time for the bar." Quincy took her hand and said, "I wouldn't delve too deeply into the reasons behind that endearment." He leaned in for a kiss and noticed her blushing again, but kissing her in public already felt natural to him. "We'd better get our list. We'll see you guys back here when we collect our trophy."

"Dream on," Truman said. "I'm winning this thing. Kennedy has her heart set on a leather jacket from Jace's store."

Quincy chuckled as they headed for the registration table. If he and Roni won, hopefully she'd be okay getting Kennedy that jacket.

"You're really lucky to have so many friends," Roni said.

"I am lucky. I know it's probably overwhelming for you to keep everyone straight, but I'm glad you're here."

"Me too. I like your friends, and I really like Red. I can see how much she adores you," she said as they stepped into the registration line. "I didn't realize you told anyone about Gram."

He drew her into his arms, and she blushed again. "You should probably get used to me kissing you and holding you in public, because I can't seem to help myself." He pressed his lips to hers and said, "I'm sorry for telling Red, but I was at dinner at their house when you texted and said your grandmother had passed away and told me not to come see you when I offered. I was going to drive over anyway, but Red talked me out of it. She said strong women know what they need and that I'd blow any chance I had with you if I didn't give you space."

"She really is like a mom to you."

"Yeah, and these guys and their wives, and Dixie, are like brothers and sisters. We watch out for each other, and as you've seen, we also give each other shit."

"That's nice. I really only have Angela and Elisa," she said as the line moved forward.

"And me, babe. And by extension, you'll have all of these friends, too, regardless of whether you ditch my ass or not. We're a loyal crew."

"Apparently you're also a big sap," Dixie said, sidling up to them.

"Hey, Dix." Quincy had been so taken with Roni, he hadn't seen Dixie approaching them. "This is Roni. Roni, this is the one and only Dixie Whiskey."

"That's Dixie Whiskey-*Stone* now, thank you very much. Hi, Roni." Dixie leaned in and hugged her, her long red hair falling forward. "I'm glad you guys made it, and that's a great jacket."

"Thank you. It was a gift from my friend," Roni said.

"Well, your friend has good taste." Dixie handed her a piece of paper and said, "This is your scavenger hunt list. Remember to take pictures, or your entries won't count."

"Okay, thanks," Roni said.

"Dix! Got a sec?" Jace hollered from across the lawn, waving her over. "Hey, Quincy!"

"Jace." Quincy lifted his chin.

"I'd better go. Everyone needs something today. Good luck!" Dixie said, and headed over to Jace.

"She seems nice," Roni said, watching Dixie walk away. "She moves in those sky-high boots like she was born in them."

"Yeah, she's a trip," Quincy said.

"Five minutes, people!" Crystal announced through the megaphone. She always stood out in a crowd, with jet-black hair, several piercings in one ear, and an affinity for dressing like a punk rocker.

"That's Crystal, Bear's wife."

"Wow, she does not look like she just had a baby," Roni said.

"You'll have to tell her that. She thinks she's gotten heavy but we all think she looks great, and Bear can't keep his paws off her." He nodded to Bear walking up behind Crystal, cradling Axel in one arm as he put his other around her and kissed her. "See?"

"They're cute together," she said as people began heading for the parking lot.

"Come on, let's go." Quincy spotted Penny and Scott standing next to Scott's car across the parking lot and pointed to her. "That's my friend Penny, Finlay's sister, and the guy with her is our buddy Scott."

Penny looked over, waved, said something to Scott, then ran toward them. "Hey, Pen," Quincy said.

Penny planted a hand on her jeans-clad hip, beaming at them. "Hi." Her eyes shifted to Roni, and she said, "I'm Penny."

"I'm Roni. You work at the ice cream shop, right?"

"Yeah, I own it." She pointed to Quincy and said, "Sometimes this big lug helps me out there."

"Really? That's so fun. I *love* your sundaes," Roni said as cars began heading out of the lot. "I think the Go Away Gloomy Day sundae is my favorite."

"I'm working on a new one called Book Boy Gets His Girl," Penny said cheekily, eyeing Quincy. "It'll be my sweetest sundae yet."

"I think that'll be my new favorite," Roni said.

"Mine, too," Quincy said, pulling her closer.

"I'd better go before Scott gets antsy. Are you guys coming back here?" Penny looked at Roni and said, "I'd love to chat and get to know each other better."

"I think so. Are we, Quincy?"

"Yeah, we'll be here. But anything Penny tells you about me is a lie."

"Ha! We'll see about that. Catch you guys later." Penny jogged back to Scott.

As they headed for Quincy's truck, Roni said, "She seems fun."

"She's a blast." He opened the passenger door and helped her in, then went around to the driver's side, and as he started the engine, he said, "You should know that everyone thought Penny and I were going to hook up, but we never have. We're just really good friends. There have been times when I've crashed on her couch or she's crashed on mine. But we've never even kissed."

"Okay," she said, and looked at the list for the scavenger hunt.

He couldn't see her expression to gauge it. "Is that an *okay*, you believe me, or an *okay*, like when girls say they're fine, but they're really pissed?" He pulled the truck in line behind the other vehicles.

She looked up from the list and said, "I trust you, Quincy. I expected that you'd have friends that are girls and guys. Besides, it's not like I'd get jealous of an *old* girlfriend."

"Well, I've never had a real girlfriend, so there are no old ones out there. I know this is new between us, but I want you to know that I'm not looking for anyone else."

"Okay. I'm glad, because neither am I." She held his gaze a beat longer, then looked at the list again and said, "This is a *long* list. Listen to a few of the things we have to do. *Serenade a stranger, go down a slide, kiss on the steps of the public library.*" She looked up and said, "That's weird for a scavenger hunt."

He was still riding the high of her not looking elsewhere and being okay about his friendship with Penny. "Sure is, but we're heading to the library first."

"Wait!" She craned her neck, looking out the window at Biggs and Red walking toward their car and said, "We need a picture of Biggs to check off *take a picture of a guy with a cool mustache*. That's fifteen points. I'll be fast!" She threw open her door and pulled her phone from her back pocket as she stepped out and ran across the parking lot toward them.

Her limp was more pronounced when she ran. Quincy wondered if it was caused by an old dance injury, but he figured it would be rude to ask and assumed she'd tell him when she was ready. He watched her showing the list to Biggs, who motioned for her to step beside him. He put his arm around her, and she took a selfie of them. Quincy loved watching her come out of her shell. As she ran back to the truck, Biggs gave him a thumbs-up, and that felt fantastic.

She climbed into the truck, breathing hard, and said, "Got it!"

He didn't hesitate or think as he hauled her across the bench seat beside him, said, "You're so fucking adorable," and plastered his mouth to hers.

When their lips parted, she sighed longingly and said, "If I jump out and take another picture, do I get another kiss?"

"Baby, you don't have to move a muscle." He pulled her into another kiss, and the truck behind them honked. Quincy tore his mouth away and glared over the seat, meeting the amused eyes of Truman and Gemma.

AFTER SHARING SEVERAL spine-tingling kisses on the library steps, forgetting to take a picture, and cracking up about it as they drove back to do it again, they made their way down the list, taking pictures of a man walking a dog, graffiti on a brick wall, and about a dozen other things. They took selfies together, kissing and making silly faces. Quincy had never had so much fun.

When they stopped at the park to go down the slide, he climbed up the ladder behind Roni and smacked her butt. She squealed, scrambling to the landing. He caught her around her waist, crushing her to him, and captured her laughing lips with his.

"That's *not* keeping your hands to yourself," she teased, though her eyes told him she loved every second of it as much as he did.

"Maybe we can renegotiate. Just for *this*." He pressed his lips to her and grabbed her ass with both hands. "It's torture looking at your gorgeous body and not being able to touch you. I won't try to cop a feel anywhere else."

She laughed and touched her forehead to his chest.

He moved his hands to her waist and said, "Sorry. Too soon?"

She shook her head and pushed his hands back down to her butt. "But fair is fair."

She grabbed hold of his ass, and his body electrified. A groan climbed up his throat, and he lowered his mouth to hers again, taking her in a long, passionate kiss. She pressed harder against his ass, and within seconds they were kissing feverishly, their hips grinding. Was this the same woman who blushed at a public kiss? When their lips finally parted, his body was vibrating from head to toe, but it was the dizzying sense of completeness that had Quincy in a fog.

"*Jesus*, Roni. What have you done to me? I've never felt like this."

"Neither have I." She went up on her toes, and he met her halfway in another life-altering kiss. "*Wow*," she whispered. "We'd better…"

"Right." He sank down to the top of the slide, pulling her onto his lap. *Holy fuck.* He was hard, and she was soft and perfect. She was going to be the death of him.

He couldn't resist cradling her jaw and taking her in another scorching kiss.

Sometime later, ten minutes or maybe thirty—he had no idea which—Roni's cheeks were flushed, her eyes lustful and beautiful, they took a selfie, kissed as they took another, and finally made their way down the slide, taking more pictures as they went. Then they headed back to the truck to knock more items off their list.

Starting with another kiss.

THE SUN WAS setting when Roni asked Quincy to pull into the pharmacy parking lot.

"What are we getting here?" he asked.

"You'll see. But we have to be fast. We only have twenty minutes to get back to the bar."

They hurried into the pharmacy, and he followed her down the aisles. She grabbed a hair removal kit.

"I'm totally cool with bikini waxes," Quincy said. "But you don't need to do that *now*."

She made a *tsk* sound and playfully smacked his stomach, heading up to the register. "It's not for me. It's on our list."

"Is there another list I don't know about?" he asked as he paid for the wax. "Does it involve silk ties? Because I could totally be down for that."

She rolled her eyes as they headed back outside.

"How about whipped cream? Is that on this new list?" he asked. "Because that'd be cool, too."

"Maybe Dixie can add that next year." She stopped beside the truck and said, "I need you to take your shirt off."

"Are we getting naked in the parking lot?"

"We have to wax a body part. It's worth *one hundred* points and could make us the winners." She waved to his shirt. "Take it off."

"Hell no. I've seen that movie *The 40-Year-Old Virgin*. I know what wax does to a dude's chest."

"Fine." She lifted the hem of his T-shirt and peeked under it. "There's not enough hair on your stomach." She dropped to one knee.

"Uh, *babe*. I can't touch you, but you're allowed to go down on me in a public parking lot? Okay." He reached for the button on his jeans.

"No I'm *not!*" She laughed, turning bright red, and began rolling up his jeans. "I'm looking for a hairy body part."

He snickered, and she gave him a deadpan look.

She ran her hand up and down his calf. "This is perfect."

"Yeah it is. Do it a little higher."

She pushed to her feet, smiling from ear to ear. "Do you have scissors, or a knife, or something?"

He covered his dick with his hands. "I like you, babe, but you're not getting near *that* with anything sharp besides your teeth."

"Ohmygod. *Quincy!*" She turned away, but she was laughing. "You are impossible."

"For you, I'm more than possible. I'm a sure thing." He pulled her into his arms and kissed her. "We're running out of time. Why do you need scissors?"

"To cut the wax strip."

He unlocked the truck and grabbed his pocketknife from the glove compartment. She opened the package and reached for the knife.

"I'll do it, babe." He couldn't even believe he was going to let her do this.

Yeah, he could, because it was Roni, and he'd have a hell of a time denying her anything.

"I can handle a knife," she said, taking it from his hands, and knelt on the ground, huddling over the strip as she cut it. Then she peered up at him from behind those sexy glasses, her hazel eyes swimming with the unmistakable combination of amusement and lust—his new favorite look—and said, "This might hurt."

He'd been through far worse than a little waxing. "Go for it, babe."

She peeled the back off the wax strip, then pressed it to the side of his calf and rubbed her hand over it for a minute or two. "Ready?"

"Babe, just do—" She tore off the wax strip, sending a burning sensation through his leg, and he cringed. "*Holy shit.* Women do that to their…?"

She giggled and took a picture. "It'll stop stinging eventually." She pushed to her feet and said, "Thanks for taking one for the team. We'd better hurry."

She handed him the strip. It was covered in hair and cut into the shape of an *R*. He arched a brow and said, "*Roni…?*"

"You said to claim my man," she said sassily, and climbed into the truck as if she hadn't just lassoed his heart and reeled him right in.

Chapter Five

RONI WALKED INTO Whiskey Bro's tucked beneath Quincy's arm, feeling completely different than she had the night of the auction. Not only was she having the absolute best evening, but they were immediately greeted by burly guys in leather jackets who embraced Quincy, or clapped him on the back, and welcomed Roni warmly. She couldn't believe how many friends he had, or how many of them went by their road names—Court, Viper, Crow, and many others—the way the Whiskey men did. She met Bones Whiskey and his sweet fiancée, Sarah, and Jed's fiancée, Josie. As they made their way through the crowded bar toward the table to turn in their pictures for the scavenger hunt, Quincy continued introducing her to what seemed like everyone there. The place was packed. Men and women were playing darts and pool, filling their plates at the buffet, and eating at tables. There were children running around, too. It was loud and busy, and everyone was friendly. There was no way she could keep all the names straight, but she made sure to remember the Whiskeys, Jed, and Scott, and each of their significant others, because she knew how important they were to Quincy.

A blonde named Isla helped them upload their pictures, and when they turned around, a little boy with a mop of light-brown hair ran by, chased by a younger sandy-haired boy.

"Whoa, little dudes, slow down," Quincy called after them.

Bones walked past and said, "I've got them. Thanks, Quincy."

"Are they his boys?" Roni asked.

"The older one is Jed and Josie's son, Hail, and the younger one is Bradley, one of Bones and Sarah's three kids."

He pointed out their two daughters, Maggie Rose, an infant bundled in Sarah's arms, and Lila, the little girl Quincy had put on his lap at the bookstore. She looked to be about two and was happily clinging to Biggs as he talked with a guy whose name Roni couldn't remember.

"I've never heard of kids running around a bar before," Roni said. "Not that I go to bars or hear about them often, but I always assume people are drinking and partying."

"Whenever the Whiskeys put on an event, it's a family affair, and quite a few of us don't drink. It's one of the many things I like about this group."

"That's another thing we have in common, because I don't drink, either."

"Miss *Woni* is here!" Kennedy hollered at the top of her lungs, pushing between Truman and Gemma, who were talking with Bullet a few feet away.

Roni had liked Truman and Gemma the instant she'd met them, when they'd come to the studio to check out classes for Kennedy. Gemma was a sweetheart, with brown hair and golden highlights, and Truman was big like Quincy and as dark as Quincy was fair. He had a beard and blue tattoos on his arms, hands, and snaking out of the collar of his shirt, but for as badass as he looked, he was kind and gentle with the kids and Gemma.

Kennedy jumped up and down in her purple dress, cheering, "Mommy! Daddy! Miss Woni is here! Are you on your playdate with Uncle Quincy?"

"Yes, I guess I am," Roni said, a handful of people around them chuckling.

"A *playdate*?" Truman asked.

"Yes!" Kennedy exclaimed. "Uncle Quincy weally wanted to have a playdate with Miss Woni."

"I bet he did," Bullet said with a snicker.

Bullet was the most intimidating looking of them all, with the exception of the mountainous bartender wearing the baseball cap, Diesel, who Quincy had introduced Roni to earlier.

"I love playdates with my wife," Bear called out from where he stood by the bar, sparking a litany of laughter and jokes among the crowd.

Quincy pulled Roni into his arms, gazing into her eyes with a devilish grin as he said, "We've been outed by a tiny human."

She laughed. "That's okay. I like playdates with you."

He kissed her, and the crowd cheered and whistled. He ate it all up, calling out to Kennedy, "Hey, jelly bean! Miss Roni and I will have many more *playdates* in the future."

"Yay!" Kennedy cheered. "Now you can show Miss Woni how you can eat ice cream all night long! *Bye!*" She ran off, leaving the guys roaring with laughter and Roni red-cheeked and burying her face in Quincy's chest.

Quincy kissed the top of her head and said, "Aw, babe. I'm sorry."

"Sorry you can eat *ice cream* all night long?" Bullet scoffed.

"Dude, that's a benefit."

"All right, Bullet. *Back off,*" Quincy said, rubbing a hand down Roni's back.

His protectiveness made him even hotter. Roni lifted her face, catching him staring down Bullet. A hint of worry fluttered in her chest. She wanted to tell him it was fine and make him stop challenging Bullet, and she opened her mouth to do just that, but before she could get a word out, Bullet cut her off.

"Sorry, Roni. Didn't mean to embarrass you." Bullet stroked his beard, his eyes now trained on Roni as Finlay came to his side, adorable with her burgeoning belly and blond hair cascading around her face. "But you gotta admit, it *is* a benefit. How do you think my wife got her nickname?"

Finlay gasped. "Bullet Whiskey, that is *not* true."

"But it's funny," Bullet said.

Roni had to admit that it was funny. She laughed along with everyone else, loving the camaraderie of Quincy's friends.

"Okay, break it up," Dixie said, pushing past Bullet with Penny and Crystal on her heels. Without her jacket, Dixie's colorful arm tattoos were visible, and they were as beautiful as she was. "It's girl time, Quince. We need to borrow Roni for a little while. You can hang out with the Neanderthals."

Roni was surprised they wanted to include her, and she was excited to get to know the other girls.

"The guys are not nearly as fun as my girl." Quincy tightened his hold on Roni, and *oh,* how she loved that.

"Last chance, Gritt. Give her a kiss or forever hold it in," Crystal said.

"Babe, are you okay going with them?" he asked thoughtfully.

"Yes, of course."

He pressed his lips to hers, then glared at the three of them and said, "I don't know what you do to indoctrinate women into your group, but go easy, okay? Don't scare her off."

Roni gazed up at him and said, "It would take a lot to scare me off."

"Well, there you have it." Dixie said, "This chick isn't so shy anymore, is she?"

"It's hard to be shy around here," Roni said as Dixie and Crystal flanked her.

Gemma joined them and said, "I can't believe you got her away from Quincy. He's had her glued to his side."

"I don't hear Roni complaining," Quincy said.

Wow. She liked this side of Quincy. He was a little possessive, but not overbearing. He was just…Protective? Thoughtful? As into her as she was into him? Yes, he was all of those things. His words came to mind, and she thought, *He's claiming me, and it feels good.*

"I'll catch up in a sec, you guys," Penny said. "I need to talk to Quincy."

As they led her away, Roni felt Quincy's eyes on her, and she glanced over her shoulder to look at him. Sure enough, though he and Penny were talking, he was watching *her.* He blew her a kiss, and she mentally caught it and tucked it away with the other romantic things he'd done.

"There she is!" Josie, a petite strawberry-blonde, popped to her feet at a table where she was sitting with her sister, Sarah. Sarah was cradling her baby.

"Is Quincy still watching us like a hawk?" Dixie asked as they all sat down.

Gemma craned her neck and said, "He's talking to Penny.

Oops, there's a peek."

Roni had to peek, too. Her heart skipped at the way Quincy was looking at her.

"Well, if that look doesn't say it all," Dixie said. "You've met all the girls, haven't you, Roni?"

"I think so, except Sleeping Beauty," Roni said, motioning to Sarah's baby. "That must be Maggie Rose. She's beautiful."

Sarah tucked her dirty-blond hair behind her ear and said, "She's all tuckered out."

"I can't believe she can sleep with all the noise in here," Roni said.

"She's used to it. I swear our house is never quiet." Sarah kissed Maggie Rose's head and said, "Have you met my other kids yet, Bradley and Lila? Biggs absconded with Lila a little while ago. I'm sure she's full of cookies by now, and Bones was keeping an eye on Bradley and Hail."

"The boys zoomed past us right before Kennedy announced my *playdate* with Quincy."

"Sorry about that," Gemma said as Penny joined them at the table.

"Oh, don't be. Kennedy's a pistol," Roni said. "I have to admit, I'm an only child, so this whole gathering is a little overwhelming, but I love kids, and I've really enjoyed meeting so many of Quincy's friends."

"This crowd can definitely be overwhelming. You're still here, so that's a point in your favor," Josie teased.

"She's got loads of points in her favor," Penny said. "Quincy is crazy about you, Roni. He couldn't take his eyes off you the whole time we were talking, and when Jed, Tru, and Scott cornered him, I heard Quincy raving about you as I walked away."

That made her feel good all over and gave her a boost of confidence. "I'm crazy about him, too."

"Did you enjoy the scavenger hunt?" Sarah asked.

"We had a blast. I thought the list had some strange things on it, though. I've never been on a scavenger hunt where they asked you to kiss your partner. Not that I minded," Roni clarified. "I love kissing Quincy, and once I saw Penny and Scott kissing by the park and taking a selfie, I figured it must be something this group does for the scavenger hunt."

"*Kissing* was on your list?" Gemma asked.

"I'm *way* more interested in the fact that Penny and Scott were kissing." Dixie cocked her head, looking at Penny, and said, "Spill it, chick."

"Why wasn't kissing on *my* list?" Crystal asked.

Josie said, "Penny, you *kissed* Scott?"

"Or did *Scott* kiss you?" Sarah asked.

They were all looking at Penny expectantly when Finlay burst through the crowd and plopped into a chair with a sigh. "My feet are killing me." She looked around and said, "Uh-oh. What did I miss?"

"Penny kissed Scott," Josie said. "Or our brother might have kissed her."

"What?" Finlay glared at Penny. "I'm your *sister*, and I'm the last to know?"

"I'm so confused," Roni said. "You guys didn't have kissing on your lists? What about waxing a body part? That was another weird one."

All eyes turned to her, and Crystal burst into hysterics.

"Oh my goodness," Finlay said, and covered her mouth as laughter bubbled out.

Josie touched Roni's arm and said, "We're not laughing at

you. This has *Dixie* written all over it."

"Did you *wax* something?" Crystal asked, doubling over with laughter.

"I waxed *Quincy*," Roni said, and everyone cracked up, including her. "It was worth a hundred points, and we wanted to win!" That caused everyone to laugh harder.

"You're going to fit right in, Roni," Dixie said. "Izzy's gossip radar must be on high alert. Here she comes."

Dixie pointed to the gorgeous bartender with straight dark hair and big almond eyes heading their way, walking like she was on a mission in a figure-hugging minidress. Roni had forgotten her name, and she was glad Dixie had reminded her.

Izzy grabbed Tracey, the petite brunette waitress who had been clearing tables when Quincy had introduced them. Roni remembered her name because she'd noticed that the scary-looking bartender with the baseball cap never took his eyes off her.

"*What* is going on over here?" Izzy asked as she slid her slinky body into a chair.

Tracey took the last empty seat and smiled at Roni. She had a cautious look in her eyes, different from the others, who all seemed so comfortable in their own skin.

"Penny kissed Scott," Dixie said.

"Whoa, *Penny*," Izzy exclaimed.

"And Roni waxed *something* on Quincy," Gemma added. "We don't know what yet."

"Ohmygod," Tracey said.

"It was his *leg*," Roni exclaimed. Then, a little softer, she said, "I waxed an *R* onto it."

The girls fell into hysterics.

"I'm going to give him such a hard time about that," Penny

said with a laugh.

Finlay pointed at Penny and said, "Great. Right after you fess up about Scott. What is going on with you two?"

"There's nothing to fess up about." Penny crossed her arms, looking like she'd been caught with her hand in the cookie jar, and said, "We had kissing on our list, too."

Dixie barked out a laugh. "That's a load of bull, but you get extra points for creativity. I made the lists, and only Quincy and Roni had kissing on theirs."

"Oh," Penny said. "*Whoopsie.*"

"Why only us?" Roni asked.

"Because we all love Quincy, and he has been dying to go out with you for months. When he told me he invited you to come tonight, I thought I'd give you guys a little nudge," Dixie said. "I'm glad it worked."

"I love that you care about him so much, but trust me, I don't need any nudging to kiss Quincy. The man makes my knees go weak every time he says, 'Hey, beautiful,'" Roni said, surprising herself with her honesty. But it was easy to talk to them, and she didn't feel embarrassed confessing the truth.

"Wow, *go*, Quincy," Gemma said. "Tru makes me feel the same way every time he looks at me. Seduction must be in their genes."

"The first time I met you and Tru, he looked at you and the kids like you're his whole world," Roni said. "But I didn't mean to out you, Penny. I'm sorry."

"There's nothing to *out*. We kissed. It's not a big deal," Penny said.

"Is that why you were at our place babysitting with him the other night?" Sarah asked. "Scott told us he needed help because Maggie Rose was colicky, but she was fine for the rest of the night."

"She *was* cranky," Penny said softly. "But Scotty's so good with her. He calmed her right down. And yes, we kissed that night, but we didn't do anything else at your house. You don't have to sanitize your couches."

"*Scotty*," Josie, Gemma, and Crystal said in unison.

Penny rolled her eyes. She sat forward and lowered her voice, and everyone leaned in. "Can we keep this on the down low? Just between us girls? I don't know what this is yet. Scott said he'd wanted to ask me out for a while. And honestly, I've been into him for a while, too, but he'd always kept his distance, so I thought he wasn't interested. It turns out he thought Quincy and I might get together. I was cockblocked by my best guy friend, and he wasn't even trying."

"We all thought you two would get together because you're such good friends," Sarah said.

"I know." Penny looked at Roni and said, "But it was *never* like that. So…*girl code*?" Penny asked.

"Of course. Consider the girl code enacted." Dixie looked around the table and said, "Nobody says a word outside of this table. That includes you, Roni. You're one of us now, so you can't tell Quincy."

It felt good to be included. Roni had never been part of a group outside of dance, and those groups weren't built on friendships that went any deeper than sharing a common goal. But as much as she wanted to be part of their girls' club, she didn't want to lie to Quincy, so she said, "I won't say anything, but what if he saw them? What if he asks? I don't want to lie to him."

"Actually, Quincy already knows," Penny said. "That's why I wanted to talk to him before. I thought he'd be hurt if I didn't tell him first, and just so you know, I told him he could tell you, Roni, as long as he swore you to secrecy. But he already knew. Apparently Scott talked to him last week and said he was into me. Bro code and all that. But you're right, Roni, Quincy would be hurt if you lied to him. Honesty is important to him."

"Following the girl code isn't lying," Dixie said sharply. "Quincy knows that."

"She's right," Finlay chimed in. "The same way our guys can't talk to us about what happens in that clubhouse out back. It's the same thing, only *we're* in control."

As they talked about what constituted lying, Tracey said, "I'm really happy for you and Quincy, and Penny, I'm happy for you and Scott, too. But I swear I must have a black cloud over my head. Not that I want a man in my life, but I escaped an abusive jerk, finally found my footing, and while you guys are falling into happily ever afters, I can't even get *tips* because Diesel scares them all away."

"The only reason Diesel scares them off is because he wants to eat you alive," Izzy said.

Tracey shook her head and looked across the room at Diesel, standing by the bar talking with Quincy and a few other guys. He was staring at Tracey, stoic faced, like a rottweiler, with cold, dark eyes.

Roni got the chills. "Quincy introduced him to me as if he was one of his friends who are like family, like you guys. He seemed nice enough, although he didn't say much. Is he dangerous?"

"Only to Tracey's panties," Izzy said with a smirk.

"Would you *stop*?" Tracey snapped.

"I'm making a mental note to seat you next to him at Thanksgiving," Dixie teased.

"Don't you dare!" Tracey warned.

"You guys are having Thanksgiving together?" Roni asked. She wasn't looking forward to the holidays without her grandmother.

"Of course." Dixie set her green eyes on Tracey and said, "And now that Diesel's back in town, he'll be there, too, sitting right next to his *dessert.*"

"*Ohmygod!* Stop!" Tracey snapped. "The guy has a revolving bedroom door. I've seen him leave work with a different woman every week. He's like a mama bear over me. It's so annoying."

"There is nothing *mama* about that man," Josie said. "He's a mammoth of muscle and grunts. He never says more than two words."

"He doesn't have to. His eyes say it all." Tracey lowered her voice and said, "*Go near Tracey and I'll rip your arms off.*" She sat back and sighed. "When he took off for those two weeks last month, I made more money than I ever have in tips. It was awesome. Now I'm back to serving mostly women again. If he doesn't let up, I'm going to have to look for another job."

"Oh no, you're not. You're family. I'll talk to Diesel, and I'll increase your salary to make up for the lack of tips in case it takes him a while to learn to back off," Dixie said.

"You can't do that, Dix, and for Pete's sake, *don't* talk to him about me," Tracey said.

"She can do it, and she should. Dixie's the boss," Finlay reminded her. "You're not quitting, Tracey. We need you here. If you don't want Dixie talking to him, I'll have Bullet set him straight."

Roni loved the way the girls jumped in to take care of Tracey. She hadn't realized how much she was missing out on. She longed for friends like these.

THE GRITTY TRUTH

"No," Tracey said. "If anyone is going to talk to him, it'll be *me*."

"But I can't let you work where you're not comfortable," Dixie said. "That's not right."

"I'm not uncomfortable anymore. I'm just mad about my tips. I'll talk to him. Not now, but one day when I find some courage lying around." Tracey's gaze moved around the table, and a small smile appeared as she said, "Like maybe next year. I'd better get back to work."

"Me too," Izzy said. "Oh, Dix. I can't make it to Thanksgiving. Jared's giving me a ride to New York to see my family."

"Oh yeah? Going to see *dick and the boys*?" Dixie smirked.

"Only if he's lucky," Izzy said.

"Are those your brothers?" Roni asked.

Dixie and Izzy cracked up.

"It's code for sex. It took me a while to catch on to their lingo, too. Jared is Jace's younger brother, and word around the bar is that Izzy and Jared have been hooking up," Finlay said as Izzy walked away. "I'd better go check the buffet." She pushed to her feet and pointed to Penny. "I'll call *you* later."

"Okeydokey, sis," Penny said.

Roni leaned forward and said, "I really am sorry for outing you, Penny."

"It's not a big deal. Secrets never stay hidden for long around this crew," Penny said. "Which is why it's your turn to spill. How did Quincy finally convince you to go out with him?"

Roni glanced across the room at Quincy at the same moment he looked over. Her pulse quickened, remembering when she'd seen him through the glass door Wednesday night. Quincy winked, and then Bones, who was holding Lila, said something, stealing his attention. When Quincy took that little girl into his arms, Roni's entire body went soft.

"*Aaand* we lost her," Dixie said.

Roni looked at the girls, knowing she was blushing, but she couldn't care less. Quincy was worth the embarrassment. It took her a second to remember what Penny had asked, and she said, "He showed up at my work with my favorite flowers, which he'd picked from a field, and a picnic set up in the back of his truck, with lights and a small fire pit, and it was the most magical night of my life."

The girls swooned as she told them the rest of the story. They peppered her with questions, which she enjoyed answering. It felt good to gush about Quincy. They talked about all the months they'd been texting and how he'd checked in with her more often after her grandmother had died. But talking about him made her long to be by his side again.

Maggie Rose woke up, and when Sarah went to change her, the conversation circled back to the scavenger hunt. Roni showed them the picture of Quincy's waxed leg, and they laughed when she told them about how he'd hollered when she pulled the wax strip off. That led to a conversation about how much waxing hurt and who waxed and who didn't, which turned into a chat about how their significant others felt about it. Roni was startled by their openness. This was so new to her, sharing private parts of her life with other women. She and Angela talked about personal things, but not like *this*. Roni liked how honest and caring these new friends were. She asked about how they'd met their significant others and loved hearing their stories, which were all very different. She'd cracked up when Crystal described the ways in which Bear had pursued her, and her heart ached when Tracey told her about her abusive past and Josie shared a little bit about Scott and Sarah having suffered abuse at the hands of their parents. Roni felt like she was gathering bits and pieces about each of them as if she were collecting berries for a friendship pie.

"I'm sure Quincy has told you that he's going to be Jed's best man in our wedding. You should come to my pre-wedding girls' day," Josie said, and the other girls all spoke at once, urging her to join them.

"I would love to, but what is that, exactly?"

"It's not a pre-wedding girls' day. It's a *bachelorette shower*," Dixie said. "Josie won't let us throw her a bachelorette party or a bridal shower because she doesn't want to celebrate her last days of singlehood and she feels funny receiving gifts. But it wouldn't be right not to have them, so we're combining her bachelorette party and bridal shower and having a *bachelorette shower*."

"Girls' day," Josie chimed in.

"You can call it whatever you want, as long as we get to celebrate you and Jed getting married." Penny looked at Roni and said, "It's the Sunday before Christmas."

"We're having it at Josie's shop, Ginger All the Days. It's next door to the bar. Jed and Josie converted their garage into the shop," Gemma chimed in.

"That's *yours*?" Roni asked. "My friend Angela and I love your gingerbread cookies. Her boyfriend buys them by the dozen. You must be swamped this time of year."

Josie nodded. "I am, and I love it, but I'm closed for the afternoon of the party."

"Wouldn't want the customers seeing the gingerbread penises we're making," Crystal exclaimed.

Roni's eyes flew open wider. "Seriously?"

"No. We're *not* making those," Josie said. "Well, Izzy and Crystal probably are, but I'm not, and you don't have to. We're making gingerbread houses. It'll be fun, and it'll give us a chance to get to know each other better."

"I'd like that. Thank you," Roni said.

Josie pulled out her phone. "Give me your number and I'll text you the details. I'd like to have it anyway, since your guy and my guy are best buds. I'm sure we'll see more of each other."

As they were exchanging numbers, Quincy, Jed, and Scott sauntered over, each holding two plates of food. Quincy's eyes locked on Roni's, and her pulse quickened.

"Hey, beautiful," Quincy said. "Do you have room for a few Neanderthals?"

Scott looked at Penny, and she quickly averted her eyes, but there was no hiding the flash of attraction.

"Where's Hail?" Josie asked Jed.

"He wanted to eat with Bradley, so he's sitting with Bones," he answered, sitting beside her.

"How's it going, *Scotty*?" Dixie asked with a smirk.

Scott set a plate in front of Penny. "Great. You?"

"It'll be better as soon as I find my man." Dixie pushed to her feet, eyes on Penny as Scott sat beside her. "My *lips* are lonely."

Crystal rose from her seat beside Roni. "Here, Quincy, take my chair. I need to find Bear so I can nurse Axel before my boobs explode."

"And I should see if Tru needs help with the kids." Gemma pushed to her feet.

"Kennedy had a cookie in each hand last time I saw her," Quincy said.

"Of course she does," Gemma said. "She's got that man wrapped around her little finger."

"She's got *all* of us wrapped around her finger." Quincy sat beside Roni and put their plates on the table. "I wasn't sure what you were hungry for, so I got some of everything, heavy on the fruits and veggies."

"This is perfect, thank you," Roni said.

He leaned in for a kiss, then brushed his scruff along her cheek and said, for her ears only, "Is it crazy that I missed you?"

"If it is, then they'd better take me to the nuthouse, too."

He kissed her again, and Jed said, "I bet Dixie wouldn't mind if you used her office for a few minutes, as long as you disinfect the desk afterward."

Quincy shot him a warning glare, and Jed chuckled.

They talked and joked as they ate. Scott was charming, and every time he whispered something to Penny, she smiled in a way that was different than when she smiled at anyone else. It was obvious to Roni that they were holding hands under the table, though she thought the others might be as oblivious to that as they were to Scott and Penny's stolen glances. Jed was funny and kept snuggling with Josie, proudly referring to her as his *future wife*. Quincy was so attentive and affectionate, keeping his arm around Roni as they ate, stealing kisses, and asking several times if she needed anything, she felt like they'd been dating for months. She wondered if there was something in the water at Whiskey Bro's, because all those tough guys sure knew how to treat their women.

"Attention." Hail's voice rang out through the microphone, from his perch in Biggs's arms on the stage.

Hail was adorable with shaggy light-brown hair that curled at the ends. Biggs was such a big man, Hail looked even smaller

MELISSA FOSTER

in his arms. Beside him, Red held Kennedy's and Bradley's hands. The stage seemed smaller and more intimate without the fancy curtains they'd had up during the auction.

Josie said, "He's such a ham."

"I think he's adorable," Roni said.

"Thank you for supporting the..." Hail looked at Biggs and said, "What's it called, Papa Biggs?"

"The Parkvale Women's Shelter."

"Oh yeah! Thanks for supporting the Parkvale Women's Shelter," Hail said proudly. He looked across the room and shouted, "Look Mama and Moon! I announced!"

Laughter rose from the crowd.

"Good job, buddy!" Jed called out to him.

"He calls you *Moon*? That is the cutest thing I've ever heard," Roni said. "I love how they included the kids tonight."

Quincy pulled her closer and said, "Family, babe. That's what it's all about."

Even with Angela, and to some extent, Elisa, Roni's family was small. She'd never imagined family could feel like this.

Biggs set Hail down, and Red sent Bradley to Biggs, taking Hail's hand. Biggs said something to Bradley, and Bradley nodded. Then he leaned toward the microphone and said, "The second-place winners are..." Biggs said something to him, and Bradley said, "Jon Butterscotch and..." He giggled, bringing rise to more laughter. "That's a funny name, Papa Biggs."

"Yes it is," Biggs said. "Now tell them the other name."

"I don't remember," Bradley said, and Biggs spoke in his ear. Bradley yelled, "Jillian Braden!"

Applause rang out as a man with dirty-blond hair shot to his feet and let out a *whoop* and a gorgeous woman with auburn hair popped up and they did a funky happy dance. Everyone cheered as they made their way to the stage. Roni recognized the guy from the auction.

Biggs set Bradley down, and Bradley yelled, "Daddy!" and darted past Jon and Jillian, making a beeline off the stage to Bones, who scooped him up and kissed his cheek.

As Jon and Jillian accepted their prizes, Biggs said a few words, but Roni was too sidetracked by Quincy stroking her shoulder to pay attention. After they left the stage, Kennedy ran to Biggs. He lifted her into his arms and said something in her ear.

Kennedy gasped and yelled, "Uncle Quincy and Miss Woni! You won!"

A thrill skittered through Roni as she turned to Quincy and he kissed her *hard*, earning even more *whoops* and cheers than the ones that had already begun exploding around them. Quincy took her hand, and they hurried up to the stage.

"You won, Miss Woni! You won!" Kennedy cheered.

"How about me, jelly bean?" Quincy teased, holding tightly to Roni's hand.

"You won, too!" Kennedy wriggled out of Biggs's arms and yelled, "Daddy, we didn't win, but it's okay! Miss Woni won!" as she ran off the stage to Truman.

Biggs laughed. "This is the second time Miss Roni got lucky at Whiskey Bro's with this big fella."

Laughter rang out from the crowd.

"I bet Quincy gets lucky tonight!" someone hollered, causing Roni to blush and everyone else to cheer.

"I already got lucky," Quincy shouted, and took Roni in a long, passionate kiss right in front of everyone.

When their lips parted, she was breathless and blushing. People were cheering and clapping, and as she gazed into

Quincy's clear blue eyes, she didn't mind the embarrassment. She felt rejuvenated, as if she'd shed a protective layer she'd worn for far too long. She liked his loud, different world, with friends who looked like they could snap a person in half and said things she'd never dream of saying, where kids ran around like they owned the place, and Quincy, her big, beautiful man, made her feel like maybe, *just maybe*, she'd found a place where she truly belonged—right there by his side.

AFTER AN INCREDIBLE evening, they left the fun chaos behind. Roni snuggled against Quincy on the way to his truck, but not even the cold night air could cool his body heat, which had amplified over the last few hours of stolen kisses and furtive caresses. Quincy couldn't remember a time when he'd been happier. He loved watching Roni joking with his friends and giggling and whispering with the girls. He could practically see her walls coming down as the girl behind the text messages came to life right before his eyes. He knew he needed to tell her about his past, but tonight had been so wonderful, he was no more ready to share his darkness than he was ready for their night to end.

She turned around as they neared the truck, walking backward and waving the gift certificate they'd won. "Kennedy is *so* going to get that jacket she wants. Maybe we can get Lincoln one, too, if there's enough money left over. Or we could both pitch in for the difference."

His emotions soared. "It's like you read my mind." He swept her into his arms and said, "I'm so into you, Roni

Wescott—" He crushed his mouth to hers as he'd been aching to do all night, kissing her so deeply, her back met the side of the truck, and she made an *oomph* sound. He tore his mouth away and said, "*Sorry.*"

She grabbed his head, pulling his lips back to hers, and holy hell, she was ravenous, kissing him eagerly, her hands pushing through his hair. Their bodies ground together, and he took the kiss deeper, getting as lost in her as he had the other night.

The sound of a motorcycle engine cut through his lustful trance, and he forced himself to pull back. Their eyes connected, both of them panting, and neither one said a word as he opened the passenger door and helped her in, then went around to the driver's side. So damn happy that she'd already scooted over to the middle, he took her in another penetrating kiss. She moaned hungrily, and that sexy sound sent desire pounding through him. If he didn't get out of that parking lot, he was going to lay her down and take his fill right there. He tore his mouth away with a curse and grabbed her seat belt, kissing her more as he fumbled with it.

He drove straight to her place, and they kissed on their way across the parking lot and all the way upstairs to her apartment. When she turned to unlock the door, he stood behind her, holding her and devouring her neck. She leaned back against him, angling her head to the side, giving him better access, but he noticed her hands were trembling and felt a pang of guilt as the lock clicked open.

"Babe." He turned her in his arms and searched her eyes for a hint of what she was thinking. But all he saw was a woman who wanted him as much as he wanted her, which meant he was in no shape to decide what *she* wanted, so he gave her an out. "I can say good night right here. I don't need to come in."

Her brows knitted. "You don't *want* to come in?"

"I definitely want to come in, but I don't want to put any pressure on you." He ran the backs of his fingers down her cheek and brushed her hair away from her beautiful face. "Roni, I don't expect tonight to end in your bed. I won't *let it* end that way. But if you would rather I leave now, I will."

A small sigh left her lips. She pushed the door open, walking backward into her apartment as she slipped off her jacket and hung it on a hook by the door. Her eyes turned seductive, and she crooked her finger for him to follow her in.

He shrugged off his jacket, hanging it beside hers, and gathered her in his arms, kissing her softly as they made their way to the couch. "If I get carried away, *stop me*, baby. Okay?"

She nodded, a sexy smile lifting her lips as she set her glasses on the coffee table and said, "But you won't."

"Not on purpose, but you have no idea what you do to me." He kissed her neck again and said, "I've never *wanted* anything the way I want you." Not even when he was using drugs.

"Neither have I. I *see* you, Quincy. I feel the way you kiss me, the way you touch me. I may not have a lot of experience with guys, but I don't need it to know that you're not going to hurt me."

"Never, baby."

He lowered his lips to hers, and they sank down to the couch, kissing like they'd never get another chance. She tasted like everything that was good and sweet in the world, and no matter how hard, how *deep*, they kissed, it wasn't enough. All those months of texting and wanting so much more and holding back came crashing in. He wanted to climb inside her, to *feel* what she felt, to pleasure her until her world spun—and then he wanted to be her grounding force, the man who held her through storms and loved her through sunbaked days and cold winter nights. He'd never felt so much so fast or grasped anything so clearly. All of those thoughts and feelings were accompanied by a shocking jolt, but he didn't fight them. He wanted to *revel* in them, and he poured that passion into their kisses as he lowered her to her back. He ran his hand down her side, and she arched beneath him as he kissed her more passionately, sinking into her, becoming one in a way he never imagined. Her hands moved along his arms and up his back, her fingers spearing into his hair.

Fuck, yes, baby, I love that.

He slid his knee between her legs, and she moaned, riding his leg, clinging to his shoulders. He was hard as stone, grinding against her thigh. She tightened her grip on his hair, igniting fire in his loins. His hand moved down the curve of her hip, over the side of her thigh, and back up, stopping short of her breast, again and again, in a maddening rhythm. She arched and rocked, moaning and mewling. He knew she needed more as badly as he did, but he didn't want to fuck this up. He tore his mouth away, dipping his head beside hers, and said, "*God*, baby. I'm dying to touch you."

She whispered, "*Quincy…?*"

He closed his eyes and said, "I'm not asking. I just want you to know."

"Look at me," she said softly, and he lifted his face. The desire in her eyes seared beneath his skin as she whispered, "*Touch me.*"

The need in her voice unleashed his desires. He reclaimed her mouth, more demanding this time, and she returned his efforts fervently, her hips bucking against his leg. He pushed his hand under her sweater, cupping her lace-covered breast, and a half groan, half growl slipped out. He'd never felt anything so magnificent. They caressed and groped, hips gyrating, mouths devouring. She made one needy sound after another, so sweet and sinful she was driving him out of his mind. He wanted to hear *more* of those sounds, to feel the strength of her passion while he was buried deep inside her. But he was in this for the long haul and refused to rush. He hadn't thought he'd touch her like this tonight, and *damn*, he felt honored. He kissed her slower, lovingly, and her sounds turned more sensual. He'd never thought so much about what he felt, but the emotions she brought out in him were inescapable. She writhed against him, her sounds turning to mewling whimpers. He soaked in every intimate sound, every touch of her delicate hands. But this wasn't enough. He wanted to give her more, to *worship* her body the way she deserved. He slid his tongue along her lips and trailed kisses down her neck, slowing to take a long, sensual *suck*, earning more enticing moans.

"Feels so good," she said heatedly.

He stayed there, loving her neck with openmouthed kisses and scintillating sucks, until she was panting. He lifted her sweater, moving down her body, kissing her belly. "You're so soft, baby." Her hands were still in his hair as he reached for the front clasp on her bra, lifting his eyes to check in with her, but her eyes were closed.

As if she knew he needed her approval, her eyes fluttered open, and her hand slid from his head. She unhooked her bra and pushed the cups to the side. Holy hell, that was hot, and her breasts were even more gorgeous than he'd imagined. He dragged his tongue over and around her nipple, bringing it to a taut peak. She bowed off the cushions, riding his leg, her hands fisting in his hair as he lowered his mouth over her breast, sucking the tip against the roof of his mouth.

"Oh *God*. Don't stop," she pleaded.

He sucked harder, kissed, licked, and teased, until her every breath was a plea or a moan, and then he loved her faster, rougher, lost in those noises. His entire body ached for her, and she was right there with him, begging for more. He shifted onto his side so he could reach between her legs, capturing her mouth in a ravenous kiss, and stroked between her legs, over her jeans. Without breaking their kiss, she reached down and unbuttoned them. He unzipped them and pushed his hand beneath her panties. She was waxed bare, and he growled at the feel of her. "So fucking sexy." His fingers slid through her wetness, teasing her as they kissed, her hips rising. When he dipped his fingers inside her, she let out a long sigh. She was tight and hot and so fucking perfect, he *needed* to taste her.

He brushed his lips over hers and said, "Christ, baby, I want to feast on you." Her eyes flew open, and his heart took notice of the nervous look in them. He kissed her softly, continuing to stroke her, and said, "One day, babe. When you're ready. I promise it'll be so good, you'll crave my mouth on you."

Her cheeks burned red, and she pulled his mouth back to hers, rocking her hips faster, fucking his fingers. He kissed her harder, stroking over the spot that caused her legs to flex. She came *hard*, her sex clenching around his fingers. Her head fell back, but his mouth went with it, swallowing her sounds, knowing he'd hear them, *taste* them, until the end of time.

He stayed with her, teasing, kissing, loving, as she came down from the peak, and he couldn't resist sending her soaring again. She clung to his head, and he kissed her harder, wanting to feel the thrills she felt, until she collapsed to the cushions. He kept his fingers inside her, kissing her softly, his feelings coming out in whispers. "So beautiful, baby...love touching you...kissing you." He withdrew his fingers and dragged them along her lower lip. Her eyes fluttered open, intense and alluring, and he kissed her again, long and slow, then deeper, more passionately, disappearing into her. He kissed her for a long time, and when he moved beside her, cradling her in his arms, she buried her face in the crook of his neck.

He kissed her forehead, knowing she was embarrassed, and said, "It's just you and me here, baby, and I adore you." He held her until her racing heart calmed, reveling in their closeness. When she finally smiled up at him, her lustful eyes at half-mast, her warm breath on his skin, he whispered, "Beautiful girl, I hope you know how precious you are to me."

Chapter Six

BETWEEN THE PAGES bookstore hosted book clubs, lectures, readings, and weekly story times for children. Usually the upbeat atmosphere and fast pace kept Quincy too busy to think about anything else, but despite the constant flow of customers, he'd been able to think of nothing *but* Roni all day. Even on his lunch hour when he tried catching up on his studies, his thoughts kept circling back to her. He'd been kicking himself all day for not telling her about his past before taking things further, but *man*, she'd turned him inside out, and he'd desperately wanted to show her how crazy about her he was. Leaving her last night had been torture. Even a cold shower hadn't cooled him off. He'd had to jerk off to find relief, only to then get a text from her thanking him for the best night of her life, which made him think about her in the throes of passion, and he'd ended up taking things into his own hands for a second time.

He gritted his teeth, knowing if he thought about her too much he'd be walking around with a hard-on for the rest of the evening.

"Dude, what's going on in that head of yours?"

Jed's voice jerked Quincy from his thoughts. "Hey, Jed. How's it going?"

"You tell me. I must've said your name three times. You a'right?"

"Yeah, man. Just thinking." Quincy picked up another book from the cart and shelved it.

"Anything I can help with?" Jed asked.

When he and Jed had first met, they'd bonded over their difficult pasts. Jed's father had died when Jed was eleven, and Jed had been in and out of trouble for years and had even spent a few months in jail before finally cleaning up his act.

"Maybe. Did anything change between you and Josie when you told her about your past?"

Jed shrugged, walking alongside Quincy as he shelved more books. "I don't think anyone wants to hear that the guy they're falling for was a thief or spent time in jail, but we worked through it. Why? What's up?"

"Roni and I got closer last night."

"I'm not surprised after spending time with you two. That's great."

"Yeah. She's amazing. You talked with her—you know how smart she is—and she's so fucking cute, she kills me." Quincy laughed a little, remembering how surprised she'd been the first night they were together, when he'd said he was cool with just kissing, and how cute she'd been when he'd kissed her onstage last night.

"Josie and I really like her, and Bear and Tru weighed in this morning at the shop," Jed said. "They dug her, too, and it was easy to see how into you she is."

"Yeah. I'm so damn lucky."

"*She's* lucky, Quince. You're a catch. Just ask any of the

million women who try to get your attention, or anyone who knows you."

Quincy motioned for Jed to follow him into the next aisle and said, "I appreciate that. I can't stop thinking about her. Her dad's a dick—a gambler and drinker. She hasn't seen him since she was a kid, and she has no idea who her mother is. She's got no family, and other than one friend and maybe her boss, I don't think she's got anyone to lean on."

"She's got *you.*"

"You've got that right, even more so now. But weird shit is going on in my head. She's got this quiet strength about her, and I know she can handle herself. But she grew up in a seedy area, and it pisses me off that her grandmother never moved her out of there. She's too good a person to have had to deal with that shit."

"Quincy, you of all people know you can't change the past. Don't even bother thinking about it. It's a waste of energy. She's out of there now, and she's safe."

"Yeah. But I made a mistake, and it's been weighing on me all day. I didn't tell her about my past before we took things further, and I feel like I should have."

"Did you sleep with her?"

Quincy put the last of the books he was shelving in place and said, "No."

"So, we're talking about making out? Kissing? Touching? If she was into it, you're fine."

"That's just it. We didn't do more than that, but it's so much more than *just* kissing or touching between us. I don't mean physically. I mean emotionally." Quincy looked around to make sure no customers were in earshot and said, "I've never…She fucking blows me away."

"That good, huh?"

"I'm not kidding, man. Kissing her is fucking unreal. If we'd been standing last night when we got into it, she would have taken me to my knees."

Jed nudged him with his elbow and said, "I'm sure you would have made good use of that position."

"No shit, but it's not about that. We spent months texting, keeping it light, and in *two* nights I feel all of this? Have you ever experienced anything that powerful with a woman?"

"Yes, and I'm marrying her next month."

"Right. Of all people, you know what I'm talking about." He paced in the aisle and said, "You know I always own up to my shit, but I'm nervous about telling Roni about my past. I'm really into her, and I want more time with her."

"And you're afraid you might never get the chance once you tell her?"

"Exactly, but she deserves to know the truth before we get in any deeper. I've never cared what people thought about my past until she came into my life, and these last few months, it's been weighing on me."

"I know. I was right there by your side as you waited out your two-years-clean mark to prove that you could do it." Jed put a hand on Quincy's shoulder and said, "Listen, you won't want to hear this, but you already know it, because I've heard you say it. If she can't see you for the man you are today, then she's not the right woman for you. End of story."

Quincy raked a hand through his hair, swallowing that sharp-edged truth, and said, "You're absolutely right. I just wish I had told her before last night. I'm already in deep, Jed."

"I knew you were last night. Whatever happens, we'll get through it. I've got your back, Quincy."

"I know. Enough about my shit. What're you doing here? Need a book for Hail?"

"No. I'm looking for a book about getting through to teenagers for the Young Knights program." Earlier this year, Jed started the Young Knights, which was like the Big Brother mentoring program, but it was run through the Dark Knights. Now there were about a dozen kids taking part in the program. "We've got a new kid who's a bit ornery. I want to make sure I'm doing things right."

"Ornery teenagers should be right up your alley. Follow me, my friend."

BY THE TIME Quincy climbed onto his motorcycle after work, he was wound tighter than a top. He and Roni had both worked until seven, and they had plans to see each other at eight thirty, but the guilt of not telling her about his past was eating away at him. He'd tried texting, but she hadn't responded, so he rode straight to the studio, hoping to catch her early.

Angela was behind the desk when he strode through the door carrying his helmet. Her blond hair was pinned up in a high ponytail. She smiled, curiosity rising in her eyes. "Hi. Quincy, the world's best first *and* second date, right?"

He loved knowing Roni had told her about their time together. "The one and only. And you're Angela?"

"Sure am. It's nice to finally meet you."

"You too. Thanks for winning me for Roni, by the way. Is she still around?"

"Yeah, she's here. She's in room three, down that hall on the right. But before you go see her, I just want you to know that she's been through a lot. I know you two have been friends for a while now, and you don't seem to be a jerk, but be kind to her, okay? She deserves the best things in life."

"I only know one way to be these days, Angela, and that's what you see is what you get." He realized that wasn't quite true, because his demons weren't visible, but he was about to fix that.

"Okay, good. Would you tell Roni I'm heading out? I'll lock the door behind me."

"Sure."

He followed the sounds of music down the hall, and there in the middle of the third room was Roni, wearing black leggings and a pink wrap top like she'd worn the other night, gliding elegantly across the floor. Her arms moved gracefully up and down, but when the tempo changed, she crumpled to the floor, head and shoulders bent forward, rolling her body upward and shifting into the splits. With pointed toes, she walked her hands forward in time to the beat, and one leg swept around her and then up, toes pointed to the ceiling. Then she was on her feet again, sinking, rising, sashaying, in a series of graceful, and then more abrupt, movements. Quincy was spellbound. She was so focused, it seemed like she was one with the music. The song started again without a pause, and her arms moved above her head in a new and different dance. Then she dropped to the floor, dragging her body along it with her hands and forearms. She turned onto her back, rising slowly, as if there were a cable in the center of her body, lifting it, her chest arching.

The lyrics came into focus as he watched her dance. It was a song about needing to lose someone in order to love herself. That could be *his* theme song. Not about a relationship with a person, but his relationship with drugs. He'd needed to lose them in order to love himself. The sentiment and the intensity of Roni's dancing coalesced, swamping him. It felt like a sign, and he knew he'd made the right decision not to let any more time go by before sharing his past with her.

When the song came to an end, Roni stood with her head bowed, her chest rising with her heavy breaths. She rubbed her hip, as if it hurt. He wanted to rub it for her.

"*Wow*, babe. That was beautiful," he said from the doorway.

Her head jerked up with an uncomfortable expression. "*Quincy*. What are you doing here?"

"I came by early to talk. I texted, but I guess you didn't get it." He walked into the room, wondering if she was already regretting what they'd done last night. "I can come back at eight thirty like we planned if this is a bad time."

"Sorry, *no*, it's fine. I'm glad you're here. I was messing around and you caught me off guard. I'm not used to people seeing me dance." She grabbed a sweater from the table and pulled it on. The soft gray tumbled around her, stopping just above her waist and hanging sexily off one shoulder.

He stepped closer and reached for her hand, finally earning the sweet smile that made his chest constrict. "Hi, beautiful," he said softly, and leaned in to kiss her, inhaling her feminine scent, which stirred a hunger for more. "If that was you messing around, then I need to see you dance for real, because you blew me away."

"Thanks, but I don't perform anymore."

"Why not? That was so powerful."

"It was *okay*. I was too stiff, my turns sucked, and I favored my left side." She leaned her butt against the table, a flash of sadness moving over her features. "I'll never be able to dance the way I used to."

He set his helmet on the table and shrugged off his leather jacket, tossing it beside the helmet, and stepped in front of her. She lifted her eyes to his, and *damn*, she was right when she'd called their connection electric. His body felt like a tangle of live wires every time they were together.

"Talk to me, babe. What do you mean, like you used to?"

She lowered her eyes. "It's not a pretty story."

He slid his finger beneath her chin, lifting her face, and said, "I have my own ugly stories. If you share yours, I'll share mine."

Her lips curved up. "What is it about you that makes it easy for me to open up?"

"I don't know, but whatever it is, I think you bring it out in me."

She hoisted herself up and sat on the table, patting the space beside her. "You might as well get comfortable."

He stepped between her legs and put his hands just below her hips. "I'm good right here, thanks. I want to be able to see your face." He squeezed her outer thighs and said, "And this is a nice benefit."

"I guess after last night we're officially past you keeping your hands to yourself."

"They're on the outside of your legs, not between them."

Crimson stained her cheeks, and she looked away, shaking her head and grinning. "I'm not used to hearing things like that."

"I'm only telling it like it is." He ran his hands down the outside of her legs and felt her bristle. She hadn't given him any indication that she regretted last night, but that flinch worried him. He held his hands up, bringing her eyes back to his, and said, "I'm not trying to do anything, Roni. I was just being *affectionate*, not sexual."

"It's not that," she said apologetically. "I love when you touch me."

He breathed a sigh of relief and sat beside her. "Is this better?"

"Yes and no," she said softly.

He laced their fingers together, pressing a kiss to the back of her hand. "How about this?"

"I like that. I liked you standing in front of me, too. It's not you, Quincy. Despite what it probably looks like after last night, I haven't been with many guys, so if I react funny sometimes, it's because I don't know *how* to react."

"It doesn't look like anything to me, Roni, other than two people who are into each other."

"Then that's good. I'm still new to this whole couple-dating thing. My whole life has been about dance, as I told you the other night. But it goes deeper than just dance classes. Remember how I said that my grandmother wanted me to get out of the place where we lived?"

"Yeah. To be honest, the way you described where you grew up made me wonder why she allowed you to live there. I get that she refused to be run out of her home, but still. It didn't sound like the best place for a young girl to grow up."

"I know. Shortly before she died, I learned there was more to why we stayed. According to my grandmother, I started dancing as soon as I could walk. I don't want to sound braggy, but she said that even when I was young I was a gifted dancer. When Elisa validated what my grandmother saw, it changed everything. It changed the way I saw myself, and it gave me a path to get out of the awful place where we lived. It's true that my grandmother didn't want to leave because she'd grown up there, but now I know that the only way we could afford my dance lessons was to stay there, because the apartment was rent controlled."

"A means to an end."

"Yes, and by the time I was twelve, I wanted that *end* with everything I had," she said so passionately, her face brightened. "I danced my butt off seven days a week. The reason I'd never roasted marshmallows or gone to a single school dance or party was that I didn't have a normal childhood. Gram and I never even went to the movies. I never saw a Disney movie until last year, when I watched one with Angela at her apartment. While other kids were out at parties playing Spin the Bottle and Seven Minutes in Heaven and when they were experiencing their first kisses and going to prom, I was here honing my skills, striving to be *perfect*, because *talented* wasn't good enough to get into Juilliard, and that was my dream. I'm not complaining. It was my choice to work that hard. I could have had a less lofty goal and had more of a life, but I was never happier than when I was dancing. When I was lost in the music and motion, I was no longer the girl who had to keep her head down and run from the bus stop to the apartment, or sleep with my head under a pillow because the gangs outside my windows were up at all hours, squealing wheels and shouting profanity."

She could have been describing Quincy's childhood, and it made him sick to think about her growing up in that situation.

"I dreamed of being onstage, telling stories through dance. I wanted to be the *best* contemporary dance soloist, to suck people into the story and make them *think* and *feel* things they never had. I lived to dance. It's all I ever wanted. Well, that and to make my grandmother and Elisa proud. I would have done anything to achieve it, and I *made it*, Quincy," she said with pride and tears in her eyes. "I got accepted into Juilliard, and I worked my butt off and achieved the impossible. *Me.* I was just a girl with a dream from a poor neighborhood, raised by her grandmother. I beat the odds, and I was so proud of myself. After graduation I got a job with a great dance company. I was on top of the world, and I came home to celebrate with Gram. She was on top of the world too, so proud of me she couldn't stop talking about it. We were going to make apple pie. She stayed home to cut up the apples, and I walked a few blocks to the store to get the rest of the ingredients. The streets south of where we lived were really bad, but north, where the store was, wasn't that bad, and we always walked when we could." She squeezed his hand, staring absently at the floor, and said, "I was on my way back from the store when I heard gunshots—*poppoppop*—real fast, seconds before the car slammed into me, and then everything went black." Tears slipped down her cheeks.

Quincy's heart shattered. "*Jesus, baby.*" Sadness engulfed him. He pulled her into his arms, holding her tight.

"I got dragged by the car. The pavement tore right through my clothes. I had to get skin grafts on my left hip and thigh. I fractured my hip, broke my leg, my foot, a few ribs, and shattered my dreams, all in the blink of an eye."

"*No,*" he choked out, not wanting to believe it.

She swiped at her tears and said, "I was messed up for a long time. I moved back in with Gram while I healed and went through physical therapy and rehab, and when I was well enough, Elisa hired me as a receptionist, and she allowed me to work on my range of motion and strength at the studio before and after work. Eventually I healed enough to teach, and Elisa offered me the apartment upstairs. I didn't want to leave Gram, but she basically kicked me out. I think she felt guilty. I tried to get her to move in with me, but she refused."

"Christ, Roni. You've been through so much. I'm sure she felt guilty, but it wasn't her fault. She did what she could so you would have a chance at a better future."

"I know." Her voice cracked.

"It's okay, babe. I've got you." He kissed her temple, rubbing his hand soothingly down her back. "I wish I could take all that pain away and wipe your memory clean, so you'd never think about it again. What happened to the guy who hit you? Did he go to jail? Was he high? Drunk?"

"No. He was a seventy-four-year-old grandfather of three. I don't know all the details, because they never arrested anyone, but I've been told that it was a drug deal gone wrong. Someone fired shots meant for someone else, and one of the bullets hit the driver in the back of the head. He was killed instantly."

Quincy gritted his teeth against the bile rising in his throat.

"That's why I no longer perform," she said, wiping her eyes. "I'm good, but not good enough."

He cradled her face in his hands, wiping her tears with his thumbs. "What do you mean? I saw you dancing like the wind. If the company that had hired you won't take you back, can't you work for another dance company?"

"I wish. Dance is all about levels of perfection. My movements are too jerky, and I get pains if I dance for too long. I'll never dance professionally again." She held up her index finger with a genuine smile that reached her eyes and said, "But there is a silver lining. I found another passion. Two, actually, that I might not have realized if I had continued down that path. When I used to help teach, it was just a way for me to pay Elisa back for all of the classes I wanted to take. But now that I put my heart and soul into it, I *love* teaching, helping girls of all ages feel better about themselves and showing them that they can shine no matter what is happening around them. And I found that I *love* children, too. Before the accident, I never had a chance to slow down and think about kids or having a family of my own one day. Children were never part of my life outside of helping to teach here at the studio, and like I said, I didn't think about whether I was enjoying *them*. I was filling a commitment. But remember the little redhead in Kennedy's class who was leaning against the wall the other night?"

"Yeah. She was a cutie."

"She is. She's a doll. Her name is Dottie, and believe it or not, standing against the wall is a *big* improvement for her. Her mom put her into my class to try to get her to come out of her shell because she's painfully shy. The first few classes, she sat on the floor huddled with her arms around her legs, peeking at the other girls. She wouldn't even look me in the eye. But now we're *connecting*. She's getting there, and it'll take time, but it feels good to know that through dance and music, she's making strides. I never would have found that type of fulfillment if I'd continued dancing professionally."

"That's great, babe. But you worked so hard. You gave up your childhood to be the best, to dance alone onstage and tell stories through your movements. I don't understand how you can walk away from that dream. Is it all or nothing in that industry? Do you have to dance with the best? Can't you perform with a smaller group? Start your own solo dance company?"

"My own? *No*. And the rest is complicated," she said softly. "To dance with a company, big or small, takes a lot of practice, and you're part of a team. Every dancer's movements are a reflection of the group. I know what I'm capable of, and I can't keep up with them, Quincy. Sometimes I get pains in my foot or my hip, my lower back. My movements are no longer fluid enough to complement other skilled dancers. I would stand out like a sore thumb, and there are days when I can't make it dancing to a three-and-a-half-minute song. I would never bring down the other dancers with my subpar performance. But I've accepted that I won't perform again, and that's okay."

She sat up and looked into his eyes. Gone were the sadness and tears, replaced with something brighter. "I'm blessed to be alive, Quincy. I've got a second chance, and I'm beyond thankful for that, because I don't think my grandmother would have survived losing me and I got a year and a half with her after the accident. All the wishing in the world can't change what happened, but I can embrace what I've been left with, and that's exactly what I am doing. And you know what else? If I hadn't been hit by the car, we probably never would have met. More glittery silver for the lining."

"You're fucking incredible, you know that?"

She lifted her brows. "Because I got hit by a car?"

"No, babe. Because you had your dreams stolen out from under you, and you're not resentful or bitter. You're focused on what you have and not what you've lost. A lot of people would have come out the other side as a different person."

"I am different than I was. I was unstoppable. Now I know I can be stopped."

He framed her face with his hands, needing to be closer, and said, "You are still unstoppable, Roni. The accident didn't stop you. It was a roadblock that you *overcame*, and look at you now." He brushed his thumb over her cheek and said, "You're strong, beautiful, and to me, an untrained eye watching you dance, you are the embodiment of perfection. I hope you don't give up on your dreams for good, because those girls you teach aren't the only ones who deserve to shine."

He pressed his lips to hers, and when she leaned into the kiss, he took it deeper, wanting to chase away the pain she'd suffered and fill all those spaces with *them*. He pushed one hand into her hair, and the other circled her waist, bringing her tight against him. His thoughts began to fracture, and he felt himself getting lost in her. It happened so quickly with them every time they kissed, like they were meant to be joined at the lips. Her hands moved up his back to the nape of his neck, and he loved the feel of her holding him, *wanting* him. She made one of her sexy noises, sending rivers of lust coursing through him and jolting him back to reality, reminding him of why he showed up early.

The last thing he wanted to do was stop kissing her, but he had to. He eased his efforts to a series of lighter kisses, keeping her close, breathing her in. He knew things would change once he revealed his past, and he wanted to soak in this last moment, memorizing the feel of her in his arms, her fingers brushing the back of his neck, and soaking in her now-familiar scent.

"Kiss me again?" she whispered.

Her sweetness did him in, and he pressed his lips to hers, kissing her slow and tender, wishing he could erase his past and just be *a guy who worked at a bookstore falling for a girl who taught dance* forevermore.

Chapter Seven

RONI HAD FOUND Nirvana. Quincy didn't just kiss her. He *enveloped* her with more than his strong arms and his delicious mouth, which caused her to make sounds she'd never heard herself make before. Emotions poured off this man, and she wanted to swim in them, to kiss him for hours, to have his hands and mouth on her like he had last night.

When their lips parted, she yearned for more. But he didn't stop there. He embraced her, holding her as tightly as he had last night, and she loved that, too. She felt safe when she was in his arms, like nothing bad could ever happen to her again.

His scruff tickled her cheek as he pressed a kiss beside her ear and said, "I'm sorry for what you've gone through, and even sorrier for what I have to tell you."

A chill ran down her spine as his arms fell away, leaving her longing for them. She'd forgotten he'd come to talk to her about something. "Is it that bad?"

He sat up straighter, wringing his hands, tilting his head in her direction. The desire she'd seen in his eyes was now shadowed with regret. He put his hands beside his legs, and his fingers curled around the edge of the table as he said, "I suppose that depends how you look at it. As you said, all the wishing in the world can't change a person's past, and I'll understand if mine is too much for you."

"That sounds ominous." She didn't know what could be so bad that it would change how she felt about him, and she hoped he was overreacting.

"I don't mean for it to, but it is what it is. Before I go into it, I want you to know that I'm sorry for not telling you before we went so far last night. I probably should have. You deserve that. But I honestly didn't think we'd go as far as we did, and I had waited so long to go out with you and was having such a great time, I wanted to experience one last night together before taking the chance of telling you everything and changing the way you look at me."

"So was that kiss just now a *last* kiss?" she asked nervously.

"I guess we'll see. You and I have more things in common than you might think. We both grew up in bad areas and we had parents who sucked. You don't know who your mother is, and I don't know who my father is. We both left that ugliness behind and built a new life, and…" He gritted his teeth, the muscles in his jaw bunching. "We've both been through rehab."

The look in his eyes told her he wasn't talking about physical rehabilitation. The pit of her stomach sank.

"My mother was an addict, Roni. She had Tru when she was fourteen. He's nine years older than me, and they lived with our grandmother, who he said was a mess, too. Tru said things got worse after our grandmother died, which was about a year before I was born. That's when our mother started using more openly, and heavily. He said she cleaned up her act when she was pregnant, but after I was born things got much worse. She was hardly ever home, and when she was, she was usually passed out cold, doing drugs, or having sex with a random druggie or a dealer."

Roni felt nauseous knowing he grew up like that. She put her hand over his, her heart breaking for him. "That sounds awful."

"It was all I knew. I didn't realize how abnormal it was because I had Tru, who I swear was born having all his shit together. Thank God, because if my well-being had been left up to our mother, I may not have survived. Tru fed me, made sure I bathed, did my laundry, got me to school, made me do my homework, taught me to be respectful, *everything*. He shielded me as best he could from all the bad stuff, but our lives were so messed up. I learned to keep my mouth shut, and somehow I knew that as long as I followed Tru's lead, I'd be okay. When he was a teenager, he met Bear, and Bear took him under his wing and taught him how to work on cars at Whiskey Automotive. Tru used to take me to the auto shop with him, and I'd do my homework while he worked with Bear. My brother was *always* there for me. He made sure that I was never alone, other than school, of course. He was my stronghold, my straight arrow to follow, and for some reason, that seemed to really piss off my mother. She was rotten to him." He pushed to his feet and paced. "I'll always carry a fair amount of guilt about that."

"But that's not your fault."

"I know it's not. Kids can't be held responsible for their parents' failings. But that doesn't change the fact that I spent years wishing I'd never been born."

That slayed her. "I'm glad you were born, Quincy, and it seemed like everyone we were with last night was glad, too."

"Thanks, babe. Believe me, I know how lucky I am to have so many good friends and to have this time with you. And don't worry. I no longer wish I was never born. A lot of things have changed." He cleared his throat as he paced. "Anyway, Tru moved out when he was eighteen, and he tried to take me with him, but my mother sent one of her crackheads after him. I remember it like a movie in my head, because the guy had a gun. I was nine years old, scared shitless, and clinging to Tru. He was big, even back then, almost the size I am now, and he's never been afraid of a damn thing. Well, except once, but I'll go into that later. Anyway, the guy was waving the gun, and Tru shoved me behind him and ran at the guy, trying to take him down. They fought, wrestled, and the guy managed to get on top of Tru." Quincy's eyes were narrow and angry, hands fisting. "He put the gun right to Tru's head, and I *begged* for my brother's life. I'll never forget the fear of seeing that. I said I'd go back home."

Tears rolled down Roni's cheeks. "Oh my God, Quincy. That's horrifying."

He nodded, jaw tight.

"You and your brother are so brave, and your *mother…*" She said *mother* with disgust, her hands fisting, too. "I want to smack her upside the head."

"She eventually got her due."

"So what happened? You went back to that awful house? Without Truman?"

"Yeah, and the guy with the gun warned Tru to stay away from me, but he didn't listen. Tru came up with a plan where I'd go straight from school to the public library, and I'd do my homework or read until it closed. Then I'd head home, eat something, and lock myself in my room. For the next few years he came by every two or three days. He brought food, money, clothes, whatever I needed, making sure I was okay and going to school, keeping clean." Sadness dulled his eyes. "Those were hard years. I knew he was risking his life every time he came to see me, and it wasn't like we could afford cell phones. I'd tell him not to come, because I was afraid for him, but he ingrained into my head that we were supposed to protect family at all costs. I'd seen him pull guys off our mom dozens of times and stand up to them fearlessly. I knew that when he said family, he meant her, too, despite how she was. Tru says Bear taught him about loyalty, but I know better, because Truman was protecting me years before he met Bear."

"It sounds like you were right when you said Tru was born having it all together."

"Yeah," he said softly. "But I was so used to following his lead, on the days when I didn't see him, I lived in fear, waiting for the ax to fall. We'd been told horrible things about the foster care system, and because of that, we'd never let any teachers or other kids know about what went on at home. And there were no outward signs for anyone to see, because Tru made sure I wasn't a malnourished, dirty kid. Like you, I've always been great at school. I like learning, and just as you disappeared into dance, I lost myself in schoolwork and books. But the whole time, I was terrified that someone would find out about how we lived and take me away, and I'd never see Tru again."

"I can't imagine living like that. I'm so sorry. I feel silly for thinking I had it bad having to run home from the bus stop or block out noise at night, when you lived in the thick of it."

"That's not silly, babe. You *did* have it bad. We both did. It was just different kinds of bad. But we survived, and that's what we need to focus on."

He came closer, though not as close as he had earlier, and definitely not close *enough*, but she sensed he needed that space.

"What I'm about to tell you is really bad, Roni. I'm ashamed of it, and I don't like bringing this ugliness into your world, but honesty is important to me, and I take responsibility for all of my failings. I'm going to ask you to please hear me out all the way to the end and not ask me to leave before I get there, because after all the bad, there is some good." He held his arms out to his sides, and she wanted to cry from the vulnerable, pleading look in his eyes as he said, "That guy who caught your eye at the auction, the one who hasn't been able to stop thinking about you since that night, is the person I was up until the point I just told you about. I was the good kid who grew up in a hellhole, with a brother who loved him and a mother who had no idea what love was. And *that* kid, the one who tried his hardest to do all the right things, eventually grew into the good, loyal man that I am *now*."

She inhaled a shaky breath and said, "Okay."

He nodded, pacing again, crossing and uncrossing his arms, his jaw clenching like he was a caged animal readying to jump a fence. Her nerves strung tighter with every silent second as she watched him eye the door, as if he were thinking about leaving instead of revealing whatever was torturing him.

But he didn't leave.

He stepped in front of her and planted his legs shoulder width apart, his arms hanging by his sides, though not limply. Not by a long shot. His fingers curled into fists, his muscles straining against the sleeves of his T-shirt, as he looked directly into her eyes without any barriers to hide behind, and said, "In between the thirteen-year-old kid and the man I am now, I got lost, and this is how it happened. I was following Tru's plan, as always. I stayed clean, did my homework, and came straight home from school, every day the same as the next, except weekends and summers, when I'd make my way over the bridge to the auto shop instead of school." He swallowed hard. "Until one afternoon when I was cutting an apple in the kitchen and my mother came through the front door arguing with a guy. He was a big bald dude, with arm and neck tattoos. He'd been there before, and I knew he was a dealer. He was a real prick. I've already mentioned that my mother slept around, exchanging sex for drugs, which is typical shit for an addict." He paused for a moment, his brows furrowed, and said, "I need you to understand what it felt like to grow up in that kind of environment."

"I can imagine how scary it was."

"I don't think you can, and not because you're not capable. Unless you've lived through it, I think it's impossible to know the bone-deep fear and disgust, the layers of deceit I had to carry out at school and everywhere I went, and the guilt all of that caused. Hating your mother is not a natural thing. When I finally realized all of that, it took me more than a year to work through all of those emotions. Anyway, you hid under your pillow to block out the noise. For me, it was like the gangs you were trying to block out were inside my house on a near-daily basis, smoking crack, waving guns and knives, fucking my mother. Sorry to be crass, but it's the truth. Usually she would take that into her bedroom, but there were times…"

Roni looked down, feeling like she couldn't breathe. "I don't want to imagine you there."

"I know it's hard. But the only way to understand my life and what went wrong with it is to know every detail." He stepped closer, lifting her chin as he had earlier, and when she met his gaze, he said, "I can leave, but I can't lie. It's your choice."

He was so honest and had been so good to her, she was conflicted, but not enough to send him away. "I don't want you to leave."

His hand slipped from her chin, and she reached for it. He looked at their joined hands; then his eyes found hers again, riddled with anguish. She didn't know why she wanted to hold it, but it made her feel better, and she held it tighter, as much for him as for her. The small smile that appeared tugged at her.

He nodded, as if he understood that she needed the connection, and said, "We were still living in the house my grandmother had left to my mother. It was small. You walked into the living room from the front door, and the kitchen was straight ahead. There were two bedrooms to the right with a bathroom in between. All I had to do was get from the kitchen to my bedroom. I figured they'd go into her room and then I could go into mine. I waited, but their argument escalated to the point that he was shoving her around. I could tell she was blitzed out of her mind because she kept challenging him. I remember thinking, *Shut up. Just shut up.* I thought she'd get us both killed. Then things happened fast. I heard them land on the couch, and it got really quiet. I stepped behind the kitchen wall because I figured they were going to have sex, and I didn't want to see it. But then I realized it was *too* quiet."

Roni clung to the edge of the cushion, fearing for all he'd been through. He was still looking her in the eye, though now his teeth were clenched.

"There was a *slap* and a scream, and I ran into the living room. He had her pinned. He was…His pants were around his knees and he was forcing himself on her. His forearm was pressed against her neck. Her eyes looked like they were going to pop out of her head, and her face was this weird mix of colors. I don't know. It's all kind of fuzzy, but I hollered at him to stop and he kept raping her, not letting her breathe. I still had the knife in my hand, and I thought, *What would Truman do?* The answer came instantly. *Protect family*," he said through gritted teeth. "*Protect family at all costs.* I tried to pull him off her, and he swung his arm out, throwing me back." Quincy's arm swung backward as he described it. "My face hit the wall, gashed open my cheek, but I heard my mother gasp a breath. That sent him into a fury. He hit her and leaned on her windpipe, fucking her like she was a rag doll. I didn't think or anything. I just pushed to my feet and went after him. I didn't want to kill him. I wanted to *stop* him, but I couldn't, and even when I stabbed him, he kept going at her, so I kept stabbing, until he finally slumped over. I couldn't breathe. I was shaking, and I stumbled backward and collapsed, thinking he'd already killed her. She was just lying there. I remember thinking, *I didn't do it. It's not real.*"

Roni's hand flew to her mouth as a sob tore through her chest. She went to him, wrapping her arms around him, and pressed her cheek to his chest. "Quincy," she said between sobs. "I can't…" His entire body was rigid, muscles corded tight. She realized he wasn't returning her embrace, and when she looked up at him, there were tears in his eyes. "Quincy…?"

He shook his head, but he didn't say a word, and she wondered if he couldn't. She reached up and touched his cheek, whispering his name, bringing his troubled eyes to hers. "Quincy, I'm not running, and I'm not sending you away. You were protecting your mother. If someone had done that to my grandmother, I would have probably done the same thing."

His stare was cold and sad as he said, "There's more."

QUINCY HAD TOLD his story dozens of times, though not in this much detail, and while it had never been easy, it had never been this hard. Every word felt like a shard of glass, and yet Roni still held him, *cried* for him, despite the blood on his hands. He hadn't wanted to say there was more. He'd wanted to keep looking into her beautiful, trusting eyes until his past disappeared. But since he wasn't Houdini, that wasn't an option.

She stepped back, and he could see she was bracing herself for the worst, standing straighter, squaring her shoulders, and lifting her chin. She was so fucking strong, even after that ugly underworld had nearly killed her.

"Is there someplace I can grab a glass of water before I tell you the rest?" he asked.

"Why don't we go up to my apartment?"

He reached for his helmet and jacket, stopping short, and said, "Are you sure you don't mind having me up there?"

She touched his stomach with her fingertips, meeting his eyes as directly as he'd met hers, and said, "Yes, I'm sure. I know there's more, and I assume it has to do with alcohol or drugs since you mentioned rehab earlier. I don't know how I'll feel after hearing the details, but if you're asking me if I still feel safe with you, the answer is yes."

His head dropped forward with relief, her words a salve to his newly opened wounds. He was so damn thankful, he gathered her in his arms, holding her as he hadn't been able to moments earlier. She may send him away after she heard the rest, but he had *this*. He kissed the top of her head, and in a strained voice laden with too many conflicting emotions, he said, "Thank you."

They went upstairs, and as they stepped into her apartment, it felt completely different than last night, like even the *room* knew he should have told her everything yesterday.

"Do you like iced tea? Or do you want water?"

"Iced tea is great, thanks." He set his helmet on the table by the door and hung up his jacket. As she got their drinks, he went to the couch where he'd lain her down last night, and more guilt swamped him. He was still standing there when she returned with their drinks.

She set them on the coffee table and said, "Are you okay?"

"No," he said honestly. "I really should have told you all of this before we went so far last night."

"I understand." She sat down and took his hand, pulling him down beside her. "I might not have told you about my accident yet if you hadn't seen me dancing. Some things aren't appropriate first- or second-date conversations. But I would have told you before we...*um*...before you saw me without my clothes on, because my scars are ugly."

"No part of you could ever be ugly. Scars are reminders of the things we've gone through that brought us to this point and made us who we are. They may not be memories we want to revisit, but they don't make us ugly. To me, *ugly* comes out in actions. Ugly was killing that man. I've done a lot of ugly things, and for years I was repulsive, even to myself. But when I look in the mirror now, I no longer see that guy. I know he's inside me, and he will lurk over my shoulder every minute of every day, weighing into every decision I make. But I have learned from my mistakes, and I'm doing everything within my power never to be ugly again."

She curled her fingers around the cuffs of her sweater and said, "I know you killed a man, but that was to save your mother. I don't feel like that makes you ugly. You're so good to me and your friends and to Kennedy and the other kids I met last night. I just can't imagine you being as bad as you're describing."

"Well, I'm going to help you imagine it, and then, if you let me, I'll help you find your way across the rickety bridge of acceptance." More shards of glass filled his mouth, and he said, "And if not, then it's my loss. But I'll still be around as a friend if you need me."

"You would still want to be my friend if I said I couldn't handle whatever you're about to tell me?"

"Of course, Roni. There's a reason I didn't keep pushing to become more than friends for all these months. I *wanted* to be friends first, to keep things light, for a few reasons. I never had real friends in my life until about two years ago. I value friendship like other people value money and jewels. You're an incredible woman, but I'm not one of those guys who feels unworthy or unlovable. I *know* I've become a good man and a good friend, and it wasn't easy to get to this point. I've fought hard to overcome my upbringing *and* my own choices and to understand and accept all of it, including who I am right now. But I'm also a realist, and I know that some baggage is too heavy for others to carry, and if that's the case, I would *never* hold that against you. My past is my burden to bear."

She nodded, brows knitted, and folded her hands in her lap, sitting up straighter as she said, "Okay, well, let's unpack that baggage and find out."

His chest constricted, and he took another deep breath, wanting to remember exactly the way she looked right then:

strong, beautiful, and willing to listen. It took everything he had to begin telling the rest of his story. "The night I killed that man, Truman found me huddled on the living room floor, my clothes bloody, my cheek torn open. The man was still lying on my mother. She'd come to by then and was screaming and crying, but I was paralyzed with fear and in shock." A lump lodged in his throat, memories pummeling him. "Before Tru even moved that man's body off our mother, he came to *me*. He dropped to his knees and pulled me into his arms. I've never felt so helpless or lost in all my life as I did in the time between when it happened and when Truman walked in. But with him there, I felt safer. I knew *he'd* know what to do."

He took a drink, needing a second, and said, "When Tru heard the screams, he thought he'd find me dead. He was so scared, checking my body for bullet holes." Quincy pushed to his feet and paced, rubbing his hand over his chest and stomach as Truman had done that night. "Once he saw that I wasn't in danger, he moved the body and calmed my mother down. She passed out again, and I told him everything. I'll never forget what he said right before he called the police. 'Don't say a word, Quincy. You're not taking the fall for this.' I argued with him, but he was worried that at thirteen I'd be tried as an adult. I'd followed his lead my whole life, and I went along with it. I never should have, but he was my guiding light. Protecting me was what he did best."

Her jaw dropped, tears welling again. "He took the blame?"

Quincy nodded, lowering his eyes, shame and guilt twining together like a noose. "The public defender said he wouldn't go to prison. He called it a 'heat of passion' murder. But our mother got clean long enough to spew lies on the witness stand. She'd always had it out for Truman. She said she wasn't in any danger, and Truman was charged with murder." Tears spilled down Roni's cheeks, sending that spear of guilt deeper into his chest.

"Oh my God, Quincy. Why would she do that?"

"I don't know. Probably because Truman having his shit together brought all her failures to the forefront. He served six years of an eight-year prison sentence for a crime *I* committed."

She shook her head. "I can't believe your mother did that."

"She was a real piece of work." He paced, wringing his hands. "Everything changed after Tru went to prison. I was a kid, completely lost. I was consumed with guilt, and I had no direction, no plan to follow. Bear took me to see Tru a couple of times, and *man*, that devastated me even more. I had put the brother who spent his life protecting me behind bars. I should have been the one in prison, not him." His voice cracked, and he tried to swallow past his thickening throat. "Every time I thought about it, I got paralyzed just like that awful day. I *despised* my mother, but I think I hated myself even more."

He stopped pacing and met her gaze, needing to feel the pain of every word, underscoring the importance of his recovery. "One day she handed me a crack pipe and told me it would take all my demons away. I knew it was the beginning of the end, but my brother was rotting in prison because of me, and I was so consumed with guilt and filled with hate and venom, I was so *lost*, I would have followed Satan straight to hell. So I took what she offered and created my own hellish prison to rot in." He curled his fingers into fists, fighting the shame and forcing himself to get the rest out. "That's when it started, and I went *all in*. I stopped returning Bear's calls and followed my mother underground. Addicts know how to disappear, living in crack houses and on the streets. It started with crack and ended with heroin. I have no idea how I survived or even what happened to the house my grandmother left us. I think my mother traded it for drugs somewhere along the way. The things I did, the blackouts…Roni, *that* is what ugly is, turning your arms into pincushions to escape the demons in your head." He held out his arms, showing her his scars from track marks. He wanted to turn away from the horror in her eyes, but he knew better. This was *his* due. "I spent most of six and a half years blitzed out of my mind, with brief periods of mild lucidity."

"Six and a half *years?*"

"Yes, years. One thought of Truman, and I'd spiral, and since he was always on my mind…Until my mother got pregnant."

"Oh God, *no.*" She covered her mouth, more tears spilling down her cheeks.

"Kennedy and Lincoln aren't Tru and Gemma's biological children. They're our siblings."

Her eyes widened. "Your *siblings?*"

"Yes. Our mother got clean when she found out she was pregnant. There was a druggie who claimed to have been a doctor before he started using, and he knew what he was doing. He helped her through withdrawal both times, and when she gave birth, he was right there to pump her full of drugs again."

"Those poor babies."

"I took off with Kennedy about a week after she was born. I wanted to drop her at a fire station or a hospital. Anywhere would have been better than living on the streets. But my mother sent her friends after me, the same way she had to Truman, only I got the shit beat out of me. Broke a few ribs, one eye was swollen shut." He rubbed the scars above his right eye and said, "So I dulled the pain with more drugs."

"Quincy," she said, openly crying. "Why didn't you get clean when she did?"

"It's not that easy when no one cares if you're alive or dead."

"But what about Bear or his parents? Couldn't you have gone to them?"

"I could have, and they would have helped me. But it would have taken clear thinking to get there, and even though my mother wasn't using, she was still pushing drugs on me. She was happier when I was high. I think it made her feel better about herself. You might have noticed our presidential names. What a joke they are. When she named Kennedy, she told me it was important to have an unforgettable name, since we'd have forgettable lives." He paced again, his gut knotting painfully. "I tried to get Kennedy away from her several other times, and when Lincoln was born, I tried to take them both." Tears sprang to his eyes. "I knew better than to let them grow up on the streets." He looked up at the ceiling as his tears fell, guilt tearing at his heart. "It was an awful cycle. I'd try to go without drugs to be there for the kids, steal food for them, formula for Linc. They cried *all* the time. I felt so fucking guilty about them, about Truman, I'd turn to drugs to..." He dragged his forearm across his eyes and forced himself to meet her crying eyes and said, "To fucking escape the repulsive person I'd become."

She looked down, and in that moment he knew he'd lost her, but he had to go on. He had to tell her everything.

"Days, weeks, years, blended together. I stole food, money, clothes. I did so many things I'm not proud of to make sure those babies survived. I stayed with them every minute I could to make sure nobody fucked with 'em. Then Tru got out of jail and tracked me down. He tried to convince me to get clean, but when you're an addict, you don't *see* what others see, and somehow you also *do* see it. It's confusing because you don't realize—or don't want to realize—you're wasting your life and hurting everyone around you, and you make *them* into the villains. But at the same time, I felt like such a waste, and the guilt ate me alive. I couldn't handle being around the brother who had worked so hard to save me. I was afraid to tell him about the kids because I'd already ruined his life, and I knew my mother's posse of crackheads would come after him if he tried to take them away. I *couldn't* do that to Tru, not after everything he'd done for me." He clenched his teeth, guilt rising to the surface again, and said, "So I told him to fuck off, and then I did what I'd learned to do best. I went deeper underground with the kids and our mother so he couldn't find us. I wasn't thinking about how bad it was for the kids, and I *should* have been. There's absolutely *no* excuse." Tears rolled down his cheeks. "When I think of how they lived…"

He turned away, trying to regain control, but the self-loathing and sadness was bone deep. Letting those horrid feelings out was the only way he'd get past them, so he faced her again, speaking faster. "Months went by, and one night I'd gone out to try to scrounge up money for formula, and when I stumbled back into the place where we were staying, I found our mother lying lifeless on the floor. She'd overdosed, and the babies were screaming their heads off on an old mattress where they'd been sleeping when I left. I felt like that thirteen-year-old kid again, lost, powerless, and as *ashamed* as I had been the night I'd killed that fucking rapist. So I called Tru. I knew he'd take the kids, and then I could disappear. Get as far away from the three of them as I could, so I'd never hurt them again."

She looked up through teary eyes and said, "But you didn't, right? That's when you got clean? When Truman came?"

He shook his head, feeling like his heart was being ripped from his chest. "No. That's when it got worse, because shit got real. I was furious at Truman for going to prison. I was a stupid kid for all those years. I felt like he'd abandoned me. As soon as I got clean, I knew it made no sense. I twisted things around in my drug-infested head and made him into the bad guy. *Him.* The guy who fucking *raised me* and gave up *his freedom* for me. It's messed up, I know, but it's the truth. He was as disgusted with me as I was with myself. He took the kids, and I got into trouble with some really dangerous people. A few days later, I showed up at his apartment stoned out of my mind, asking to borrow money so I could pay off my debt. He lived above Whiskey's Auto, where I live now. But he did the right thing and sent me away. I went back over the bridge, away from Peaceful Harbor, to the hellhole where I'd spent the last six and a half years, and tried to hide from the dealer. But his guys found me and dragged me back to him. There was all sorts of shit going on—a dozen or more guys were there. They started arguing with each other, and I saw a chance, so I took off running. They came after me, but I got away. I have no idea how long I ran or how I evaded them. It was a nightmare, followed by weeks of hiding out, terrified. Eventually they caught up with me again, beat the hell out of me, and left me for dead. I don't know how I survived that or walking miles back over the bridge to the auto shop. I don't remember most of that night. I thought that was the end, that I'd die and the torture I caused everyone would finally be over. But I guess I passed out in front of the shop, because that's where Tru found me, and when I woke up, I was in the hospital, and he was right there with me."

Roni inhaled shakily, tears streaming down her cheeks. "Thank God he found you."

He nodded. "The first thing I asked was if I was alive. It's a strange question, but I really thought I'd died that night, and when he said *barely*, I thanked God, and I thanked Tru. He asked if I was sure I wanted to be alive, because I was doing everything within my power to kill myself. When I didn't answer, he leaned over me in the hospital bed, looking directly into my eyes, and said he wasn't ready to lose me."

Quincy looked up at the ceiling again, blinking against tears. "After all I'd put him and the kids through, *he* wasn't done with *me*. For all those years I thought he'd hated me as much as I hated myself. But he *still* loved me. Talk about a second chance. That's when I saw the light and agreed to go to rehab, which was another kind of hell. I had to deal with all those feelings that had drowned me for so long. Tru came to see me as soon as they allowed him to, and I gave him shit, blamed him for my drug use. That's all part of the process, and it *sucked*. But he *never* gave up on me. He was still the guiding light he'd always been. And after rehab and with the help of therapy, I turned a corner, and once I did, I saw the devastation I had caused. I'll never get over what I put Tru and the kids through. What I put Gemma through, and all our friends who were there for them when I was on drugs."

Roni wiped her eyes, staring at her fidgeting hands in her lap, *not* looking at him. He didn't blame her, and he waited in silence for a long time, until she finally lifted her devastatingly sad eyes and said, "When was that?"

He sat beside her, thankful when she didn't look away. "Two years ago on Halloween night was when he found me and

I went to rehab. The reason I didn't push for more with you after the auction was because the chemistry between us was so strong that first night when we talked. I'd never felt anything like it before. Then we started texting, and our texts were light and fun, and I loved every second of them. It was nice getting to know you without this hanging over my head, and I made the decision to wait until I'd been clean for two full years before really trying to get you to go out with me. I wanted to hit that milestone. I know it's not a long history of being drug free, but it was important to me to be able to tell you I'd been clean for two years rather than a year and a half. *I* knew I'd stay clean, but it takes a lot of trust to believe in a junkie." It was torture to get the words out, but he wasn't about to stop until he told her everything. "When your grandmother died, not being able to help you through it was like asking me not to breathe. We barely knew much about each other, but I already had feelings for you. I wanted to be there for you. It was a good thing Red, and to some extent Jed, talked me out of it, because I would have told you all of this then, and that would have just added to your pain."

She looked down at her hands again and said, "This is a lot to take in."

"I know it is, and I realize that the time we've had together was a gift. I'm not going to try to push you into giving me a chance, but I want you to know a few things. I'm determined to stay clean for myself *first*, for Truman and the kids, and for all of our friends who have helped us get to this point. I have a roof over my head and a job I love. I aced my GED, and I'm taking classes toward an accounting degree. I'm also committed to helping others stay clean. I run NA meetings every Wednesday night in the basement of the Lutheran church, and I'm a sponsor to another person in recovery. I have the most incredible support system with my brother and our friends, and I haven't thought about using drugs as a way to resolve my problems even *once* since I've gotten clean. I don't *feel* like I'm fighting that urge to use drugs. I feel like I've moved past that, like it happened in another lifetime. But you need to understand that just because I feel that way doesn't mean an addict doesn't live inside me. Addictions are lifelong villains, and they lurk in every hard, dark moment for a chance to attack."

She lifted her eyes to his, the fear in them warring with empathy and something bigger he didn't want to try to name.

"I know this is hard to hear," he said vehemently. "But I want, and *need*, to be honest with you, because if you decide to give us a chance, you should know these things."

He explained how overcoming addiction was a process of learning to accept responsibility for his actions, learning to manage the addiction, to identify and avoid triggers, and find other means for dealing with stress and the triggers that can't be avoided.

"I was a kid with no direction when I got sucked into drugs. I'm *not* that kid anymore, Roni. As much as I love Truman, I no longer need to fall in line and follow his lead. I've hit rock bottom. I've gone through rehab and therapy. I've dealt with the guilt and the shame of my actions, and every day I do the work needed to stay clean. Killing that man and allowing Truman to take the fall was the catalyst to my undoing. He took the blame with the best of intentions, and he was willing to hold our secret forever, but I couldn't do that to him. Remember when I said Truman had been afraid of one thing and I'd get to it later?"

She nodded.

"He was terrified he'd lose the kids. Kennedy and Lincoln didn't have birth certificates. When he had them checked out by one of Bones's friends, a pediatrician, the doctor made an educated guess at their ages. We say they're three and five because they needed dates to celebrate birthdays, and Tru used the date he found them. But they're probably closer to two and a half and four and a half right now. Time didn't exist back then. I can't remember exactly when they were born."

She shifted on the couch, and he knew how hard this was for her to hear. He gave her a moment before saying, "While I was in rehab, Tru asked me to apply for guardianship because he thought he wouldn't get approved with his criminal record. The record he had for a crime he *didn't* commit. I'd been clean for a few weeks by then, and I could see things more clearly—the family I had, the friends I wanted, the life I hoped for—was all right there for the taking. But I knew that if I allowed Truman to live the rest of his life under the shadow of my crime, I'd end up unable to look in the mirror again, and that could send me right back into the life I'd finally gotten out of. So a month after entering rehab, I checked myself out. I confessed to Gemma first, because she thought my brother was a killer, and he didn't deserve that lie hanging over their relationship. Then I went to the police and told them everything."

He paused, remembering how nervous he'd been. "I was sure I'd go to prison, and that would have been okay with me, as long as the kids were safe and Tru had a clean slate. But with the help of Gemma's stepfather, who's an attorney, the court granted Truman post-conviction relief and vacated his sentence, and he was awarded guardianship of the kids. He and Gemma are raising them as their own so the kids have the love and stability that we never did. The state could have put us both on trial, but the prosecutor exercised his prosecutorial discretion and declined to pursue charges. Our attorney said that my age at the time of the crime and Truman's prison sentence factored heavily into that decision."

"You risked going to prison to clear his name."

He nodded. "Yes, but it was as much about taking responsibility and clearing my conscience, which was important for my recovery, as it was about clearing his name. I live a clean life in every way now, Roni. I don't even lie. I've been tested for diseases, and thank God I'm clean. I haven't had sex since shortly after I got out of rehab. It was only a couple of times, and *yes*, I used protection. But it was just sex, and it made me feel empty and bad about myself. That probably doesn't sound very manly, but one of the things I've learned through recovery is to stay away from things that make me feel bad. I don't care if people think I'm a pussy for being celibate all this time. The only thing that matters is that every day when I wake up and look in the mirror, *I* like the person staring back at me. And after I confessed, I put myself back into rehab and completed the ninety-day program."

Roni was quiet for so long, wringing her hands, Quincy was sure she was mustering the courage to say it was all too much.

"So, you're pretty sure you'll stay clean?" she asked in a soft, shaky voice.

"It's my intention to, and I hope I will. But no matter how determined I am and how much I believe I will *never* fall into that hellish life again, I can't make airtight promises. That wouldn't be fair to you. But I can assure you that I have no reason to go back to that life, and I have more reasons than I can count to stay clean."

She looked down, but not before Quincy saw her lower lip trembling. He moved off the couch and knelt in front of her, taking her hands in his. Tears spilled down her cheeks, gutting him anew. He lowered his forehead to her hands, trying to push aside his torment enough to find the right words to say. She rested her cheek on his head, clinging to his hands, shaking with her sobs, and he went up on his knees, pulling her into his arms.

"I'm sorry, baby. I'm so fucking sorry." He held her as she cried, her body shaking and quivering, her tears drawing his own. They didn't move until she'd cried her very last tear, and then he held her longer—for both of them. Sometime later, she calmed, and he leaned back far enough to see her beautiful, red-rimmed eyes, wanting to make the promises he knew he couldn't. Instead, he did what he had to and said, "I'm going to get out of here and give you time to figure out what you want."

"I'm sorry for getting so upset," she said in a broken voice.

"Don't be. I know it's terrifying."

"The whole thing breaks my heart. You living that way, and the kids…" She covered her face with her hands, shaking her head.

"I'm sorry, but I had to be honest with you," he whispered, and forced himself to his feet, despite the sorrow weighing him down like concrete. The walk to the door felt like he was going to face a firing squad, though in reality, he already had.

Chapter Eight

MONDAY MORNING, AFTER another sleepless night, Roni headed into the studio two hours before it opened. "Broken" by Seether and Amy Lee blared through the room, where she was trying to stop the hurricane of anguish that had been storming through her all weekend. Sweat beaded her brow as she threw herself into every move, trying to obliterate visions of Quincy as a young teen following his mother into the very places Roni feared, images of the man she'd already come to care for drugged out and living in squalor, and battered and bruised when he'd tried to save the babies. Her vision blurred with tears as haunting sounds of the kids she'd already grown to care for crying echoed in her ears.

The music silenced abruptly. "I thought I'd find you here."

Roni whirled around. Between the blur of tears and the torment in her heart, she couldn't even *try* to cover up what she was going through. Angela's face blanched.

"*Ohmygod.* What happened?" Angela hurried over and threw her arms around Roni, breaking open the dam that had held in her sobs. "You were on cloud nine when we talked Saturday. Did Quincy do something? Is that why you avoided my calls yesterday?"

Roni tried to talk, but all that came out were more sobs.

"I will *kill* him. I swear to God—"

Roni pushed from her arms, shaking her head and gulping air to calm herself down. "He didn't hurt me."

"Then why are you crying? I haven't seen you like this since your grandmother died. And why didn't you take my calls yesterday?"

Roni grabbed a towel from the table and pressed it against her eyes to dry her tears. "I couldn't talk about it. I wasn't ready, but I can't dance it out, either."

"That's what *I'm* here for. You don't have to dance things out. Talk to me. Did something happen with Quincy?"

Roni told her all the sordid details Quincy had shared. When she finished, her heart was lodged in her throat and she was completely depleted. She leaned back against the wall and sank to the floor. "I can't stop seeing him as a kid with all that awful stuff going on around him, following Truman around because he was his *everything* and having to *kill* that guy to save his mother." More tears slipped down her cheeks.

"It's horrible. Every bit of it."

Roni swiped at her tears. "He must have been terrified from the time he was old enough to know what fear was right up until he got clean."

"I can't imagine living like that."

"It's like the universe was against him from day one. I just wish...I'm just so sad, Ang."

Worry hovered in Angela's eyes. "Roni, I knew you were falling hard for Quincy, but this is kind of a game changer, isn't it? I mean *drugs*...? Are you thinking of seeing him again?"

"I don't *know*," she snapped, but the truth was, she *did*

know. He'd texted her yesterday to say he'd ordered Kennedy's and Lincoln's jackets. Two seconds later another text had rolled in, saying that the previous text was just an excuse because he couldn't stop thinking about her, but he didn't want to put pressure on her. She'd physically ached when she'd read it. She *was* struggling, caught in the worst kind of web, trying to reconcile years of drug abuse with the incredibly stable and strong man she'd come to know.

"*Yes,*" Roni finally admitted. "I think I am. I *like* him, Ang. I *more than* like him, and I know we haven't been going out long, but all those months of texting makes it feel like we have. I don't want to walk away, but I'm afraid. What if he goes back to using drugs?"

"Okay, well, that's a *start.*" Angela got up and paced. "Roni, you worked your butt off to get away from all of that. Do you really want to invite the possibility of drugs into your bedroom?"

Roni looked up and said, "Aren't you supposed to be on my side?"

"I *am* on your side, more than *you* are, I think." Angela crouched beside her, and in a calmer voice, she said, "You just told me that Quincy killed a man and that he said he can't make any promises about never doing drugs again. How do you know he's not unstable?"

"He was *thirteen* when it happened. His mother was being raped, and he tried to get the guy off her. He *saved* her, Ang. Do I think he should have called the police instead? *Maybe.* But the way he described it, she would have been dead by the time they arrived. It's not like he's a serial killer or he killed for the thrill of it. He was traumatized by what he'd done. The courts didn't even put him in jail."

"Okay. *Fine.* That was kind of heroic, but do you really want to live your life wondering if he'll fall off the wagon?"

"Of course not," she said softly.

"Then your decision should be easy."

"In *what* world? Do you remember when you and Joey first started going out? Remember what you said to me after your first date? You said you never knew you could feel so connected to another person, and you *hadn't* spent months texting with him like Quincy and I have. You and Joey hadn't even really talked until a week before you started going out."

"Of course I remember. I still feel that way a year later, but he didn't pull the rug out from under me and tell me he killed someone and was a druggie for years, living in crack houses with two babies."

Roni put her head back and closed her eyes. "If you could have seen him Friday night with all his friends and their kids." She met Angela's gaze and said, "And with *me*, Ang. He treats me so well. When we were doing the scavenger hunt, and at the bar afterward, I felt like we'd been dating for months. It's so easy to be with him, and I was so happy during the scavenger hunt and when we were at the bar. All those scary-looking bikers that we saw at the auction were there, and they're not scary when you get to know them. They're like one big family. I loved being around his friends, getting to know the people who love him—and trust me, they do love him." And they'd loved her, too. Josie had texted Sunday morning with the information about her bachelorette/bridal shower, and while Roni had been thrilled to hear from her, it had also made her even sadder, so she hadn't responded. "They think the world of him, and that means something because several of them have known him since Tru first met Bear when Quincy was only nine. Those bikers fight to keep our streets safe. If Quincy was a threat, he wouldn't be around them. And his friends knew how hooked on me he'd been for all those months. He even talked to Red Whiskey, who's like a mother to him, about wanting to see me after Gram died. It's like we were already dating back then for both of us. And he *waited* until he was clean for two full years before trying to go out with me. Doesn't *that* tell us something about him, too?"

"I guess," Angela said. "But how do you know they aren't *all* recovering addicts?"

"I don't, but so what if they are?" Roni said softly. "Does that matter if they're not using drugs *now*? I met the greatest group of girls, and they even invited me to a bachelorette party and bridal shower they're combining into one celebration, where they're going to be making gingerbread. Does that sound like a group of bad people to you? Quincy doesn't drink, either, and he told me the truth about everything, knowing it could end things between us. He didn't have to do that. He could have waited until months down the line, or even kept it to himself forever."

"That's true, and I *was* very pro-Quincy before you told me all of this. You know that. I like that he has been there for you all these months and that he didn't pressure you to jump into bed with him. But I'm your best friend, and I need to watch out for you and say the things you don't want to hear." She sat beside Roni and said, "There are a *lot* of guys out there. You could find someone who doesn't have that kind of baggage, a guy who treats you just as well as Quincy does, who won't make you wonder if he's going to get caught up in drugs again. Someone who is hardworking and who will always be there for you. You deserve that, Roni. You deserve someone you can count on."

"I know I do," Roni said softly. "But I'm not as convinced as you are that Quincy isn't that person. I feel so much for him, and I truly believe that he's a good person. I feel it in my bones. I *know* your points are valid. I'm not trying to convince myself otherwise. I'm just being honest with you. On one hand, even after hearing all of it, I'm still falling for him. And on the other hand, I'm terrified of what that could mean. I'm so confused right now. I don't know what to do."

"Well, I'm glad you're not sweeping the reality of what *recovery* means under the carpet. From what I've heard, and it sounds like from what he told you, it's a forever thing."

"He drilled that, and the fact that he can't promise me anything, into my head. Even if he wanted to promise, you and I both know that there are no guarantees in life. Look at what happened to me. My life changed in an instant."

Angela took her hand and said, "It sounds like his did, too."

"Does it really sound that way to you?" Roni sighed. "I guess that makes sense. You grew up here in Peaceful Harbor, with a big backyard and friends in all the surrounding houses, and two parents who went to work from nine to five and loved you with everything they had. You've never had to run home from a bus stop out of fear or heard gunshots outside and wondered if they'd make their way into your home. To me, it sounded like Quincy's life was a ticking time bomb. When he told me about his childhood, it broke my heart. I don't know how he and Truman stayed out of trouble for all those years. I had my grandmother telling me who to stay away from, but they had no adults to guide them."

"Clearly Truman focused on keeping his little brother alive, and as they grew up, they had each other."

"Until they didn't," Roni said sadly.

Angela put her arm around Roni and said, "I will support whatever you decide. Just promise me that you won't sell yourself short."

"The funny thing is, I feel like I was selling myself short *until* I let him into my life."

RONI MOVED THROUGH the afternoon vacillating between wanting to text Quincy and not wanting to open that door until she understood what it really meant to be in recovery. She'd skipped lunch and gone up to her apartment, where she'd googled everything she could think of on the topics of drug addiction, recovery, and the percentage of people who relapsed. Just reading about the process of recovery had made her anxious. She took solace in the fact that Quincy had actually made it through to the other side. But that didn't mean Angela's worries weren't pecking at that solace like crows at roadkill all freaking day.

Elisa peeked into Roni's classroom, looking as regal as ever in a sharp navy peacoat buttoned all the way up. Her silver hair was pulled back in a severe bun, her makeup perfectly applied over high cheekbones and thin lips. A royal-blue scarf circled her long neck, giving her a splash of youthfulness. "Before I leave for the day, is there anything you want to tell me?"

Roni's stomach clenched. She knew she'd been quiet, but she'd thought she'd done a good job of hiding her anguish.

Before she could think of a response, Elisa said, "Like you changed your mind about the Winter Showcase?"

Relief washed over her. "I don't think so, Elisa. I'm sorry. I'm not ready for that."

Elisa walked into the room. Even at sixty-nine she still danced every day, which kept her tall frame strong and lean. She put her arm around Roni, speaking in a soft, maternal tone. "When are you going to stop comparing yourself to what you used to be capable of and start seeing the beauty in what you are capable of now?"

They'd had this conversation every few months since Roni's accident, and this was the first time Roni really *heard* it. But it wasn't dance she was thinking of. It was Quincy, and there *was* beauty in the very capable man he'd become.

Elisa was looking at her expectantly, but Roni didn't want to get into a big discussion twenty minutes before her next class—the class Kennedy was in. Roni was still trying to wrap her head around all that Quincy had told her, including the fact that Kennedy and Lincoln were his siblings. She'd been trying not to think about whether he would pick up Kennedy after class today. Roni went for levity and said, "I do see the beauty in what I'm doing now. I love teaching."

Elisa gave her the expressionless look she'd come to expect in answer to her evasive responses. "Honey, you know what I mean."

"I do. But I'm not ready, Elisa. Thank you, though, for encouraging me."

"You've been quiet today. Are you okay? Is your hip bothering you?"

"No. It's fine. I'm just tired. I had a big weekend."

Elisa flashed a curious smile and said, "I heard you won the scavenger hunt."

"How did you hear that?"

"The winners were listed on the *Peaceful Harbor Gazette*'s website. Will I have a chance to meet this Quincy Gritt you partnered with?"

Roni's throat thickened. "Um, maybe one day."

"Hello?" Gemma said from the doorway. "Sorry, Angela was at the front desk and she said I could come back and talk with Roni for a minute. I didn't mean to interrupt. I can wait in the lobby."

"I was just on my way out," Elisa said, and as she left, Gemma walked into the room.

"Hi," Roni said, wondering why she was there early and where Kennedy was. She hoped Gemma and Truman wouldn't pull Kennedy from her class because of what was going on with her and Quincy. "Where's Kennedy?"

"She's playing with Emmie in the lobby. Lira is watching her." Emmie was another student in Roni's class, and Lira was her mother. "How are you doing?"

Roni breathed a sigh of relief and feigned her best upbeat attitude. "I'm great. How are you?"

Gemma's green eyes turned serious and compassionate. "I'm well, but are you *sure* you're okay? I don't mean to be nosy, but Quincy came over Saturday night, and he was really upset. He and Tru talked for half the night. He came back over Sunday and spent all day with the kids, which is how I know he's hurting. They're like his little doses of happiness."

Roni's shoulders sank. She hated that he was as tortured as she was. "The truth is, I'm not okay, Gemma. I'm sad and confused, and…"

"I understand. Quincy doesn't know I'm talking with you, but I wanted to because, well, we all really enjoyed getting to know you Friday night, and I've sort of been through what you're going through. When Truman and I first met, he told me that he'd killed the man who was attacking their mother. I didn't find out the truth until much later. I don't know how Quincy survived with all the guilt he'd been carrying, much less how he found the courage to confess to me and the police. He didn't even know me. But he told me everything, and Truman was furious at him for confessing."

"Because he wanted to protect Quincy?"

"Always. The same way Quincy, who was no longer a scared, confused kid, wanted to protect Truman, and me and the kids."

Tears threatened, but Roni fought against them. "Is it wrong that I hate their mother?"

"No. In fact, you're in good company with those feelings." Gemma softened her tone and said, "I'm not here to try to convince you to give Quincy a chance. This is *your* life, Roni, and it's a huge decision to be with someone who has a history like Quincy's. But I thought you might need to hear from someone who was there for some of it. I didn't know what to make of Truman when I met him, much less Quincy. I came from an affluent family who snubbed anyone who was below their economic status. But I have *never* been loved as wholly as I am by Truman, and I've *never* been loved by family as deeply as I am by Quincy. I was there when he hit rock bottom. We found him unconscious on the lawn, and to be honest, it terrified me. I wasn't sure I could be involved with someone whose brother was an addict. It's a world I didn't understand. But I thank God *every day* that my love for Tru and the kids was stronger than my fear of what having Quincy in our lives could have meant if he hadn't gotten clean. Then Quincy went to rehab, and that was hard. There was a lot of pent-up anger and guilt between them, but Quincy never faltered. He was determined to get clean. He surprised us all when he confessed and again when he put himself back into rehab to finish his ninety-day program because it proved that his strength and conviction to leave that life behind was that much more powerful than the allure of drugs. He's a good man who did terrible things to himself, and those things hurt others, but he's in a better place now."

Roni felt like she was going to cry. "He said he can't promise he won't use drugs again."

"That's true. No one in recovery can make that promise. I know it's painful to hear, but I can tell you that in the time I've known Quincy, he's never once taken a step backward. He doesn't drink, he's honest to a fault, and for what it's worth, he's never brought a woman around us until you."

Roni had been thinking about his honesty, too, and knowing he'd never brought another woman around his friends confirmed what she already knew. Their connection was more powerful than anything she'd ever known. It was stronger than both of them. "Thank you for telling me all of this, Gemma. I miss him already, and it's only been a day and a half." It felt good to say that out loud. She missed his constant texts, his voice, and seeing his soulful eyes. She missed his *friendship*, his kisses, and the smile that stirred butterflies in her belly, but just as all that longing took hold, the crows swept down to feed again.

Chapter Nine

QUINCY SHOVED HIS laptop across the desk and pushed to his feet after typing and deleting the same line four times while trying to write a paper for his business ethics class. He could no sooner concentrate on schoolwork than he could on anything else besides driving his ass over to the dance studio and talking to Roni. She hadn't responded to his texts on Sunday. He was anxious, and at the same time he felt completely wrung out and *empty*. He'd talked to Tru, to Penny, and to Jed, but nothing could soothe the ache of longing eating away at him. He'd barely slept the last two nights, and it didn't help that Simone had needed extra support yesterday.

He checked the time, threw on his leather jacket, grabbed his keys, and headed downstairs. Truman, Jed, and Bear all turned as he walked into the shop. There was no escaping the concern in their eyes. He'd seen it so many times in the weeks after he'd gotten out of rehab, he could spot the *are you on the edge* looks a mile away. He hadn't been tested like this since those first few weeks, and they all knew it. Dealing with the trials and tribulations of reentering the world without the safety net of being so drugged up that nothing could faze him had been a massive undertaking, but he'd fucking *nailed* it. This thing with Roni was totally different, and it was kicking his ass, but he'd have himself put in a straitjacket before he'd use drugs again. Although he wasn't a fool. Anything that fucked with his head and his heart at the same time required backup.

Jed lifted his chin and said, "How's it going, Quince?"

Shitty. "It's goin'."

"Don't worry, man," Bear called out to him. "The way Roni was looking at you Friday night, she'll be calling before you know it."

He wasn't so sure about that.

"Hey, bro," Truman said as he closed the distance between them. "You okay?"

Truman searched Quincy's eyes, and it took everything Quincy had to keep from snapping at him. He loathed feeling that way toward his brother, but what he hated even more was making Truman worry about him.

"I'm standing here, aren't I?" Quincy gritted his teeth. "Sorry, Tru. I'm agitated, pissed off that I made shitty choices and thrust this nightmare on Roni. But I've got it under control. I'm heading to an NA meeting."

"You are?" The relief in Truman's eyes was palpable. "That's great, man. I'm proud of you. Do you want me to come with you?"

"No, thanks. I'm good. But I appreciate the offer. Would you mind if I pick up Linc from Red after the meeting?"

Truman stroked his beard, grinning. "Need a little buddy time?"

"That's always great, but I actually need a little *Red* time."

"No problem, man." Truman stepped closer and said, "What can I do to help?"

"Exactly what you're doing, offering to help, being there to listen like you did this weekend. I hate to make you worry, but it's good that you do. And as much as I hate being checked on, knowing everyone cares is important." He looked at Bear and Jed, who were respectfully looking away. He raised his voice and said, "I'll get through this, you guys. Don't worry. I'm not going to fuck up anyone's life. Most importantly, my own."

The question is, how can I convince Roni of that?

"My door is always open, buddy. We believe in you," Bear said.

"One hundred and fifty percent," Jed agreed.

Truman clapped a hand on Quincy's shoulder and said, "Two hundred percent, bro."

With a nod, Quincy headed out to his truck.

ATTENDING THE NA meeting was exactly what Quincy needed to center himself. Every time he walked into a meeting, he was reminded of his first time, when he'd desperately wanted to succeed and feared he might not be strong enough. He'd looked around the room and had seen people from all walks of life working the program, validating the things he'd learned in rehab. And just like the first time, he walked out after the meeting feeling even stronger and more in control than he had when he'd walked in.

Thank fucking God.

He drove to the Whiskeys' house on the outskirts of town, trying to ignore the voice in his head telling him to drive to Roni's instead. He wanted to see her, to make the promises he shouldn't. He wanted to do whatever the hell it took to make her *his* again, to hold her in his arms and see her smile, to wipe away her devastation and disappointment. As he drove down the long tree-lined driveway and parked in front of the Whiskeys' modest two-story home, he tried not to think too much about *why* he felt the need to see Red, because doing so would bring his thoughts back to his worthless mother. He was just thankful Red and Biggs were in his life.

He thought about Roni and wondered who she'd talk to now that her grandmother was gone. Angela? Elisa? He tried to imagine her discussing his past with them, and his gut twisted. Who in their right mind would encourage her to give him a shot when she'd worked her ass off to escape the very life he'd walked willingly into?

He climbed from the truck and headed up the walk toward the front door. Tinkerbell, Bullet's rottweiler, bounded around the side of the house, barking.

"Hey, Tink. I didn't see Bullet's truck." Quincy bent to love up the pooch as Red came around the side of the house holding Lincoln's hand. Red wore her leather jacket, while Lincoln was bundled up in a thick wool sweater, his russet hair peeking out from beneath his navy-blue hat. A familiar happiness came over Quincy at the sight of them, taking even more of the edge off.

"I wondered who caught Tink's attention," Red called out.

He waved, and Lincoln broke free from her grasp, toddling faster toward Quincy with his arms outstretched and an adorable toothy grin. "Incy!"

Tinkerbell ran after him, and Red hollered, "Tink, *slow down!*"

The dog slowed to a trot.

"Hey, buddy." Quincy scooped Lincoln into his arms and

kissed his cheek, inhaling the sweet scent of innocence. "Are you being good for Nana Red?"

Lincoln nodded and rattled off something too fast for Quincy to understand.

"What was that?" Quincy showered Lincoln's cheek with kisses, making him squeal and giggle. "Maybe Nana Red can translate for me."

"He ate lunch with Papa Biggs on the patio today. Right, honeybun?" She tickled Lincoln's belly, and he giggled again.

"Where is Biggs today?" Quincy asked as Lincoln grabbed hold of his hair and tugged. He reached for Lincoln's hand and kissed his tiny fist, earning another heart-melting grin. Lincoln immediately grabbed Quincy's hair again.

"Papa Biggs is inside changing Axel's diaper," Red said, running an assessing eye over Quincy.

"Play wif Tink!" Lincoln tried to wriggle free, and Quincy set him on his feet. Tinkerbell licked Lincoln's face, and he toddled toward the backyard with the pooch by his side.

"I see you're babysitting Tink today, too," Quincy said as Red embraced him.

"If you think Bullet is protective of Finlay, you should see Tink. She won't let Finlay out of her sight. Poor Fin needed a break. It's nice to see you, sweetheart."

"Sorry I didn't call first."

"Oh, honey, you never have to call." She looped her arm around his, and they followed Lincoln and Tinkerbell. "Biggs hasn't stopped talking about your new gal since she took his picture."

"I'm not so sure she's my gal anymore."

"Oh, baby, is that the trouble I see brewing in your eyes? I'm sorry. You two looked so close, I was betting she was *the one."*

He was, too. "I've never felt anything like what I feel for her, and it was there even before we started going out," Quincy admitted. "It happened fast, without any warning. Then we had our first date, and I swear to you, Red, the earth shifted beneath my feet. That's some crazy shit."

"Sounds like your little lady's snagged your heart." She waved to the patio chairs and said, "Why don't we sit down and chat. Would you like some lemonade or a soda, honey?"

"No. I'm fine, thanks." He leaned forward, elbows on knees, watching Lincoln plop down in the grass and toss a ball. Tinkerbell picked it up, ran around the yard, and brought it back to him.

Biggs walked outside, his cane in one hand, baby Axel in the other, and said, "How's it goin', son?"

Son. He wondered if Biggs knew how much that endearment meant to him every damn time he said it. "Things are a little complicated right now, Biggs."

"Then this ought to make your day. Nothing's simpler than a baby. Feed 'em, change 'em, love 'em up." Biggs handed him Axel, bundled up in a thick sweater with a blanket around him. Wisps of dark hair stuck out from beneath a cute black beanie with MINI DARK KNIGHT embroidered on the front. Biggs sat beside Red, leaned in for a kiss, and said, "The boy looks good with a baby in his arms, doesn't he?"

"Aw, Biggsy, don't go rushing him into parenthood." Red's expression warmed as Quincy cradled Axel. "But yes, all our boys look good lovin' our babies."

Axel yawned, his tiny eyes squeezing shut.

"You know, I never knew what a family was supposed to look or act like, beyond Tru," Quincy said, stroking Axel's cheek. "I always knew he loved me, and I knew our mother had it out for him. But as a family, we were so broken. Tru showed me how to love, but you two and your family showed me how to love like a *family* loves. You showed me what a family could and should look like." He looked at Lincoln rolling around on the grass with Tinkerbell, then at Biggs sitting with his arm around Red, her hand on his leg, and Quincy's chest constricted. "I want that one day—a real family, kids of my own to love, teach, and be there for. I want to be a man my family can rely on, like you, Biggs, and Tru, and the rest of them. A man people respect and want to be around. Not anytime soon, of course. I've got a lot of ground to cover before I can be that man. But maybe five or six years from now, after I'm done with school and have several years in recovery under my belt."

"You're doing all the right things, Quincy," Red reassured him. "Do you want to tell us what happened?"

"I told Roni about my past." He looked at Axel. If he was lucky enough to have his own family, one day he'd have to tell his children about his past, too. "I didn't sugarcoat it. I told her about the guy I killed, the kids living on the streets, and everything else, and for the first time in my life, I wish I was one of those guys who could lie."

"No you don't," Biggs said gruffly. "Lying would tear you up and send you right back to the streets, because it's *not* what you're made of, son."

"I know. Thank you," Quincy said, choking up at Biggs's support. "I didn't mean it. But the tears and the fear in Roni's eyes when I told her will haunt me forever."

"As they should. More fuel for the staying-clean fire," Biggs said with a serious stare.

"Right, but it sure would be easier if I felt like I didn't deserve to be loved. Then I could just walk away. I know I fucked up for too many years, but I'm a *good* man. Your family, Tru, Gemma, everyone has shown me that I'm worthy of giving and receiving love."

"I believe you always knew you were, darlin'," Red said. "Otherwise you wouldn't have gotten clean or stayed clean."

Quincy held out his finger, and Axel grabbed hold. "It's crazy that I've got this empty place inside me right now. Like I left a piece of myself with her."

Biggs studied him for a beat and said, "Are you fighting the dragon?"

"No. I have no desire to use drugs. Drugs can't fill this void. It's different from when Tru went to prison. I'm different. This emptiness is different from anything I've ever felt. But somehow I know nothing can fill it. It's like a space inside me reserved for us, for me and Roni, and I know that sounds crazy."

"That's not crazy, son. I saw love between you, too," Biggs said. "You might not know it yet, and she might not either, but it was as real and present as that baby in your arms."

"I think I might have lost her," Quincy admitted, the words cutting him like a knife. "I told her I'd give her space, but it feels wrong not to go plead my case and tell her how much she means to me."

"Don't push, honey, and don't give up hope," Red encouraged. "Matters of the heart don't run on a timeline, and they can't be forced. Look at Bear. He waited months for Crystal to finally go out with him. The boy was so lovesick, it dripped off him. And Bullet wanted to plow in guns blazing to claim Finlay, but for the first time in his life, he learned to listen, to be gentle, and ease in as best he could. He was kind of like a Mack truck plowing at half speed, but that's what love does to a person. It shows them what they *can* be for the right person. It might take Roni a day, a week, or a few months before she knows what she can handle and what she wants. But if she chooses to walk away, then she wasn't the right person and we were all wrong. That'll hurt, baby, maybe worse than anything else you've ever felt. But we'll still be here for you."

"I know. I appreciate that."

"What are you looking for today, son?" Biggs asked. "What can we do to help you through this?"

Quincy sat back and said, "When I was growing up, other kids talked about what it was like to be with their parents, and I never understood their feelings of comfort or the sense of reassurance they gained from just watching television with them or having family dinners where they talked about their days. But thanks to you two, I get it now. I guess I needed to hear that I was doing the right thing by giving her space, letting my past breathe its fire between us, and waiting to see if she wants to walk through it with me." He brushed his lips over Axel's forehead. "If you don't mind, I'd appreciate just sitting here for a bit, talking or not. It feels good to know I'm welcome."

Red wiped her eyes and said, "Now I want to call that little lady and plead your case for you."

They all laughed, unraveling the tightness in Quincy's chest just enough to fit in a little more hope.

Chapter Ten

THE HOPE QUINCY had taken away from his time with Biggs and Red had remained strong as Monday bled into Tuesday, but when Tuesday gave way to Wednesday and he still hadn't heard from Roni, that hope began to fray. By the time Wednesday evening rolled around, he told himself that Roni was probably done with him, but no matter how hard he tried to accept it, he just couldn't. Unfortunately, he didn't have the luxury of being distracted tonight. The NA meeting was starting in ten minutes, and he needed to be fully present for the other people in that room who counted on him. This would always be a big part of his life. A tug-of-war where drug dealers preyed on the weak, and Quincy tried to impart enough strength to those in recovery—and to himself—to make it through another day, another week, another year, becoming stronger with every passing hour. How could he have expected Roni to understand when she'd escaped the claws of the drug world without ever faltering and filled her life with music, dance, and happiness?

"I ran into a friend I grew up with the other day," Simone said, drawing Quincy from his thoughts. She looked good, less nervous and more confident than she was last week. "Her roommate is moving out after the holidays, and she offered to rent the room to me."

"Is she someone you ever partied with?"

"No, but I was honest with her about where I am in my recovery, and she's supportive. She doesn't drink or use drugs. I think by then I'll be ready to be out of the shelter and be on my own."

"That's good, but is the apartment in Parkvale or in Peaceful Harbor?"

"Parkvale."

Quincy gritted his teeth. "Sims, you know that if you leave the shelter and stay in Parkvale, you'll be out from under the protection of the Dark Knights. Have you heard *anything* from Puck or his guys?"

She fidgeted with the seam on her jeans and said, "No, but I know he's watching me. I can feel it. What about you? He called you my *pretty boy sponsor* the night he showed up at the shelter. I bet he's watching you, too."

"I haven't seen him around, and I don't think he'll come over the bridge into Dark Knights' territory. I want to be supportive of you moving out, and I think it's great that you're doing so well. But have you considered moving to this area? I'm sure you can find a job here."

As much as Quincy would like to help her find a job in Peaceful Harbor, she had to take those steps herself, at least for now. When Quincy had started running NA meetings, he'd asked Biggs if the Dark Knights could help find people in recovery jobs and housing. But after a long discussion about the realities of recovery, they'd agreed that because of the nature of the beast, and in an effort to keep Biggs's business associates and Peaceful Harbor safe, they would help only after completion of rehab plus six months of commitment to the NA program.

"It would cost me twice as much to live here," Simone said, and she was right. The Harbor was a lot more expensive than Parkvale. "And I can't live at the shelter forever."

"I get that, but you never know. It might be worth asking around."

"I will. I promise." She pushed her curls out of her eyes, and they sprang right back into them.

"Can't ask for more than that. Come on. I have to get the meeting started."

He called the meeting to order, and everyone took a seat around the circle. They began with a moment of silence, and after the readings and announcements, Quincy asked if anyone would like to share.

Jacob, a clean-cut guy in his early thirties, said, "I'd like to."

Quincy nodded.

Jacob remained seated, as they did when they had a small group, and said, "I'm Jacob—" The door opened, and he paused.

"Sorry."

Quincy spun around in his chair, and the air rushed from his lungs. Roni was walking tentatively toward the group. He pushed to his feet and said, "Excuse me for one second," quickly closing the distance between them.

"Hi," she said softly, gazing eagerly at him from behind her glasses. "Sorry for interrupting."

"It's okay. It's good to see you. I want to talk with you, but I can't during the meeting."

"I know. I'm here *for* the meeting. I read online that it was an *open* meeting." There were open and closed NA meetings. Open meetings were open to anyone interested in finding out about the program, while closed meetings were for only those who identify themselves as addicts or believe they might have a drug problem.

Quincy couldn't believe his ears, or that she'd researched the meeting. "It's an open meeting, but I don't understand."

"How can I truly understand what you've been through and the challenges you'll face unless I've spent time in your world?"

She smiled briefly and hurried to one of the empty seats, apologizing to the group for interrupting, as if she hadn't just blown him away. He returned to his seat, trying to shake off his shock and feeling like the luckiest son of a bitch on earth.

"Hi, I'm Jacob," Jacob said to Roni. Then to the group, he said, "I've been clean for forty-one days. I got hooked on oxys after I injured my back playing football with my buddies. Things went from bad to worse, and you all know how that goes." He wrung his hands. "My wife and I have been together since we were fifteen. We've got two little girls, and we're both committed to my staying clean…"

As Jacob talked, Quincy stole a glance at Roni. She was listening intently to Jacob. He couldn't believe she was actually there. He didn't know what it meant to her, but the fact that she'd shown up in support of him, and of her own accord, meant everything to him.

"I'm a real estate agent, which means I'm on the road showing houses and meeting with clients," Jacob said. "I think we all know that when someone has gotten clean and then starts using again, the first thing they do is cut off communication with the people supporting them. My wife is all too familiar with me disappearing for days on end. But she's checking up on me too much. If I'm supposed to be showing a house and I don't answer my phone, she drives by wherever I'm supposed to be. I know she's doing it because she loves me and she's scared I'll use again, but it's making me crazy. I've asked her to attend Nar-Anon, but she's too embarrassed. It's a stressful situation." He looked pleadingly at Quincy. "I know no one is supposed to offer suggestions or comments when we share, but I love my wife, and I'd really appreciate help figuring out how to handle this."

"Of course. Thank you, Jacob." Quincy looked at the others and said, "It's important to remember that recovery is as hard for friends and family as it is for the person going through it. Jacob's wife wants to support him, and that's crucial to his recovery, and it's only natural for her to look for the red flags she may have missed the last time around. It's also reasonable that Jacob is frustrated by that. You can see the vicious cycle. Frustration can lead to needing an escape, which can lead to using again, and the pisser is that she's trying to keep him from using."

"I've told her all of that, which is why I wish she'd join a support group so she can hear it from someone else. Maybe then she'd understand it," Jacob said.

"I agree that's the best route," Quincy said. "But we're the ones who used drugs, and we have to understand that it's perfectly reasonable for our loved ones and friends to be uncomfortable or embarrassed attending support meetings. They may feel shame, like our drug use was a personal affront, that *they* weren't enough to keep us clean, or we didn't love them enough. They may even feel like they drove us to it, pushed us to the brink. They're hurt and angry that you would risk your family's foundation for something they don't under-stand. If you and those around you haven't already experienced being embarrassed by your drug use, chances are you all will at some point. Jacob is doing the right thing by asking for help. The reason this group is here, the reason the program works, is because we help each other through all aspects of recovery. When someone wants to support you and either doesn't know how, or needs a more private way to handle it, there are alternatives like attending meetings outside of your hometown or utilizing online support groups. I can recommend books on the subject after the meeting, and of course, Jacob, your wife, or anyone else, can come talk to me before or after any meeting."

"Thank you. I'll suggest all of those things to her," Jacob said.

Quincy looked at Roni, still unable to believe she was there, and said, "Before the next person shares, when a new person joins the group, they usually introduce themselves. Would you like to tell the group your name?"

Roni sat up straighter, looking beautiful and nervous in a cream sweater and brown jacket, her hair falling in soft waves over her shoulders. "Hi, I'm Roni. I've never used drugs, but the man I'm dating is two years into his recovery."

Holy shit.

She fidgeted with her purse in her lap as their eyes met, and she said, "I'm just starting to read about and learn what *recovery* really means, and I'd be lying if I said I wasn't scared out of my mind about the possibility of him relapsing."

Oh, baby, I know you are, and I will never let you down.

"But I trust him," she said, holding his gaze. "And I want things to work." She looked at the others, her eyes lingering on Simone for a moment. "So I'm here to learn, and I hope that's okay."

"It's more than okay. *Thank you*," Quincy said, his voice so thick with emotion, he was sure everyone else heard it too.

"Maybe you can talk to my wife," Jacob joked.

As the others welcomed her, Quincy futilely tried to tamp down the hope consuming him. When their eyes met again, sending his pulse skyrocketing, he gave up trying to rein in anything and reveled in the fact that Roni believed in him, and she was there, making a big fucking effort for *them*.

RONI HAD BEEN so scared to walk into the meeting, she'd had to take a minute outside before entering. She hadn't realized it until she'd sat down, but she'd assumed the people there would remind her of the people she'd grown up around, dirty and maybe even drugged out, which made no sense given that this was a meeting for people who were in recovery. But fear was a powerful thing, and it had strange effects on people's minds.

Fear also did wonderful things, like plaguing Roni at the idea of not having a chance for something more with Quincy. She'd felt totally off-kilter these last few days, and she'd missed him desperately. Before they'd started seeing each other, going days without receiving a text from him had been difficult. But after getting to know him, after kissing him and being held by him, every day without that connection was pure torture. She hated knowing she'd caused Quincy angst while she figured out what to do, but she was glad she'd taken the time to think. The minute she'd spotted him across the room, all those tangles inside her had started to unfurl, and she'd felt like she could finally breathe again.

She'd quickly recognized the girl that she and Angela had

seen at the bookstore and learned her name was Simone. As she listened to the stories of the people in the meeting, she was in awe of their honesty and fortitude to make it through the horrible situations they described. She didn't like thinking about Quincy having been in any of those situations, but she needed to accept the truth and find ways to support him. As he ended the meeting, and they all stood up and held hands, saying the Serenity Prayer, she was even more in awe of Quincy. He'd put himself into every minute of the meeting, talking out situations thoughtfully and tactfully, giving guidance, hope, and strength, where so many other people—shamefully, her included until now—would turn away, maybe even *run* in the opposite direction, rather than offer a hand to pull these people across the rocky gorge between addiction and recovery.

She'd thought she was falling for him before, but that was nothing compared to how she felt now, having seen past his loving heart, right through to his generous soul.

Members exchanged hugs and thanked Roni for coming to the meeting. She stood off to the side while Quincy spoke with a few of them, and she noticed Simone heading her way. Roni was a little embarrassed because of how Angela had questioned her the other day, and she could tell that Simone recognized her.

"Am I right in assuming Quincy is your boyfriend?" Simone asked with a friendly smile.

"Yes. Was I that obvious?"

"I noticed it in Quincy's eyes the second he saw you. I think it's great that you came to support him and learn about recovery."

"Thank you. I have a lot to learn, and I'm not sure of the best way to support him, but I figured this was a start."

"You're doing exactly what he needs. He's done the hardest part, and he's making a real life for himself, surrounded by good people. Just letting him know you care and you understand what it means to be with him will help."

"Thanks, Simone. I'm sorry about how my friend acted toward you the other day. Angela has been my best friend for a long time. She's very protective of me." Angela had apologized to Roni yesterday for coming down hard on her about Quincy's past, and although she was still nervous about it, she'd been supportive ever since. She'd even talked to Joey about him, and Joey had told her that everyone had baggage and that Roni should trust her heart, which was exactly what Roni had decided to do.

"That's okay," Simone said. "Now more than ever I realize those are the type of friends you want on your side. The ones who will do the things to protect you that you might not do yourself. If not for Quincy, I wouldn't have made it this far."

Roni stole a glance at Quincy and said, "Did you know him when he used drugs?"

"Yes, on and off. It's a strange life when you're an addict. You don't have friends. You have people who can find you your next hit. Quincy was the only person who would ask after me and stand up for me if a guy got rough. When I hit rock bottom, I came to him, and he helped me get into rehab and set up at the women's shelter."

"I'm glad he was able to help you."

"Me too," Simone said. "I know you said you were scared about what all of this means, and you should be. To ignore the seriousness of his past wouldn't do any good for him or for you. Quincy's a great guy, and I know he has a lot of supportive friends, but I'm really glad he has someone special in his life. He deserves to be happy, and it gives us all hope. Recovery is a hard road, and from what everyone has told me, finding someone who is willing to walk alongside you on that journey is rare."

"Thank you. I hope one day you find that, too," Roni said as the others headed for the door.

Quincy sauntered over with a curious and grateful look in his eyes, rousing those butterflies, and said, "Is Simone filling your head with lies about me?"

"I was just telling Roni that I think it's great that she came to the meeting," Simone explained. "You're lucky, Gritt. Don't screw this up."

He smiled, and then his expression turned serious and he locked those clear blue eyes on Roni. "I don't intend to."

"Good boy," Simone said, pulling her coat on. "I have to get to the bus stop. It was nice meeting you, Roni. Maybe I'll see you around."

"Nice meeting you, too." As Simone walked out, leaving them alone in the room, Roni said, "I saw her at the bookstore that day Angela and I stopped by."

"So you were the chicks she told me about who had come in just to gawk at me." He stepped closer, causing her temperature to spike, and said, "I can't believe you're here. I thought you'd given up on me."

"I didn't, not for a second. I just needed time to put all the pieces into place before jumping in with both feet and putting my whole heart into us." She touched his hand, needing the connection, and said, "You talked about feeling lost after Truman went to prison. I understand that. When I was hit by the car, I lost so much of myself, I didn't know who I was or where I fit, but I still had Gram. Then I lost her, and I felt so alone. But you were there for me. I didn't realize it then, but we were building more than a friendship for all those months. It's scary to think I could lose you to drugs at any moment, but no part of me wants to walk away and lose out on what we were becoming. So if you can be patient with me as I learn about recovery and have questions or need reassurances, then I want this, Quincy. I want us. I want *you*."

"Christ, baby." He gathered her in his arms, holding her like she was *all* he'd ever wanted, and said, "I'll be patient—"

She pressed her lips to his, unable to wait another second. She didn't need to hear what he'd do, because she already knew. He'd already shown her the man he was. When their lips finally parted, the rest of those tangles inside her loosened and shifted, becoming lovely, welcome bows.

"Thank you, babe. Thank you so damn much."

"Don't thank me. Just keep being honest. I might need time to process things, but I want to be here for you."

"I will always be honest." He kissed her again, softer this time, and said, "My place isn't far from here. Can we go there to talk?"

"I'd like that. I want to spend time in your world, Quincy, see where you live and get to know all of you. And if you have a hard day or *hour*, I might not know the right things to say, but I want you to teach me, because all of that bad stuff that you went through led to the person you are today, and I really like that guy."

Chapter Eleven

QUINCY FOLLOWED RONI into his loft-style apartment above Whiskey Automotive, still in a mild state of shock that she'd shown up for the meeting. Talk about jumping in with both feet…

"So this is your sanctuary," she said quietly, leaning in playfully.

He'd wondered if it would be awkward to be together after everything she'd learned about him and sitting through the NA meeting, and he was glad it didn't feel that way.

"You could call it that." He helped her off with her jacket and hung it, and her purse, by the door. As he hung up his jacket, he said, "You can look around."

There was nothing fancy about his apartment, no walls separating anything but the bedrooms and bathroom from the open living space. The kitchen was just a counter, refrigerator, oven, and a few cabinets to the left of the entrance that led to the shop. Truman had left some of his furniture for Quincy when he'd moved out, including a wooden coffee table, an orange armchair, which now sat in front of the balcony doors, and a comfortable brown couch. Jed had helped Quincy build floor-to-ceiling bookshelves on the wall to the right of the entrance. The shelves were full, and more books were stacked on the floor.

"Cute kitchenette," Roni said, walking slowly past the kitchen and table for two. She looked across the room. "Wow, that's a *lot* of books."

"It makes me look like a hoarder, right?"

She flashed an easy, natural smile, which made him feel even more at ease. She ran her hand along the back of the orange chair and said, "No, it makes you look like a guy who loves to read and grew up hanging out at a library. Your safe haven."

"I'd say that's accurate. I never had books of my own when I was growing up, so now they're my guilty pleasure. And you're right, they are my safe haven. I had a lot of extra time on my hands when I got out of rehab, and I kept my mind busy with reading."

"My boyfriend the bookworm," she said in a singsong voice. "I like knowing that."

"And I like hearing you call me your boyfriend."

"Good, because I like saying it." She turned around and parted the curtains, peering out the balcony doors into the darkness. "What's back there?"

"A junkyard. This apartment is kind of a rite of passage. Tru lived here when he got out of prison, and he made it into a home for the kids before he and Gemma rented a house closer to the preschool. The Whiskeys put in a nursery in the auto shop downstairs so Tru wouldn't have to leave the kids, and everyone helped watch them while they worked. Now that the kids are older, Red babysits them."

Roni turned with a surprised expression. "He took the kids to work with him? I love that."

"Yeah. He couldn't part with them. He said he didn't know what they'd been through, and he was worried something would trigger a bad memory for them. He even wrote fairy tales for the kids with nothing bad or sad in them."

Her hand covered her heart, and she said, "Oh my gosh. I love that, too."

"I'd give just about anything to have caused that reaction," he said more to himself than to her.

"You *have* caused that reaction, many times. You just didn't see it," she said, touching the couch, as if she needed to touch everything he owned.

And he loved that, too.

"I melted on the spot the very first day you picked up Kennedy from dance class, when she leapt into your arms, and every time you've picked her up since then." She walked toward him and said, "When you told me you were taking Kennedy and Lincoln out on a date, you got the same melty reaction."

She took his hand as they sat down, and the intimate touch brought another wave of relief after not knowing if he'd ever have a chance to hold her again.

"I love that the kids are so important to both of you," she said softly.

"Tru and the kids are three of the best reasons for me never to touch drugs again. I have a lot to make up for, and I have great appreciation for the love they give me," he said honestly. "I want to be sure they know that. I'll never do wrong by them again."

"I'd imagine they know that. But, Quincy, while I might get warm and melty over a lot of things, what I feel for you goes beyond that. I hope you don't think that I'm holding your past against you in any way. I've found a place for your past, and for us, in here." She patted her chest over her heart. "I know you did what you could with the kids given your addiction, and Tru did what he could. But that doesn't make him better than you or make me think less of you. The truth is, you get that swoony reaction from me with almost everything you do and say. I love the way *you* love your friends and family, and while it felt amazing to be welcomed into their close-knit circle Friday night, what made it so special was that those were the people *you* love."

His chest felt full to near bursting. "Damn, babe. That's…Thank you."

"Don't thank me. It's how you make me feel. I'm sorry it took a while for me to see things clearly. But when you first told me that you'd been clean for two years, I weighed that against the six and a half years you'd used drugs, and at the time, it hadn't felt like very long. But what I've read online since then and the stories I heard tonight have shown me that two years in the life of a person in recovery are probably equivalent to about five years in the life of someone who isn't battling addiction, struggling every single day to overcome something stronger than they are. And from what I've read, in the first few months of recovery, maybe struggling every single *hour* is more accurate."

"You really do understand," he said with as much awe as disbelief.

"I'm *trying*. I still have a lot to learn, but I've been thinking about a few things you said the other night. You might think Truman was born having all of his ducks in a row, but he lived a different childhood than you did. It sounded like he had your grandmother to help guide him, at least a little, before you were born. But you had *no* adults to guide you. And yes, Truman did remarkable things, but he was still a kid raising a kid in a house overrun by drug addicts."

She took off her glasses and set them on the coffee table. Then she took his hand and said, "Please listen to what I'm about to say, because it's important. Truman is wonderful, but he had nine years before you came along to figure things out. I'm not saying it was easy for him, because I'm sure it was hell. But he has *nothing* on you, Quincy Gritt, because you were born into the worst kind of chaos, and you've caught up in record time. In two short years, you've not only lined up your ducks and set them on a path to a strong, stable future, but you're also helping others get their ducks in a row. *That* is what great men are made of, Mr. Gritt, and I am honored that you chose me to be by your side on this journey."

His heart cracked wide open, her every word burrowing deep inside him, planting roots. Truman was his pillar of strength and character, the man he'd forever held on a pedestal, and this incredible woman thought *he* belonged there, too. "You can't imagine how much that means to me."

Her long lashes fluttered as she looked down at their joined hands, her cheeks pinked up as her beautiful eyes met his, and she said, "Then maybe you can show me. I miss you, Quincy."

"God, baby, I miss you, too." His arm circled her as their mouths came together, softly at first, in a kiss full of unspoken promises and unyielding hope. He deepened the kiss, pouring his pent-up emotions into their connection, and she kissed him more passionately.

Their tongues collided, hard and hungry. She grabbed his hair, drawing a groan from his lungs and a moan from hers as she leaned back, bringing him down over her, and holy hell, he loved that *taking*. Everything felt different—the ferocity of their kisses, the way she clung to him, even the thundering of his own heart felt bigger, *louder*, as if it was beating hard enough for both of them. Their hands were everywhere, caressing, groping, *claiming*. She was so soft and luscious, and she was right there with him in their mutual devouring. Minutes turned to much longer, and the world faded away, until there was only him and Roni and the wild passion consuming them.

He didn't know how long they lay there making out, their bodies grinding and rocking in perfect sync. She was making those sexy noises, turning his blood to fire, and he never wanted it to end. He kissed her slower, more sensually, his tongue sliding over hers, then delving deep and possessive, drawing out their pleasure. She arched beneath him, moaning and holding him tighter as they both took the kiss deeper. She was his heaven and his earth, a delicacy he treasured and a grounding force he hadn't known he needed. He wanted—*needed*—her with him tonight, in his arms, and he didn't care if they kept their clothes on till morning.

When their lips finally parted, he cradled her in his arms, tucking his head in the crook of her neck, both of them breathless, and said, "Stay with me."

"Hm?" she said, eyes still closed.

"Stay with me tonight, baby. I just want to hold you."

Her eyes fluttered open. "All night?" she asked with a sweet curve to her lips.

"All night." He read a hint of hesitation in her eyes and brushed his lips over hers. "We don't have to do anything sexual. We can watch a movie or whatever you want. I like being close to you. I want you in my arms tonight, and I want to wake up with you by my side."

She touched her hip, reminding him she was self-conscious about her scars, and that pained him. He didn't even notice her limp anymore. When he looked at her, he just saw Roni, his sweet, sexy, strong girl with the bravest, most loving heart he'd ever encountered.

"I'll give you a pair of my sweatpants and a T-shirt to sleep in." He gazed deeply into her eyes, wanting her to truly *hear* what he said next. "But just so you know, when you finally show me those scars, I'm going to kiss each and every one of them, and I promise you, I will not think they're anything short of beautiful because they're part of *you*."

She touched her lips to his and said, "You're using your melting powers on me again."

"I'm just being honest, babe. But I don't want to pressure you. If you'd rather stay at your place tonight, that's fine." He tightened his hold on her and said, "But not yet. I'm not done holding you."

She ran her fingers along his jaw and whispered, "I'd rather stay."

Chapter Twelve

A SLIVER OF sunlight snuck in through the curtains in Quincy's bedroom, streaking across his broad back, snaking over Roni's hip, and dropping off the edge of the bed, as if its sole purpose was to create an illusion that she and Quincy were *one*. That was fitting, because it was exactly how she felt. Quincy lay sleeping with half of his chest on hers, one long leg bent at the knee, resting over her. His hair fell over his face, and he had the slightest curve to his lips. He'd been wrapped around her all night, making her feel safe. She'd been a little nervous about staying overnight, but she hadn't wanted their night to end, either. He'd made her feel comfortable, and she was glad she'd stayed. The sweatpants and shirt he'd lent her were ridiculously big, but she liked wearing his things and being in his home. It had been wonderful lying on the couch together, kissing, talking, and *sort of* watching *The 40-Year-Old Virgin*. They'd laughed a lot, and it felt good not to be holding back any longer. Attending that meeting had changed things for her, confirming that she'd made the right decision. She could tell it had changed things for him, too. His touch felt more intimate, and even the way he looked at her seemed deeper and more open.

When they finally went to bed, she'd wondered if he would try to have sex with her, and she hadn't been sure that she *didn't* want to. But he hadn't even tried. As important as it was to know she could trust him, she'd been buzzing with desire since the moment he'd walked out of the bedroom wearing nothing but a pair of black sweatpants riding low on his hips, his hot body and sexy tattoos on display. She wanted to know more about those tattoos. What did the sunflowers on his chest symbolize? Why did he have roses on his shoulders and hands? She wanted to know the symbolism behind each and every tattoo covering his arms, too. When she'd asked him, he'd said that most were drawings Truman had made for him when he was young, but then he'd wrapped his big, loving self around her, and thinking had gone out the window.

His body heat had seared through her clothing all night long, and she'd been acutely aware of his arousal pressed temptingly against her. She didn't want clothes between them anymore. She wanted to feel his heated flesh against hers, to *experience* the emotions that seeped off him every time he looked at her, and to allow her own desires to be set free.

"Morning, beautiful," Quincy said groggily, snuggling in.

His rough hand slipped beneath her shirt, skimmed up her belly, and came to rest over her heart, setting off fireworks inside her. She *wanted* him, and she didn't want to be self-conscious about her scars, but she was. Quincy hadn't noticed them the other night, but it had been dark and they'd both been caught up in the heat of the moment. There was no place to hide in the light of day, and that made her anxious. But he'd bared his soul, revealed all of the uglier parts of his past, and she didn't want to hide those parts of herself from him anymore, either.

He kissed her cheek and went up on his elbow, captivating her with the desire in his eyes, and said, "Your heart is beating fast. You okay?"

"Just a little nervous." She mustered all of her courage and said, "I want to feel your skin against mine." Before she could chicken out, she pulled off her shirt.

Hunger flared in his eyes, and he lowered his gaze to her chest. She didn't look away, needing to see his reaction as he took in the disjointed, *decrepit*-looking sunburst of scars above her left breast, leaking down her side to her ribs. Appreciation, empathy, and lustful flames rose in his eyes as he drank her in. He didn't flinch, he didn't even blink, and something warm and heartfelt joined forces with the underlying current of electricity between them.

"*Baby*, you are absolutely gorgeous."

Relief exhaled with a sigh, the honesty in his voice making her want him even more. She didn't look away as he traced the thin white scars and puckered skin over her breast with his index finger, touching every line, every indentation, the emotions in his eyes deepening. He followed the gnarly trail down her side, along the smooth, unmarred skin between her ribs and her waist. When he brushed his fingers over the indentation where a piece of metal had pierced her skin, she closed her eyes and he pressed a kiss there.

"Open your eyes, beautiful."

She did, and the way he was looking at her made her *feel* beautiful, *special*, and *wanted*. He didn't say a word as he kissed the trail of scars from her ribs up and over her breast, kissing every inch, until her whole body thrummed with desire and something much bigger.

"There is nothing ugly about these scars, baby," he whispered as he kissed them. "No need to hide them."

She touched the scars over his eyebrows and on his cheek, remembering what he'd said about the gash he'd gotten the night the man had attacked his mother. "The wall?" she whispered. He nodded, and she leaned up, kissing each of those scars.

He continued loving her with his mouth and hands, passionately and sensually. It was freeing and wonderful, and she somehow knew that was because it was *Quincy* touching her. It was the best feeling she'd ever experienced. He didn't touch her like he was on a mission to have sex. He touched her like she was precious and he was trying to memorize every bit of her, scars and all. When his hand slid down to her hip, her belly clenched nervously. Not because she didn't want to go further, but because she *did*, and that meant showing him the area covered in the worst of her scars.

He must have felt her reaction, because instead of going further, he rose and brushed his lips over hers, whispering, "Thank you for trusting me."

She wanted to feel his touch, his *acceptance*, of the worst of her scars. She leaned up and touched her lips to his, and like an unearthed volcano, her imprisoned desire poured out in urgent, messy kisses. He must have been holding back just as much as she was, because in the next breath, their bodies took over. Her hips rocked against his hard length. His hand played expertly over her breast, squeezing and rolling the throbbing peak, sending pinpricks of *need* racing beneath her skin. He made a raw, sexual sound that vibrated through her. She grabbed at the sheets as he lowered his mouth to her breast, sucking and kissing, sending her body into a writhing, moaning frenzy.

When he grazed his teeth over the sensitive peak, pleasure shot through her core.

"*Quincy*," she pleaded as he teased her right up to the edge of madness, intensifying his efforts with her every sound until "*More*" flew demandingly from her lips.

She reached down and pushed frantically at her sweatpants, delirious from the *want* consuming her. He covered her hand with his, stilling it, and pressed his lips to hers in a painfully tender kiss that went on for so long, when their lips finally parted, she was dizzy with desire.

"I want to undress you, and I don't want to rush through it," he said, and kissed her again, deeper and rougher, cradling her against him, as if he were telling her he was serious, he was in charge, and she could trust him.

He moved lower, kissing her belly, running his tongue around her belly button as he untied the bow holding up her sweatpants, and slowly peeled them down. Desperate to see his reaction, she watched as he found her scars. And like before, he didn't flinch, didn't look away, just brought that sweet, loving mouth of his to the rough patches of skin, as tenderly as he had to the rest of her.

"You're beautiful, baby. Every inch of you," he said huskily.

He continued stripping down her sweatpants and taking her panties with them, kissing and touching each and every scar on her hips and legs, and all the smooth spots in between, until she lay naked, her heart beating frantically. In those moments, she knew there was no greater luxury than being adored by Quincy Gritt. He kissed his way up her legs, his mouth lingering on her inner thighs, making her needy parts clench with anticipation. As his kisses inched closer to her center, she could barely breathe. She fisted her hands in the sheets, *Ohgodohgodohgod* playing like a mantra in her head, along with things she didn't want to think about, like *What if I taste bad? What if—*

He slicked his tongue along her wetness, and her hips shot off the mattress, causing her to smack him in the nose with her cooch. His head snapped back, and he let out a painful sound, rising onto his knees, his hand covering his nose, confusion staring back at her.

"*Ohmygod.* I'm sorry!" She slammed her legs together, rolling onto her side, and covered her face. "I'msorryI'msorryI'msorry!"

"Did I hurt you, babe?" he asked far too kindly for what she'd just done.

She shook her head, mortified. "I've never…"

"*Never…?*" He lay on his side next to her, bringing them face-to-face.

She spread her fingers, peeking out from between them, and whispered, "Done *that*."

A wolfish grin appeared, and she closed her fingers, blocking him out, but nervous laughter escaped, and she peeked at him again. "I'm so embarrassed. Do you want me to leave?"

"Do you *want* to leave?"

She shook her head. "I want to be invisible."

He chuckled and moved her hands, gathering her in his arms, and kissed her. "If you were invisible, I wouldn't be able to see where to touch you." He slid his hand down her back and caressed her ass. "Or where to kiss you." He kissed her again, slower and sweeter. "Did it feel that bad when I licked you?"

Her cheeks burned, but she managed to shake her head and whispered, "That *good*."

"Aw, babe, we're just getting started. I'm going to light your world on fire, if you let me."

The wickedness in his eyes made her entire body shudder. "You're not afraid I'll break your nose?" She giggled, which made him laugh, easing her embarrassment.

"Hold on. Let me just get my nose guard." He pushed up on his palm as if he were going to get it, making her laugh harder.

"If you didn't have a bionic tongue, you wouldn't have to worry about it."

"You like my tongue, huh?" He started kissing her neck, which tickled, and they rolled around, kissing and laughing, obliterating her embarrassment.

And then his mouth covered hers, turning all that laughter into insatiable passion. He buried his hands in her hair, taking their kisses deeper, their bodies grinding together. She ached for more, and hungry sounds climbed up her throat. He trapped her bottom lip between his teeth, tugging gently, sending shivers of delight rippling through her.

His eyes bored into her. "I'm going to make you feel so damn good, baby."

"*Yes*" came out greedily.

He slithered down her body, tasting and kissing. Her pulse raced, anticipation pounding through her as he spread his hands on her lower belly, and his thumbs moved in a hypnotizing rhythm on either side of her sex. She curled her fingers into the sheets as he lavished her with tantalizing kisses all around her center. Her eyes closed, every touch of his lips taking her higher, drawing a gasp of exhilaration.

"I love kissing you, tasting you," he said between kisses. He moved his thumbs outward and licked beside her sex, making her squirm with desire. "I cannot wait to devour you."

The hunger in his voice and his dirty talk had her lifting her hips, craving his promises. When he sealed his mouth over her inner thigh and *sucked,* lightning scorched through her. "*Oh God...*"

She felt his hot breath between her legs and clamped her mouth shut, fisting her hands tighter in the sheets and pressing her butt deeper into the mattress to keep from embarrassing herself again. His tongue slid along the sacred place that yearned for him, sending fire racing through her core. An unstoppable moan parted her lips, and he did it again and again, stroking and sucking, sending all her fail-safes out the window, but not *his.* As she arched and moaned, trying to lift her hips, he held them down. She loved that he was taking care of *both* of them.

"That's my girl." He eased his grip and said, "Enjoy me, baby. Let yourself go."

He slid his fingers inside her and did something magnificent with his mouth at the same time, electrifying her entire body. He continued zeroing in on all her needy spots, taking her on a wild roller-coaster ride of sensations, wreaking havoc with her ability to think. Blood pounded through her veins, tingles clawed up her limbs, and heat ignited in her core. She felt a tantalizing tug low in her belly, as if her insides were trying to reach him, and her toes curled under. She could barely breathe, had never felt anything like this before.

"Come for me, baby," he said roughly.

His fingers moved quicker, and his mouth covered that mind-blowing bundle of nerves, devouring her so rough and scintillating, her heels dug into the mattress and pleasure crashed over her, tearing indiscernible sounds from her lungs. He didn't relent, mercilessly devouring her, sending her up, up, *up* until she shattered into a million pieces, and "*Quincy*—" flew desperately from her lips.

Her voice echoed in her head as her body thrust and bucked, until she finally, blissfully, collapsed blurry-eyed and boneless to the mattress. He kissed his way up her overly sensitive body, reigniting her with every touch. When he pressed his lips to hers, she expected to be turned off by the taste or scent of herself. But as his tongue swept over hers, the taste of her mixed with the rugged, sensual taste of him, and it was absolutely perfect.

NEVER BEFORE HAD Quincy felt someone else's pleasure as his own. Emotions whipped through him like a hurricane. He brushed his lips over Roni's, and the truth came out. "I'm so into you, baby, you fucking own me."

"I want *all* of you, Quincy."

His heart stumbled, unable to believe they were there in that moment. The look in her eyes untethered him, and he took her in a fierce, loving kiss. They continued kissing as he stripped off his sweatpants, both of them expelling greedy sounds when he broke their connection to grab a condom from the nightstand drawer. Roni's eyes were riveted to his cock. She reached up and touched it, one single stroke, light as a feather along his length, igniting his entire body anew. He gritted his teeth as she touched him again, tentatively. He had a feeling she'd never experimented like this before, and the fact that she wanted to do it with him brought an onslaught of new emotions.

"That feels good, baby," he encouraged her.

She sat up and wrapped her fingers around him, her curious eyes meeting his as she stroked him again, a little tighter this time. He lifted her hand to his mouth and licked it from palm to fingertips and placed it on his hard length, wrapping his own hand around it.

"Tighter," he said hungrily. "Like this."

He showed her what he wanted, moving her hand tighter along his length. She breathed harder, stroking faster, and licked her gorgeous lips. He gritted his teeth, craving her mouth on him, but not wanting to ask for too much. Her eyes moved to their joined hands, and he let go. Her tongue swept across her lips, and her innocent, eager eyes darted up to his, then to his shaft again. She was killing him second by second, dragging him so deep into her, he knew he'd never climb out. He brushed his fingers down her cheek and said, "What do you want, baby?"

Without a word, she leaned forward and ran her tongue around the broad head. His chin dropped with a hiss, and her beautiful, unsure eyes flicked up to his.

"It's good baby, *so* good. I'm yours, Roni. Touch me, play, explore, whatever you want." *Just don't stop.*

She licked his length, and then she slowly lowered her mouth over the head and about a third of his cock, sucking and sliding him in and out of her lips. Quincy stroked her jaw and slid his hand beneath her hair, fighting the urge to thrust, to pull her mouth further over him. "That's it, baby. *Holy...*You feel so *fucking* good." She took him deeper, moving quicker. Excruciating pleasure tore through him, and "*Jesus...*" escaped through gritted teeth. "Careful, babe. You're going to make me come, and as much as I want that, I really want to make love to you." The words slammed into him. He'd *fucked* and he'd *taken*, but he'd never *made love* to anyone. As Roni drew him out of her mouth, her beautiful, trusting eyes met his. His chest constricted, and he knew the words had come straight from his heart.

"I want that, too," she said softly.

He sheathed himself and came down over her, that hurricane inside him whipping violently. He didn't push those feelings away. He wanted to get swept up in them, to lose himself in her and feel everything she had to give. Their mouths joined ravenously, but when her arms circled him, instead of thrusting and burying himself deep inside her, he had the overwhelming urge to see her face as their bodies came together for the very first time. It was another foreign desire, and he reveled in it.

He kissed her softly and cradled her face in his hands, gazing into her eyes as he entered her *slowly*. Her eyes widened, and he said, "You okay, baby?"

She nodded, her hands sliding into his hair. "Better than okay."

His fucking heart was going to explode. He thrust deeper, burying himself to the hilt, and the world tilted on its axis. She let out several fast breaths, holding him tighter, her eyes brimming with untamed desire.

"*Oh*," she said with surprise. "You feel so good. I never knew it could feel like this."

"Christ, baby. Neither did I."

A thousand sensations ravaged him as their mouths came together, and their sweet kisses turned feverish. He tried to go slow, but it was like their bodies were not only made for each other, but they also knew *exactly* what to do. She met every thrust with a tilt of her hips, every demanding kiss with a devouring of her own. Her softness conformed to his hard frame, allowing him to sink into her entire being. He pushed his hands beneath her ass, lifting her hips so he could take her impossibly deeper, earning one sinful sound after another. He pumped his hips faster, and her head fell back, her fingernails digging into his shoulders.

"Quin....*Quin*—"

Her inner muscles clamped like a vise, and she cried out as her climax consumed her. He didn't even try to hold back. They'd have plenty of time for long lovemaking and fiery fucks. Pleasure crashed over him, *into* him, stealing the last of his control. He gritted out her name, thrusting animalistically as their passion ravaged them.

When the last of the aftershocks claimed them, he dipped his head beside hers, their hearts racing in tandem. He kissed her cheek and neck, their bodies still connected as he cradled her in his arms and rolled them onto their sides. As the world came back into focus, he gazed into her loving eyes and knew without a shadow of a doubt he'd never be the same again.

Chapter Thirteen

RONI SAT ON the floor of her classroom Saturday just before noon, scrolling through the pictures of her and Quincy they'd taken at the scavenger hunt and in the days since. She loved who she was with him, who he was with her, and everything about their coupledom. Their happiness radiated from every picture. It had been only a few days since they'd come back together, but they'd become so close, it felt like much longer.

"Did you find the songs?" Angela asked as she walked into the room. She looked cute in black leggings and a pink tank top, with her hair pulled back in a barrette.

She winced. She was supposed to be finding songs for a teenage contemporary dance duet for the winter performance. They were going to work through lunch on the choreography. "I got sidetracked. I sat down to look for them, but then Quincy sent me a video message asking how my day was going, and I got distracted looking at pictures of us. The video was so cute, I watched it three times. In it, he's holding Sarah's little girl, Lila. Sarah brought her into the bookstore because Lila missed him. How cute is that?"

"Ridiculously adorable. I want to see Loverboy and Lila."

Angela sat beside her, and Roni showed her the video of Quincy holding Lila. Roni's heart fluttered as he said, *Hey, babe, miss you. How's your day? Wave hi, Lila.* Lila waved. Quincy blew Roni a kiss, and Lila puckered up and blew one, too. Then Lila kissed his cheek, and he flashed a devastatingly happy grin. He said, *Say bye-bye.* Lila said it and he winked, said, *Bye, babe,* and ended the video.

"*Girl,* he is *so…*" Angela sighed.

"I know." Roni had told Angela all about the meeting, their first night, and first sexy morning together. Angela had again apologized for coming across so harsh about his past, but Roni was kind of glad she'd said all those things, because it had helped her to realize that she did need to know more about recovery and what it entailed.

"Seriously, Roni. He's brawny, melts like butter for little kids, *and* sends you to work every day with your head in the clouds. That man is a definite keeper."

Elisa peeked into the room and said, "While you girls are at it, find a song for Roni's solo."

"Elisa…" Roni shook her head.

Elisa shrugged with a mischievous glimmer in her eyes and said, "It was worth a try."

As Elisa walked away, Angela said, "She's not going to give up."

"I know, and I love her for it. But I'm just not ready."

"If it's up to you, you'll never be ready. You're too good not to get out there and strut your stuff. It's like hoarding cookies when you know your friends would love them." Angela pointed to Quincy's picture and said, "That guy right there deserves to see you onstage, in all your spectacular glory. And I don't mean *naked.*"

"Why not? He'd *like* seeing me naked onstage if it was a *private* performance." The idea sent a thrill through her. She still couldn't believe he not only didn't mind her scars, but he continued to touch her all over like they didn't exist.

"Can I tell you how great it is to hear you say that after how worried you were about your scars? I love that Quincy adores *all* of you. I feel like you should give him extra lovin' tonight as a thank-you from me."

Oh, how she'd *love* to do that. But she didn't know if they were seeing each other. They'd spent the last three nights together, but they hadn't made plans for tonight.

She held up her phone, and Angela said, "What are you doing?"

"Making him a video message."

"Oh my God." Angela laughed. "You two take *cute couple* to a whole new level."

"Thank you," Roni said, wiggling her shoulders. She started the video and waved. "Hi. My day's been great. Even better after seeing your video. This is so much better than texting. Let's keep doing it. Angela and I are working through lunch on the winter performance choreography."

Angela popped up over Roni's shoulder and said, "Hi, Quincy!"

"Okay, I'm keeping it short. Have a great day!" Roni waved and blew him a kiss, then ended the video. She sent it to him and said, "Can I ask you something about relationships?"

"I already told you. *Do it often and do it dirty.* It makes everything better."

"You're such a weirdo. I think we have *that* down pat."

"You're in the *salivating over each other* stage, when you want to spend every second together, and even that doesn't feel like enough. That's the greatest feeling."

"That's exactly how I feel, but he hasn't said anything about seeing me tonight, and it's Saturday night. I want to ask him, but I don't want to sound clingy, and it's totally fine if he wants to spend time with his friends or do something else without me. But shouldn't we talk about it? Should I expect him to say he'll see me Sunday, or Tuesday, or whatever day he wants to? Does he want space and he's not telling me? What if he thinks *he's* smothering *me?*"

"You definitely should know where you stand, especially on a weekend night," Angela said firmly. "He pursued you for months, and you can't stop talking about how special he makes you feel. I bet he's chomping at the bit to get you into his arms tonight. Bring it up. Tell him what you just told me. Guys don't always plan, the way we do."

"You're right. I'll talk to him after work. We should get started before we waste our whole lunch hour."

Angela got her phone, and they started looking through their playlists. "I've got one," she said. "How about 'Delicate' by Taylor Swift?"

Roni wrinkled her nose. "I'd like to see them dance to something more powerful. Maybe 'I Was Here' by Beyoncé?"

"That's not bad. Let's add it to the list."

They chose a handful of songs and then began narrowing down their list. They were listening to their final three choices, putting together dance moves to see which felt best, when Elisa walked in with Quincy. When Roni's eyes connected with Quincy's, she was sure the wood floor would ignite a path between them. *Good Lord.* She'd just seen him hours ago, had made love with him that morning, and *still* he stole the oxygen from her lungs, all rugged and manly in his leather jacket, hair brushed back, faded jeans clinging to his thick thighs. It was all she could do to keep from running over, scaling him like a mountain, and sealing her mouth over his.

"Sorry to interrupt, ladies," Elisa said with a knowing smile, tearing Roni from her lustful thoughts. "It seems this fine young gentleman didn't want his *girlfriend* or her bestie to go hungry."

Angela gave Roni an *I told you so* look as they went to him.

"Sorry to bother you, babe." Quincy held up the bag he was carrying from the bookstore's café and said, "Two salads and croissants. Hope that's okay."

Elisa said, "I'll leave you three to chat."

"Thank you, Elisa," Quincy said. "Next time I'll bring enough for you, too."

"Such a sweetheart," Elisa said. As Quincy turned his attention to Roni, Elisa gave her a thumbs-up.

Reveling in her approval, Roni said, "Thank you, Quincy. You didn't have to bring us lunch."

"But we're glad you did!" Angela exclaimed. "Thank you."

"I won't stay. I know you're busy, and I have to get back to work. I'm sorry to just show up, but I missed you, and I thought you might say you were too busy for me to stop by. I didn't want you to go without eating."

"Yeah, right, like she'd ever say *that*," Angela said with a laugh. "Why don't you give me the bag, and I'll take it into the kitchen so you can smooch your girl."

He handed her the bag, and as she walked out, he said, "Best friend ever," and drew Roni into a sweet kiss, stirring those butterflies that seemed to live in her belly these days.

"I'm glad you're here. I was missing you, too," she said. "I'd never tell you not to come see me unless I was teaching."

"Good because apparently I can't even go a few hours without seeing you. I don't know what you're doing to me, but I hope you never stop. What time can I see you tonight?"

The air rushed from her lungs. "Thank goodness."

"Why do you sound relieved?"

She looked up at him, feeling silly for worrying, and said, "I thought you might not want to see me tonight because you hadn't said anything about it."

"Babe, how can you think that? I'll have to try *harder* to show you how I feel," he said with a sexy smirk.

"That's *definitely* not a problem." She felt her cheeks flame. "I know how much you like me, but I don't know what's normal in relationships. I only know that when we're apart, I can't wait to be together again, and I didn't want you to think I was too needy by asking about it."

"That's not needy, babe. That's being into me." He lowered his voice to a whisper and said, "I fucking love that." He gave her a quick kiss. "I don't know what's normal for other people, but I know what I'd like *our* normal to be. Seeing you seven days a week sounds perfect to me."

She laughed softly, sure he was kidding, though his words filled her with joy.

"I mean it, Roni. I want us to be a *given*, not a question. What do you want?"

"To be a given," she said, doing a happy dance inside. "But if you want time by yourself or with friends, I'm okay with that, too. I'm used to being on my own, and I'm not going to get jealous or clingy. It's not that I *need* you with me every second or need to know what you're doing every minute. I just like being with you. I guess I never realized I'm such a planner, but I'd like to know if we're going to see each other or not."

Angela walked back into the room and said, "Okay, you

two. Time to wrap it up. This dance isn't going to choreograph itself."

"I'll walk you out," Roni said to Quincy. "Back in a minute, Ang." She walked Quincy out to his truck, so relieved she had a bounce in her step.

"Get in here, beautiful." His arms circled her, and he said, "I don't ever want you worrying. If you're concerned about something, talk to me. In case you haven't noticed, I'm a big communicator. It helps me keep a clear head."

"I will from now on. Promise."

"Good. I have to get back to work, but I wanted to ask you one more thing. Thanksgiving is right around the corner. I know it's your first holiday without your grandmother and it might be a tough one, so we don't have to go anywhere if you'd rather spend a quiet night in. But Dixie and Jace are hosting Thanksgiving at their new house, and if you want to be around people, everyone will be there—the Whiskeys, Tru and Gemma and the kids, and almost everyone else we hung out with after the scavenger hunt. Lila and Bones share a birthday right after Thanksgiving, so we celebrate their birthdays that night, too. Nothing fancy, just presents and cake."

Thanksgiving was about two weeks away. She was touched that he'd thought about her feelings and couldn't believe he was willing to forgo seeing all the people he loved to be with her. "I would love to go with you. It will be sad without Gram this year, but I'll make her famous apple pie, and you and I will be together, which will make it much better. This will give me a chance to get to know your friends better, too."

"Great. How about we make the pie together?"

She fluttered her lashes flirtatiously and said, "Does that mean you want to get your hands dirty in my kitchen?" She could hardly believe how open she'd become in the last few days. The sexy things she said and did with him felt so natural, she wondered if he'd discovered hidden parts of her, or if his loving attention caused her to grow as a woman. She figured it was probably both, and she hoped they'd continue down that path for years to come.

"I want to get *you* dirty in your kitchen," he said, eyes brimming with the sinfulness she adored.

"I've never fooled around in my kitchen before. That will be a fun first to conquer. We might need to do a trial run on that pie before Thanksgiving. Want to stay at my place tonight?"

His eyes darkened. "Baby, what are you trying to do to me? Now I'm going to have that thought on my mind all day."

"Lucky me." She bounced on her toes and said, "Then you'll be all ready to go by tonight."

"Why do you love torturing me?" He lowered his lips to hers, sinking into a deep, toe-curling kiss.

"Considering that you got me all hot and bothered with that kiss, I think *you're* the one who loves torturing *me*," she said sassily. "And you don't see me complaining."

"You're hot and bothered, huh?" Heat flared in his eyes, and he grabbed her butt.

"Keep those grabby hands to yourself, mister." She pushed out of his arms, laughing. Loving his playfulness, she walked backward toward the studio and said, "I need to go back to work."

He strode toward her like a lion stalking his prey, save for that coy grin. "I'll be quick."

"You're never *quick*. You're hours of pure, naughty enjoyment, and now I'm going to think about *that* all day. *Ugh!* You need to leave." She shooed him away with her hands. "*Now,* before we end up horizontal in your truck and I get fired."

He laughed and blew her a kiss. "See you in the kitchen tonight, beautiful."

As he climbed into his truck, she knew there was no way she'd be able to think about anything other than that naughty promise and the hunger in his eyes for the rest of the day.

Chapter Fourteen

QUINCY PULLED ON his jeans, listening to the sound of Roni's music playing in the other room. He couldn't believe it had been almost three weeks since their first date, eight wonderful days and seven sinfully loving nights, since they'd talked about being a *given*. The word had become one of his favorites. He loved how their lives were blending together. Video messaging had become their *thing*, and he loved that they had a *thing*. Their days were busy, but they came together in the evenings. Roni had gone to another meeting with him, and her support brought them even closer. She was just as low-key as he was about where they stayed. They'd spent some nights at her place and some at his, depending on who was working later. Sometimes he studied in the evenings, and she worked on choreography or read, or they hung out with his friends, who had become her friends, too. Angela and Joey had even joined them for a bonfire at his apartment Friday night with Jed and Truman and their families, and Penny and Scott. The girls were excited that Roni was coming to Josie's party. It felt amazing to have Roni become such an integral part of his life, and he loved that there was no weirdness between her and Penny. He was also glad Penny and Scott had finally told their friends that they were seeing each other. He'd never seen Penny blush until that night. Scott definitely had a hold on her, and he was thrilled for both of them.

Quincy ran his hand through his hair, still wet from the shower he and Roni had taken, and grabbed his shirt as he walked out of his bedroom. His heart thudded faster at the sight of Roni wearing one of his T-shirts, dancing bare-legged and beautiful in front of the counter, her wet hair swaying over her shoulders.

She bent over the counter to write in her choreography journal. She worked so hard to get things right for the kids. He wished he could convince her to get on that stage and show the world how incredible *she* was.

Maybe one day…

She wiggled her butt as she wrote, sparking memories of last Saturday night, when they had planned to make her grand-mother's pie and had ended up devouring each other in her kitchen instead.

He dropped his shirt on the couch and went to her, running his hands down her hips as he kissed her neck, knowing that drove her wild. She smelled fresh and sexy, like promises of sunny afternoons and loving nights, scents of a future he never thought he'd have—and now couldn't imagine without her in it.

"Hey, beautiful. How's your hip this morning?" They'd gotten a little wild last night. He tried not to be too rough, but sometimes they got carried away. Roni never complained, but sometimes after they'd made love, or after a long day of work, he'd catch her rubbing her hip. He almost always gave her a rubdown in the evenings, and one night he'd drawn her a hot bath. They'd soaked in it together, and that seemed to help ease her pain, too. Aside from making love with her, there was no greater pleasure than taking care of her, emotionally and physically.

"I think my body's getting used to us," she said. "I'm okay, but I could use a few more kisses right here." She moved her hair over one shoulder, baring her neck for him.

He was falling hard for her beautiful mind and loving soul, but the areas that were scarred—her body and her confidence—held special places in his heart. He gave all of them extra love, letting her know how beautiful she was, inside and out, as often as he felt it, which probably made him sound like a broken record. But he didn't care. He enjoyed lavishing her with loving truths. It had been hard for her to walk around without pants on in front of him at first, but last Tuesday night after they'd made love, they'd talked about it as openly and honestly as they talked about everything else. She was a little embarrassed, but by morning, when she'd woken up to him kissing the scars on her back, she'd understood that when he'd said he thought every inch of her was beautiful, he'd meant every word.

He kissed her jaw and said, "Nothing could have prepared me for how incredible it feels to wake up next to you."

They'd just made love in the shower, and still his body thrummed with renewed desire. He usually had Sundays off and wished he hadn't offered to fill in for another employee today. But he was getting off at three, and they were taking Kennedy and Lincoln on a date together.

"Mm," she said, leaning back against his chest, rubbing against him.

He turned her in his arms and said, "I wish I could spend the whole day with you."

"Me too. But at least you'll be home early. I'm excited for our date with the kids."

He had a surprise in store for her. "We'll have fun. What are you doing today?"

She pressed her lips to the center of his chest and said, "Missing you."

"Damn, you have all the best answers. Are you going to hang out here?"

"Just for a little while. I need to go to the studio to talk with Elisa about a few things. Can we meet at my place after you get off work?"

"Sure. Sounds good. Now, tell me, gorgeous girl..." He lifted her onto the counter and wedged himself between her legs. "How am I supposed to leave when you're dressed like this?" He ran his hands up her legs and over her thighs.

Her eyes darkened. "*Quincy.*"

"Hm?" He brushed his thumb between her legs and felt her clench through her panties.

"You're going to leave me all hot and bothered."

"You should know me better than that." He slipped his thumb into her panties, over her slick heat.

"*God...*"

"Aw, baby, you need me," he said, stroking her. She squirmed, holding his gaze, and bit her lower lip. "You're so fucking sexy."

He glanced at the clock on the stove, calculating how much time he had before he had to leave. He didn't have time for another shower, but he had time to pleasure her. He hooked his fingers into her panties and tore them down her legs, earning a surprised *squeak.*

"Breakfast time," he growled, and spread her legs to look his fill.

"You'll be late," she said halfheartedly, running her hands through his hair the way she knew drove him out of his freaking mind. Her hands were as lethal as the rest of her.

"Have faith, sweetness." He crushed his mouth to hers and pushed his fingers inside her, earning the sounds he craved. He'd learned just how to make her come, but stopped short, needing to taste her, to feel her come as he devoured her. He tore his mouth away, and she whimpered. With one hand on her ass, he hauled her to the edge of the counter and lowered his mouth to her promised land.

She fisted her hands in his hair and wrapped her legs over his shoulders as he feasted on her. "*Don't stop. There, there...Oh God!*"

He ate at her harder, fucking her with his tongue, teasing the sensitive nerves that kept her at the peak, her essence spreading over his tongue.

Heaven.

"DO YOU THINK I'm turning into a sex maniac?" Roni asked Angela over the phone later that afternoon. She was at her apartment, getting ready for her date with Quincy and the kids. Their brainstorming of choreography had somehow turned into a discussion about Quincy.

Angela laughed. "You ask the funniest questions. I get it, because I think I asked you the same thing when I was seventeen and first having sex. Remember?"

"You didn't *ask*," Roni reminded her. "You told me you

were turning into one. So, do you think I am?"

"Of course not. You're a healthy, sexually active young woman. But I am a little concerned about how excited you are over going on a kid date."

Roni was elated that Quincy wanted to include her. "You know I love Kennedy and Lincoln. Weren't they adorable making s'mores at the bonfire?" Lincoln had taken a liking to Roni, sitting on her lap, talking a mile a minute, giggling, and sharing s'mores, and she'd loved every second of it.

"I think you mean *s'Moons*," Angela said.

Jed had coined the name *s'Moons* because Josie had made gingerbread cookies and the kids had used them instead of graham crackers.

"Kennedy would lecture you about calling them that, and Lincoln would try to do the same, but it'd come out as one long word that made no sense." Angela laughed and said, "I swear that kid talks as fast as lightning. Joey's in love with him."

"I can't wait until you guys have kids. I can be Aunt Roni." She sat down to put on her boots and said, "Why do you think it's weird that I'm excited to go on the date with Quincy and the kids? Family is important to him, and I love that about him."

"I don't know. Maybe because you're twenty-four, not thirty. But I guess it doesn't matter what you do with him, does it? You've been floating on air since you two worked things out. I'm *so* glad you didn't listen to me."

"I listened to your concerns. But the heart wants what the heart wants, and mine wants Quincy more than you could ever imagine." Roni had gone to a second NA meeting with him Wednesday night, and it had been helpful. But she probably wouldn't go to many more. Between the information she'd gotten online, the books she was reading, the things she'd learned at the meetings, Quincy's sponsorship of Simone, which included phone calls and spur-of-the-moment meetings when she needed support, and from simply talking with Quincy about his recovery, she was getting a clear sense of what recovery entailed. She knew things could change for him at any second, and she was glad Quincy didn't try to sugarcoat it. He'd told her that a smell, a taste, or even the sight of something could trigger what he called *the beast*, and his addiction could take over again, even though he had yet to feel drawn to drugs. She knew the risks, and they scared her, but Quincy was worth it, and the support of his family and friends buffered that fear.

"I doubt it's more than I can imagine, considering you come into work every day all bright-eyed and revved up like he has a magical peen," Angela said, bringing Roni's mind back to the moment.

"It must be magic, because you always say that after you and Joey fool around, all you want to do is cuddle and all he wants to do is sleep. But I swear when Quincy and I do it, we get rejuvenated."

"Yes, I've heard all about Mr. Gigantic Schlong and your hours of sexcapades and post-orgasmic pizzas."

Roni flushed with memories of their sexy morning. She hadn't shared any specifics about their sex life with Angela other than saying things like, *We thoroughly enjoyed each other multiple times* or *His mouth should come with a warning label*, but it felt good to participate in girl talk, rather than just listening to Angela's stories. Roni felt like she was catching up on some of the things she'd missed out on when she was growing up, like actually having a boyfriend and private jokes and experiencing what it was like to want to share her life—and her bed—with someone. She was so used to being alone, she hadn't been sure how she'd feel spending every night with Quincy, but it had happened so naturally, she couldn't imagine it any other way.

"Do you ever wish you had more experience? That you'd been with more guys?" Angela asked.

"No. I care about Quincy, and that makes it special." Roni knew that certain things she and Quincy did weren't *new* for him, but he'd told her they *felt* new because he was doing them for the first time with a clear head and a woman he cared about. "I have to be honest, Ang. I always thought you were making up how much you enjoyed sex." She headed out of her bedroom and said, "But if it's half as good as ours, then I know you probably weren't."

"I *definitely* don't have to embellish. Joey is a sex *god*. We barely made it into my apartment Friday night after we left the bonfire. Speaking of my sexy-ass fiancé, can you believe he's got stacks of Christmas gifts already bought and wrapped for his family? I swear he's Mr. Christmas."

"I'm sure he has yours bought and hidden away. He spoils you."

"And I love every second of it. Can you believe Thanksgiving is only four days away? This year went so fast. I'm *so* glad we have a four-day weekend. I'm planning on enjoying stay-in-bed Friday with my sex god."

"Isn't that how you spend every day when you're both off work?" Roni teased, pacing her living room.

"Usually," Angela said. "But we're going to pick out our Christmas tree next weekend, and you know it'll be up until all the needles fall off."

Roni was excited to spend Thanksgiving and Christmas with Quincy. "I think it's fun that Joey loves the holidays so much. Remember the artificial tree Gram had? That thing was so old, it practically fell apart when we cleaned out her apartment."

"I remember. You wanted to give it a funeral."

"I did not." Roni laughed. "I was just sad to get rid of her things."

"I was only kidding. Do you think you and Quincy will pick out a tree together?"

"I hope so. I've never picked one out before. I wonder what he does for Christmas. Knowing him, he probably spends it with Tru and Gemma and the kids, which sounds perfect to me. Oh gosh…I just thought of something. Given the way his mother was, I wonder if he ever celebrated Christmas." Her chest constricted. "I hope he did. It would be sad if he didn't."

"Boy, you two really are made for each other. You both missed out on so much when you were growing up."

"I know. But I'm going to make this Christmas extra special for him."

"I thought he was the best man in a wedding on Christmas."

"He is. Josie and Jed are getting married, but I'll think of something fantastic just for Quincy. Did I tell you the kids' leather jackets arrived the other day? They are so stinking cute! We're saving them for Christmas presents. I can't wait to see their faces when they open them."

"You know Lincoln won't give a hoot about a jacket. He'll have more fun with the box you wrap it in."

"I know. Why do you think Gemma and I were whispering at the bonfire? I was asking for more gift suggestions."

"Of course you were. You're always one step ahead of me."

Roni looked out the window and saw Quincy climbing out

of his truck. A smile crawled across her face. "Quincy just got here. Thanks for brainstorming with me today. I appreciate it."

"Anytime. You were my girl before you became Lover-boy's."

"You're the best, Ang. I have to run. Have fun shopping with your sex god."

"Have fun on your kiddie date with your magic peen."

Roni laughed as she ended the call.

She was so excited to see Quincy, she threw open the door and hurried onto the landing. He took the stairs two at a time, eating up the space between them.

"There's my beautiful girl." He reached for her at the same time as she launched herself into his arms. He carried her inside without breaking their kiss, her feet dangling above the ground. When he set her down, he kept her close with his arm around her waist and said, "*Mm.* Your kisses do me in every damn time. I missed you."

"I missed you, too. How was work?"

He shrugged. "Busy. Did you hear they're calling for snow next week?"

"No, but I love snow, so I don't mind."

"You're so cute. Did you have a good day?"

"Yes. I came up with some fun ideas for my five- and six-year-old class and brainstormed a few things for the Winter Showcase with Angela. She's going to get her tree with Joey next weekend. She asked if we were getting a tree together."

"Did she? You know what that means."

"That she's my friend?"

He chuckled. "Considering Christmas is more than a month away, it means we're a *given* in her eyes, too." He brushed his lips over hers and said, "I fucking love that, and I know what we're doing next weekend."

"I hope it's getting a tree!"

"Forget cute. You're the *cutest*. Yes, we're getting a tree."

She squealed and threw her arms around him again. "Can we go to the Helms Tree Farm? I went there on a field trip in elementary school. They have hot cider and horse-drawn wagons!" She bounced on her toes and said, "Please? I've never picked out a tree before. Gram always used an artificial one."

He laughed. "We'll go anywhere you want, if it gets me that gorgeous smile."

"Yay!" She hugged him again. "Thank you!"

"You've got it, babe. I've never picked out a tree, either. It's kind of fitting, isn't it? Our first Christmas together, and the first time we've picked out trees."

"Yes, and I'll take lots of pictures. We're going to have so much fun!" She toned her excitement down a notch and took the opportunity to ask, "Did you celebrate Christmas when you were young?"

"Not with my mom, if that's what you want to know. Tru and I would sit outside on Christmas Eve, and he'd point to the stars or the clouds and make up stories that were nothing like our lives. He'd tell me that one day we'd make our own happy stories in real life."

"Fairy tales just for you. He was always a storyteller."

"Yeah, he was. Every year he'd draw me a picture and leave it next to my bed Christmas morning." His face turned serious, and he said, "Christmas ended for me after he went to prison, and then last year I celebrated with Tru's family and all of our friends. It was great, but this year will be even better." He pressed his lips to hers.

"Do you still have Tru's pictures? I'd love to see them."

"No. When I got tied up in drugs, I lost everything. Losing them is one of my biggest regrets. But I had the ones I could remember tattooed on me so I'd never forget them."

"Would you mind telling me what some of them mean?"

He held out his hand, showing her the rose on the back of it, and said, "Before Tru moved out, and for as long as I can remember, every time things got hairy around the house, he'd take me to a church a few blocks away from where we lived. They had beautiful rose gardens. He'd make up stories about us living in some faraway place filled with roses, allowing me to escape the nightmare of our lives and live in those fantasies for a while. I loved those damn stories. After he moved out, he came up with a way to speak in code around our mother so she wouldn't know what we were talking about. He'd ask if I went to see the roses, but what he was really asking was how things had been in the days between our visits. If things had been bad, I'd say I got pricked by the thorns. But if things hadn't been that bad, I'd say the roses were in full bloom. The funny thing is, we used the same language whether it was summer or winter, and she never caught on."

She hugged him. "I hate that you had to live like that."

"We can't pick our parents. But I had Tru."

"And he had you. I'm sure it helped that he had you to focus on during the rougher times."

"I think that's true. You'll notice there are no thorns on my roses. I want to carry the good forward, not the bad."

"I love that you put so much thought into them. What about the tattoo of a woman's face and a little boy on your arm? Was that based on one of Tru's drawings, too?"

"Yup. A mother and son seen through the window of a ship. When he gave me that picture, he said if he had the power to give me one thing, he'd put me on a boat to someplace faraway with a new mother. He made up stories about her, too. And you know the wheel in motion that's tattooed on my upper arm? When I was in rehab he drew that to remind me to keep moving forward."

"He's always looking out for you. You're lucky to have each other and to know you always will. I wish I had a sibling. It would be nice to know someone was always there for me."

"That's what I'm for, babe. You want to know about the sunflowers on my chest? You're always tracing them."

She nodded eagerly.

"Tru didn't draw those. I read about them right after I got out of rehab, and it felt like a sign. They symbolize optimism, faith, happiness, and they're natural soil decontaminators, removing toxins like lead, arsenic, and even uranium. They've been used at some of the world's biggest environmental disaster sites, like Chernobyl. Since I'm living a clean life, that spoke to me, and they always grow toward the sun."

"Now, that I knew."

"Did you know the giant ones can grow to twenty feet tall?"

"Whoa. No. One day you should have a garden with them in it."

"Maybe one day *we* will," he said with a wink, making her all fluttery inside. "I'd like to think that I can reach unimaginable heights and reach for the sun, too."

"You mean with work?"

"Not really. I guess I mean with life, staying out of the darkness of my past. I don't have lofty goals of owning a business or anything like that. I love working at the bookstore, and they've already told me that I can move into their accounting department when I'm ready. Dixie's also hinting that when she and Jace start a family, she'll need me to take over the accounting for the auto shop and the bar. But I'll probably always keep one foot in the store. As you've already figured out, books make me feel safe and happy. I can fall into a fantasy world or fill up on facts, and I never want to stop learning. I've got a fairly good brain, and I don't want to waste it ever again."

She added that to the long list of things she loved about him. "The other night Tru said that even as a kid you were the smartest boy he'd ever known."

He shrugged and said, "He says shit like that all the time."

"I believe him, Quincy. You're always studying and learning, and the way you're living your life proves how smart you are."

"Or maybe it just proves I'm determined." He swept her into his arms, giving her a chaste kiss, and said, "Enough about my tattoos."

"Wait! Do you have one for the kids?"

"Of course, and one for Tru and Gemma and each of the Whiskeys. The chains around my left arm. There's a link for each of them, and just beneath the chains you'll see a garden, which has a flower for Jed and my other friends who I've gotten close to. And in that garden—"

"There's a penny. I've seen it. For Penny, right?" she asked, loving that he knew she wouldn't get jealous over that.

"Exactly. We'd better get a move on so we're not late picking up the kids. Uncle Quincy can't be late."

"Is that weird for you that Kennedy and Lincoln are your siblings, but they call you Uncle Quincy?"

"No. It's a blessing," he said. "I pray they don't remember a thing before coming to live with Tru."

"That makes sense. Will you guys ever tell them the truth?"

"I'm going to leave that up to Tru and Gemma to decide. But Tru knows that I think we should tell them everything when they're adults and they can handle it. They deserve to know the truth."

She slipped her finger into his belt loop and said, "Does it worry you that it might change your relationship with them?"

"Sure, but I can't let my fears keep us from doing the right thing." He glanced at her bag sitting on the floor by the door and said, "Did you pack clothes to stay at my place for the next couple of nights?"

"Yeah, let me just grab my books so I don't forget."

She went to get the books, and as she put them in her bag, he glanced at them and said, "You got more books on overcoming addiction? I could have gotten them for you at a discount."

"I know, but I found them for only two dollars each at a secondhand store online." She pushed to her feet and said, "Elisa recommended them."

"You told her?"

"Is that okay? She likes you so much, she was talking about how nice a young man you are and asking about where you grew up. I didn't want to lie."

He took her hand, emotions rising in his eyes as he said, "It's more than okay. I'm glad you're not ashamed of me."

"Quincy, you've done—you're *doing*—something amazing. You're beating the odds. I'm not ashamed of what you've gone through. Getting mixed up in drugs can happen to anyone. It happens, and I don't mean to sound casual about it, but drugs are everywhere. I'm sorry you went through it, but I'm not going to act like it didn't happen or like it's something I have to hide. I'm proud of all you're doing for yourself and for others."

"Jesus, baby. What did I do to deserve you?"

"Don't be silly. There's no deserving unless it goes both ways."

"How did Elisa know about those books?"

"When she was younger she had a friend who started using cocaine to lose weight for dance, and it turned into an addiction. Elisa helped her get clean and get a job outside of the industry. She's supportive of us. She'll always worry about me and the people in my life, but we talked for a while. It was reassuring to hear that her friend hasn't gone back to using drugs."

"You can't imagine how much it means to me that you're so invested in my recovery."

"Yes, I can, because I see it in your eyes and hear it in your voice. We'd better get going, *Uncle Quincy*."

He grabbed her jacket from the hook and held it up for her. As she put it on, she said, "Where are we taking the kids?"

"You'll see."

"Mysterious, aren't we?"

"I'm an open book." He swatted her butt and pulled the door open. "Let's go, sunshine. We've got kids to entertain."

Chapter Fifteen

LATER THAT AFTERNOON, Quincy carried Lincoln and Roni held Kennedy's hand as they left the Harbor Theater, where they'd watched the original *Toy Story* as part of a *Toy Story* marathon. Kennedy had gotten all dolled up for their date in a purple dress with black tights and black biker boots that her aunt Crystal had given her, with a cute quilted black coat over it.

"Did you like it, Miss Woni?" Kennedy asked. "I heard you sniffling. Were you cwying?"

"I loved the movie," Roni said. "But I was sad for Woody. I didn't like the way Andy pushed him aside for a new toy."

"It's okay, Miss Woni. They're fwiends now." Kennedy smiled up at her, her pigtails swaying as they walked along the sidewalk.

"Did you like the movie?" Roni asked.

"Uh-huh," Kennedy said. "I've seen them all, but Uncle Quincy wanted *you* to see it. He said you guys didn't get to see movies, or go to pawties, or dances, or *anything* when you were kids, and he wants to do all those fun things with you. I want to do them with you, too!"

Roni looked at Quincy, and he lifted one shoulder, as if his sharing his feelings for her with Kennedy and setting up the date for her as much as for the kids wasn't a big deal. For all his casualness, his eyes were full of affection. She was falling so hard for him, she wondered if he, and everyone else, could see it in her eyes, too. She'd been as enthralled with him and the kids as she'd been with the movie. He was patient and loving with them, always kissing and hugging them, making sure they were comfortable. She thanked her lucky stars that she hadn't walked away, because she'd have missed out on the best things in her life.

Kennedy took Quincy's free hand and said, "I think Miss Woni needs ice cweam to cheer her up."

"That's a great idea, jelly bean." Quincy looked at Lincoln, perched in his thick arms, and said, "What do you think, buddy? Do you want ice cream?"

Lincoln's head bobbed excitedly. "*Iwikeiceceam!*"

Quincy nuzzled against his cheek, earning sweet little-boy giggles. "I think you have a career as an auctioneer ahead of you, monkey boy."

They walked down to Luscious Licks, and when Quincy reached for the door, Lincoln said, "Down!" and wriggled free. He and Kennedy ran inside.

Quincy pulled Roni in for a quick kiss as they followed them inside. "Did you really like the movie?"

"Yes, very much. But I liked hearing what you told Kennedy even more."

"I want to do all those things with you, babe. I don't have a lot of money, but I'm going to do my damnedest to make sure you never miss out on anything ever again."

"Look who it is," Penny said with a wink at Roni and

Quincy as she came around the counter and hoisted Lincoln into her arms. "Two of my favorite tiny humans."

Kennedy jumped up and down and said, "We're on a date! We saw *Toy Story*!"

"How fun! Tell me all about it," Penny urged. "Is that the one about Shrek?"

"No, silly," Kennedy said. "It's about Andy and Woody and Buzz Lightyear…"

As Kennedy went on about the movie, and Lincoln bounced in Penny's arms babbling at record speed, Quincy took off the kids' jackets and Lincoln's hat and set them on a chair. He ran his hand over Lincoln's staticky hair, and Lincoln flashed a toothy grin, reaching for Quincy with grabby hands. Quincy took him from Penny, and Penny crouched to give Kennedy her full attention as she told her about the movie. Lincoln beat the top of Quincy's head like a drum, and Quincy tickled his belly, making him squeal with delight.

Roni could watch them together all day long. "You're so good with him," she said as she put her jacket with the others.

"Thanks, beautiful," Quincy said with a sexy grin.

Lincoln threw himself in Roni's direction, arms outstretched, and said, "WantBooful."

Roni warmed all over.

"Did he just say…?" Quincy's brows slanted. "That's *my* girl, buddy."

"There's enough of me to go around," Roni said, taking Lincoln and settling him on her hip. He wrapped his arms around her neck, grinning like he'd won a prize.

"Guess I can't fault the boy for knowing a hot babe when he sees one," Quincy said as he took off his jacket, looking handsome and delicious in a gray Henley.

"I wanna be a hot babe like Miss Woni," Kennedy chimed in.

Quincy scowled, and Roni and Penny exchanged an amused glance.

Roni tried not to laugh at the quandary in Quincy's expression and offered Kennedy her hand. "How about we check out the ice cream?"

Penny patted Quincy on the back and said, "Breathe, Uncle Q. She's only five."

"I want a special movie sundae," Kennedy exclaimed. "A happy-ending sundae!"

Quincy slid such a heated look at Roni, her pulse quickened.

"Looks like Uncle Quincy wants one, too," Penny said with a chuckle.

Quincy's eyes never wavered from Roni's as he said, "Only from my girl."

"Uncle *Quincy*, Miss Woni doesn't make sundaes," Kennedy said. "Only Penny does."

"I think I'll leave Uncle Quincy's happy ending to Roni," Penny said.

The kids chattered as Penny made their sundaes, and Quincy put his hand on Roni's back, whispering about happy endings and making out in the back of a movie theater when the kids weren't with them. She loved their secret sexiness.

Quincy sat between the kids as they ate, simultaneously wiping Lincoln's mouth and responding to Kennedy's litany of remarks and stories, adding more reasons for Roni to swoon over him. He even let Lincoln feed him ice cream, and he gleefully missed a few times, feeding Quincy's scruff instead of his mouth.

Roni gave him the remaining napkins and got up to get more.

Penny was finishing up with a customer. When the customer left, Penny said, "Let me get you a wet paper towel. Quincy will let Lincoln get ice cream all over him before he's done."

Roni glanced at him again as Penny went to the sink and said, "He's a natural with them."

"Yeah, he'll make a great dad someday. Just one of the many reasons so many single ladies in the Harbor show up for his readings at the bookstore."

"I know," Roni said, feeling a pang of jealousy. Quincy glanced over and blew her a kiss, pushing that jealousy away. "I had fun getting to know you and Scott better at the bonfire. I really like him. You two seem happy together."

"Thanks. We are, but it's still new. It's weird transitioning from friends to something more." Penny handed her the wet paper towels and a dry washcloth.

It was funny, because Roni hadn't felt like it was weird for her and Quincy, but they hadn't known each other nearly as well as Penny and Scott did. Roni had learned that friendships ran deep among their friends. Penny had called Quincy a number of times since they'd been together, and she lit him up in a different way than Roni did—a friendly way, like Angela did for Roni. She was glad they had each other.

"It turns out I like Scott *way* more than I thought I did," Penny said.

"It's funny how that creeps up on us, isn't it?" She glanced at Quincy and said, "I'm head over heels for *you know who.* Even hearing his voice makes me happy."

"I'm glad because he is crazy about you, too. He was really distraught after he told you about his past. I'm glad you took a chance on him, because he's worth it."

"I know he is. But I don't like thinking of it as me taking a chance on him. Don't we all take chances with every relationship? I know the risks of dating someone in recovery are different, but he's not a *chance*. He's who I *want* to be with, and I'll support him however I can."

"I'm glad to hear that," Penny said.

"What about you and Scott? Do you think it's serious? He seems great with the kids."

"He is, but I don't know if we'll ever get that far. I don't think kids are in Scott's future," Penny said forlornly.

"Why not?"

"I think the abuse he went through with his parents scares him. He makes comments about how being an uncle is enough for him. And I've always wanted kids, so…"

"I hate that they went through so much. But we don't *all* become our parents. I get why Scott's scared, but look at Quincy and Tru. Quincy might have fallen down a rabbit hole, but he climbed out, and he's on a great path. Look at Sarah and Josie. They're great with their kids. If they can move past the way their mom treated them, I'm sure Scott can, too." She glanced at Quincy as he tried to stick his spoon in Lincoln's ice cream, and Lincoln covered it with his hands, making Kennedy roar with laughter. "I keep wondering how Quincy and Tru learned to be so patient and loving when their mother was so awful. I don't think Quincy gives himself enough credit where the kids are concerned."

Penny turned her back to Quincy, speaking just above a whisper, and said, "He feels bad for not getting them into a safer situation sooner than when Tru found them."

"But he tried several times. His mother kept sending people

after him," Roni said quietly. "He got beat up for it, and he never left the kids alone."

"Really? I didn't know he tried to get them out."

Roni's nerves prickled. "*Oh.* I assumed he told you." She hoped she hadn't made a mistake.

"He didn't, but that sounds more like the Quincy I know."

Lincoln put his hand in his ice cream, and Kennedy yelled, "Lincoln!"

Quincy picked up Lincoln's hand by his wrist and said, "Hey, beautiful, think we can get those napkins?"

"Igoticeceambooful!" Lincoln said.

"I see that," Roni said with a laugh. He was so stinking cute. She went to the table and wiped Lincoln's hands, then tapped him on the tip of his nose. "There you go, little man."

Kennedy popped out of her seat and said, "Penny, wanna see me dance?"

"Let's get those sticky hands clean first," Roni said, and Kennedy held her hands out for her to wipe them.

With clean hands, Kennedy sashayed and twirled around the room and said, "Look at me, Penny! Look what I can do! Will you come to my dance show?"

Lincoln toddled behind her, yelling, "Metoo!"

"Absolutely," Penny said, wiping down the table as they danced.

Quincy put his arm around Roni and said, "There's never a dull moment around them."

Her nerves prickled again. "I think I made a mistake."

"Just now?" he asked as the kids giggled and danced around the store.

She nodded.

"I doubt that. What happened?"

"I thought Penny knew that you had tried to get the kids away from your mom. I'm sorry. I didn't know it was a secret."

"Only Tru and Gemma know, but it's fine. Don't worry about it."

"But you guys are so close," she whispered. "Why didn't you tell her?"

He held her tighter and lowered his voice. "Because she's a *friend*. She didn't need to know all the gory details." He glanced at Penny, sweeping Lincoln into her arms and dancing with him, then turned his honest eyes on Roni and said, "She was never going to be in my bed or in my life the way I'd hoped you were going to be. I wanted you to make your decision knowing absolutely everything, the good and the bad, so there were no surprises, no skeletons that could ruin us later."

"I appreciate that, and I'm sorry for mentioning it to her."

"You didn't do anything wrong, babe. You can talk about my past with anyone." He pressed his lips to hers, soothing her worries.

Kennedy yelled, "Miss Woni, dance with us!"

"IdancewifBooful!" Lincoln wriggled out of Penny's arms, making a beeline for Roni.

Quincy squeezed her hand and said, "Looks like we have a dance party to join."

Chapter Sixteen

QUINCY LOOKED UP from the apples he was slicing Thanksgiving morning to watch Roni swaying to the beat of "Cornelia Street" streaming from her phone as she mixed ingredients for the apple pies they were making. How had this become his life? Sharing his time with this incredible woman? Going to sleep with her in his arms and waking to her sleepy snuggles and insatiable kisses? Sometimes he caught himself hoping the other shoe wouldn't drop, but in the next breath she'd say or do something intimate or adorable, and he'd remember that shoes didn't fall randomly from the sky. He was in control of those shoes, and they were remaining firmly on the ground.

"I feel you looking at me," she said with her back to him, still swaying to the music. "I love it, but we need the apples so we can get the pies in the oven."

Yeah, they were *that* in tune with each other. He went back to slicing the apples.

They'd stayed at her apartment last night so she would have all of her grandmother's baking utensils. They'd slept in, but as soon as her eyes had opened, she'd been so excited to make her grandmother's famous apple pie, she'd snagged her sexy glasses, thrown on baggy sweatpants and a black tank top with DANCE HAIR DON'T CARE written across the chest, and dragged his ass out of bed. He'd tried to entice her into making love, but she was a bundle of nervous energy. While she was thrilled to be included in the Whiskey's holiday celebration, she wanted to make sure the pies were just right. *Come on!* she'd urged, giving him his sweatpants, then tugging him out of bed by the hand. *It'll be fun, and I promise to make it up to you once we know the pies are perfect!* She was so damn cute, there was no place he'd rather be than right there with her in the kitchen, soaking up all her sunshine.

"Hey, babe, is it bad that I can't stop thinking about the movie *American Pie?*" he asked.

"What movie? I don't think I've seen that one."

"*American Pie.* The scene where his friends tell him that uh, *you know*, feels like warm apple pie."

She turned with a wooden spoon in one hand, her nose wrinkled in confusion. "What feels like apple pie?"

"You've seriously never heard about this scene?"

"Guess not, sorry." She shrugged and went back to mixing. "What's so great about it?"

"Baby, you will never look at apple pie the same again."

She gave him an incredulous look. "I doubt that."

"Okay, beautiful. It's your appetite." He chuckled and said, "The main character is played by Jason Biggs. He's in high school, and he asks his buddies what it feels like to get to third base with a girl. They tell him it feels like warm apple pie. Then he comes home, and there's fresh apple pie on the counter."

She turned around, eyes wide. "He *didn't.*"

"Oh yes, he did, and not just with his fingers."

"*No!*" She laughed and made a grossed-out face. "Ew!" She put her hand on her hip, sassily arching her brow, and said, "So? Does it?"

"What?"

"Does it feel like warm apple pie?"

"How would I know? I've never fucked a pie." He laughed and pulled her into his arms, crushing his lips to hers. "We're watching that movie together this weekend."

"*Fine*, but you're not putting your *you know what* in my pies."

"Baby, nothing could possibly feel as good as being buried deep inside *you*." He took her in a moan-inducing kiss and then smacked her ass as she went back to making their perfect pies.

"Time for the *secret* ingredient," she said coyly.

"What's Gram's secret?"

She glanced over her shoulder and said, "I can't tell you that. It wouldn't be a secret anymore."

He wound his arms around her from behind, sliding his hands up her shirt, fondling her breasts, loving the appreciative noises she made. "Maybe I can pleasure it out of you."

"Uh-huh," she said breathily.

He sank his teeth into the curve where her shoulder met her neck, sucking gently. She writhed against him, reaching behind her to hold on to him.

"That's it, baby, touch me."

She twisted out of his grip, eyes full of lust, but pointed the wooden spoon at him and said, "Keep all that hotness over there. We can't...I need to get these in the oven."

He stalked toward her. "I just want to know the secret ingredient."

"*No* you don't," she said with a giggle.

He swept his arm around her, tugging her against him. "You're right. I want *all* your secrets, Veronica Wescott, every damn one of them. And then I want to make our *own* secrets, our own traditions, our own everything."

She went soft in his arms. "You're making me all melty again. I love when you say things like that."

"And I love when you're all melty for me."

She gazed up at him with her beautiful, trusting eyes, stirring something deep inside him. He always wanted to devour her, but right now he just wanted to *love* her. The realization didn't hit with the force of a hurricane; it hit as swift as the wind, touching every iota of his being, lifting and filling him up in ways that made him feel *whole*. Oh yeah, he was definitely falling in love with her, and nothing had ever felt so right in all his life.

"Tapioca, extra sugar, and cinnamon," she said softly, drawing him from his thoughts. "Those are Gram's secret ingredients."

"And love," he said. "You said she made her pies with love."

"Always," she said just above a whisper.

Their eyes held so long, he wondered if she felt it, too.

"Oh gosh. The pies." She laughed.

He shook his head to clear his thoughts. "What?"

"The *pies*. We have to finish them and put in the secret ingredients. You put me under some kind of spell, and my head goes right up to the clouds." She gave him a chaste kiss and turned back to the bowl.

"This Girl Is on Fire" came on, and she began dancing again, humming along as they put the apples into the mixture, and she stirred them. He loved watching her dance. He'd arrived early to pick up Kennedy from her class yesterday just so he could watch Roni in action. Roni was great with the kids, and she'd finally gotten Dottie to dance with the other girls. He wasn't surprised. He didn't know how anyone could resist her charms. Elisa had seen him standing in the doorway and had stopped to chat. She'd raved about Roni, telling him how driven she had been from the time she was a little girl, and how quickly and immensely she'd stood out among her classmates. She said Roni had a *rare gift* when it came to dancing, and she went on to describe how hard Roni had worked to get into Juilliard, practicing night and day for hours on end, year after year. Elisa had said she'd pushed herself to painful limits after the accident so she could dance again, and that she'd hoped Roni would dance in the showcase. Angela had made comments about that at the bonfire, too. He knew Roni loved teaching, but he couldn't shake the feeling that she shouldn't let go of her dream completely. There had to be another angle where she could get on that stage and feel good about it.

Roni turned and tilted her head, looking quizzically at him, and he realized he was staring at her. "Like what you see?"

"Hell yes."

She dragged her gaze down his bare chest and licked her lips, stirring the heat that was always simmering inside him for her, and said, "So do I, except something is missing."

"Your hands on my body?"

"That, *too*," she said with a giggle. "I guess you were so busy staring at me, you didn't hear me ask you to please get the dough for the crust I made last night out of the fridge. We need to roll it out and get it ready."

"Sorry, babe. I didn't hear that." He grabbed it from the fridge and said, "I get a little lost in you."

"You don't hear me complaining."

As she showed him how to roll the crust, line the bottom of the pan, and flute the edges, he stole kisses and nuzzled against her neck, earning as many eye rolls as needy sighs. He poured the apple mixture into the pie crusts while she swayed to the music, humming and bobbing her head as she cut the remaining dough into strips using a fluted cutter that created decorative edges.

"Hey, babe. Elisa really wants you to dance in the Winter Showcase. Maybe you should give it some more thought."

"I'm good, thanks."

He put the empty bowl in the sink and leaned against the counter as she began placing strips of dough over one of the pies and weaving them to create lattice. "But you said you like teaching the kids that they can shine no matter what. Don't they deserve to see you, as their mentor, doing just that?"

She kept her eyes trained on the pie. "Did Elisa ask you to talk me into it?"

"No, and that's not my intent. But she did tell me how hard you worked to become so good at dancing, and I know you said you don't want to bring others down, but I keep thinking that seeing you dance can't help but lift those kids up."

She continued working with the dough, remaining silent.

"Is there more to this than just not being perfect or bringing others down?" he asked. "Because you're perfect to me, and Elisa said you're still head and shoulders above any dancer she's ever worked with."

"You have no idea what it's like to have to basically learn to walk again, much less dance."

His chest constricted. "You're right, but I know how hard it is to face something much bigger than me every day of my life and to make a conscious choice to beat it no matter what the cost or embarrassment. Because my dream is to remain drug free, and I'll die before I'll let anything drag me back into that hellhole."

She lifted her eyes to his and said, "I'm sorry. I didn't mean it like that. I know how hard recovery is."

"Then open up to me, baby." He reached for her hand, drawing her into his arms, and said, "You pushed through rehabilitation for a reason, and you've taken on the challenge of a lifetime with me, which proves you're not the kind of person who shies away from them." He kissed her forehead. "I will support you one hundred percent either way. I just want to understand your decision."

Without a word, she went back to weaving the dough. She remained silent until she was almost finished with both pies, and then, speaking softly, she said, "Physical therapy was so hard, Quincy. It really took a toll on me. I fought with everything I had to regain my mobility and flexibility. But it was like swimming against the current. I'd make strides, then fall back because it hurt too badly to keep going." Her voice escalated angrily, but it was not loud. "I struggled with depression, which was so foreign to me, I swear it took everything I had just to keep my head above water. I thought I'd never dance again, and that terrified me, because without dance, I had no idea who I would be."

"That's understandable. Every time I thought about getting clean, I was terrified about who I'd be without drugs. But after I blew off Bear, I had no one to take the other side of the rope, no light at the end of the beast-infested tunnel to remind me why the fight was worth it."

She put the pies in the oven, avoiding his gaze as she set the timer.

"But *you*, babe," he said, taking her in his arms again, making her *see* him. "You've *thrived*. You have the world at your fingertips, and you're not alone. You have the support of me and all our friends, of Elisa, Angela, and all those little girls who look up to you as their guiding light. I wish you'd give it a shot and not put those dreams you worked so hard for away for good."

"It's not that easy. Dance has always been *my* guiding light, my stronghold," she said, using the same words he used to describe Truman. "It's always been something that has consistently made me happy, and the thought of being humiliated onstage will absolutely ruin that for me. I know myself, Quincy. Once that happens, I'll *never* get that joy of dancing back. But right now I have it, even if I'm only dancing for myself between classes or after work, and I'm okay with keeping dance for myself and teaching. I don't get anxious when I teach, but every time I even think about getting up onstage, I fill with anxiety that my leg will give out or my foot or hip will hurt."

"That's how you felt around me, remember? You were okay texting, but you were nervous with me in person."

She nodded, smiling.

"And look how good we are together. You're human, babe. If you get up onstage and your hip or foot hurts, the people watching you—"

"Will pity me," she said strongly. "And I don't want that."

"Like hell they will. Trust me on this, beautiful. They'll be so enthralled by what you're doing. You're the only one who will notice your flaws. You're the expert, a perfectionist, but the rest of us are thrilled just to be given the chance to see you dance."

She traced a sunflower on his chest and said, "But what if I can't finish a performance?"

"Then you'll get your applause early."

"You make it sound easy," she said with a smile.

"Not easy, babe, just realistic. Do you think Elisa or Angela is going to be critical of your dancing? Or Kennedy or Dottie? All of them are going to cheer on Miss Woni."

She laughed.

"I'm serious, Roni. I get that you don't want to be humiliated. Nobody does. And the last thing I want for you is to have the joy of dance stolen away. But I don't think you've given yourself a fair shot. Maybe you can start small, do a private dance for me."

She blinked at him, her lips curving playfully. "Like a striptease?"

"Hell yes, but only in addition to the real dancing you do. I show up early just so I can watch you dancing. When you're telling the story of the song through dance, it's mesmerizing. I can't look away."

"But I'm your girlfriend, so you see it through different eyes than everyone else."

"Maybe, but if other people see even half of what I see, they'll be blown away, too." He tucked her hair behind her ear so he could see her face better and said, "Baby, you are too magnificent to let fear lead you. I wish you could see yourself the way others do, the way it sounds like you used to. I want to support you the way you support me, and if that means letting this go, I will. But tell me, Roni. Is that really what you want? Never to dance on a stage again?"

She lowered her eyes so fast he knew she hadn't given up on her dream.

"That's what I thought." He kissed her forehead, bringing

her eyes back to his, and said, "I would give anything to see you onstage if and when you're ready, and that hope comes with an offer of a full-body rub before and after the performance."

She slid her finger into the waist of his sweatpants and kissed his chest. "You'd give *anything*?" She ran her fingers over his pecs and said, "There's a reason I didn't give you a shirt to put on this morning."

"*Anything.*" God, she owned him. She knew just how to distract him from the conversation.

A seductive smile played at her lips as she traced the tattoos on his arm, her eyes following her fingers along his forearm. "I really liked that thing you did the other morning when we made love in the shower."

Instant. Hard-on.

He pulled her against him so she could feel what she was doing to him and said, "That thing with my mouth, or when I picked you up and took you against the wall?"

Her eyes blazed up to his. "*Both.*"

"Christ, baby," he growled, and captured her mouth, lifting her into his arms. She wound her legs around his waist, and he carried her toward the bedroom, tearing his mouth away only long enough to say, "Does this mean you'll think about the showcase?"

"That'll cost you two orgasms."

He scoffed. "What am I, lazy? We're going for *four*."

Chapter Seventeen

DIXIE AND JACE'S house was just like their family, or maybe like a mug of hot chocolate on a cold winter's day—big, warm, inviting, and at the moment, filled to the brim. Quincy hadn't been kidding about everyone being there. Roni had never been in a house filled with so many people or so much love. When she and Quincy had arrived, they'd been passed from one embrace to the next and greeted with unexpected excitement, which was wonderful. The children had cheered, and Lincoln had toddled over yelling, *Boofulhere!* causing uproarious laughter. The kids had dragged Quincy off to play by the enormous Christmas tree. Even though the girls had been good to Roni since they'd met, and she'd gotten closer to Penny, and Josie had even texted a few times just to chat, Roni had still been a little nervous about feeling like an outsider since Thanksgiving was such a family-oriented holiday. But Red and the girls had swept her into their circle. Jed and Crystal's mother, Pamela, an upbeat blonde, had chatted Roni up about the pies she and Quincy had made, and Roni had given her the recipe. She and the girls had gabbed about their relationships and Josie and Jed's upcoming wedding. Now they were tossing out names for Finlay and Bullet's baby.

"Bullet calls you Lollipop, so how about Cake Pop?" Penny teased, earning a scowl from Finlay and laughs from everyone else.

"I think if it's a girl, she should have a feminine name, like you and Penny do," Gemma said. "Maybe Tiffany or Elizabeth?"

"Those get my vote," Pamela said. "Or even something old-school, like Margorie or even Melody."

"I like both of those. How about a unisex name like Jordan or Parker?" Josie asked.

"I love unisex names, but Bullet doesn't," Finlay said. "We were talking about baby names while he was putting together the bassinette that Sarah and Bones gave us at the baby shower, and I suggested the name Charley for a girl or boy, and he said"—she lowered her voice an octave—"our little sweetheart is not growing up with a dude's name."

"That's my boy for ya," Red said with a chuckle.

"You could go with Trigger if it's a boy," Crystal chimed in. "That ought to check his manly name box."

"My baby is *not* being named after part of a gun." Finlay rubbed her belly and said, "It fits my husband well, but this is an innocent baby. I'd like to honor you or Biggs, Red. What's Biggs's real name?"

"Biggs's given name is Byron, but, honey, you honor us every day by being good to our son," Red said compassionately. "You should name this baby whatever name speaks to you and Bullet."

"Don't name him Byron," Dixie said. "That's an awful name. He'll get teased. Why do you think my dad goes by Biggs?"

Finlay put a hand on her hip and said, "Have you met my husband? I could name our son Jezebel and nobody would tease him," causing more laughter.

"Whatever you do, Fin, don't name him after some type of *fuel*," Tracey said, eyeing Diesel, who had been watching her as closely as the other guys were watching the kids. "I need a glass of water. I'll be right back."

As they discussed names, Roni stole a glance at Quincy, down on all fours with Hail and Bradley riding on his back. Jed, Truman, and Bones were talking by the enormous Christmas tree, watching the kids like hawks as Kennedy directed Lincoln to crawl under Quincy's stomach and told Hail to say *giddyap*. Lila crouched in front of Quincy in her adorable frilly dress, peering at his face, and he reached over to tickle her with one hand. She toddled away squealing and giggling, plastering herself against Scott's legs. Scott hoisted his giggling niece onto his shoulders. Quincy glanced at Roni, grinning like he was having the time of his life. It was a sight Roni knew she'd never forget, and one she wanted to see for years to come.

"Uh-oh, you guys, *look*." Josie pointed to Diesel hulking over Tracey in the kitchen as she filled a glass with water from the dispenser on the refrigerator door. Like most of the men, Diesel was wearing a black leather vest with Dark Knights patches, which made him look extra intimidating.

"He's six foot six and she's what? Five two *maybe*? Can you imagine those two in bed?" Crystal laughed. "Talk about riding a bronco."

"By the look on Diesel's face, I'd say that's *exactly* what Diesel is imagining right now," Dixie said.

Gemma and Penny agreed. Red just shook her head.

"Girl talk sure has changed," Pamela said, sharing a knowing glance with Red.

"I don't understand how Tracey doesn't realize he likes her," Sarah said. "Unless we're wrong about that."

Dixie crossed her arms and said, "We're not wrong."

"I think Tracey does realize it, even if she can't admit it to herself yet," Penny said. "The way he's looking at her makes it hard to miss."

Just like yours and Scott's furtive glances, Roni mused.

Finlay rubbed her burgeoning belly and said, "That must be what Bullet and I looked like to you guys at first."

Tracey turned around, clutching her glass in both hands, her back pressed against the refrigerator, eyes wide as saucers as Diesel said something Roni couldn't hear. "Shouldn't we help her out of that situation?"

"Tracey might look scared, honey, but she's not," Red said emphatically. "Our girl can hold her own with him, the same way Finlay did with Bullet. Diesel's rougher than our Bullet, but he'd never hurt a woman. He's a protector through and through."

Tracey scurried out of the kitchen, heading directly for the girls with a scowl on her face, and squeezed between Red and Roni. Roni glanced at Diesel, who wore a satisfied smirk. When he noticed Roni looking at him, his face went stoic again.

"What was *that* about?" Penny asked.

"I don't know. He's so weird," Tracey said. "He asked me if I had a date for Josie's wedding, and when I said how could I possibly have a date when he doesn't let guys speak to me, he just stood there staring at me."

"*Visually devouring* would be more accurate," Dixie said.

"She's right. He *was* looking at you like that," Roni agreed. "Did he want you to go with him to the wedding?"

"Of course not," Tracey insisted. "But I think I finally understand why he's always watching me. Red, you told him about my abusive ex-boyfriend when I started working there, didn't you?"

"Yes, I did, and I told him to keep an eye out, so you didn't run into any trouble," Red said.

"See? That's exactly what he's doing," Tracey said. "I think he wanted to make sure he had time to check out my date, as if I even want one. I'm going to have to yank his chain so he backs off, like you do with aggressive dogs. Does anyone have one of those collars with spikes inside it?"

Red laughed. "I told you she could handle herself with him. Tracey and I have talked at length about our mountain of a man, and she wants to deal with him on her own."

"Exactly," Tracey said.

"Believe me, if I thought any man posed a threat to any of our girls, I'd be the first to step in." Red looked at Roni and said, "That includes you, sweetheart. You're family now."

Surprised, Roni said, "Thank you. I've never been around a family like yours. It's amazing how you all take care of each other."

"It's special, isn't it?" Tracey said. "I had no idea it could be like this until they brought me into their clan."

Pamela and Crystal exchanged a warm glance.

"Neither did I. It was overwhelming for me at first," Sarah admitted. "But then I learned to trust, and that led to accepting that this is what family is supposed to be about."

"That's right, honey," Red said. "And, Roni, that charming man of yours is *our* boy, and he will always be an important part of our family. He's not alone in his recovery or any other part of his life. He slipped through the cracks once, but never again."

Roni loved hearing that, though she knew it from the way they treated him. Before she could respond, Crystal said, "What are the guys powwowing about?" She pointed to Bullet, Bear, and Jace, who was holding baby Axel.

"Knowing Bullet, he's figuring out how to lock Finlay away for the rest of her pregnancy," Dixie teased.

Finlay giggled. "He loves so hard. He's going to be the best daddy."

"Have you seen Bear with Axel?" Crystal asked. "He jumps at the chance to change diapers, bathe him, and play with him."

"Bear's good with Axel, but he's got nothing on three-times-daddy, Bones," Sarah pointed out.

"Speaking of kids," Tracey said to Roni. "Your boyfriend sure loves them." She nodded in Quincy's direction. He was talking with Scott and Truman, holding Kennedy and Lincoln under his arms like footballs, their legs kicking as they giggled up a storm, while Hail and Bradley ran in circles around the three men.

"He's so good with them." Roni looked at Gemma and said, "We had a blast on our date with Kennedy and Lincoln."

"They did, too." Gemma smiled and said, "Lincoln can't stop talking about *Booful*, and Kennedy is already planning your next date with them."

All the girls commented about Lincoln's cute nickname for Roni.

It was funny how the same nickname could make her feel special in two totally different ways. She glanced at Quincy again as he put the kids down and scooped up Lila, kissed her cheek, then set her down to play with the other kids. His eyes turned serious as he talked with Scott and Truman. Then his gaze shifted to Roni, his expression softening. She loved that she seemed to be on his mind as often as he was on hers.

"That was an excessively *dreamy* sigh, Roni," Finlay said.

Roni realized she was staring at Quincy and tore her eyes away, only to find all eyes on her. "Sorry. He's just so…"

"Hot?" Tracey suggested.

"Yes, definitely, but he's more than that. There's something about him and the way he cares about others. I can hardly believe that in less than a week we'll have been dating for only a month. It feels like we've been together for much longer."

"That's because he charmed you via text all summer," Penny said.

"He sure did," she said.

"He can be pushy, but he means well," Penny said.

"He doesn't push, but he definitely nudges," Roni said. "He makes me want to do things I didn't even realize I wanted to do."

"Quincy and his *dirty deeds*," Crystal teased.

"Not *that* kind of pushing. I mean, maybe that, too, but…" Roni felt her cheeks burn.

"They do send videos to each other all the time," Josie pointed out. "Jed said Quincy stops whatever he's doing to watch your videos."

"This just got a lot more interesting," Dixie said.

"Not *those* kinds of videos," Roni insisted. "We use video messages instead of texting. It's more personal. Anyway, what I meant was, he sees more in me than I let myself see anymore."

"What do you mean, *anymore*?" Josie asked.

Roni hadn't realized she'd never told them about her accident. She filled them in on what she'd gone through and said, "Quincy's trying to get me to perform again. On the one hand, I'm really nervous about it. But on the other hand, a big part of me wants to do it for him, which feels weird because I've never wanted to dance *for* someone else. I wanted to make my grandmother and Elisa—my dance instructor—proud, but dancing has always been something I've done for myself."

"That's how you know you've found your person," Red said. "The one who will help you become the best you can be and would walk through fire for you."

Roni thought about that for a second and said, "I think he would walk through fire for me, and for all of you, too. He's that good a man."

"And your person comes with all of us," Gemma said cheerily.

"Speaking of *us*, did Gemma talk to you about the costumes for the Winter Showcase?" Crystal asked.

"No. Is there a problem?" Roni asked. "We had some issues with ill-fitting costumes for the Summer Showcase, but Elisa worked that out with the costume company, and I thought she sent home a note to parents not to order until four weeks prior to the event."

"I haven't ordered Kennedy's yet," Gemma reassured her. "I hadn't said anything about this to you because you're seeing Quincy, and I didn't want you to think we were trying to use your relationship to our benefit, but when I was looking through the company's website, I realized that Crystal and I could make the costumes much cheaper. We can get the materials in bulk through the boutique and save the families quite a bit of money."

"Do you know if Elisa would consider having them made locally?" Crystal asked.

"I think she'd love that, and, Gemma, I wouldn't have thought you were using my relationship with Quincy. When I was young, we couldn't afford as many dance classes as I wanted to take, so my grandmother made *all* the costumes in exchange for tuition. I think Elisa and the parents would appreciate saving money and doing things locally. Why don't you give me your number. I'll mention it to her and let you know what she says."

"Perfect. Thank you," Gemma said.

As they exchanged numbers, Jace sidled up to Dixie cradling Axel in his arms and kissed Dixie's cheek. He looked to be in his late thirties, with longish dark hair and serious eyes that Roni had noticed were on Dixie as often as Quincy's were on her.

"My husband the baby hog," Dixie said lovingly. "If you think Quincy likes kids, Jace hasn't put this baby down since Bear and Crystal walked in the door."

Jace cocked a grin and said, "Maybe this time next year we'll have our own little one to carry around."

"I have a contract to fulfill, remember?" Dixie leaned into him. "I can guarantee the face of Silver-Stone won't be quite as appealing in your Leather and Lace outfits with a big baby belly."

Jace's eyes heated. "Wanna bet?" He gave her a smooch, and Dixie laughed. "You're sleeping with the boss. I'll modify the contract."

"*Stop.*" Dixie sounded more playful than irritated. "How about we give Nana Pamela her grandbaby?" She took Axel from him, kissed Axel's forehead, and handed him to Pamela.

"I have missed you," Pamela said, snuggling Axel.

Dixie took Jace's hand and said, "Come on, big boy, you need to carve the turkey."

As she dragged Jace toward the kitchen, he said, "I'll make a Leather and Lace maternity line."

Dixie looked over her shoulder and said, "Help! I need reinforcements!"

Roni laughed as the other girls followed her toward the kitchen.

"Let's go, baby girl." Red put her arm around Roni, guiding her toward the girls, and said, "One of our own needs backup. That means us, even if I'd rather have more grandbabies."

DINNER WAS DELICIOUS, noisy, and wonderful. Between the kids' hilarious remarks, the guys making dirty jokes and speaking in code so the kids wouldn't catch wind of them, and the girls giving it right back, Roni had never laughed so much. Quincy was as attentive as ever, holding her hand or draping an arm around her for most of the meal. He whispered sweet and sexy things in her ear, kissing her cheek often. Everyone had a field day teasing them about how affectionate they were, which Quincy ate up as he had at the bar, kissing her more just to egg them on.

"You keep that up, and you'll be the next ones with a bun in the oven," Bear said with a mischievous grin.

"We've got that covered," Jace exclaimed.

Dixie rolled her eyes and said, "No babies for you until we fix up my other *baby*."

"You're the only woman on earth who calls her house a baby." Jace looked around the table as he said, "When we moved out of her little house in town, she said she felt like she was abandoning her baby."

"I can't help it if I'm attached to it," Dixie said. "I'm proud of buying my house."

"I was wondering if you were going to sell," Truman said.

Dixie shook her head. "Sorry, Tru. I'm not ready to let it go. We're going to fix it up and rent it out for a while."

"If she has her way, we'll rent it until our unborn children are old enough to move into it," Jace said with a shake of his head.

"I love that idea!" Dixie exclaimed, causing a round of chuckles and jokes.

"Of course you do." Jace eyed Diesel and said, "Hey, D, you gonna be around for a while? Are you looking for a place to rent?"

Diesel shook his head. "Nah. I'm good at the clubhouse, thanks."

"He's already installed a revolving bedroom door," Tracey said more to Roni than anyone else, but everyone else heard, and silence fell over the room.

Diesel set his dark eyes on her, and that satisfied smirk returned as he said, "Jealous, baby girl?"

Tracey lifted her chin, meeting his gaze and narrowing her eyes. "In your dreams, *Unleaded*."

Everyone cracked up, though Tracey and Diesel seemed to be having some sort of stare down.

"Okay, everyone, settle down," Biggs said sternly, his eyes moving around the table as they quieted. "It's been a hell of a year, hasn't it? We've welcomed new family members, new grandbabies, and we're blessed with another on the way. We've got two weddings on the horizon and new couples around the table." He lifted his glass toward Quincy and Roni, then to Penny and Scott. "And I would just like to say that I am thankful for each and every one of you and for those who aren't here to celebrate with us."

"Want to make bets on who gets engaged next?" Bear asked, looking at Roni and Quincy and Scott and Penny.

Scott put his arm around Penny, pulling her closer, and said, "I just got this gorgeous woman to go out with me. Give us a minute, would ya?"

Everyone laughed.

"Penny, if you want to marry my brother, just move in with him," Josie said. "Sarah and I are living proof that once you live with Scott, getting married is right around the corner."

More laughter ensued.

Roni loved their banter and the way the other couples sitting around the table were just as close as her and Quincy. Even though Sarah and Bones had Lila between them, he'd reached across the back of the high chair and stroked Sarah's shoulder, catching her attention to blow her a kiss. Truman and Gemma were whispering around Lincoln. Bullet had kept one hand on Finlay's belly the whole meal, making an announcement every time the baby kicked. There were no Hallmark moments around this family, that was for sure. They were too real for that, giving each other a hard time and laughing so heartily it startled the babies. Roni loved that about them, too. After dinner they sang "Happy Birthday" to Lila and Bones, and Lila loved her birthday gifts almost as much as she loved her cake. They'd had fun shopping for her birthday presents. Quincy had been adorable picking out the perfect dress-up doll and several of her favorite books. There were several desserts, and Roni was glad her and Quincy's pies were a hit. All of the girls wanted the recipe.

When they'd finished eating, Biggs took the kids into the living room and read to them, while Red and Pamela cared for the babies, and Bullet made Finlay put her feet up. Everyone else helped clean up. Once the kids had left the room, the guys unleashed more dirty jokes without using code words, causing Roni and some of the other girls to blush as much as they laughed. Even Diesel cracked a smile, which did little to soften his granitelike features.

It was the most wonderful Thanksgiving Roni had ever had. While she missed her grandmother, with Quincy and all of her new friends, there was no room for loneliness. Once the last dish had been washed, Quincy took her hand, leading her out of the kitchen, and said, "I want to show you something."

He was striking in his jeans and black sweater as he led her upstairs, down a hall, and through a door that led up another flight, into the glassed-in crow's nest she'd seen when they'd arrived. Before she could say a word, he hauled her against him, taking her in a warm, sensual kiss that lasted so long she tingled from head to toe.

"Sorry, babe," he said. "I've wanted to do that all evening."

She wound her arms around his neck, running her fingers through the back of his hair, and said, "I'm glad you wanted more after all the kisses we shared during dinner."

"Those were appetizers." He pressed his lips to hers again. "Are you having a good time?"

"How could I not? This family of yours is what dreams are made of. There's so much love and support, it's like the stories Tru used to make up for you. I wish you could have grown up with them so you would have always had the love you de-served."

"God, *baby*, that big heart of yours gets me every time." He kissed her again and said, "Your lips, too." He kissed her slow and sweet, and then he tucked her against his side, and they went to the windows, gazing out as snowflakes drifted down from the sky.

"It's snowing," she said excitedly.

"I requested snow just for you." His phone rang, and he cursed quietly. "Sorry." He pulled it out of his pocket and glanced at the screen. "It's Simone. I need to take it. The holidays can be hard."

"Of course. Want me to wait downstairs?"

"No way." He kept her close as he answered the call. "Hey, Simone."

He was quiet, listening, and Roni felt his body go rigid. He stepped away from her, jaw tight, eyes serious, and said, "Are you hurt?" He paused, his chest expanding with fast inhalations. "Stay with Sunny. I'm on my way."

As he ended the call, Roni said, "Is she okay?"

"She had a run-in with her ex and she's shaken up, but she's at the shelter and safe now. I'm sorry, baby, but I have to go and make sure she doesn't slip backward because of this. Would it be okay if Tru gave you a ride home?"

"Absolutely. Can I go with you to be there for her? For both of you?"

"Christ, baby. You'd do that?"

Red's words came back to her, and she said, "You're my person, Quincy. I'd do anything for you."

He tugged her into another embrace. "I'd do anything for you, too, but as much as I appreciate the offer, I don't want you around any of this. Her ex is a drug dealer, and he has eyes on the shelter. I don't want him seeing you there."

"Are you in danger?" she asked as they went downstairs.

"No. But I need to make sure she's not." He strode into the living room, still holding her hand, shoulders back, chest out, looking even taller than normal, and said, "*Diesel, Tru,*" in a deep, commanding voice Roni didn't recognize.

She had a feeling he didn't realize he was still holding her hand as Diesel and Tru closed the distance between them, and every other man in the room followed as if they had been summoned, too. Quincy quickly explained the situation.

"That motherfucker's *done,*" Diesel seethed, hands fisting.

"Before you go that route, Diesel," Quincy said sharply. "Think you can reach that female cop you're friends with in Parkvale?"

Diesel nodded.

"We might need her tonight. I'm going to try to convince Simone to file a complaint and get a restraining order. I think she'd be more comfortable with a woman," Quincy explained. "Can you get extra eyes on the shelter and at Simone's work for a while?"

"Consider it done. She'll be escorted to and from work, and I'll set up shifts so she's never alone." Diesel put his phone to his ear and stepped to the side.

"Does she need a doctor?" Bones asked.

"No, but thanks," Quincy said. "I'm heading over to make sure she stays clean."

"We're coming with you to patrol the area to make sure there's no more trouble," Bullet said, nodding to Bones, Bear, and Jed.

"Scott and I will make sure our girls get home safe," Biggs said gruffly.

Holy cow. They worked together like an expertly choreographed dance team.

"I don't think we need everyone, but I know better than to argue." Quincy looked at Truman and said, "Would you mind giving Roni a ride back to her place?"

"No problem, bro," Truman said.

As if he'd dismissed them, the guys went to their significant others. Quincy pulled Roni into the dining room and said, "You sure you're okay?"

"I'm fine, but the way they sprang into action makes me wonder if this is really dangerous." She squeezed his hand and said, "Don't lie to me, Quincy. I can take it."

"I will *never* lie to you. They're just making sure that asshole and his guys aren't hanging around. It's what they do, babe. The Dark Knights are here to protect people. I'll be fine. I promise."

"Okay, but please be extra careful, and come to my place after you're done."

"I don't know how long this will take. It could be two or three in the morning."

"I don't care how late it is. I need to know you're safe."

"Okay." He gathered her in his arms, holding her tight. "I...Thanks for understanding, babe."

He gave her a quick kiss, grabbed his jacket, and headed out the door with the others, leaving her struggling with an unexpected lump in her throat as Truman, Gemma, and Biggs sidled up to her.

Truman said, "Are you doing okay?"

"Sort of. I'm nervous for them and Simone."

"You wouldn't be human if you weren't," Truman said.

"I remember the first time I saw the guys charge out the way they just did," Gemma said. "It scared me."

Roni was glad she wasn't the only one who felt that way.

"The thing is, by the end of that night I realized that all those leather-clad guys banding together like that shouldn't have been scary," Gemma explained. "They're like Superman on steroids. The scary guys are the ones they're going after and protecting the rest of us from."

"And you don't worry that they'll get hurt?" Roni asked.

Gemma nodded and said, "Of course I worry, but they're keeping people safe and saving lives."

"Are they going to fight?" Roni asked.

"Only if they have to, darlin'," Biggs said, draping an arm over her shoulder, a pillar of strength for her to borrow from. "Don't you worry. By now Diesel has about thirty Dark Knights on their way to Parkvale. They're going to be just fine."

His voice was as rough as sandpaper and as comforting as his embrace. More pieces of Quincy's life were falling into place, including where Quincy's caring nature and his drive to support and help others had been nurtured. She was falling for this family as deeply as she was falling for Quincy.

Chapter Eighteen

IT WAS NEARLY two thirty in the morning when Quincy climbed out of his truck and headed across the parking lot toward Roni's apartment. When he'd first gotten out of rehab, he'd bent Truman's and Jed's ears after meetings and rough days. But he'd never had anyone to come home to. Now he made an effort to leave the nightmarish reminder of his past behind as he ascended the steps toward the woman who was front and center in his dreams of the future. When Roni answered the door, eyes filled with worry but looking beautiful in sleeping shorts and a tank top, and threw her arms around him, he'd never been more grateful in his life.

"Hi, baby. Sorry it's so late." Truman had texted him to tell him he'd tried to get Roni to stay at their place so she wasn't alone, and when she said she would be fine, Gemma had offered to stay with her. But Roni had insisted she was okay. Quincy knew his strong girl well enough to realize she wouldn't have wanted to be a burden on them.

She put her hands on his cheeks, searching his eyes, and said, "Are you okay? Is Simone okay?"

He leaned in and kissed her. "We're both fine. Let's go

inside."

"Can I get you anything? I don't know what to do in this situation. Do you want some water?" she asked as he hung up his jacket.

"I just want you, babe." He took her hand, and they went to the couch. "Have you been awake all this time?"

"I couldn't sleep. I was too worried. Is Simone okay? Was she hurt?"

He hated making her worry. "She's okay. He grabbed her when she got off the bus and tried to get her to go with him in his truck. He roughed her up a little, but he didn't hit her. She's got some bruises on her arms from the force of his grip."

"Oh no." Roni covered her mouth with her hand. "Poor Simone. Maybe you should let her stay at your place so she's safe."

For the millionth time since they'd been together, he felt like his heart was overflowing. "You are really something. I love that you want to help Simone, but as her sponsor, I can't do that."

"Can *somebody*? The Dark Knights?"

He explained the agreement he and Biggs had come to about people in recovery being six months' drug free before putting them into the homes or businesses of club members and Peaceful Harbor residents. "Diesel and I talked about getting her out of Maryland altogether. Biggs's brother Tiny runs the Redemption Ranch in Colorado, which works with people in recovery. They have a great program with therapists and physicians on staff. But Simone isn't ready to leave the area."

"Even though it's not safe here?"

"This is a process, babe. Recovery is hardest at the beginning, and she's just starting to find her footing. That big a change could set her back. She wants to stay clean, and she did the right thing by resisting him and calling me. Diesel's got her covered from now on, and I was able to convince her to get a restraining order against her ex, which is what took so long. Diesel's got some connections to try to push it through the system, but it'll still take a week or two."

"Oh, good. That was smart. Do you know the person who did this to her?"

"Yeah. He's the dealer I owed money to. The one who had me beat up and left me for dead."

"*Quincy*," she said angrily. "You said you weren't in any danger."

"I wasn't. You saw the guys leave with me. They had my back."

"I can't believe I have to point this out to you, but that guy left you for dead and you're still *alive*. That sounds dangerous to me, especially if he's watching that place and knows you helped Simone." Panic rose in her eyes, and she said, "*Oh no.* Do you still owe him money? What if he comes after you?"

"Roni, baby, I *don't* owe him a thing, and he won't come after me." He took her hands, holding them reassuringly tight, and said, "He knows I'm her sponsor. He's probably had eyes on me since I started helping her, but that's his *only* beef with me. I have no connections or debts to him or anyone else in that world. When I was in rehab, Tru was worried the guy would come after my family, so he went to Biggs and borrowed money to pay off my debt. Biggs had Bullet take care of it, and I've since paid Biggs back every cent. *Nothing* is going to happen to me. I would never put myself in his line of fire, much less put you or anyone else in danger."

"Okay, thank goodness." She let out a breath of relief.

"You don't have to worry, babe."

"That's never stopped me before." She climbed into his lap and put her arms around him, resting her head on his shoulder. "I was really scared tonight."

He kissed her forehead, stroking her back, and said, "I know. I'm sorry."

"I'm glad you're both okay."

She held him tighter, and it broke his heart knowing what he had to say next, but there was no way around it. "Roni, I know you said you're all in, but if this ever gets to be too much for you—"

She covered his lips with her finger and lifted her loving eyes to his. "What am I, lazy?" she said, throwing his own words back at him. "You're not getting rid of me that easily, Quincy. You're stuck with me."

As she lowered her lips to his, he said, "There's no place else I'd rather be."

Chapter Nineteen

THE HELMS TREE Farm was everything Roni remembered and so much more. It had snowed on and off all weekend, and by late Sunday afternoon, Peaceful Harbor was blanketed with several inches. The Helmses' two dogs, each with a big red bow on its collar, greeted guests with wagging tails and sloppy kisses. Festive music blared from speakers, and colorful holiday lights twinkled against the flurries falling from the sky. People of all ages were bundled up in hats and scarves, meandering in and out of the gift shop and milling around the walk-up window of the weathered snack shack, drinking hot chocolate and warm cider. Children were running around playing, and families were sledding behind the gift shop. Others headed out to the fields, trekking between rows of lush trees with tufts of white gathered on their branches, while lucky tree hunters returned pulling their prized six- or seven-footers. There were horse-drawn wagon rides, the horses decked out with bells and bows, and a make-your-own wreath station under a pavilion. Roni snuggled closer to Quincy. He was smiling as he took it all in, flurries glistening on his gray beanie and black winter jacket.

This was exactly what they needed after a few stressful days.

Since it was one of the busiest shopping weekends of the year, Quincy had worked all day Friday and Saturday, and today he'd worked until three. But Roni didn't mind. It had given her time to shop with Angela for Christmas decorations and a gift for Josie's party. She'd also picked up a few stocking stuffers for Quincy, which she was excited to give him. They'd stayed at his place the last two nights since she had the weekend off, and Quincy had surprised her with a key to his apartment Friday night so she could come and go while he was working. She loved being there. It was starting to feel more like home than her own apartment. Their evenings had been intimate and wonderful, but Simone had called a few times late at night, and it had taken Quincy a while to settle down afterward. There was a code of anonymity that went along with sponsorship, and while Quincy didn't share details of their conversations, he'd explained that with substance abuse, when drugs are held out like carrots to a horse, even if the person in recovery is strong at the moment and turns away, the urges don't stop there. Roni didn't mind Simone's calls. It had given her another level of perspective, and she liked how invested Quincy was in Simone's recovery. He worked so hard; he *needed* today even more than she did. When he set those clear blue eyes on her and pressed his lips to hers, she could already see the good it was doing.

"Ready to get our tree, beautiful?"

"What do you think?" She tugged him toward the table where they were handing out tags to put on the tree they selected. The staff would cut down their tree as they enjoyed everything else the farm had to offer. She'd been anxiously awaiting this moment ever since Quincy had said they were going there, and she was too excited to walk.

"Come on!" She ran down a row, swiping her hand along

the branches of the trees, sending the snow on them raining down. "Do you want a big tree or a small one? Fat or skinny? I think the sign said they had different types, too. Do you know anything about trees? Should we get one for your place and one for mine?"

He laughed and swept her into his arms, grinning from ear to ear. "I want *this*, baby—*you*, this happy and by my side, every single day."

He kissed her hard and possessive, which turned slow and spine-tinglingly sensual, and just when she was sure they'd melt the snow beneath their feet, he pulled away, leaving her heart full and her knees weak.

"I'll buy you as many trees as you want," he said. "Where do you want to wake up Christmas morning?"

Her head was still swimming in his declaration, but she managed, "In your arms."

"*God*, woman." He touched his forehead to hers and said, "You're killing me. I want that, too. Do you want trees at both of our places?"

"Not necessarily. We spend more time at yours, and I like being there. It feels more like home."

"One tree it is."

They sealed their decision with another kiss, and as they walked hand in hand, she told herself not to get carried away by this new level of togetherness, but it was hard not to when she wanted him by her side every day, too.

They took their time going up and down the rows, trying to pick out a tree, but none felt perfect.

"This one's nice," Quincy said, pointing to a massive tree that was at least a foot taller than him.

She wrinkled her nose and said, "It feels overdone, like that one guy in every high school who's the star of everything, his hair is too perfect, and his teeth are too straight."

Quincy chuckled. "It doesn't sound like I missed much."

"Actually, I wish you'd had a chance to go through high school because you like learning so much. But if you had gone, you'd probably have had a zillion girlfriends, and one of them would have wrangled you into marriage by the time you were twenty-one. You'd have two kids by now, and I'd see you down the aisle in the grocery store where I'd stopped on my way home after a solo dance performance, and our eyes would meet. My heart would go absolutely crazy for the blue-eyed guy who looked like he had a heart of gold. But you, Mr. Loyal Gritt, would have given me a friendly, but not flirty, smile and gone on your way, buying puppy chow—because you'd definitely have a puppy—kid-friendly foods, and probably something special for your wife—who, by the way, would be smart, and loving, and everything you've ever dreamed of."

He frowned. "And what would happen to you in that fantasy of yours?"

"I'd go home and think about the dreamy guy who had stolen my heart, and I'd compare every other man to him for the rest of my life."

He pulled her into his arms and said, "That's the saddest story I've ever heard."

"You didn't hear the end yet."

He cocked a brow.

"When day turned to night, I'd crawl into bed and rest my head on my husband's shoulder. Just as he'd turn to kiss me, our two little ones would run into the bedroom and climb between us. The puppy would paw at the edge of the bed because she's too small to jump, and my husband would scoop her up and let her lick his entire face. I'd look over our kids' heads into his clear blue eyes and say something like, *I love our life*, and he'd lean over the two most adorable children in the world and say, *I love my wife*. And then he'd kiss me, and our kids would yell, 'Ew, Dad!' and he'd kiss me again, because my kisses have always done him in."

"Hell yeah, they have, and I'm ready to be done in again." He kissed her ravenously, parting only at the sound of giggles. He eyed the three kids running past them and said, "Two, huh?"

She loved that he was playing along. "Too many?"

"I'm thinking three." He hooked his arm around her shoulders and walked in the direction the kids went. "Maybe four."

"Let me just scratch *dance* off my future to-do list."

"*Nonono.* Two's good."

They both laughed, and then they checked out more trees, passing by so many, Quincy finally said, "We're running out of options," at the same moment she saw *their* tree and exclaimed, "That one!"

She pulled him over to it. "Isn't it perfect for us?"

"It's a little crooked."

"That's part of its charm, and that's why it's meant to be ours. Neither of us have followed straight paths to get where we are, but we're perfect together. This tree is taller than you, but I think it'll fit in your apartment, and it has a long pointy branch for the star, or whatever we want to put there."

"It's missing a branch." He put his hand in the hole where the branch was missing and said, "I guess that means it's been through a rough time, like us."

"Exactly," she said proudly.

"You're right. It's perfect. Let's make it ours."

As he tied the tag on the tree, Roni scooped up a handful of snow and packed it into a snowball. When he turned around, she threw it, nailing him in the chest. His jaw dropped, and he swiped at the snow stuck to his jacket, laughing as he scooped up a handful of snow.

"We're doing this, huh?" he said, his eyes narrowing as she packed another snowball.

"Oh *yeah.*" She threw another snowball.

He ran toward her, and she squealed, sprinting ahead. A snowball hit her back and she cracked up. Grabbing more snow and packing it on the run, she hurled it behind her. She missed him, but in his hand was another one. She squealed again, running in a zigzag pattern and scooping up more snow, dodging his snowball. Their laughter filled the air as they chased each other through the rows. When she turned to throw another one, he was *right there*, and he tackled her to the ground in fits of laughter. She rolled away and tried to get up, but he yanked her down on top of him, her back to his chest, her legs flailing.

"I'll get you!" she said through her laughter.

He spun her in his arms, so they were face-to-face, crushing her to him. His warm, smiling lips brushed hers, and he said, "What'd you say, beautiful?"

She wiggled and squirmed, trying to break free. Realizing it was a futile effort, she said, "I *almost* got you!"

He rolled her beneath him, looking devastatingly happy as he said, "Almost my ass. You've already got me, baby. With your crooked tree and sweet apple pies, I never stood a chance."

And neither did she, as the man who'd claimed every last piece of her smothered her laughter with steamy kisses until there was no room for anything else.

QUINCY HAD HEARD about the joys of Christmas and the magic of the holidays, but until today, he'd never fully experienced them. The last couple of hours had been a whirlwind of fun, and Roni's enthusiasm for absolutely everything was contagious. They'd made two wreaths, one for her house and one for his. That was something Quincy had never imagined himself doing, but with Roni he'd enjoyed every freaking second of it. They'd also gone sledding. After every sled ride, Roni's face had lit up, and she'd exclaimed, *Again!* until they'd gone so many times, her hip had ached from trudging up the hill. They'd taken a hot-cider break beneath the sparkling lights, people watching and playing with the dogs. He hadn't realized Roni was a dog lover, but she'd gotten right down on the ground with him to love them up. Now, as they walked around the gift shop filling their basket with ornaments of dancing snow women, a snow couple sharing a sled, Santa Claus reading, a round-faced boy and girl with red hats and green pajamas kissing in front of a Christmas tree, and many others, the magnitude of his emotions hit him head-on.

"We *have* to get this one." Roni held up a wreath ornament that looked a lot like the wreaths they'd made with gold pinecones and red ribbons, but the ornament had a round-faced couple hanging on it with their arms and smiling faces sticking out the front of the wreath and their bodies and legs out the back. They wore red-and-white Santa hats and green mittens, and they were holding up a white banner with OUR FIRST CHRISTMAS printed in red and the year printed in black beneath it. "They'll put our names on the white part of the hats.

And next year we can come back and get this one and have them put the year in the heart." She held up a snow-couple ornament with fuzzy Santa hats, rosy cheeks, and green scarves, holding a white heart with red-and-white striped edges like a candy cane.

That organ that had been tripping him up so often lately around Roni stumbled once again as he realized they weren't just decorating a tree. They were paving the way for tradition, making room for plans of tomorrows and holidays to come.

"I love them both." *And I love you.*

"Yay!" She set down the snow couple and kept the wreath ornament. "Come on." She took his hand, hurrying toward the craft table, and said, "Let's get our names put on the banner."

Two bags of ornaments later, they headed out of the gift shop. The sun was starting to set, and people were loading trees onto their cars.

"Wow, the sunset is gorgeous." Roni pointed to the fiery sky in the distance as they walked by the loading area. She nudged Quincy and said, "Hey, isn't that the guy who won second place at the scavenger hunt?"

He followed her gaze to Jon Butterscotch. He was standing a few feet away talking with a tall blonde who looked annoyed as she sent trees through a tree baler. "Yeah, that's Jon."

Jon waved them over as they walked past and said, "Hey, Quincy. Great to see you."

"You too, Jon. This is my girlfriend, Roni. Roni, this is Jon Butterscotch."

Jon lifted his brows and grinned. "Ah yes, the hundred-point kisser."

Roni blushed. "That's me. I saw you at the bachelor auction a few months ago."

"That figures," the blonde uttered as she shoved a tree through the baler.

"Aw, don't get jealous, Tater Tot," Jon said flirtatiously. "Next year *you* can try to win fifty shades of sweetness."

The blonde rolled her eyes and moved a netted tree to the side with the others.

"Quincy, do you know Tater?" Jon asked. "We go *way* back to when she was just a sweet young thing."

The blonde narrowed her eyes and said, "Call me that again, and you're next in the baler." She turned a warm smile to Quincy and Roni and said, "I'm *Tatum* Helms. Nice to meet you both."

"Hi. I'm Quincy, and this is Roni."

"Do you own the tree farm?" Roni asked, eyes dancing with excitement.

"My family does," Tatum said. "I'm in town helping out for a little while."

"I was just arranging for her to deliver my tree to me Friday night." Jon winked at Quincy.

Tatum put another tree through the baler and said, "Not happening, Butterscotch."

Quincy chuckled.

"I've been dying to come here for years," Roni said. "Your family makes it so special. We've done almost everything and bought nearly every ornament you have." She waved to the bags in Quincy's hand. "It must have been amazing growing up around all these festivities every year."

"Not for this Scrooge," Jon said. "Tater hates Christmas."

Jon had big ones to keep calling her that with the visual daggers she was sending his way.

"Really? Why?" Roni said empathetically.

"I don't *hate* Christmas." Tatum glanced at Jon with narrow eyes and said, "Let's just say some bad memories have soured it for me."

"Aw, come on. You love me," Jon said jovially.

Tatum scoffed. "As much as I love stepping in a steaming pile of—"

"Got it," Quincy interrupted. "Good luck, Butterscotch. Nice to meet you, Tatum."

As they walked away, Roni said, "He's pushy."

"That's Jon. He's a good guy. He's just full of himself." He hugged her against him and said, "If I ever act like that, smack me, will you?"

"You bet I will. It's getting dark. Maybe we should get going."

"Not quite yet, beautiful. I haven't had a chance to kiss you beneath the stars while we ride in a horse-drawn wagon."

"And here I was thinking today couldn't get any better."

Chapter Twenty

AFTER LEAVING THE tree farm, they stopped for pizza and then headed to Quincy's apartment to set up the tree. They moved the orange chair to the other side of the room and set up the tree stand they'd bought at the farm in front of the balcony doors. Quincy thought Roni was going to jump out of her skin the way she was bouncing on her toes as he finished putting up the tree.

The second he was done, she said, "It's perfect!"

"You've got a good eye, babe. I think it'll just fit once we put the star we bought on top."

She slid her arm around his waist, snuggling against him, and said, "I can't wait to decorate it."

"Aw, hell. We forgot to buy lights for the tree." He chided himself for the stupid mistake and said, "I'll run out and get some."

She stepped in front of him, grinning up at him, and said, "Stay right here. I have a little surprise for you." She went to the bedroom and came out a minute later carrying four enormous shopping bags. "I picked up a few things while you were working this weekend. Lights for the tree and some to go around the headboard of our bed."

Our bed. He loved that.

She put the bags on the couch and said, "I got decorations for the walls, garland for the bookshelves, stockings, and there's another bag in the bedroom with Christmas throw pillows for the couch. I even got Christmas cookie cutters so we could bake cookies together."

He drew her into his arms. "You could have done anything on your weekend off, and you chose to do all of this for us?"

"I got a little carried away, didn't I?"

"No, babe. It's awesome. *You're* awesome. I've never had a real Christmas like this. I didn't even know what to get, and you…" He pressed his lips to hers. "Thank you."

"I definitely went a little overboard," she said as they started unpacking the bags. "Before we got together, I was dreading the holidays without Gram. I thought if I was lucky, maybe I'd get a text from you, if you hadn't already given up on me by then." She was talking fast, putting packages on the table. "But then you burst into my life with your decorated truck and marshmallows and hand-holding and kisses and made me fall in love with you, and since it's our first Christmas together and I wanted it to be perfect for you, I—" Her head spun toward him, eyes panicked. "Ohmygod! I didn't mean to say that." She pushed to her feet and paced as he tried to find his voice, her confession singing through his head. "We haven't been dating long. I messed up. Girls aren't supposed to say it first, are they? I'm sor—"

He hauled her into his arms, silencing her with the firm press of his lips. His heart thundered in his chest. *You love me. Please don't take it back.* He intensified the kiss, savoring her confession. When their lips parted, he kept her close. She was looking at him like he was the answer to all her prayers, which was so fucking fantastic that he wanted to holler it from the rooftops, because he knew without a doubt that she was the answer to his.

"I love you, too, Roni. I've felt it for a while, and I don't know or care who is supposed to say it first. The only thing that matters is that we're in this together. *You*—beautiful, talented, big-hearted Veronica Wescott, who I have thought about every single day for the past six months—*love me*, despite all my faults and my ugly past. I love you so much, baby, I ache with it."

"I love *all* of you, Quincy, but what I feel is so much bigger than those three words. I love that we understand each other and what we've each had to overcome. I love how we support each other. How when I hear your voice, my heart goes wild, and when you reach for my hand, that simple touch fills me with so much happiness, I want to *live* in those moments." Tears dampened her eyes, and she said, "When you're studying and I'm reading or working on choreography, even though we're just sitting on a couch or lying on a bed doing our own thing, we're doing it together, and it feels *so* good, like I've finally found the place where I belong."

"You have, baby, and so have I. Let's make this our best Christmas *ever*."

"I have a better idea." She went up on her toes and kissed him, and then she picked up a string of lights and said, "Let's make this our best Christmas *yet*, only to be outdone by next year's."

And that was exactly what they did, winding colorful lights around the tree and hanging the ornaments they'd bought, stealing kisses in between. They strung lights over the kitchen alcove, around the balcony doors, and around the bedroom doorframes. They decorated the bookcase with garland and a few ceramic holiday knickknacks. Roni had thought of everything, including a red runner for the table, a red-and-white tree skirt with silver glitter, and a wreath hanger for the door from the shop.

Quincy went into the bedroom to get the bag of throw pillows and saw that she'd already hung up lights around the headboard. She must have done it before he'd gotten off work, which made sense, since she'd met him downstairs and they'd gone straight to the tree farm. As he grabbed the bag of pillows, he noticed a light-blue frame on the nightstand and picked it up. It had the year written in white across the top and held a picture of them kissing on the slide the night of the scavenger hunt. *God*, he loved her.

When he returned to the living room, she'd turned off the overhead lights. The Christmas tree shimmered with color, as did the other lights in the room. Roni was placing two stocking hangers, which looked like presents, on the edge of a bookshelf.

"Can you grab the stockings?"

"For a kiss." He leaned in and kissed her.

He set down the bag of pillows and picked up the stockings. She'd had their names embroidered on them. She was full of surprises. As he handed her a stocking, he said, "Thank you for putting up the lights in the bedroom, and I love the picture."

"It's one of my favorites," she said as he gave her the other stocking.

"You're making this place a real home."

"Is that okay?" she asked softly.

"It's better than okay."

They hung up the stockings, and she stepped back, admiring them, and said, "There."

"Perfect." He slipped his arm around her as they turned to take it all in and said, "One more thing, beautiful."

"The pillows," she said. "I almost forgot."

She was so cute. He'd meant the star, but she was so happy, flouncing around as she placed red-and-white pillows on the couch and a white one shaped like a snowman on the orange chair. When she stepped back to admire them, he grabbed her by the waist from behind and lifted her off her feet. She squealed as he put her on his shoulders.

"Quincy!" Their laughter filled the room. She tried to lean over his head to kiss him, which only made them laugh harder. "What am I doing up here?"

"You have a star to put up." He carried her to the kitchen, where the star lay next to the second wreath they'd made. They were going to hang that one at her place.

"How could I forget the star?" she said as he handed it to her and went to the tree. "Our artificial tree was only about three feet tall. I've never done this before." She leaned forward, reaching for the top branch.

"Careful, babe." He grabbed the trunk near the top, bending it forward so she could put the star on.

"This is so exciting. I wish we could take a picture."

"Your wish is my command." He pulled his phone from his pocket and took a picture of her holding the star and another as she put it on the top of the tree.

He set her down so he could connect the plug for the star, and she took pictures of him doing it. Then they stood arm in arm, admiring their tree. "Baby, that's the most beautiful tree I've ever seen."

"That's because it's ours." She looked around the room and said, "I've always liked Christmas, but it's never felt like this."

"This room is full of love, babe, and that makes everything better." His arms circled her. "*You* make everything better. I love everything about you, and it feels incredible to say that and not have to hold back."

"I hope you never hold anything back from me." A spark of something dark and sexy glimmered in her eyes. "I got you one more surprise to prove it." She ran her fingers down the center of his chest all the way to the waist of his jeans, sending heat to his groin. "Give me a few minutes to put it together."

"That sounds promising."

She looked over her shoulder, cheeks pink, and said, "Stay there."

RONI HURRIED INTO the bathroom, her nerves flaring as she washed up. Quincy was on the phone with his back to her when she slipped into the bedroom to change. She pulled out the holiday lingerie she'd bought with Angela that would turn her into a human Christmas gift. Or rather, a *naked* human gift-wrapped with a red satin bow. She opened the package with trembling hands, placing the two long strips of satin on the bed.

Oh Lord.

This had seemed like a much better idea when Angela was egging her on.

Inhaling deeply, which did nothing to calm her nerves, she stripped off her clothes. She picked up the shorter satin strip, trying to remember how to wear the darn thing, and looked at the packaging for directions.

There were none.

Great.

She wrapped the satin around her chest twice, crossing the strips diagonally over her breasts, and tied them in the middle. That wasn't so hard, but the other, longer strip would be trickier. She threaded it up between her breasts, under the other ribbon, and over her shoulder. Then she reached between her legs to grab the end, but it kept swinging out of reach like a freaking leaf blowing in the wind. She threaded more satin over her shoulder and tried again to grab it.

"You okay in there?" Quincy asked through the closed bedroom door.

She froze. "Don't come in! I'm fine." She unthreaded the strip and laid it on the bed. Then she lowered herself onto her back on top of the satin strip. She grabbed the bottom of it and the other end, which was over her shoulder, and wiggled off the bed holding both, bent over. She caught sight of herself in the mirror and stopped cold.

Holy crap. I look like the Hunchback of Notre Dame.

Was she *really* doing this?

She looked in the mirror again and cringed, turning away. It had looked so sexy in the store, and she wanted to do this so badly for Quincy, to let him know she was *his* through and through. She was *not* going to let the ribbon rob either of them of the special gift.

She straightened her spine, holding the top piece draped over her shoulder, and threaded it down between her breasts under the other satin strip, then fed it down between her breasts again. She pulled the bottom end up between her legs, covering her private parts, and ran it up the center of her body, over the ribbon covering her breasts, and threaded it down behind that ribbon, then tied the two ends into a big red bow. She looked in the mirror and could not believe she was standing there wearing nothing but two strips of satin. Her chest and cheeks were bright pink. But she was not going to let that dissuade her from turning on her incredibly sexy boyfriend with a gift he'd never expect.

She fluffed her hair, trying to ignore the feel of the ribbon riding her butt crack as she put on the skimpy, see-through red kimono she'd bought, and closed her eyes for one brief moment to try to calm down.

As if anything could work that miracle.

She drew upon every trick she'd ever learned about calming stage fright, which was nothing like setting out to seduce the man she loved, and threw a silent prayer up to the powers that be that she wouldn't pass out from nervousness.

She grabbed her phone, queued up "Santa Baby" by Eartha Kitt on repeat, and did her best to *strut* out of the bedroom. Quincy was standing by the bookcase. He looked up from the book he was holding, and it fell from his fingers as she slinked toward him. Flames ignited between them as she twirled around. She held his predatory gaze, swaying her hips and shoulders, opening the kimono, and shimmying as it dropped to the floor.

"*Holy...*" he said huskily as she put her hand on his stomach, dragging her fingers along his side and back as she pranced around him, and then twirled.

"You li—"

"I fucking *love*." He hauled her over his shoulder and carried her into the bedroom.

"Quincy! Wait, I have a dance for you!"

He laid her on the bed and took off his shirt, coming down over her. "Devour now. Dance later." His eyes bored into her as he untied the bows.

Oh, how she adored him! He made the pesky outfit worth the trouble.

"You're so fucking sexy." He captured her mouth in a ravenous kiss, futilely trying to tug the satin free without breaking their kiss. He tugged and yanked, frustration rolling off him as he tore his mouth away and growled, "What the ever-loving hell? I need scissors."

She giggled and began unwrapping herself. "Take your clothes off."

He pushed from the bed, getting naked in three seconds flat, and reclaimed her mouth. His erection rested against her center, thick and enticing. She wanted to do so many things: slide down and feel him filling her until they were one, taunt him until he was begging her to make love to him, and *this*— allow his magnificent mouth to make her shudder and shake with pleasure. But tonight was supposed to be about him, so as his hands roamed over her body, she tipped her head back, arching beneath him so he'd rise. She knew her man so well. He was a passionate, caring lover and always gave her room to move. She rose, too, and pushed his chest, taking him down on his back. He reached for her ass as she straddled his legs, kissing his chest, teasing his nipples with her fingers and tongues. His cock twitched eagerly beneath her.

"Oh, yeah, baby, that feels good." He grabbed her hips, tugging her forward. "I need my mouth on you."

Her body ignited. "I have a better idea."

"You want to fuck me, baby?" He squeezed her hips, lifting his beneath her.

She loved his dirty talk, and he knew it. He was a master at it, whispering such naughty things he could get her wet without ever touching her. "I want to love you with my mouth, and I want you to love me with yours."

He made a guttural sound, and she wanted to repeat what she'd said just to hear him do it again. She shifted and turned, straddling his face, and wrapped her hand around his cock. He grabbed her hips, lowering her center to his mouth, as she took him to the back of her throat. They'd explored each other's bodies so often, they knew them by heart. Some nights they made love multiple times, and others they just lay in bed talking and kissing. But tonight, especially after they'd declared their love, she wanted *everything*.

He moaned against her, and the sound vibrated up her core, heightening her arousal. She quickened her efforts, stroking him faster, sucking harder, and then teasing the tip, making him moan and thrust.

"Christ, baby, you're gonna make me come."

He was always so careful not to let himself go, but she wanted to feel that passion, to taste his arousal. She wanted him to lose his mind.

"Good," she said around his length, earning that sinful sound again.

He ate at her more rigorously, bringing his fingers into play, teasing and taunting the way he knew drove her mad. She matched his efforts by quickening her own, and soon they were both moaning and thrusting, on the verge of release. He hit the spot that sent heat searing through her, and she cried out around his cock as her climax engulfed her. She cradled his balls the way she knew he loved, and he followed her over the edge. His hips jerked and thrust as she swallowed everything he had to give, and they stayed there, loving each other through the very last shudder.

Then he reached for her, bringing them face-to-face, and rubbed her jaw, taking her in a sweet, sensual kiss. Her body tingled and hummed, and she ran her hand over his hip and grabbed his butt, pressing them together. As always happened, their bodies took over, turning that kiss to a feverish devouring, and within minutes he was hard and she was aching for him.

He sheathed his length, and as he lowered himself to his back, guiding her over him and onto his shaft, he said, "I want to watch you come," sending heat raging through her. She lowered her lips to his, her hair tumbling around them as they found their rhythm. He tangled his fingers in her hair, and she freaking loved that possessive hold. He intensified their kisses, thrusting harder, and moved one hand to the top of her ass, pressing down as he thrust up. The pleasures engulfing her were overwhelming, and she rose up, arching her back, using his chest for leverage as she rode him. He kept one hand on her ass, the other teasing her nipple.

"So fucking sexy," he gritted out.

He sat up, covering her breast with his mouth and sucking so hard, her orgasm crashed over her, pummeling her in erotic waves of heat and ice, sending her up, up, *up*, then careening down, until she collapsed, panting and shuddering against him. His strong arms circled her as he shifted her back to the mattress, showering her with kisses and whispering in between every touch of his lips. "Love you...never get enough of you...so beautiful, baby."

When her eyes fluttered open and his face came into focus, he laced their hands together and made love to her until they were both blissfully sated and too worn out to move.

A long while later he took care of the condom, and they lay together, nose to nose, kissing and whispering, the lights on the headboard casting colors around them and "Santa Baby" still on repeat in the living room.

"Now that we've crossed *Roni wrapped up in a bow* off my Christmas wish list..." He kissed her smiling lips and said, "What's on yours?"

"You've already granted me more wishes than I ever knew I had."

Chapter Twenty-One

RONI AND ANGELA sat across the table in the break room of the studio, going over the final details for the production with Elisa. It had been three weeks since Thanksgiving, and everything in Roni's life felt like it was falling into place. She and Quincy were stronger than ever, and the Winter Showcase was coming together beautifully. Elisa had met with Gemma and Crystal the week after the holiday, and Roni and Angela had since met with them twice about the costumes. Not only were they able to save the families money, but they were also willing to do fittings for each of the girls. As a bonus, Roni had gotten closer to Gemma and Crystal. They texted often and had even met for lunch a few times.

"You two have done a phenomenal job, and with the gals at Princess for a Day on board to make the costumes, I think this is going to be our best showcase yet," Elisa said.

Angela and Roni exchanged excited glances.

"You girls work so well together. I'm proud of you both." Elisa closed her notebook, her eyes shifting to Roni as she said, "Your grandmother would be very proud of you for the way you've triumphed since her passing."

"Thank you," Roni said. "I hope so."

"Of course she would. She was proud of you for everything you've ever done," Angela reminded her.

"And she'd be even prouder if you added a certain solo to our lineup," Elisa said with a hopeful glint in her eyes.

"Maybe one day, but I'm not ready yet. I'm just getting used to dancing in front of Quincy." She and Angela had been working longer hours to prepare for the showcase, and Quincy had wanted to know every little thing about the productions and the dancing she used to do. He loved to watch her dance so much, one night she'd surprised him when he'd come to see her on her dinner break, and she'd performed one of her favorite dances just for him. She enjoyed dancing for him so much, she'd given him several more private shows at his apartment, many of which had ended halfway through with them naked and wrapped in each other's arms.

"He's a lucky and very special young man," Elisa said.

"He's got you swooning over those lunches and dinners, doesn't he?" Angela teased.

Quincy had brought enough food for all of them on the days when Angela and/or Elisa were working through their meals. He'd gotten to know both of them better, and Roni was touched that he made such efforts with the people who were important to her.

Elisa pushed to her feet and said, "He has me swooning over the way he treats Roni. Everything else he says and does comes second to that."

"Hear, hear," Angela said.

Elisa said, "Has Mr. Wonderful told you where he's taking you on your date tonight?"

"Not yet, but I've never seen him this excited or this mysterious." About two weeks ago, Quincy had told her he had a surprise for her, that she should dress nicely and prepare to be *wow*ed. Didn't he know that he *wow*ed her every day with his thoughtfulness and unending support and love for her and everyone else in his life? They'd taken Kennedy and Lincoln out last weekend to a do-it-yourself craft shop, where the kids had made Christmas gifts for Truman and Gemma, and they'd all had a blast. Quincy had made Roni a dancer out of clay, and she'd made him a heart-shaped ornament for their tree with RONI LOVES QUINCY painted in it. With Quincy's help, Kennedy had then made one that said KENNEDY LOVES RONI + QUINCY. Lincoln would have no part of being left out, so they'd made another that said LINCOLN LOVES BOOFUL + INCY.

"I can't wait to hear all the details," Elisa said. "I love a good surprise."

"And I want to hear all the details you can't tell Elisa," Angela said with a wink.

As they walked out of the room to close up for the night, Elisa said, "You girls think I'm too old to enjoy a good time. Just you wait and see what you're capable of at my age." She hugged them both and went into her office.

"She's hilarious…and *right*," Angela said. "I know I'll still be all over Joey until the day I die."

"Me too. Quincy, not Joey." She glanced at the clock, wondering how Quincy's meeting with Simone was going. He'd gone with her to see the apartment she was moving into after the holidays. The restraining order had come through last week, and Roni had seen the relief on his face when he'd gotten the news, and he'd gone to see Simone that night to make sure she knew not to let her guard down.

"Did you decide what you're wearing tonight?" Angela asked. "Please tell me you're going with the over-the-knee boots."

"I am, but not because you call them eff-me boots. I'm wearing them because they go with my black long-sleeved dress with the jagged bottom."

"You're wearing your body-hugging eff-me dress with the flouncy, easy-action skirt, and you won't admit to your boots being eff-me boots?"

Roni swatted her arm and whispered, "*Shh.* That's *not* why I'm wearing the dress. I'm wearing it because I know he'll love me in it."

"Almost as much as he loves effing you in it." Angela laughed and bumped Roni's shoulder with hers. "I love making you blush."

"So does he." She looked down the hall at the door that led to her apartment, but it felt like she hadn't lived there in months. They'd stayed at Quincy's place every night since they'd put up the tree, with the exception of Wednesdays when she'd stayed late to dance, and he'd come over after his NA meetings. "I better go. I have to shower and get ready."

"Why are you looking at that door? You practically live at his place."

A thrill darted through her every time Angela teased her about that. "I know, and I love it." She flashed a cheesy grin and said, "My black dress and *non*-eff-me boots are at my place. I'll see you tomorrow and let you know what the big surprise was."

As Roni headed down the hall, Angela said, "Don't forget to wax all your naughty bits."

Roni shook her head, laughing as she headed up to her apartment, glad she'd already taken care of *that*.

LATER THAT EVENING, Quincy walked into her apartment wearing a dark suit and crisp white button-down, with his hair slicked back and a sinful look simmering in his eyes as he drank her in. "*Christ*, baby, you take my breath away."

She could do little more than stare at him. He was *that* striking.

"Cat got your tongue?" He reached for her, pressing his lips to hers. "Maybe this will help." He lifted his other hand and opened a clear container. In it was the most gorgeous wrist corsage she'd ever seen, with tiny blush-pink and white roses, a hint of green leaves, baby's breath, and a blush-pink ribbon. "You missed out on your prom and other dances, so I assumed you'd never been given a corsage." A lump lodged in her throat as he placed it on her wrist and said, "And now the first and only corsage I've ever given is to the first and only girl I've ever loved."

She threw her arms around him, tears slipping down her cheeks, and said, "Thank you. It's beautiful. *You're* beautiful." She drew back, wiping her eyes, loving what he'd said even more than the corsage.

"How about we go with manly, handsome, or studly?"

She laughed. "You're all those things, but you literally stole my ability to speak when you walked in the door. You're always great-looking, don't get me wrong, but in that suit, you look like you belong on a billboard or a movie screen, and the fact that you wore it for me makes me feel so special."

"You're the most special person in my life. I'm glad you like it. I bought it for Jed and Josie's wedding, and I wanted tonight to be a night you'd never forget."

She could hardly believe that Christmas and the wedding were only nine days away. "There's already no way I'll ever forget tonight."

"We're just getting started, and you look incredible, baby. How many more sexy outfits do you have hidden away?"

"A few," she said. "Which reminds me, I need to grab my bag from the bedroom. We're staying at your place, right?"

"Unless you prefer staying here," he said, following her down the hall.

"This doesn't even feel like home anymore. It feels like a stopover."

He pulled her closer and said, "Then let's make it official. Move in with me, baby. I love you and you love me, and we're together every night anyway. Let's make my place *our* place."

Goose bumps chased over her skin. "Really?"

"It's what I've wanted for weeks. When we're apart, something inside me feels unsettled. But at the end of the day, when one of us walks through that door and into the other's arms, everything feels right again. I almost asked you the night we got our tree, but I didn't want to rush you."

"*Rush me*, Quincy, because in my head I'm already there." Happiness bubbled up inside her. "I guess we'd better bring my bookcase, huh?"

He lifted her off her feet, twirling her around as they kissed. As he set her down, he said, "You just made me the happiest guy on earth. We'll bring your bookcase and everything else. We'll start moving tomorrow after work, and I'll finish up while you're at Josie's party Sunday afternoon. I'll get Tru and the guys to help."

He picked up her bag and draped an arm around her. As

they headed down the hall, she said, "They might have plans."

"Then I'll move you in myself. I'm not giving you time to change your mind."

"Like that would ever happen. You're stuck with me, buddy. And I'm paying half the rent."

He scoffed. "Like hell you are."

She put her hand on her hip and said, "Rent is nonnegotiable. If you want me to move in, then you have to accept my terms."

"You drive a hard bargain. *Fine.* I'll put my half into buying you things."

She gave him a disapproving look.

"Love you." He kissed her and helped her on with her coat.

As they headed down to his truck, she asked, "How did it go with Simone? Did you like the place she's moving into?"

"It was fine. I don't like her in that area, but I stopped by the bar on my way back and talked to Diesel. He assured me that they'd continue watching out for her. She hasn't run into any more trouble, but her ex is a real prick. He might be waiting for her to get out from under the protection of the Dark Knights. Hopefully by then she can find a place in Peaceful Harbor or head to Redemption Ranch."

"I'd be terrified if I were her. I read online that the person you take a restraining order out against is notified when it comes through. If he's as awful as he seems, he's probably not done trying to get her to use drugs again."

Quincy helped her into the truck, looking at *her* like she'd hung the moon, and said, "I guess it shouldn't surprise me that you read up on restraining orders, given the way you've read everything you can get your hands on about recovery. Simone said she feels more protected now than ever before. She's playing it off like she's more afraid he'll come after the Dark Knights instead of her."

Panic rose in Roni's chest. "Will he? What about you? Are you in danger because you're her sponsor?"

"No, babe. I told you that, and there's no way in hell he'd go after the club, either. Simone is doing what she has to in order to stay strong enough to make it from one day to the next. She's trying to make herself feel safer. It's a natural coping mechanism. That's why I'm checking on her more often, to make sure she doesn't backslide. Which reminds me, we made plans to meet at the shelter Sunday early afternoon."

She breathed a little easier. "I'm glad you're checking on Simone. I worry about her. I don't know how you can see the people at the meetings and not want to keep tabs on all of them."

"It's not a matter of not wanting to. They have to want to stay clean more than they want drugs. I'm not their savior. I'm there to give hope, to make sure the discussions move smoothly, and provide an environment conducive to recovery. To Simone, I'm a mentor, the person on the other end of her rope who's there to listen, to impart what I've learned through NA, and to help her find her way. I'm here *for* her, but the only person who can *save* Simone is *Simone*." He smiled and said, "Now, my sweet, sexy love, it's time for your surprise."

Chapter Twenty-Two

QUINCY WAS SO damn happy with their decision for Roni to move in, it *almost* quelled his nervousness about the surprise he had in store for her after dinner.

The streets of Peaceful Harbor were decorated for the holidays, with twinkling lights along the main drag. When he pulled into the parking lot of Dimitri's, a cozy Mediterranean restaurant overlooking the harbor, Roni's jaw dropped, her eyes glittering with awe. The restaurant was built to look like a Mediterranean home, with stucco walls, a clay-barrel roof, arched openings surrounding a patio with wrought-iron railings, and a double-arched entrance, which was lined with festive lights.

"Quincy, we can't afford this place."

He parked, so damned happy she said *we.* "Tonight's a special night and we *can* afford it. We went months texting and not going on a single date. I have a nest egg of date money with your name on it. I may not earn six figures, but I make enough to treat you to an occasional *spectacular* night. And one day, when I'm done with school, we'll make enough so we can rent a little house with a yard for our puppy and bedrooms for our future babies, and I'll be able to take you to fancy places more often."

Love rose in her eyes. "I don't need fancy, Quincy. I only need you."

"I know, but I want this for you, babe. You may not remember, but before we started going out, I had asked you over text if you could go to one restaurant in our area, which would it be, and you said—"

"Dimitri's," she said softly. "I don't know what to say. I've never been anywhere this fancy."

"You don't have to say a word. Your eyes have always told me what you're thinking, and I love you, too." He kissed her and went to help her out of the truck.

They headed into the dimly lit, intimate restaurant. There were only about twenty tables, with candles in the center. White lights surrounded the windows overlooking the harbor. Moonlight danced along the surface of the inky water.

Quincy helped Roni off with her coat, and she whispered, "Everyone is dressed to the nines. Do I look okay? Why am I so nervous?"

"Maybe because you know you're the most beautiful woman in here and all the others are jealous." They hung up their coats in the coat room and, out of view from the hostess, he pulled her into his arms, kissing her passionately until she went soft against him. Then he brushed his lips over hers and said, "Better?"

She sighed. "*Much.*"

They were seated by a window, just as Quincy had requested when he'd made the reservation. The view of the water was beautiful, but nothing compared to the view across the table of the girl who had stolen his heart and showed him what living a full life was really about. They shared appetizers of roasted tomatoes and sage and Halloumi-roasted broccoli with caramelized leeks. Roni couldn't stop raving about the food and the atmosphere. He was glad he'd chosen well. He'd learned a lot about her over the past several weeks, like the way she played with the ends of her hair when she was concentrating and how her feet and arms moved when she was thinking through a dance routine, even if she was sitting down. She liked to lie in bed in the mornings and let the day *drift in*, reveling in the peacefulness because she'd spent so many years afraid to hear what was outside her window. He'd learned about her eating habits, too, like the fact that she loved pasta and bread, though she preferred whole wheat to white, and she preferred fruits and vegetables over protein. She and Quincy were frugal eaters, having grown up on shoestring budgets, but they liked to experiment when they cooked together, which often led to them messing around or making love and then eating one of Roni's secret indulgences—pizza or tacos. He'd also noticed that she wasn't big on sweets unless they made them, like the pies and cookies they'd made. He'd never paid so much attention to everything about a person before, and with Roni, it wasn't like he even tried. He just adored everything about her and noticed it all.

They talked over dinner, sharing chicken with artichokes and olives and herb lamb cutlets with roasted vegetables.

"If you really want to start moving tomorrow evening, then I should start packing tonight or tomorrow morning," she said.

"We'll figure it out, babe. We can stay at your place tonight and pack for a few hours if you want."

"How about if we pack, then go back to your place for the night, although I know I'm going to be too excited to sleep."

"Yay for me," he said with a raise of his brows.

"Where will we put my furniture? I have to tell Elisa and Angela." She lowered her voice, leaning forward, and said, "Oh, Quincy, I'm so happy!"

He moved his chair closer and took her hand. "Me too, babe. We'll put some of your furniture in the second bedroom or put yours in the living room and mine in the bedroom. Whatever you want."

"I don't know. I wouldn't care if we had no furniture."

They nuzzled and kissed and finished their meals, sharing balsamic berries with honey yogurt for dessert. By the time they left, they were both stuffed.

When they got to the truck, Roni put her arms around his neck and said, "Thank you for such an amazing night. You have officially *wow*ed me."

"We're not done yet."

Her eyes widened. "We're not?"

"Nope. I have one more surprise for you." He helped her into the truck and went around to the driver's seat, hoping with everything he had that she would like what he had in store for her.

She must have asked him five times where they were headed as he made his way through town, but he just squeezed her hand, letting her wonder.

When he pulled down the road that led to their destination, she said, "Are we going to the Harlequin Playhouse?"

"Sure are."

"That's where we hold our showcases. I danced here when I was young, but they don't have productions Thursday nights."

"This is a special show."

"What are we seeing?" she asked excitedly.

"It's a surprise." He parked in the near-empty lot.

As he helped her out of the truck, she asked, "Are we early?"

"Maybe a little."

Quincy loved the way her face lit up as they entered the luxurious lobby, with deep-red carpet, dark-wood walls, and fancy chandeliers. A door to their right opened, and Raya Singh, the manager of the playhouse, walked toward them in a fitted blue dress. She had olive skin, straight black hair, and high cheekbones and reminded Quincy of Elisa, only younger. He'd met with Raya several times to arrange the surprise for Roni.

"Quincy, Roni, it's so nice to see you." She embraced Quincy. Smiling warmly at Roni's curious expression, she said, "You have quite a thoughtful boyfriend."

As Raya embraced her, Roni looked over her shoulder at Quincy and said, "Have you been scheming with Raya?"

"You'll see," Quincy said.

Raya lowered her voice conspiratorially and said, "He's very good at scheming. Let me take your coats, and then you can go into the theater and make yourselves comfortable."

"Thank you, Raya," Quincy said, helping Roni off with her coat and handing them to Raya.

"Your corsage is beautiful," Raya said.

"Thank you." She took Quincy's hand and said, "It's the first one I've ever been given."

"That makes tonight an even more memorable evening. I hope you enjoy the show."

They headed into the empty theater, and as they made their way toward the front, Roni said, "I'm so nervous. What have you done?"

"I fell in love," he said, because what other answer was there?

THE LIGHTS DIMMED, and the curtains drew back, revealing a pearlescent screen. "Are we watching a movie?" Roni whispered.

Quincy put his arm around her. "Remember when I said I wished I could go back and see all of your performances? This is even better, because I get to watch them with you."

She had no idea what he meant, but before she could ask, the screen lit up, and six-year-old Roni appeared, standing center stage in her lavender Summer Showcase leotard and skirt. Music began playing, and the little girl lifted her face, so serious and focused. Roni's pulse raced as she watched her younger self dance. She remembered that production. She'd been just as nervous back then as she was now, but Gram had said, *There's nothing you can't do if you want it bad enough.* As Roni watched, the dance turned to a montage of her dancing during her childhood intermixed with still shots of her and Gram. Tears spilled down Roni's cheek, and Quincy kissed her temple and rested his head against hers as they watched her bloom before their eyes into a teenager dancing alone on the stage.

God, I was so good.

An hour or more passed as years of group dances and solos played out before them. Roni couldn't believe her eyes. Quincy had even included footage of her and Angela performing together and still shots of them before and after the shows. How did he get all of the footage and pictures? The screen went dark, and just as she turned to ask him, it lit up again with one of the dances she'd performed while at Juilliard. Fresh tears fell as memories returned of the competitive edge she'd needed, the constant nervousness she'd endured from trying to meet and exceed everyone's expectations—most of all her own—and the glorious, insurmountable feeling of accomplishment, of shining among elite dancers, that had made it all worthwhile. When a picture of her graduation certificate from Juilliard appeared on the screen, a sob fell from her lips, and she covered her mouth. She'd tucked that away in a box in her closet. There was no way he could have found that.

Quincy held her tighter and whispered, "Love you."

Her chest felt like it might burst as the audition she'd done for the dance company in New York appeared on the screen. The lump that had lodged in her throat expanded painfully as she watched herself gliding gracefully across the stage, her movements perfect.

Where did you get this?

She swiped at her tears, but there was no stopping them as the screen lit up with a montage of still shots of Roni in the hospital in the days after the accident, her ravaged body casted and covered in bruises and scrapes. The song "Perfect Skin" by Olivia Lane played. Quincy held Roni tighter as an image appeared of her sleeping in a hospital bed and another of her tear-streaked cheek, looking away from the camera. There were pictures with Gram and Elisa holding her hand by her hospital bed, and a selfie Angela had taken of them lying side by side. Roni's chest ached as pictures of her in physical therapy appeared, and of her learning to walk, making painful faces, smiling, and sticking her tongue out. *Angela must have given you these.* She remembered Angela taking that picture, cheering her on, and saying goofy things just to make her laugh. Angela had been Roni's rock throughout her grueling recovery.

Pictures of Roni trying to dance again filled the screen, and then more video footage, this time from the studio, of Roni struggling through her pain. There was so much footage documenting months of her recovery, he could have only gotten it from Elisa, but she didn't know how Elisa could have taken it. The way it was pieced together showed Roni's transition from when she'd been too injured to walk to her gliding gracefully across the floor, throwing herself into every move, and all of the painful stages in between. She wiped her eyes, enthralled with herself as she danced in the studio after hours when she thought nobody could see her. Then Quincy brought out another surge of emotions with a montage of her teaching the teenage hip-hop class, ballet class, and Kennedy's class. He'd even included the moment when Dottie had finally joined the others.

When the screen darkened, she let out a breath she hadn't realized she was holding, and in the next second, the song "Lose You to Love Me" came on, and the screen came to life again with Roni dancing in the studio more recently. Quincy appeared in the doorway behind her, looking utterly and completely awestruck as he watched. She was so lost in dance, she hadn't even noticed he was there. What he'd said that night sailed through her mind. *You're strong, beautiful, and to me, an untrained eye watching you dance, you are the embodiment of perfection.*

He held her tighter and whispered, "I think I fell harder for you right then."

Tears spilled down her cheeks, though she'd thought she didn't have any left, she'd shed so many already.

When the music faded and the lights came on, she noticed Quincy's eyes were damp, too. He cleared his throat and blinked them dry, looking at her a little nervously. "I hope that was okay."

She wiped her eyes, her throat raw with emotion. "How did you do all this?"

"Elisa had footage of the events and security footage from the cameras in the studio. I had the idea the day I first met her, and we've been working on it ever since. Remember when she walked me back to see you that first time? I had already asked her if she could help me with it. Angela helped, too. Her parents had video from most of the performances."

"And my graduation certificate from Juilliard?"

"Elisa pulled some strings and got me a copy. I had it framed. It's hanging on the wall in *our* apartment."

Tears flooded her eyes.

"She helped me get the audition tape, too," he said. "I didn't mean to upset you. I wanted to experience what you had over the years, to walk through *your* fire together, and I wanted *you* to see exactly how remarkable you are."

As she pushed to her feet, confusion rose in his eyes, but as she lowered herself to his lap and put her arms around him, his confusion turned to understanding. She hugged him tight, feeling truly *seen* for the first time in years. Quincy saw her insecurities, her strengths, and her flaws, and she was so in love with him, she wanted to let him know she saw all of him, too, especially his loving, supportive soul.

She lifted her tear-streaked face, meeting his smiling eyes, and said, "You're the remarkable one. You have not only *wow*ed me, but you've become the very air that I breathe. I'm going to dance in that showcase, Quincy, and I'm going to do it for *you*. So if I can't finish, I expect you to lead the early applause."

Chapter Twenty-Three

"HEY, QUIN?" RONI called out from the bathroom late Sunday morning. "Did you find the shoes?"

He loved when she called him that. They'd been packing Roni's apartment and bringing boxes over since Thursday night. They'd unpacked most of it, and after he visited with Simone this afternoon, he was meeting Truman and some of the guys at Roni's place to move the rest of her furniture while she was at Josie's party. He looked at the boxes he'd already opened, and the stack he hadn't, wishing they'd remembered to label them. But labeling got lost in the excitement of moving in together.

"Not yet, babe," he called out to her, his eyes drifting to the Christmas tree, which had accumulated several small gifts under it from each of them over the last few weeks. He loved picking out gifts for her and seeing how excited she was when she snuck his out there.

He tore open another box, finding leotards and other dance paraphernalia. Two boxes later, he found her shoes and dug through them looking for the tan ankle boots she wanted to wear to the party. He found her ankle boots, but more interestingly, he found a pair of black stilettoes and imagined her in them.

He carried them into the bathroom and found her bending over, fishing the hair dryer out from under the sink, giving him an eyeful of her gorgeous ass peeking out from beneath a towel. This was just one of the reasons they'd started keeping condoms in the medicine cabinet. He brushed against her, running his hand beneath the towel and up her thigh.

"*Quincy*," she said softly as she rose, eyeing him through their reflection in the mirror.

"I found the box of shoes." He dangled the stilettoes from his fingers. "What do I have to do to get you to wear these?"

"Those were for a Halloween costume."

"How about you slip your pretty little feet into them for me?" He kissed her neck, snaking his other hand higher, teasing between her legs, earning that blush he adored.

"Don't you have to get ready to go see Simone?"

Pressing his hard length against her ass, he delved his fingers into her wetness. "I have plenty of time."

She pressed her hands flat on the counter, breathing harder as he homed in on the spot that made her moan. He lowered his mouth to her neck, nipping and licking.

"Quincy," she panted out, spreading her legs wider.

He set the heels on the floor and stripped off his sweatpants, whispering, "Open your eyes, beautiful." She opened her eyes, heat flaring in them as she sent her towel to the floor. He rubbed his cock against her ass and said, "How about those heels, baby?"

She slipped her feet into them, and *fuuck*. She was always sexy, but holy hell, this nearly did him in. He groped her breast with one hand, using his other hand between her legs as he ground his cock against her. She rocked and made those little needy sounds he loved.

"You're so fucking sexy, baby."

He sank down, kissing the curve of her ass, nipping the soft cheeks, earning a long, sensual moan. He spread her legs wide, licking between them, and wound his hands around her, teasing between her legs as he licked and kissed and explored.

"Quincy, I need you," she panted out.

"I wish you were on birth control so I could sink into you with nothing between us," he said, his voice rough with desire as he rose up.

She turned around, palming his erection, and said, "I was thinking the same thing."

He crushed his mouth to hers as they drove each other out of their minds, stroking and teasing. When she guided his cock between her legs, he withdrew his fingers, rubbing his length along her center, wetting it from base to tip, and a groan rumbled out. He thrust his hips, the length of him riding along her slick heat, and tore his mouth away. "I need to fuck you right now." He lifted her and set her on the edge of the counter, reaching for a condom.

"You said you have time." She raised her brows seductively and said, "Might as well make the most of it." She pressed her lips to his, then guided his face lower.

"I fucking love you. Put your hands behind you, baby, and hold on tight."

He moved her legs over his shoulders and took his fill, fucking her with his tongue, teasing her with his fingers, and taunting her with his teeth, taking her right up to the edge.

"*Need more…now…Quincy, please!*"

Only then did he devour her the way she needed. His name sailed from her lips as she came, her body quivering and quaking as she rode the wave of her climax. He stayed with her, taking her right up to the verge again, and then used his mouth to keep her there, her body shaking and panting as he sheathed himself.

"Hurry," she pleaded.

His arms circled her as her legs wrapped around his middle, and he drove in deep.

"Need to be closer," she said, winding her arms around his neck and lifting off the counter.

He pounded into her, turning with her in his arms to use the wall for leverage, and slanted his mouth over hers. She sucked his tongue, knowing full well that it drove him fucking mad, and he thrust harder, *faster*, heat searing down his spine. Her head fell back as she cried out, and he followed her over the edge, surrendering to their ecstasy.

She went soft in his arms, snuggling into the crook of his neck, both of them breathing hard. He was overcome with emotions. He'd never known love could be so powerful, it radiated around him.

He pressed his lips to her cheek and said, "Want to lie down, and I'll rub your hip before we shower?"

She shook her head. "I want to stay right here."

He felt her love in every word she said, every breath she took, and in these moments when he craved taking care of her as much as she longed for their closeness, he knew he'd become as deep a part of her as she had to him.

GINGER ALL THE Days smelled as sweet as Roni imagined

Santa's workshop would smell, and it was the most adorable shop she'd ever seen. Pink walls and white built-in shelves displayed all types of gingerbread houses, castles, wagons, baby strollers, cookies, bowls, ice cream cones, and more. The curtains were striped pink, white, and brown to match the awning out front, and the display cabinets were nearly empty, as Josie had almost sold out that morning. Sarah and Dixie had done a great job of decorating. Pink and white balloons with BRIDE and WIFE TO BE printed on them were tied to chairs and bobbing from the ceiling, their long ribbons hanging down, and a silver banner with CONGRATULATIONS written across it hung in front of the glass that separated the shop from the kitchen.

Chatter and laughter filled the air as the girls decorated their goodies. Roni was working at a table with Tracey and Penny, decorating gingerbread houses, while Finlay sat on a chair with her feet propped up and a tub of icing balancing on her belly, which she was eating by the fingerful. Across the room, Sarah and Josie were making a gingerbread castle, and Izzy and Crystal were making erotic gingerbread items and giggling up a storm, while Gemma and Dixie decorated cookies. Dixie ate them as fast as they iced them.

When Roni had arrived, they'd squealed and congratulated her on moving in with Quincy, and she'd shared in their excitement. Between dinners with Quincy and the other couples, to bonfires and Sunday lunches, Roni had developed close friendships with all of them, and she'd grown to not only love their brash comments and honest conversations, but also to participate in them. And as she licked icing from her fingers, she looked forward to having more get-togethers with them in the future.

"Roni, how's it coming along?" Josie called out.

The walls of her gingerbread house had already collapsed three times, and she'd just finished lathering the seams with more icing. "I think I've got it this time!"

"Me too!" Izzy tipped her head back and held a penis cookie upside down over her open mouth, dribbling watered-down icing off the tip and catching it with her tongue.

They all cracked up.

"I bet Jared appreciates that talent," Dixie said with a smirk.

"Oh, *please*. I tossed that Stone weeks ago." Izzy made a big show of biting the tip off the penis cookie.

"You did?" Tracey asked. "Then who were you out with until two o'clock this morning?"

Izzy ate another bite of her cookie and said, "Not Jared."

"Guess Santa Stone won't be coming down your chimney," Crystal teased, making them all giggle.

"She can hang with me Christmas Eve," Tracey said. "I've got nothing going on."

Izzy walked over and put her arm around Tracey. "Damn right, roomie. We'll have ourselves a fun party. We should go to Whispers." Whispers was one of the hottest night clubs in Peaceful Harbor.

"Um…you know that's not really my thing," Tracey said.

Izzy patted her on the head and said, "I know, but I'm trying to fix that," and went to check out the two-level castle Josie and Sarah were making.

"Roni, are you and Quincy still coming over Christmas morning to open presents with the kids?" Gemma asked.

"We wouldn't miss it for the world," Roni said.

"Good," Gemma said. "Lincoln made a special gift for his *Booful*."

"He says the cutest things." Finlay dipped her finger into the icing again.

"So does his uncle, about Roni." Penny looked at Roni and said, "Every time Quincy buys you a present, he calls to tell *me* because he's so freaking excited, he's afraid he'll tell you by accident."

"I know. He told me he called you," Roni admitted. "But I do the same thing to Angela. I'm having so much fun shopping for him. I swear we're like kids when it comes to the holidays."

"Jed said he's never seen Quincy so happy," Josie said.

"I believe it, because Angela says the same thing about me, and it's true. I never thought I could feel like this. I remember when I went to Juilliard, I was ecstatic. I thought it was everything I could ever want. But it was different, you know? Nothing compares to coming home every day to Quincy. I wake up, and I'm smiling. I go to bed, and I feel safe and happy and good all over. I never imagined having a boyfriend, much less falling in love and living a life that feels like a dream. This sounds corny, but it's like Quincy and I were made for each other. I even told him I'd do the Winter Showcase."

"You did?" Penny exclaimed. "That's awesome. He must be thrilled. We all have tickets to watch Kennedy dance. I can't wait to see you perform."

"I think Lincoln might lose his mind seeing you dance," Gemma said. All the girls chimed in excitedly.

"Sounds like we'll have a full house." Roni was happy they'd all be there, but a nagging thought was clawing to get out, and she knew this was a safe place to release it. "I'm a little nervous about it. Quincy is so excited. I hope I don't disappoint him."

"Girl, *please.*" Penny shook her head. "Quincy is so in love with you, you could get onstage, do one twirl, take a curtsy, and he'd applaud like you'd danced in *The Nutcracker*."

The girls all agreed. Roni knew it was true, and she could already feel herself calming down. "You're right. He loves me unconditionally."

"Hey, maybe I'll get a sister-in-law soon," Gemma said excitedly.

Roni laughed. "We *just* moved in together."

"Maybe *Potty* is next up on the marriage list," Finlay said with a tease in her eyes.

Penny glowered at her. "I told you not to call us that."

Finlay giggled, eating more icing.

"You two were very affectionate at dinner Friday night," Sarah said. "Bones and Bear have already made a bet about who will marry first, you and Scott or Roni and Quincy."

"Tell them to save their money and bet on Roni and Quincy," Penny said.

"Uh-oh," Crystal said. "Is Scotty having bedroom issues?"

"*Crystal*," Josie snapped. "He's my brother, and I don't want to know that."

"Well, if it makes Penny unhappy, she has to be able to talk about it," Sarah said. "We didn't have loving role models. But maybe the guys could give him pointers."

"Bullet sure could," Finlay said with a snort-laugh.

"Truman, too," Gemma agreed.

"Bear knows *all* the dirty tricks," Crystal said. "You should see how he—"

"Stop!" Dixie said. "There *is* a brother ban on sex talk."

"Josie and Sarah, cover your ears," Penny advised them, and Josie covered her ears. Sarah pulled Josie's hands off her ears as Penny said, "Scotty is totally awesome in that room and every other room. I never imagined falling for a guy as hard as I am."

"Then why did you pull out of the wedding race?" Izzy asked.

Penny glanced at her and Finlay, and Finlay rubbed her belly, a frown forming on her face. Roni and Penny had talked more last week about Scott not wanting a family, and Roni knew how heavily it was weighing on her. From the way Penny began focusing on her gingerbread house, it was obvious she didn't want to talk about it.

In an attempt to get the focus off her friend, Roni said, "There's not really a wedding race, is there?"

"Of course not," Crystal said. "But once one of our guys claims a woman, it never seems to take long before they've got a ring on her finger and a baby in the oven."

The girls laughed.

"I'm sure you've noticed that Jace is chomping at the bit to climb on that baby bandwagon," Dixie said.

"Well, Quincy and I have talked about it. He wants to have five years drug free before we start a family, which I'm totally on board with. We're both so young. I love kids, but I *want* that time alone with him before we have babies to care for. I've gone my whole life without feeling the way I feel with him. Call me selfish, but I'm not ready to share that yet."

"Aw, I'm going to cry," Finlay said.

Penny tossed her napkin. "Here you go, hormone hoarder."

"I think it's really smart to wait," Gemma said supportively. "You've both been through a lot, and you deserve to enjoy each other."

"She's right. There's plenty of time for babies," Penny said. "And I'm sure Kennedy and Lincoln will be happy to fill all of your tiny human needs."

"So will Axel," Crystal chimed in. "Feel free to come over

between three and four in the morning, which he's recently declared as *party time*."

They laughed and talked as they finished their gingerbread creations and cleaned up.

"Let's open presents!" Dixie announced.

"I told you I didn't want presents," Josie insisted as Sarah led her to a chair.

Sarah gave her shoulder a loving squeeze and said, "Sit down and enjoy it, sis."

Dixie handed her a black-and-white gift bag with a pink ribbon and said, "This isn't for you. It's for Jed."

Josie peeked into the bag and said, "Ooh la la! I see a Leather and Lace label." She pulled out a slinky black lace negligee.

The girls *ooh*ed and *aah*ed, but all Roni could think about was where she could get something sexy like that to wear for Quincy. The way he'd gone crazy for her heels and ribbons, she knew he'd love it. She missed him again. Even with all these girlfriends, she couldn't wait to get back home and see him, and see her furniture moved in.

"I'm going to have to google that company," Roni whispered to Tracey.

"I'll hook you up!" Dixie said loudly.

"I told you secrets are hard to keep in this group," Penny said.

Roni shrugged and said, "It's okay. We're living together. You guys know we mess around."

"Hey, Roni?" Gemma said, looking at her phone. "Tru just texted asking if he had the wrong time to meet Quincy. Have you heard from him?"

"He went to the shelter. He might be running late." Roni reached into her back pocket for her phone, but it wasn't there.

"I must have left my phone in the car. Let me grab it and see if he sent a message."

She went outside and ran to the car, the cold air stinging her cheeks. She grabbed her phone, and as she closed the door, she caught sight of something in the driveway near the road. She squinted to see better, and as she walked toward it, she realized it was a person. The hair on the back of her neck stood on end when she recognized the clothes Quincy had been wearing when she'd left. She screamed, "*Quincy!*" and ran toward him, hollering, "*Help! Someone help!*" His jacket was gone, his shirt torn, and he wasn't moving. She fell to the ground beside him, and the sight of rubber tubing tied around his arm, just above his elbow, gutted her. "*Nonononono!*"

The girls barreled out of the building, and Roni shouted, "*Call 911!*" She turned Quincy over, but he was deadweight, out cold, his lips darker than normal. "*Ohgod, nonono!* Quincy, wake up! *Please wake up!*"

The girls were talking frantically into their phones as Penny dropped to her knees and grabbed his arm, checking his pulse. "I got a pulse!" she yelled, tears pouring down her cheeks.

Dixie shouted, "Is he breathing?" with the phone pressed to her ear.

"I don't know!" Roni said, tears blurring her vision as she lowered her ear to his mouth. "A little, but just barely. *Hurry. Please hurry!*"

"Do you know what drugs he took?" Dixie asked.

"No!" she said angrily. "He *wouldn't* take any! *Please*, hurry!"

As Dixie rattled off Quincy's drug history, Diesel and Tracey sprinted down the driveway from the clubhouse. The other girls shouted, calling out Quincy's name, trying to rouse him.

Roni cradled him against her chest, rocking forward and back, chanting, "Don'tdiedon'tdiedon'tdie." Everything else turned to white noise as she pleaded with him to wake up. Tracey tried to pull her off him as Diesel sank down beside him, but she fought to hold on. "No. He needs me!"

"Step back or he'll die," Diesel barked.

Roni fell back on her hands, tears flooding down her cheeks. Gemma and Penny crouched between her and Quincy, sirens blaring in the distance.

"Let Diesel check him out," Gemma said. "He's going to be okay, but you need to give Diesel space."

"What'd he take?" Diesel demanded.

"I don't know. Don't let him die! Please help him!" Roni pleaded, pushing to her feet as motorcycles and trucks roared into the driveway.

Tires screeched, and Truman, Bullet, Bones, Bear, Scott, and Jed bolted toward them.

"Babies in the truck!" Bones shouted to Sarah on his way to Quincy.

There was shouting and cursing. The girls tried to console Roni, but she fought them, needing to get to him, unable to think past the prayers and *Please don't die*s running through her head.

"He's not breathing! Starting compressions!" Bones hollered as he started CPR.

"*No!*" Roni's knees gave out, and she crumpled to the ground, sobbing.

"Goddamn it!" Truman turned with fire and fear in his eyes and shouted, "When did he start using again?"

"He didn't! He *wouldn't!*" Roni insisted. "I know he

wouldn't."

"He's breathing again!" someone hollered as the ambulance arrived, and then there was a flurry of activity and Quincy was loaded onto a stretcher and into the ambulance.

"Can I go with him? I want to go with him," Roni pleaded frantically, but she was ignored.

As the ambulance doors were closed, she heard an EMT say, "He's not breathing."

Roni grabbed ahold of Penny, a crushing sensation making it hard to drag air into her own lungs. Penny embraced her, and then other arms circled them, everyone talking all at once. "He'll be okay." "Let's get to the hospital." "Everything's going to be all right."

As Truman and Gemma helped her into their truck, all Roni could think about was the EMT's last words. If Quincy didn't make it, she didn't know how anything would ever be okay again.

Chapter Twenty-Four

QUINCY WAS LYING in a bed in the emergency room with two broken ribs—and a broken heart that hurt worse than any broken bone ever could—wondering how the hell his life got so fucked up, when Truman strode through the curtain, jaw tight, eyes blazing with anger and disappointment, cutting Quincy to his core.

Truman's eyes narrowed as he hulked over the bed, getting right in Quincy's face, teeth gritted, as he said, "How many times, Quincy? How many times are you going to try to off yourself and put us through this? Thank God for fucking Narcan." Narcan was the medication the EMTs gave Quincy to counteract the life-threatening effects of the overdose. "Do you have any idea what Roni is going through right now?" Truman thrust his arm out, pointing in the direction he'd come. "She's out there bawling her eyes out, trying to convince everyone that *you* didn't do this. I love you, man, but what the hell? You nearly *died.*"

Narcan had not only saved his life, it had also left him clearheaded enough to know that while Roni might be championing for him now, that would soon change. "I didn't fucking do it," Quincy seethed.

Truman cocked his head.

"Did you notice my truck wasn't there? Do you really think I'd fuck up Roni's life? I love her, man. Do you think I'd do that to you again? To Gemma? To the kids? To everyone in our fucking lives?" He pushed up to a sitting position, wincing with pain, and grabbed his ribs.

"I didn't want to believe it, but we've been here before. You still had the fucking rubber around your arm." Truman's eyes filled with tears.

"I *didn't* do it, Tru. Puck and five of his goons dragged my ass out of my truck at a stoplight when I was on my way to see Simone. *Puck* did this. He tried to make me look like just another junkie who overdosed so he wouldn't get caught. He was sending a message to the Dark Knights saying back off or Simone is next. I swear to God. I love you, man, and the last thing I would *ever* do is put you through this again." His eyes filled with tears, and he didn't care, because he was so fucking sad and mad, he was going to lose his mind. "They drove me to some god-awful place and knocked me around. Then they threw me in the car, shot me up with heroin, and tossed me out the door in front of Whiskey Bro's. The police told me I made it as far as Jed's driveway. I don't remember how I got there. The only thing in my head was that I needed to get to Roni to make sure she was safe." He swiped at his eyes. "Two years and forty-nine days clean down the drain because of one fucking asshole."

Truman's nose flared, his teeth clenched, and the muscles in his neck and arms bulging as his hands fisted. "I'll fucking kill him."

"*No*, you *won't.* You're not going to prison, Tru—not for

me or anyone else. *Puck* is. I was recording a video message for
Roni when I saw him and his guys get out of their cars in front
and behind me and come up on my truck. I left the recording
going and stuck the phone in my pocket. That's why I had the
doc call the cops. Now they've got evidence."

"He'll come after you again, Quincy. That's not going to
put him away long enough."

"No, but a murder charge will." Quincy gritted his teeth,
closing his eyes against the burn of tears. "When he was
roughing me up, he admitted to killing the guy who was driving
the car that hit Roni. Remember when I came to you to borrow
money and you sent me away? The next day, his guys found me.
I got away, but they chased after me. I heard shots, but I never
looked back. I just kept hauling ass." He swallowed the bile
burning his throat, remembering the montage of pictures of
Roni in the hospital and her long, hard road to recovery. "He
said that bullet was meant for *me*, Tru. Roni lost her career
because I was a goddamn addict. How the hell am I going to tell
her that?" He looked away, ashamed and gutted.

Truman sat on the edge of the bed and tugged him into an
embrace.

"You didn't pull the trigger," Truman said sternly. "You
didn't fucking do it, Quincy. You don't even know if he was
telling the truth. He's been watching you, and Roni went to
those NA meetings. He probably saw her there and got the dirt
on her."

"I think he had eyes on me the whole time I've been helping
Simone. He definitely knew about me and Roni and her
accident. That's why he told me. It crossed my mind that he
could have lied, but the cops called the detective who had
worked the case and confirmed that Roni's accident was

September nineteenth, two years ago. You found the kids September fifteenth two years ago, and—"

"You came asking for money three days later, September *eighteenth*."

"They found me the next day. The timeline matches no matter how much I wish it didn't. It's *my* fault, Tru. Any way you cut it, if I hadn't been there, she'd be living her dream, dancing professionally, and not out there crying over my sorry ass."

Truman took him by the shoulders, leveling him with a dark stare. "You listen to *me*. You're *not* a sorry ass. You've been through hell and back, and you not only found your way out of it, but you became one of the best, most loyal and honest men I know, and Roni knows that, too. I will tell her with you, and we will get through this together. She loves you, man. You had that fucking tubing around your arm, and she *still* refused to believe you used again. She loves you so damn much. Don't let this send you back to the dark places that swallowed you whole before. You don't deserve that."

His throat constricted. "I'm *not* going to use again. I'm going back to rehab for thirty days. I've already made the call, and I also spoke to my boss at the bookstore. She knows I've been in recovery, and she'll hold my job for me. I'd appreciate it if you could let me say goodbye to the kids tonight and give me a ride to the rehab center. A month should be enough time for me to get my shit under control and for you to help Roni get her stuff back into her place, so she can move on." He clenched his jaw as more tears came. He swiped angrily at them. "She doesn't need me and my shit in her life. She'll never be able to look at me again after I tell her."

"You don't know that," Truman said, looking as pained as

Quincy felt.

"Yes, I do, and I appreciate the offer to tell her with me, but I've got to do this alone. I'm sorry, Tru. The last thing I ever wanted was to put you through this again."

Truman shook his head, embracing Quincy again. "I love you, man, and I know going back to rehab feels like a step backward, but I'm so damn proud of you."

The lump in Quincy's throat expanded with Truman's praise, and he held him tighter. "Thank you." He released his brother and wiped his eyes. "Can you do me a favor? The police and that detective they called are waiting to question Roni about her accident. They agreed to let me talk to her first, so can you send her in? I'll be with her when they question her, but we'll need a ride home, if you don't mind. They're keeping me for an hour or two for observation, and then I'm out of here."

"You bet."

"And, Tru." His brother lifted his chin. "One more thing. When I'm in rehab, can you look after her and Simone for me? The cops picked up Simone, and they said they'll have eyes on her and Roni, but you know that isn't enough."

"Absolutely. She's family, man. We've got her back."

RONI PACED THE waiting room, trying to hold her shit together. If one more person told her that everything would be okay, she was going to scream. All of their friends were there; even Biggs and Red had come. The support Quincy had was insurmountable, but how could anything be okay? She'd seen the tubing.

She couldn't even *think* about it.

He'd almost *died*.

Truman had explained on the way to the hospital that the EMTs gave Quincy something to counteract whatever drugs he'd used, which was good, but even though she'd seen the puncture wound in his arm, she still didn't believe that Quincy would do drugs again. And the worst part was, she *knew* she was in denial. All of the literature had said not to take a relapse personally, but this wasn't about *her*. Quincy using drugs was personal to *him*—and that's what hurt so badly. That's why she didn't want to believe it. He was too invested in his recovery. Why would he relapse?

Red walked over and put a hand on Roni's back. "Can I get you anything, sweetheart?"

Roni shook her head. "I just don't believe it, Red. The battle going on in his head must be vicious. One side fighting to stay clean, the other giving in to the lure of drugs." The words fell out so fast, she couldn't stop her voice from escalating. "And where's his truck? I heard two officers asking for him at the registration desk. Did he commit a crime? Was he carjacked? Did he even see Simone? Was *she* using again? Nobody will tell me anything!"

"Oh, baby girl." Red put her arms around her, stroking her back as she cried on her shoulder. "All I know right now is that he never made it to the shelter, and they found his truck still running in the middle of the road in Parkvale."

"I don't understand *any* of this. I'd know if Quincy was in a bad place, even if he didn't tell me. I'd sense it. I know I would." Roni wiped her eyes as Truman came out through double doors, his shoulders rounded in his flannel shirt, his face

MELISSA FOSTER

a mask of pain. "Truman!" She ran to him. "How is he? What's happening? Can I see him?"

"He's good. He wants to see you. I'll take you back." He looked over her shoulder at Bullet and Diesel, and some sort of silent message passed between them that included a single nod and made the men stand taller, their hands fisting.

As Truman walked her through the emergency room, she said, "What was that? What were you saying to them?"

"It's best if Quincy tells you."

He opened the curtain, and she saw Quincy sitting on the edge of the hospital bed wringing his hands, a bruise and scratches streaking the side of his face. He lifted his grief-laden eyes, and tears flooded hers as she ran to him and threw her arms around him, sobbing.

"I'm sorry," Quincy said, holding her tight. "I'm so fucking sorry."

She held him tighter, unable to speak through her sobs, anger, sadness, and confusion. She needed this—to be in his arms, to *see* that he was alive. His scruff scratched her cheek as he kissed it, and the familiar feel drove her heartache deeper. She clung to him until she got a handle on her sobs, at least mostly. She pushed free from his grip, holding his arms, but the tears in his eyes slayed her.

"You almost *died.*"

His jaw clenched. "I'm sorry, beautiful. I promise, I did *not* use those drugs."

"I want to believe that, and I don't believe you would, but I've read all about denial, so don't play me for a fool." Tears spilled from her eyes. "That hurts too much."

"I'm not. Simone's ex, Puck, injected me with them."

The air rushed from her lungs, tears flooding her eyes again.

"It's true, baby. He tried to kill me in order to send a message to the club."

"Oh my God." She hugged him again, crying harder. "I knew you wouldn't use them! Is that why the police are here? Can they arrest him?" She realized he wasn't embracing her. His body was rigid. She leaned back, searching his anguished eyes. "What's wrong? Oh God, did they hurt Simone? Where is she? Did they *kill* her?"

"No, baby, she's safe."

She swiped at her eyes. "Then why aren't you hugging me?"

He lowered his eyes, the muscles in his jaw bunching. "I'm going back to rehab, Roni. Starting from ground zero again. I'll need to work the program when I get out, and you don't need my shit in your life."

Sobs burst from her lungs.

"You can move back to your place, move on with someone who doesn't—"

"Shut up!" she seethed. "You shut your mouth right now, Quincy Gritt. I am *not* quitting on you, and you are *not* pushing me away because of some convoluted honorable idea in your head. You are my other half, and you *love* me. I know you do, so if we need to go to NA meetings seven days a week, or twice a day every day, then that's what we'll do. But you are *not* alone in this, and you are *not* getting rid of me that easily."

Tears spilled from his eyes. "But, Roni—"

"*No!*" She wedged herself between his legs and took his face in her hands. "*No*, Quincy. No *buts*. Yours is the face I see in my future, and I know you want that, too. Two kids and a puppy. I don't care if we're back to square one. *You* didn't do this to yourself, and you're not throwing away our future because of it. Our five-year plan starts *now*, like it or not."

His strong arms circled her, crushing her to him. "I love you."

"I love you, too," she said, their hearts hammering frantically. "Please don't say you don't want us again. *Please.*"

"I'll always want you, Roni." He took her by the arms and pulled back, agony billowing off him. "But there's more."

"Whatever it is, we can handle it."

"I'm not so sure. Your accident, it happened September nineteenth, right?"

"Yes. Why?"

His jaw tightened again. "Puck admitted to firing the bullet that killed the driver of the car that hit you."

"*Ohmygod.*" Roni covered her mouth, more emotions swamping her. *They finally found the person responsible for the accident.* "Is that why the police were asking to see you?"

He nodded, swallowing hard, and let go of her arms. "Remember I said that I owed Puck money, and when his guys found me and dragged me back to him, I got away?"

"Yes...?"

Tears poured from his eyes. "The bullet that hit the driver was meant for me. I didn't know. I promise, I didn't know. Puck told me when he was roughing me up, and the timing makes sense. The police verified it. If I hadn't been there that day, if I hadn't run, you'd still be dancing professionally."

His words knocked the wind out of her, and she stumbled back, hand on her chest. The room careened, making her sway. She stared at a speck on the floor, trying to ground herself, but her head was spinning, and her heart felt like it was shredding. *They were shooting at Quincy.*

"You lost everything because of me, baby," he said regretfully. "There is no apology big enough to make up for that."

The bullet was meant for you. She could barely hear past the blood rushing through her ears. "But you'd be dead," she said more to herself than to him. She lifted her eyes to his, the world coming back into focus. "That bullet was meant for you. If you hadn't run, you'd be dead."

"And you'd have the life you always wanted."

There were no tears stinging her eyes, only vehemence burning her chest, emboldening her. "The life I wanted *then*, not the life I want *now*. Not after meeting you."

"Baby, I saw the pictures of the hell you went through because of me. How can you even look at me without hating me?"

"I love you too much to ever hate you." She stepped between his legs and picked up his arms, moving them roughly around her. "You didn't pull that trigger, and you weren't driving that car. We are meant to be together, Quincy Gritt, and if you don't want that because you don't love me, then tell me right now, to my face. Don't hide behind all the stuff that was thrown into our paths and redirected us, because those paths brought us together, and they *cannot* be changed. We can't look back. We can only look forward. I never would have known that I wanted two babies and a dog and a recovering addict with a heart so goddamn big, he's willing to throw the woman he loves away in order to save her from hurting any more. Well, I have news for you, Mr. Heart of Gold. You have brought me more happiness and given me more love in the last seven months than I could have *ever* hoped for, and I am prepared to not only stand by your side but to walk through fire with you today, next week, and years from now. So do *you* love *me* enough to work through whatever guilt you feel *together*, or do you need me to walk aw—"

Her words were lost to the urgent press of his lips and the

tight squeeze of his arms. "I love you," he said between desperate kisses and salty tears. "I want you, baby."

She pushed her hands into his hair, kissing him harder, and then she tore her mouth away and said, "If you *ever* ask me to walk away again, I swear I'll knock your teeth out."

He laughed, which made her laugh, and their mouths came together in a softer, more loving kiss, their salty tears slipping between their lips in a kiss full of apologies for the past, gratitude and hope for the future, and love so big and real, nothing could ever come between them.

Chapter Twenty-Five

FIVE DAYS CLEAN. Let's make it six was Quincy's first thought as he awoke.

He'd had the same thought every morning since entering rehab, changing only the number of days. *One day at a time.* Just as he had each of the other mornings, he lay with his eyes closed, thinking of all of his reasons to stay clean. He was on top of that list, because if he couldn't for himself, there was no way he could do it for anyone else. That was the only reason he came before his remarkable girl. Memories of their first date sailed through his mind. He'd never forget the astonished look on her face through the glass door when he'd appeared. Her nervousness had endeared her to him even more than everything else about her already had. Roasting marshmallows, joking around, and those sinful kisses played like a movie, followed by her exuberance at the scavenger hunt and her mesmerizing dancing. But nothing beat her trust and acceptance the day she'd showed up at the NA meeting and the support she had given him every day since, except maybe the love in her eyes every time they'd made love. He could still hear her laughter when they'd gone sledding at Helms Tree Farm and recall the

fun they'd had while picking out their tree. His chest constricted with memories of hanging ornaments on their Christmas tree
and that sexy ribbon outfit she'd worn to seduce him. He knew
better than to mentally unwrap that ribbon when it would be
another twenty-four days until he saw her.

He shifted his thoughts to his other reasons to stay clean:
Truman, Gemma, the kids, and all of their friends, making it a
little easier to push away the urges to use drugs again, though
easier was a relative term.

After visualizing every one of his friends and family members, he remembered it was Christmas, and sadness tiptoed in.
He could feel his sensitive girl thinking about him, probably
wearing one of his T-shirts and sleeping on his side of the bed.

He lingered on that thought.

His side of the bed. Her side of the bed.

Twenty-four more days.

The longing for her had become a dull ache in his chest, his
constant companion. At least he knew Roni wouldn't be alone
today. Before Truman had dropped him off at rehab, she'd gone
with him to see the kids so he could say goodbye. His heart had
broken, but he hadn't lied to them. He'd never lie to them.
He'd told them that Uncle Quincy needed a little help and
would be gone for a while, but that he loved them and would
think about them every day, and before they knew it, he'd be
back to play and go on special dates. Roni had said she was still
going to Truman and Gemma's house on Christmas to
represent both of them, which made him love her even more.
He hadn't thought that was possible. But he was learning that
his love for her was as unstoppable as her endless love for him.

He opened his eyes, finally ready to greet day six, and inhaled deeply as he threw his legs over the side of the bed. He

stared at his bare feet, a memory of sitting on the couch with Roni whispering through his mind. They'd been leaning against opposite sides, playing footsies as she'd read and he'd studied. She'd flashed that brilliant smile, and it had lit up her beautiful hazel eyes behind her sexy glasses as she'd said, *This is another first. I've never played footsies before. We're going to fill our lives with firsts and forevers.*

He inhaled deeply, wishing they could play footsies now, and glanced at the clock on the bedside table. There was a wrapped gift beside it that hadn't been there last night. He picked it up and opened the card, recognizing Roni's swirly handwriting. His pulse sped up as he began reading.

Merry Christmas! You can imagine how excited I was to hear that Biggs had arranged for this to be delivered to you. I swear that man has connections everywhere. I hope you like the present. They've been on my mind since you told me about them. You'll see what I mean when you open the gift. You must have given everyone a mandate to take care of me (I love you so much for doing that!), because in the last five days I've had more dinner invitations than I could possibly accept. I don't feel much like being with other people, but I went to someone's house every evening because I knew you'd want me to. When I went to Biggs and Red's house, everyone showed up. It was like Thanksgiving all over again, except somber, because you were so sorely missed. You should know they did their best to cheer me up. Angela has been texting me video messages and pretending to be you. They're really funny. I'll show you when you get home.

I miss you every minute of every day, but I'm SO proud of you, Quincy. You are the strongest, bravest person I know, and I am so lucky to share my life with you.

Tears burned his eyes. *She* was the strongest and bravest, and *he* was the lucky one.

I sleep in your shirts, and I dream about you every night. I swear when I wake up, I can feel you thinking of me as I am of you. I love you, Quincy, today, tomorrow, and always.

Forever your beautiful, Roni

Quincy wiped his eyes and cleared his throat to try to ease the tightening of it. How the hell did he get lucky enough to be with her? That was an answer he'd never receive, but he'd spend his life showing her just how much he adored her. He smelled the card, catching a hint of Roni. Maybe he imagined it, and if so, he didn't care. He felt her all around him.

He set the card upright on the nightstand so he could see it when he went to bed and picked up the package, sending a silent thank-you out to Biggs as he opened it.

Inside was a shirt box, and when he removed the top, he found a white wire-bound book with QUINCY'S CHRISTMAS MEMORIES printed in red script across the middle with garland and holly beneath it. He took it out of the box and opened the cover, his heart constricting at the sight of the first drawing Truman had ever left by his bed. Tears welled anew as he took in the picture of Truman's face on a bird's body, soaring through the sky with Quincy as a little boy riding on his back. Below the picture was the story Truman had told him about how he wished he could fly them away to someplace where drugs didn't exist. Quincy inhaled a ragged breath as he turned the page, met with another of the pictures he'd lost, one of the rose gardens, and another story he'd never forgotten. For the next half hour, he marveled at pictures and stories from the past he wished he could forget, and at the same time, he never wanted to let go of the moments behind each of the images in the book.

When he came to the last page, his heart filled up, and laughter tumbled out. Truman had drawn a picture of Roni sitting on Quincy's shoulders. He was holding the trunk of the tree near the top with one hand as she placed the star on it, and in his other hand was his phone as he took a selfie of them. Below the picture the caption read *Our first perfect Christmas tree*. Beside them were two connected red hearts. The heart on the left had *Roni* written inside it. In the connected space between the two hearts, *loves* was written vertically, and inside the right heart was *Quincy*, all three words written in black in Roni's swirly handwriting.

He swiped at his tears, and then he lay back on the bed to take a second look through the most glorious Christmas gift he'd ever been given.

RONI SAT ON the couch sipping a warm mug of hot chocolate, staring absently at the lights on the Christmas tree and the gifts beneath it, wishing Quincy were there. And then the guilt rolled in for having that selfish thought when he was doing something far more important for them. She tried to push that guilt away, hoping the present she'd dropped off yesterday had brightened his morning. Truman had worked hard for the last few weeks on those pictures, and she'd wanted to see Quincy's face when he opened the gift. But she was sure he needed to see them now even more.

This was supposed to be his special Christmas, filled with nothing but good memories and *firsts*. She was glad he was taking care of himself and putting his recovery above all else, but that didn't stop her from missing him more than she'd ever missed anyone or anything in her life. Even more than she'd missed dancing after the accident. Unfortunately, missing Quincy brought an onslaught of other emotions. Uglier emotions she'd been trying to hide from everyone else, even Penny, whom she'd been talking with daily because she was as worried about Quincy as Roni was. Talking about the things they missed about him and their hopes and fears about his recovery had created a sisterly bond Roni was thankful for. But she kept the harsher feelings to herself because Penny and everyone else had enough on their plates worrying about Quincy, trying to make sure Roni was okay, and making arrangements for Simone to go to Redemption Ranch in Colorado, which, thankfully, Simone had finally agreed to. Roni could tell Elisa and Angela about the feelings she was hiding, but she didn't want to worry them any more than she already had, either. They had been wonderfully supportive. Elisa had even told her to take some time off, which Roni didn't do. The last thing she needed was more time alone.

When she was alone, those harsher emotions trampled in—sadness, anger, and hatred—and the ugliest of them were aimed at Patrick "Puck" Fulton. When the detective had questioned her, it had dredged up the fear and pain of her accident. It was still haunting her. Late at night she'd hear the screeching tires and feel the pain of the impact and the devastation of losing everything she'd worked for. It drove her hatred for Puck even deeper. She hated him for so many reasons. Nearly killing

Quincy and stealing two years of his recovery were at the top of that list, but it didn't stop there. He'd killed an innocent man, stolen away the career she'd worked so hard for, and disrupted the life she and Quincy were building, and she was livid at him for making Quincy feel guilty for something he didn't do. Thankfully, she'd learned that when the police had raided Puck's home and car, they'd matched ballistics from one of his many guns to the bullet that had killed the driver of the car that had hit her. They'd also found Quincy's DNA. Between that and the audio Quincy had gotten of Puck kidnapping Quincy, shooting him up with heroin with the intention of killing him, and bragging about killing the driver of the car that had hit Roni, the police had enough evidence to prosecute, and hopefully put him away for a very long time. That gave her a modicum of relief, but not enough to diminish the hateful anger that was eating her alive.

She'd never been good at harboring negative emotions, and she needed to find a way to deal with or get rid of them. She had no idea how to do that because there was no way in hell she'd forgive that monster.

The only thing she knew for sure these days was that she'd been right to believe in Quincy, and she was lucky to have so many people in her life that cared about both of them. Angela and Joey had dragged her out with them last night to spend Christmas Eve at Angela's parents' house. Roni hadn't been feeling festive, and she hadn't wanted to go, but in the end she was glad she had. Angela's boisterous family had known her for so long, they knew just how to make her laugh, and she'd needed that. Though coming home to an empty apartment had left her sad and lonely once again.

She finished her hot chocolate and was putting her mug in

the sink when a knock sounded on the balcony door. She glanced at the clock on the stove, wondering who would show up at seven o'clock Christmas morning. She crossed the room and peeked between the curtains. Angela waved from the other side of the glass. She was wearing a red Santa hat and holding a plastic container. She lifted it, doing a happy dance as Roni opened the door.

"Merry Christmas, sugarplum! It's freezing out here," Angela said, pushing past her. She eyed Roni with a disturbed look on her face as she set the container on the table. "What do you have going on here?" She waved a finger at Roni. "A little Britney Spears hot mess mixed with Billie Eilish style and Helena Bonham Carter hair?"

Roni looked down at her outfit and said, "These are the sweatpants Quincy lent me the first night I stayed over, and this is his softest T-shirt, and…" She reached up and touched what had been a bun last night but was now a tangled mess hanging off the side of her head, and she and Angela both laughed.

"Aw, Roni. I'm sorry he's not here." Angela hugged her. "I'm sorry. I know nothing can replace Quincy, but at least you have the world's greatest best friend, who made you cinnamon buns." She took off the top of the container, releasing a mouth-watering aroma.

"You are a goddess. Thank you." Roni reached for one. She took a bite, and the sweet treat was exactly what she needed. "Mm. These are the best."

"I made them with extra love, which means extra cinnamon and frosting." Angela took off her coat and said, "Aren't you going to see Gemma and the kids this morning to open presents? I'm not sure they're going to appreciate your new look."

"I have a few hours before I need to be there." Roni grabbed plates and napkins, and as they sat down, she said, "Shouldn't you be with Joey celebrating Christmas?"

"I loved him up and he went back to sleep. So here I am, with my girl." She pulled a small gift out of her pocket and set it on the table. "Merry Christmas!"

Roni popped to her feet, feeling happier already, and went to the tree to get Angela's gift. "Merry Christmas to you, too." She handed it to her and said, "It's for you and Joey."

"Count of five?" Angela said as Roni sat down.

Roni nodded. They'd been counting to five instead of three since they were little, though neither could remember why. They counted together, *"One. Two. Three. Four. Five!"* and tore open their gifts. Roni watched Angela open hers rather than taking the top off the gift Angela had given her.

"*Whoa.*" Angela withdrew the red-and-black Leather and Lace camisole and panties from the box. "Roni, I can't accept these. I've seen their stuff online. They're really expensive."

"Dixie and Jace hooked me up with a huge discount. I even got something for myself, for when Quincy comes home."

"In that case, I *love* it. Thank you." Angela leaned forward and hugged her. "Open yours."

Roni opened the box and withdrew a key chain that had half of a best-friends heart. "It's beautiful. Thank you."

Angela reached into the pocket of her sweatshirt and placed an identical box on the table. "This is the other half. It's for Quincy. We'll always be besties, but with love comes another type of best friend, and I want you to know that I love you guys together, and I will happily share my bestie status with your man."

"Oh, *Ang.*" Roni hugged Angela, tears stinging her eyes. "I love you so much. Thank you. This means the world to me."

"I'm glad you like it. Listen, Roni. We both know you're not telling me everything about how you feel with Quincy being in rehab and finding out the bullet was meant for him, and that's okay. Gram grew you up tough, and I know you like to hole up and process grief in your own way. You tried to do it after your accident, and again when Gram died. I totally get it."

"I'm sorry," Roni said softly.

"Don't be. Every friendship has some sort of push-pull. You're the pull-away girl, and I will forever push my way into your life, even when you tell me not to, because even though you have lots of new friends and a man who adores you, nobody can take the place of the girl who gave you your first pad when you got your period during dance class."

They both laughed.

"I can't believe you brought that up," Roni said as another knock sounded on the balcony doors. She got up to answer it and said, "Is Joey meeting you here?"

"Nope."

She moved the curtains and saw Truman on the other side, a black hat pulled low on his brow, the collar of his coat up, his beard tucked against his chest. "Hi," she said as she pulled the door open, a gust of cold air sweeping in. "Come in."

"Hi, Roni." He nodded to Angela and said, "Hey, Angela. Merry Christmas."

Angela smiled and said, "Hi, Tru. Same to you."

Truman turned a serious gaze on Roni and said, "I'm really sorry to interrupt, but I need you to get dressed and come with me."

The tone of his voice sent panic spreading through her. "What's wrong? Is it Quincy?"

"Yeah, it's Quincy."

Chapter Twenty-Six

ROUTINE WAS ESSENTIAL to Quincy's recovery. The first time he'd gone to rehab, he'd had to figure out what routine even meant. Now he knew all about routine, but creating one that didn't include time with Roni or a video message from her was agony. He took advantage of just about every therapy the center offered, from twelve-step yoga and emotional regulation to music therapy and gym time. Some days he'd hit the gym twice. He was using the bench press when he was called to meeting room number three.

He knocked, and someone said, "Come in."

Quincy opened the door, staggering at the sight of Roni standing a few feet away, gorgeous in a red sweater and black jeans, tears visible behind her glasses. "Baby…?"

They ran to each other, and she launched herself into his arms, their mouths crashing together. Their salty tears slipped between their lips. His heart felt like it was going to explode.

"How did you get in here?" He looked around the room and saw Truman standing by the door with so much happiness in his eyes, it was palpable.

"Biggs pulled a few more strings," Truman said.

With one arm around Roni, Quincy went to him, embracing both of them, because there was no way in hell he was letting go of her. "Thank you, man. For everything. Those pictures are..." He tried to find the right word and realized he didn't need to. Truman had been there every step of the way, just as he was now. His childhood stronghold and straight arrow to follow, the boy-turned-man who had taught him how to love, protect, *and* lead himself *and* others. He may not need to follow Truman any longer, but he was damn thankful he'd stuck by his side so they could enjoy the future they both deserved.

"Merry Christmas, bro," Truman said. "They're giving you half an hour, so I'll give you two some privacy."

As he left the room, Quincy wrapped his arms around Roni again, holding her tight. "God, I've missed you."

"Me too," she said through tears. When he tried to lean back so he could see her face, she held him tighter, whispering, "I'm not letting go."

"Neither am I, babe." He sat in a chair with her on his lap, and they held each other for a long time without saying a word. But Quincy was aware of the minutes ticking by, and he needed to *see* Roni's eyes to know if she was really okay.

He drew back and framed her beautiful face between his hands, wiping her tears with the pads of his thumbs. A knot formed in his gut at the sadness storming in her eyes. "I love my gift. Thank you for having Tru draw the pictures and write the stories, and for putting it in the book. The last picture is my favorite."

Her lower lip trembled, but she drew her shoulders back, making a valiant effort at producing a smile, the fakeness of it tearing at him.

"Mine, too," she said softly.

"You should open the gifts I put under the tree." When she lowered her eyes, he lifted her chin and said, "Talk to me, baby. How are you doing? Are you going to work? Spending time with Angela or the girls? Do you need anything?"

"I'm okay. I'm going to work and seeing people for dinner."

"Truth, baby, remember? We made a promise to be honest."

Tears flowed down her cheeks, and a sob burst out. She threw her arms around him, burying her face in his neck. "I'm not okay. I *miss* you, and I have so much anger and hatred inside me for Puck and all the things he's done to you, to me, to that poor man he killed. I don't know what to do with it. I'm scared I'll never let it go." She gasped and said, "And now I've spilled my guts when I should be asking about how you're doing. I'm sorry."

Her confession left him raw, heartbroken, and determined to help her. "Look at me, beautiful." She leaned back, and he dried her tears. "I'm fine," he reassured her. "I've got this, Roni, and I would worry about you whether you told me what's wrong or not, because I see it. I feel it. You're a part of me, babe, and that doesn't stop because we're miles apart." He pressed his lips to hers, thinking about the ways she relieved stress and remembered how she'd said she'd danced late at night after her grandmother had passed away to push through her grief. "Are you dancing after work?"

She shook her head. "There's no time. Everyone's being so nice and supportive, and I thought you'd want me to be with them, so I usually go right to someone's house when I get off."

"Listen to me, baby. I love that you're seeing people because you know I don't want you to be alone, but that's *my* selfish desire to fill a gap for you while I'm in here. But it might not be the right gap. I need you to take care of *yourself* first and foremost while I'm in here taking care of myself, and if that means that you dance instead of seeing friends, then do it. Don't let that bastard's ugliness eat away at you and destroy your beauty. You *need* to get that anger and hatred out of your system, and dancing has always been your outlet. Promise me you'll make time to do that."

Nodding, she inhaled deeply, letting out a long sigh as she took his hand and pressed it to her chest. "Feel how fast my heart is beating?" She held it there as her heartbeat calmed, and then a genuine smile appeared, and she said, "You knew exactly what I needed. How could I have forgotten about the one thing that I relied on for so long?"

"Because we haven't been stressed the last several weeks, and your extra time spent dancing has been for fun. But you're in recovery again, babe. You relived the accident when the police questioned you, and I could see how it dredged up all that hurt and anger. When you pile that on top of the fact that your boyfriend is on day six of his recovery, that's a lot for you to deal with. You need to dance and use that outlet as much as you can." He rubbed her hips and said, "And be sure to pamper yourself afterward—take warm baths or get a massage. I'll pay for it."

"I'll dance, but I only want your hands on my body." She hugged him again and ran her fingers through his hair.

He closed his eyes briefly, reveling in her touch. "Babe, it might also be a good idea for you to talk to someone. A therapist. Did you talk with anyone after your accident?"

"They had someone at the hospital, but not really."

"I know from how you kept to yourself after your Gram

died that you like to handle things privately. But some knots are too tough to unravel alone. Are you open to talking to someone?"

She met his gaze and nodded. "Yes. Thanks to you, I'm learning about how important communication is."

"We'll get the name of a therapist that's familiar with grief and recovery before you leave here." He glanced at the clock, and his heart sank, but he tried to keep that disappointment out of his voice as he said, "Our time is almost over. Take lots of pictures for me when you celebrate Christmas with the kids, and at Jed and Josie's wedding tonight. Who's stepping in as best man?"

"Actually, they postponed the wedding. Jed said he can't get married without his best friend there."

Quincy hated that he'd screwed up their wedding, but he loved Jed's commitment to him. "Fucking Jed."

"They're doing it the day he proposed."

"Which time?" He told her about Jed's first spontaneous proposal, and the second, planned one.

"The first time. They're getting married in February."

"Okay, well, it sucks that I ruined their wedding, but I'm glad I'll get to see them get married. Have you heard anything about Simone or Penny? Are they okay?"

"Yes. Diesel's flying with Simone out to Redemption Ranch tomorrow, and Penny and I talk every day. She's worried about you, but like the rest of us, she has faith in you."

"I appreciate that. I hate that I put everyone through this. At least I'll be out in time to see you perform in the Winter Showcase."

"*You* aren't putting us through anything, Quincy. You didn't take those drugs. Puck did this, and they've arrested him." She filled him in on what Truman and Biggs had told her. "And you know what?"

"I know a lot of *whats*. The most important being that I love you, beautiful."

She pressed those gorgeous lips to his. "I'm glad rehab hasn't dimmed your melting powers. It's only twenty-four more days. They're *important* days, and yes, they will be treacherously hard, but I'll see a therapist and get back to dancing, and you'll work on your recovery, and after twenty-four brutal days, we'll be even stronger. That's a small price to pay when we have forever to look forward to."

Chapter Twenty-Seven

NEW YEAR'S DAY brought eight inches of snow and ice, and winter remained in full force throughout the month of January. But like a beacon of things to come, as Quincy walked out of the rehab center after completing his thirty-day program, the sun was shining, his girl was smiling, and the brisk winter air had never felt so good. They made their way to Roni's car, and he tossed his bag in the back seat and hauled her into his arms, lifting her right off her feet and kissing her as deeply and as passionately as he'd been dreaming about for too damn long. She made those sinful sounds he loved, touching his arms and back.

She tore her mouth away, her eyes dark and hungry, and said, "Your muscles are so *big*."

"I guess those twice-a-day workouts paid off."

"They sure did. I can't wait to get your clothes off."

God, he adored her.

"Let's get out of here, beautiful, and spend the next twenty-four hours naked in each other's arms."

They settled into their seats, and as they drove away, Roni talked at breakneck speed about how happy she was that he was coming home, how great therapy had been, and how excited she was about dancing *for him* in the showcase.

"Angela and I took Kennedy and Lincoln out for two dates, and the kids and I had a slumber party one night so Tru and Gemma could have a break. We had so much fun."

She glanced at him, her brow furrowing, and he realized he was staring, but he couldn't look away. He squeezed her hand, sure he was grinning like a fool.

"Am I talking too much? I'm just so happy you're out, and I want to fill you in on everything."

"You could never talk too much." He lifted her hand, kissing the back of it. "I've missed your voice as much as I've missed everything else about you. You've gotten even more beautiful, babe. I just can't stop looking at you."

She blushed and turned down a side road.

"Where are we going?"

"I need to make a quick stop before we go home," she said. "It'll only take a minute."

When she turned down Dixie's old street, lined with the cars and trucks of his friends and family, he realized something was up. "I guess Tru and Gemma bought Dixie's house after all, huh? Leave it to Jace to get her to sell and speed up his baby timeline."

"Speaking of babies," she said, parking behind Bullet's truck. "I can't believe I forgot to tell you that Bullet and Finlay had a baby girl. She's the cutest thing I've ever seen." They got out of the truck and headed up the walk. "Her name is Tallulah Wren, and they call her Lulu. She's got a shock of black hair, like Bullet, and Finlay's big blue eyes. Bullet never puts her down. I think he's more of a baby hog than Jace is."

"I can't wait to meet her," he said, drawing Roni into his

arms. "Babe, before we go inside and get sidetracked with everyone, I want to thank you for believing in me and sticking by my side. I wish I could have been there for you this last month while you were dealing with all those bad feelings. I will do everything within my power to be here for you from now on. You're my other half, my *love*, the face I see when I close my eyes, and the only person I ever want in my arms at night. I adore you, beautiful, and I hope that when we're old and gray, you look back on our life together and have no regrets, because I sure as hell won't."

Tears welled in her eyes, and as she swiped at them, she said, "The only regret I'll have is walking in there with smudged eyeliner."

She went up on her toes and pressed her lips to his. As soon as they walked through the door, everyone yelled, "Welcome home!"

Quincy was passed from one set of loving arms to the next as everyone congratulated him and said how proud they were of him, sending a rush of emotions through him. The last time he had gotten out of rehab, he'd barely known these friends who had become family, and now he couldn't imagine a life without them. Everyone was talking at once. Several of the kids piled in for a group hug. The girls said they missed him, and the guys joked around and talked shit. It was great to be back with everyone, even if they still had him cornered in the foyer.

Bullet held baby Lulu in one arm, adorable in a pink sleeper. She had so much black hair, it looked like a wig, and the way Bullet was holding her made it clear she wasn't leaving his arms even as he hauled Quincy into a one-armed embrace and said, "Love you, dude."

"You too. Congrats on this adorable little one." Quincy

tickled the baby's feet. "Tallulah, huh? Great name."

"Yeah, Kennedy came up with it. I'd have called her any-thing that little sweetheart wanted. We'll catch up," Bullet said as Penny pushed past him and plastered herself against Quincy.

"I'm so glad you're back," Penny said with tears in her eyes.

"Me too, Pen. You and Scott good?" He looked at Scott standing at the edge of the foyer with Truman, Bear, and Bones, all of them grinning.

"Mm-hm." Penny sniffled, tightening her hold on him.

"Let me in there." Dixie threw her arms around both of them and said, "You finally got your girl after all those months and just *had* to give her a big old test, didn't you?"

He chuckled. "Missed you too, Dix."

"Okay, blubbering Bettys, let Mama Red in there." Red pried them off Quincy and hugged him even tighter than they had. "I'm glad you're home, sweetheart. We're all here for you."

Hell if he didn't get choked up all over again. "Thanks, Red."

Jed sidled in, and Quincy accepted that *choked up* was prob-ably how he was going to spend the next several hours. "Sorry about your wedding, man."

Jed clapped him on the back. "No worries. I'm just glad you're okay. Love you."

"Love you, too," Quincy said as he was pulled into another embrace. Several hugs later, he stood before Truman, who was holding Lincoln, and his heart felt like it might beat right out of his chest.

"You did it, bro." Truman pulled him into a one-armed hug and said, "I'm so effing proud of you."

"Soeffingproud," Lincoln said, making everyone laugh.

"Get over here, little man." Quincy settled Lincoln in his

arm and pressed his cheek to his, whispering, "I've missed you, buddy."

"Me too!" Kennedy hollered as she ran over, arms up.

"Get up here, jelly bean." Quincy hoisted her into his other arm and kissed her, too. "I've missed you guys."

"Isleepedinbooful'sbed!" Lincoln rattled off loudly, earning more laughs.

Quincy winked at Roni, standing with Penny and Angela, loving that she'd included her and Joey in their celebration, and said, "I go away for a month and you move in on my girl? I'm going to have to teach you about respect, little man. It's a good thing I love you."

Lincoln wriggled out of his arms and said, "Loveyouuncaincy!"

"Come into the house! I wanna play!" Kennedy said as Quincy set her down, and she ran out of the foyer.

Everyone headed for the living room, but Quincy reached for Roni, wanting a moment alone with her.

"Take your coat off and stay awhile," she said. "Is this too much? Everyone wanted to see you."

He hung up his coat and said, "It couldn't be more perfect. Thank you, and I'm so glad you included Angela and Joey."

As his mouth came down over hers, Biggs hollered, "Quincy Gritt, get in here, son."

Quincy grinned against her lips. "I want more of those later."

He draped his arm around her shoulders, kissing her temple as they entered the living room, where a WELCOME HOME banner hung above the fireplace, and on the mantel was the picture of him and Roni kissing on the slide that had been on their nightstand. There were several other pictures from the apartment there, too, and new ones of him and Roni that they'd taken since the scavenger hunt. The room fell silent as his gaze moved over Roni's couch and his orange chair. Everyone watched as he tried to make sense of his and Roni's furniture being there. Their books filled the shelves, and his GED was framed and hanging on the wall beside Roni's diploma from Juilliard. Their crooked Christmas tree with the same presents underneath it that had been there when he'd gone into rehab was tucked into the corner of the room.

"Welcome home, Quincy," Roni said softly, gazing up him. "I thought we could use a fresh start, so I rented Dixie's house. It's only two hundred dollars more than what we were paying for your apartment, and I can pay the difference. Your belief in me and my dancing really got to me, and with your encouragement and some helpful things I learned about myself in therapy, I decided to talk with Raya and Elisa about putting together a solo contemporary dance performance a couple of times a year at the playhouse. It'll be my own thing, not through the dance studio. Elisa supports it, and Raya thinks it's a great idea."

They both had tears in their eyes as he said, "Baby, all of this, and *that?*"

She shrugged. "Is it too much too fast?"

He gathered her in his arms. "No, baby. It's perfect, just like you. But you're not paying the extra rent." Chuckles from the guys and *aww*s from the girls rose around them as he kissed her, earning whistles and cheers. "This year we rent the house," he said quietly. "Next year maybe we'll get a puppy." He touched his lips to hers, and the room went silent. "And then a ring, and the next year a wedding." He tightened his hold on her. "Plenty of time to practice making babies as we make our way to our future." More hoots and cheers rang out, and he crushed her to him. "Thank you for accepting me and my baggage."

She gazed up at him with so much love in her eyes and in her heart he was drenched in it as she said, "I love you and all your gritty truths, Quincy, and I always will."

As he lowered his lips to hers, Lincoln yelled, "Ikissbooful!" and just like that, Quincy was finally, ecstatically, *home*.

Bonus Content for THE GRITTY TRUTH

I loved the images Truman and Roni had drawn for Quincy, I had to commission two of them and bring them to life. Follow the link below to see the two I chose.

www.MelissaFoster.com/bonus-content

Ready for More Whiskeys?

If this is your first Whiskey book, the series began with **TRU BLUE**, Truman and Gemma's love story. Information about that story is provided on the upcoming pages, along with information about **RUNNING ON DIESEL**, the next book in this series, featuring Diesel and Tracey, and **IN FOR A PENNY**, a novella featuring Penny and Scott. If you'd like to meet the Colorado Whiskeys at Redemption Ranch, pick up **SEARCHING FOR LOVE**, and get to know the Whiskey cousins, the Wickeds, in **A LITTLE BIT WICKED**, the first book in The Wickeds: Dark Knights at Bayside. Happy reading!

Fall in love with Tracey and Diesel in
RUNNING ON DIESEL

Desmond "Diesel" Black is a Nomad with the Dark Knights motorcycle club. He protects others with his life and always rides alone. Tracey Kline left the only family she had for a man who broke more than her spirit, leaving her untrusting and on her own. When a twist of fate reveals pieces of the other no one else sees, will they be able to help each other mend their past hurts and learn to trust the chemistry and connection that's too strong to deny?

IN FOR A PENNY, A WHISKEY NOVELLA

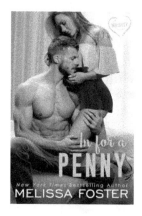

When everything you want is right in front of you, but it's still out of reach…

Penny Wilson has a successful business, more friends than a girl could ask for, and a boyfriend she's madly and passionately in love with. Scott Beckley is honest, loyal, hands down the best lover on the planet, and absolutely gaga over his nieces and nephews. Scott's a keeper…as long as Penny doesn't ever want to hear those three magical words that would take their relationship to the next level. Scott escaped abusive parents at seventeen and was forced to find his way alone in the world. Even though it's been more than a decade and he's reunited with his estranged sisters and built a good life in Peaceful Harbor, Maryland, he's still tortured by his past. Penny knows he loves her with everything he has, but for a girl who wants a family and a guy who is afraid of having one, love might not be enough.

Ready for More Dark Knights?

Fall in love with Truman, Gemma, Kennedy, Lincoln, and the rest of the Whiskeys in TRU BLUE

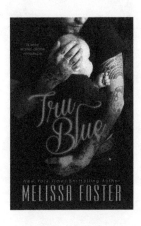

There's nothing Truman Gritt won't do to protect his family—including spending years in jail for a crime he didn't commit. When he's finally released, the life he knew is turned upside down by his mother's overdose, and Truman steps in to raise the children she's left behind. Truman's hard, he's secretive, and he's trying to save a brother who's even more broken than he is. He's never needed help in his life, and when beautiful Gemma Wright tries to step in, he's less than accepting. But Gemma has a way of slithering into people's lives, and eventually she pierces through his ironclad heart. When Truman's dark past collides with his future, his loyalties will be tested, and he'll be faced with his toughest decision yet.

**Meet the Colorado Whiskeys at Redemption Ranch
And fall in love with the Bradens in SEARCHING
FOR LOVE**

A deliciously sexy, funny, and emotional second-chance
romance

Zev Braden and Carly Dylan were childhood best friends, co-explorers, and first loves.

Their close-knit families were sure they were destined to marry—until a devastating tragedy broke the two lovers apart. Over the next decade Zev, a nomadic treasure hunter, rarely returned to his hometown, and Carly became a chocolatier, building a whole new life across the country. When a chance encounter brings them back into each other's lives, can they find the true love that once existed, or will shattered dreams and broken hearts prevail?

Get ready to fall hard for the Wickeds!

What do a cocky biker and a businesswoman who has sworn off dating bad boys have in common? According to Chloe Mallery, not much. But she couldn't be more wrong...

Justin came into the Wicked family after a harsh upbringing by a thieving father. He's gone through a lot to become a true Wicked, and he's made them proud. Now he's ready to show the woman he loves exactly what type of man he is. But Chloe has worked hard to move past her difficult upbringing, and she's wary of getting involved with a man who looks like he's walked right out of it. When tragedy strikes, will their trying pasts draw them together, or will Justin's protective nature be too much for Chloe's independent heart to accept?

Love Melissa's Writing?

Discover more of the magic behind *New York Times* bestselling and award-winning author Melissa Foster. **The Whiskeys are just one of the many family series in the Love in Bloom big-family romance collection** featuring fiercely loyal heroes, sassy, sexy heroines, and stories that go above and beyond your expectations! See the collection here: www.MelissaFoster.com/love-bloom-series

Free first-in-series ebooks, downloadable series checklists, reading orders, and more can be found on Melissa's Reader Goodies page.

More Books By Melissa Foster

LOVE IN BLOOM SERIES

SNOW SISTERS

Sisters in Love
Sisters in Bloom
Sisters in White

THE BRADENS at Weston

Lovers at Heart, Reimagined
Destined for Love
Friendship on Fire
Sea of Love
Bursting with Love
Hearts at Play

THE BRADENS at Trusty

Taken by Love
Fated for Love
Romancing My Love
Flirting with Love
Dreaming of Love
Crashing into Love

THE BRADENS at Peaceful Harbor

Healed by Love
Surrender My Love
River of Love
Crushing on Love
Whisper of Love
Thrill of Love

THE BRADENS & MONTGOMERYS at Pleasant Hill – Oak Falls

Embracing Her Heart

Anything For Love
Trails of Love
Wild, Crazy Hearts
Making You Mine
Searching For Love
Hot For Love

THE BRADEN NOVELLAS
Promise My Love
Our New Love
Daring Her Love
Story of Love
Love at Last
A Very Braden Christmas

THE REMINGTONS
Game of Love
Stroke of Love
Flames of Love
Slope of Love
Read, Write, Love
Touched by Love

SEASIDE SUMMERS
Seaside Dreams
Seaside Hearts
Seaside Sunsets
Seaside Secrets
Seaside Nights
Seaside Embrace
Seaside Lovers
Seaside Whispers
Seaside Serenade

BAYSIDE SUMMERS
Bayside Desires
Bayside Passions

Bayside Heat
Bayside Escape
Bayside Romance
Bayside Fantasies

THE STEELES AT SILVER ISLAND
Tempted by Love
My True Love
Always Her Love
Enticing Her Love
Caught by Love
Wild Island Love

THE RYDERS
Seized by Love
Claimed by Love
Chased by Love
Rescued by Love
Swept Into Love

THE WHISKEYS: DARK KNIGHTS AT PEACEFUL HARBOR
Tru Blue
Truly, Madly, Whiskey
Driving Whiskey Wild
Wicked Whiskey Love
Mad About Moon
Taming My Whiskey
The Gritty Truth
Running On Diesel
In For A Penny

SUGAR LAKE
The Real Thing
Only for You
Love Like Ours
Finding My Girl

HARMONY POINTE
Call Her Mine
This is Love
She Loves Me

THE WICKEDS: DARK KNIGHTS AT BAYSIDE
A Little Bit Wicked
The Wicked Aftermath

WILD BOYS AFTER DARK
Logan
Heath
Jackson
Cooper

BAD BOYS AFTER DARK
Mick
Dylan
Carson
Brett

<u>HARBORSIDE NIGHTS SERIES</u>
Includes characters from the Love in Bloom series
Catching Cassidy
Discovering Delilah
Tempting Tristan

More Books by Melissa
Chasing Amanda (mystery/suspense)
Come Back to Me (mystery/suspense)
Have No Shame (historical fiction/romance)
Love, Lies & Mystery (3-book bundle)
Megan's Way (literary fiction)
Traces of Kara (psychological thriller)
Where Petals Fall (suspense)

Acknowledgments

I hope you enjoyed Quincy and Roni's story as much as I loved writing it. I'm looking forward to bringing you many more Whiskey love stories, including the upcoming Colorado Whiskeys at Redemption Ranch, whom you can meet in SEARCHING FOR LOVE, a Bradens & Montgomerys novel.

If this is your first introduction to my work, please note that all of my books can be read as stand-alone novels, and characters appear in other family series, so you never miss out on an engagement, wedding, or birth. You can find information about the Love in Bloom series and my books here:
www.MelissaFoster.com/melissas-books

I offer several free first-in-series ebooks. You can find them here:
www.MelissaFoster.com/LIBFree

I chat with fans often in my fan club on Facebook. I hope you'll join me there.
www.facebook.com/groups/MelissaFosterFans

Follow my author page on Facebook and Instagram for fun giveaways and updates on what's going on in our fictional boyfriends' worlds:
www.facebook.com/MelissaFosterAuthor
www.instagram.com/melissafoster_author

If you prefer sweet romance, with no explicit scenes or graphic language, please try the Sweet with Heat series written under my pen name, Addison Cole. You'll find many great love stories with toned-down heat levels.

The sketches included at the end of this story were created by Oliver Harbour, an exceptional artist, caring friend, and all-around amazing guy. Thank you, Ollie, for sharing your talent with me.

Thank you to my awesome editorial team, Kristen Weber and Penina Lopez, and my meticulous proofreaders, Elaini Caruso, Juliette Hill, Marlene Engel, Lynn Mullan, and Justinn Harrison. And as always, heaps of gratitude to my family for your endless support, and for putting up with me and my crazy hours and chats about fictional characters.

Meet Melissa

Melissa Foster is a *New York Times* and *USA Today* bestselling and award-winning author. Her books have been recommended by *USA Today's* book blog, *Hagerstown* magazine, *The Patriot*, and several other print venues. Melissa has painted and donated several murals to the Hospital for Sick Children in Washington, DC.

Visit Melissa on her website or chat with her on social media. Melissa enjoys discussing her books with book clubs and reader groups and welcomes an invitation to your event. Melissa's books are available through most online retailers in paperback and digital formats.

Melissa also writes sweet romance under the pen name Addison Cole.

www.MelissaFoster.com
Free Reader Goodies: www.MelissaFoster.com/Reader-Goodies

CPSIA information can be obtained
at www.ICGtesting.com
Printed in the USA
LVHW031948080321
680887LV00007B/1618